ARIES 181

TIANA WARNER

Rogue Cannon Publishing

Canada

This is a work of fiction. While much of the technology described is real, the characters, events, and incidents are products of the author's imagination. Any resemblance to actual persons or events is coincidental. Companies are either products of the author's imagination or used in a fictitious manner.

First published in Canada in 2019
Rogue Cannon Publishing, Abbotsford, BC

tianawarner.com

Chapter 1
The Aries Research Lab

A dead engineer was an inconvenient way to start the week.

From the passenger's seat of his Bentley, Tony used his phone to post a new job opening.

"Get her car out of the parking lot. Torch it so it looks like tragedy struck on her way in."

"Yes, sir," said Reah, weaving through traffic as she took him to the Aries office.

Accidents were uncommon in the research lab. The work involved too much time behind a computer for that. But when the occasional 'whoops' did happen, it was an annoyance. Covering them up was a pain. Finding a willing and qualified replacement was worse.

"Warehouse," said Scott when Tony entered the lab to check the damage. "She was modifying the propellant."

Tony stifled a curse. Of course it was the propellant—the substance too stubborn to realize its own potential.

"Show me."

He and Scott crossed the lab with its white lights reflecting off white tiles, white walls, white tables, and white lab coats. The five other engineers kept working, unease leaking from their pores like sweat. With only seven of Tony's two hundred employees cleared for the lab, the hole left by their dead colleague was more of a chasm.

Tony was unruffled. Their non-disclosure agreements were thorough enough for a situation like this.

"What's the damage?"

"She, uh—she was completely burnt, Doctor Ries."

That much was obvious. Scott's fluorescent-pale skin and lab coat were smudged, leaving a goggle-shaped clear spot around his eyes. Holes split the toes of his shoes, revealing socks with hamburgers printed on them.

"Was anything else destroyed?"

An empire of technology filled the warehouse. These were his top achievements, past and future. No accident, no matter how messy, could quash the pride he felt every time he entered it.

He flung open the double doors. The stench of burnt metal and hair tickled his gag reflex.

"Minor damage to the surrounding area," said Scott, dabbing his sweaty brow with a singed sleeve. "No property was ruined."

Delightful.

It took a moment to blink the warehouse into focus. Dim, cold, and vast, the place could have passed for a storage facility. Walkways snaked between mounds of technology.

An early prototype of the Aries satellites—what the world came to know as the Aries 180 fleet—stole Tony's attention as he entered. The size of a bald eagle and mounted on a podium, it was the one now-useless technology he refused to incinerate. He caressed it as they passed.

Yet, despite all that filled the floor, the place was a cold vacuum, a void. Like the invisible substance called dark matter, every space in the warehouse represented an irksome gap in knowledge. Empty corners, walkways, every molecule of dead air held promise. As creator of the Aries universe, Tony intended to use any means necessary to fill those gaps.

Tony's watch vibrated. He looked at it to find a text.

Reah: *Need your clearance to get her purse. Locker 4.*

He replied, *5 mins*, and quickened his step.

The temperature rose as he and Scott drew deeper into the warehouse. A drone whirred overhead, taking photos at intervals. More drones hovered beneath the three-story ceiling, LED lights marking their presence. He would have to review the surveillance images later to see what happened. He might enjoy popcorn with it.

They stopped at the explosion site. The concrete floor rippled, like it had melted and hardened again. Every adjacent surface was dented and singed. Five dry chemical fire extinguishers lay nearby. Most intriguingly, a black, body-shaped imprint traced the floor like a shadow, a dusting of ash in its center.

Tony scattered the ash with his toe. "Looks like this place was pretty lit."

Scott cast him a sideways glance.

The culprit was the twelve-foot vat towering beside the scene of the accident. Smoke wisped from the top, Tony's hopes and plans disappearing with it into the black ceiling. The heat wrapped around him like a wool blanket.

"So the propellant isn't going well," said Tony, like a challenge.

"It just reacted badly," said Scott. "I'm confident we'll get it in time."

"Hm." *Don't placate me, Scotty.* What churned inside that vat represented tens of millions of dollars.

Sure, every aerospace company had rocket propellant, but no one had this. This was his next opportunity for international success—his next Aries 180 fleet, so to speak. If only the damn stuff would stop failing him. The setback choked his sense of control like a vice around his throat.

His father had told him there was no point in going into business unless you were going to be the best. Rather, the advice had been something like, "You wanna run a business, you gotta do whatever it takes to get on top. Might as well quit and be a shit-scraper if you're gonna be a pussy about it."

Tony held that wisdom close. Using methods no one else was brave enough to try, he was on his way to upgrading Aries from a humble Canadian startup to the world's most cutting-edge aerospace company.

His watch vibrated.

Steve: *Korean Space Agency wants you to join the call.*

Korea would have to wait. He was already late for an appointment with the bank.

"What are you going to do to fix it?" he said to Scott.

"We're, uh, looking into it."

"I hired all of you because you're the smartest engineers in the world. You're telling me you don't know?"

Scott hesitated. Tony hated hesitation.

"There are other engineers who might know more about high-energy liquid tetrapropellant, Doctor Ries."

4

"I've scoured universities. I've head-hunted in the Silicon Valley. They're too—" Tony waved a hand. "They're not ready for the scope of the job."

Scott didn't need to know how many applicants failed the psychological evaluation. A PhD and a 150 IQ meant squat when the candidate couldn't pass a basic obedience experiment.

Tony's watch buzzed again. He ignored it.

If he wanted this propellant, he would have to get his engineers something to work from. Sometimes, they needed a push. Call it inspiration, or pieces of the aerospace puzzle.

This was a gap in the matter that made up his universe. It needed to be filled.

"Give me a week. I'll get you the data."

Global Nanosats was making headway in liquid propulsion. They could be of use.

He pulled out his phone to check his calendar. An email notification appeared, reminding him of a development meeting in twenty minutes. He swiped it away.

Stress tickled the base of his brain. He would have to make time to get that data between his other appointments, or cancel a few. This was more important.

He'd known for a while that he was overexerting himself. His universe was expanding faster than he could manage. If he wasn't careful there would be a stellar collision. He couldn't keep filling these voids alone.

He needed someone to help him get this information— someone smart, fearless, and malleable. He needed a personal assistant.

Chapter 2
Jess Takes on a T-Rex

Jess peeked into the empty meeting room, laptop hugged to her chest. She double-checked the tablet on the door.

Image Analytics Team Weekly Catch-up – Monday, 11:00 AM – 11:15 AM.

Yes, this was it. She sidled in and looked at each chair, not wanting to take anyone's spot.

A real team meeting, in a real office, as a real software engineer! The room glistened, the wooden table a clean slate, the whiteboard waiting to be filled with information, a screensaver of inspirational photos drifting across the 4K TV. After everything it took to get here—after the accident had almost prevented her from returning to university in September—she'd made it. She was standing in Aries Inc., one of four interns to make it through the interview process, and she was ready to spend these next few months conquering the tech world.

Beyond gaining programming skills, this was her chance to be part of something groundbreaking. Aries might not have been the first to launch earth imaging satellites, but they were the first to image the world every hour at three-centimeter resolution—and those 180 all-seeing eyes were winning contracts worldwide, able to track everything from deforestation to foreign nuclear activity. The day Doctor Anthony Ries was awarded a Nobel Peace Prize, Jess fully intended to show everyone the headlines and boast, "I helped build that company."

Voices carried down the hall. Jess smoothed her blouse and gripped the back of the chair in front of her, trying to look as though she hadn't been acting like a lost Cocker Spaniel. In walked Floyd, her team lead, alongside Wyatt, one of her orientation buddies from last week and the other intern to land on this team.

"Morning, Floyd! Morning, Wyatt!" said Jess, in her most *I'm-a-team-player* voice.

They took seats at the head of the table while Jess took the one she'd placed her hand on and set down her laptop. The four other guys on the team entered with coffees in a chummy way that suggested they'd had a pre-meeting meeting in the lounge.

Someday, Jess would be part of pre-meeting meetings.

"Jessica, can you take notes?" said Floyd.

Jess glanced at Wyatt. Wearing an *Overwatch* tee and sipping hot chocolate, he looked like a teenager at Take Your Kid to Work Day. Jess gave Floyd the benefit of the doubt and decided she must have looked more prepared to take notes.

She let go of the ends of her sleeves, which she'd balled in her fists, and opened her laptop with a smile. "Sure."

"All right, let's get this going," said Floyd. "Chris?"

Chris had long, wavy hair and a mid-length beard that was probably supposed to look hipster, but paired with his white bohemian-style shirt, gave him a striking resemblance to Jesus.

Great, now she was going to remember him as Jesus Chris.

"Cool. So, I figured out how to use reflectance values for water recognition," said Jesus Chris. "I found a bug and sent that to Marco, but overall it's looking good. The algorithm is able to pick out lakes, rivers, and ponds."

Chris working on water recognition algorithm, typed Jess.

Ah, reflectance values.

Working with NASA's remote sensing images last term taught her that while ordinary photos contained red, green, and blue bands, the ones taken by earth imaging satellites also contained a bunch of values beyond the visible spectrum, like infrared. *Multispectral data.* That was where the Image Analytics Team came in.

"We build AI to analyze all this data and detect what's in each image," Floyd had explained during her onboarding last week.

So when farmers in Alberta needed to analyze trends in failing crops, Aries was there with infrared-based intelligence. When a rainforest preservation project wanted to know about illegal deforestation, Aries was able to monitor the tree canopy and send alerts. With Jesus Chris's new algorithm, changes in bodies of water could be tracked and monitored without human intervention.

These algorithms, along with the hardware manufactured in the lab, kept Aries speeding along at a rate that would turn it into an unstoppable aerospace giant.

"You need it tested?" Floyd nodded toward Wyatt, who was using his finger to scoop a marshmallow from the bottom of his mug. "We'll get Wyatt and Jessica on it this week. Stanley?"

Interns to do Quality Assurance, Jess added with a flourish. She would test this code, all right. She would test the heck out of it.

Stanley was avoiding everyone's eyes, his face buried in his notebook. Maybe it was the buzz cut and mustache, but he looked like one of those karate masters who could snap a block of wood with his forehead.

"I improved ship detection performance by 300%," he said.

Silence.

All right, a shy-and-to-the-point kind of guy. Shy Stanley.

"Good," said Floyd. "What's next?"

"Traffic."

"Let's go with human detection next. Everyone does ships and cars. We need to get into the market with a USP."

USP. What did USP stand for? Unique … something. Proposal?

Shy Stanley shook his head. "Not yet."

"Why not?" said Floyd. "You've done vegetation, haven't you? It's just a calculation."

Wait—Jess abandoned her attempt to figure out what the S stood for—*identifying people in satellite images?* She'd totally done that in her machine learning class.

Her heart leapt at the prospect of engineering something with such high impact. Would they let her take this on? Sure, they'd hired her as a tester, but a project like this would add glitter to her resume. And Jess needed a solid resume like a rocket needed Newton's third law of motion. Her gaze flicked to her inbox, where an email from her landlord went unanswered: *Rent increase*. Below that, *University of British Columbia Tuition Reminder*. Below that, *Your Credit Card Bill is Due*.

Pulling her laptop closer, she opened the webpage for the Canadian Junior Engineering Scholarship. Not only would the $50,000 prize pay off her student debt, but this would also make her look like an absolute queen to future employers. A picture of a smiling young woman topped the page, taunting her. Thick-rimmed glasses, long dark hair with bangs—they might as well have put a photo of Jess.

Working on a machine learning algorithm for Aries Inc. would qualify her. Candidates had to be nominated, so she would have to work hard and suck up to the right people before her four months here were up. It so happened that working hard and being sociable were her specialties.

"I'll put it on the schedule, but right now I don't have the bandwidth," said Shy Stanley.

Jess almost raised her hand but caught herself. She drew a breath. "Last term I did a project on—"

"This is a priority," said Floyd.

"We've promised traffic detection to a few customers."

Jess tried again. "I feel like I might be able—"

"Oh. How long will that take?" said Floyd.

"At least a month."

Jess leaned forward, as if to physically insert herself into the conversation. "I—"

"Hang on," said the guy beside Shy Stanley, who had a British accent. "Jessica, your CV said you did a machine learning project with satellite imagery, right?"

"Yes," she said loudly. "We used spectral signatures to determine—"

"I've seen her resume, thanks," said Floyd.

"Then Bob's your uncle. Get Jessica on it," said British Man. God, she would need to figure out his name.

Shy Stanley shrugged. "She can work from our existing algorithms."

"That's a decent project. Good work experience for her," said Jesus Chris.

Jess looked at Floyd, trying to put a cork in her desperation so it didn't show on her face. But it bubbled inside her, making her knees bounce under the table. This was potential for serious programming street cred. QA testing Aries algorithms was one thing, but to develop one herself?

Floyd shook his head. "Jessica is QA."

"She has time for both," said Jesus Chris. "Plus, Wyatt can pick up any slack. Right, Wyatt?"

Wyatt smiled placidly. "No prob."

The room fell silent. It seemed everyone was on board except Floyd.

Jess pushed down her rising indignation. His hesitation was probably nothing personal. As team lead, he would look bad if Jess failed. This was her first real day on his team and she had yet to prove herself.

She let go of her balled-up sleeves and sat taller in the chair. "I'd like to do it."

Understatement. She was inwardly screaming, stretching across the table to grab Floyd by his pressed collar and beg him to let her do this. *Don't you understand? I need this scholarship!*

More than anything, she wanted to feel proud of herself again. Besides, any more debt and she'd have to ditch her girlfriend and take up residence on her sister's couch.

Floyd addressed Jesus Chris as though he hadn't heard her. "If you want another developer, we should hire another developer. But Jessica is QA."

"I'm a developer," she said. "I'm going to UBC for engineering."

Then she smiled, afraid her tone came off aggressively.

The men looked at her.

Shy Stanley said, "You want it done, here's your chance, Floyd."

Floyd glared around the room. Several long seconds passed before he nodded once. "I want you to balance your tasks, Jessica. Don't let QA fall behind."

Jess nodded eagerly.

"Look at Stanley's code," said Floyd. "Detecting people in these images is going to be a lot different from ships or plants. Lots to consider."

I know, she wanted to say. *I spent all last term working on it.*

For the sake of modesty, she smiled and said, "Thanks. I think I have some ideas."

British Man and the other guy, who had the sunken look of someone perpetually sleep deprived, finished their status updates and Floyd assigned more QA testing to Jess and Wyatt. Jess could have fist-pumped as the meeting drew to a close. A week into her job and she had her own project! And this was a topic she knew. She'd already made the basic algorithm for detecting humans in multispectral images. The code would need cleaning up, because the final hours of the project had been rushed, but it could pick out humans with decent accuracy. The point of deep learning was that the algorithm would find patterns and fine-tune itself over time, but Jess wanted to improve the baseline. For starters, it tended to label animals as humans. She would also need to adapt it for incoming Aries satellite images instead of the ones her prof had distributed for the project.

Jess wouldn't fail the team, or herself. This tool would be the most impressive thing Floyd had ever seen.

She wound the spider web of hallways back to her office, making two wrong turns that she hoped no one in the nearby offices noticed.

The maps and space posters and random nerdisms wallpapering everyone's offices reminded her she would have to order decor for her own. She didn't want her coworkers to look at her bare walls and think she was without personality. Maybe this would be the place to unroll that life-sized TARDIS poster that was under her bed.

The only personal detail in her office so far was the mantra she'd written on a stack of sticky notes and left on her desk.

'Be Kind and Always Smile'.

A good daily reminder.

She picked up her phone and texted her girlfriend.

Jess: *I got a real dev project today!*

She opened Slack, the tool the company used for chatting and collaboration, and posted the meeting minutes to their team channel. Then she clicked through all the unread messages that had accumulated. She'd been a little keen when she got her account last week and had joined nearly every channel—including one called #littlearms dedicated to the T-Rex emoji. Someone named Dan had added a message with four T-Rexes this morning, and ten people had reacted to it with T-Rexes.

Jess considered adding a T-Rex reaction, too. She hovered over the icon. Would it look like she was trying too hard? Would others in the channel wonder who this Jessica Curie person was? Or this could get her in with the crowd. They would think she was one of them because she understood their T-Rex humor.

Or did she? Was this some inside joke she wasn't a part of?

Her phone buzzed.

Mandeep: *A promotion already? You'll be getting a permanent offer tomorrow, at this rate!*

Jess considered responding humbly, but she'd lowkey been fantasizing about life on a six-figure salary since she got the job offer. If she impressed Floyd and Doctor Ries enough with this project, they might give her a glowing reference for a job at Google. Or she could work her way up the Aries corporate ladder and become the Senior Vice President of … Satellites, or something. This early in her engineering career, her potential was endless. Someday, she would afford a down payment on a house for herself and Mandeep. Not downtown Vancouver, of course—that was for billionaires and people who enjoyed having twelve roommates—but somewhere in the suburbs.

Jess: *Get ready for the house of our dreams. xx*

Finally, her life was back on track.

She put down her phone. Someone else had reacted to the T-Rex message with a T-Rex. Deciding to commit to Aries culture two-feet-in, she did, too.

Wyatt appeared in her office door. "Lunch?"

Jess glanced at the time. Noon already!

They made their way to the lounge, a bright, open space with a cafeteria on one side and dozens of booths and tables on the other. It had the college vibe of a company started by millennials, with the adornments of one that made more money than it knew what to do with. The ceiling and walls were painted like outer space, with stars, galaxies, planets and comets, the ISS and other satellites, and (allegedly, if someone was inclined to count them) all 180 Aries satellites.

The two other interns weren't there yet, so Jess and Wyatt went to claim their usual round table in the corner. The lounge was mostly empty, the full-time employees trickling in.

"BRB," said Wyatt, disappearing toward the bathroom and leaving Jess to claim the table alone.

She unwrapped her veggie sandwich, looking forward to hearing what everyone was working on. Grace was in her final year of university, so she would have gotten an exciting project right away. Hopefully not too exciting. Nothing scholarship-worthy.

Floyd entered the lounge and caught her eye. She smiled. He glanced around, frowned, and strode over.

"Hey, Jessica," he whispered, sinking into a squat with an arm over the back of her chair.

She swallowed the bite of sandwich hard. "Hi."

"I think it would be beneficial for you to mingle with the full-time employees. Part of your work experience is to sink into the culture. Know what I mean?"

Her face grew hot. "Oh. Sure."

Floyd gave her a smile that didn't reach his pale, colorless eyes. "Great."

Jess let his words sink in as he strolled over to the microwaves to heat his food. Did he think she was antisocial? Did he not see all of the interns sitting together every day last week?

Horrifyingly, her eyes started to burn. She stuffed her sandwich in her bag, letting a dark curtain of hair cover her burning face as she leaned down.

"Wyatt," said Floyd, his voice carrying.

Wyatt, on his way back from the bathroom, changed course and met up with Floyd.

"How's the first week?" said Floyd. "Settled into your office?"

Jess stood and peered around the mostly empty lounge. A group of guys sat in the far corner, but Jess noted their red badges. They were from the research lab—the only place the interns weren't allowed to tour during orientation.

"The Red Badges represent our Research and Development Team," the admin, Beth, had said. "The lab is full of classified technology, so they have a special security clearance. Don't try and get in, and don't ask questions, or Doctor Ries will have your head."

Metaphor or not, Jess had no desire to get anywhere near being decapitated by the company founder.

In the middle of the lounge, three people sat at the long table. Jess's heart raced. They were laughing and looked friendly—but god, they must have been at least ten years older than her.

Strong, confident, independent. You've got this.

She put on her best smile and strode over.

"Can I join you?"

They looked surprised, but the one nearest, a red-haired girl who looked like she spent a lot of time in a CrossFit gym, pulled out the chair beside her.

"Sit! You're Jessica, right?"

"You can call me Jess."

"I'm Kit. This is Anita and Omar. We're on the Cloud Team."

Anita wore a high-waisted skirt, blouse, and oversized glasses that put Jess's fashion sense to shame. Omar wore the software developer attire Jess was more familiar with: shorts, sandals, a company-issued sweater with the Aries logo on the chest, unzipped to reveal a t-shirt he'd clearly gotten for free at a conference.

Kit, Anita, Omar. Kit, Anita, Omar. Jess hammered their names into her brain until they were securely in place.

She pulled out her sandwich again, but the lump in her throat was too thick to let her eat it. She opened her bottle of fizzy water instead.

"What school are you from?" said Kit.

"UBC. This is my first work term."

"Good for you!" said Anita. "Not an easy thing, Anthony Ries' interviews."

Jess allowed herself the surge of pride.

"Hey, what's a single biscotti called?" said Omar, popping open a bag. "Is it a biscotto?"

"Biscottus," said Kit.

"Why are you eating biscotti for lunch?" said Anita.

Omar stirred his coffee with it. "I already ate. I got hungry at ten."

Kit sipped her protein shake, giving Omar a judgy look.

"What's the Cloud Team working on?" said Jess.

"We're building an open data portal," said Anita.

"You know, so the public can use our imagery to spy on their exes and stuff," said Kit.

Jess was familiar with open data, having used the City of Vancouver portal for a class project, but she'd only used KML files—that was to say, geographic data—of bike paths and library locations.

"You're giving the satellite images away for free?" said Jess, feeling like this wasn't a great business model.

"The portal gives weekly images instead of the real-time ones people get if they pay," said Omar. "The idea is that companies will use our data, get hooked, and enter a contract with us to buy more."

"Which team are you on, Jess?" said Anita.

"Image Analytics. I'm splitting my time between QA and a new algorithm."

"Ah, Floyd's team," said Omar.

Jess thought she saw Anita and Kit share a look, but then it was gone, and Omar said, "What's the algorithm?"

She launched into explaining her human detection project, and lunch passed with easier conversation than anticipated. They were interested in what she'd studied at

UBC, and she liked learning what the Cloud Team was up to. She would have to learn more about web development. Maybe she could take a course when she went back to school next term.

When Kit and Omar stood, Anita reached across the table to Jess.

"One sec," she whispered.

Jess sat back down. Anita opened her mouth, closed it, looked around the room, then turned back to Jess. She was silent for so long that Jess raised an eyebrow.

"I know, it's always freezing in here," said Anita, speaking at last.

"What—? Oh." Jess unclenched her fists, letting go of her sleeves. She'd gotten into the habit of balling them in her fists to hide her scars. It made her look like she was always cold.

"I've tried a few times to get Admin to ease off the air conditioning."

Jess had the impression this wasn't what Anita had stopped her to say, but she went with it. "Maybe they're trying to make the office feel like outer space to inspire the engineers."

Anita laughed.

Deciding she could trust her, Jess opened her hands to reveal the scars. "It's a habit. I shattered my forearms last year. They did surgery to fuse the bones with titanium rods."

Anita's eyebrows pulled down. "Oh, I'm sorry."

Jess balled her fists again, preferring not to look at the mangled skin of her palms. Her wardrobe had become all long-sleeved shirts to hide the pairs of lines running up each forearm.

"It's okay. The doctor said I'm improving my dexterity faster than expected."

Anita's mouth quirked. "Why doesn't that surprise me about you?"

"The only thing I can't really do is punch—or lift heavy weights. Everything else is normal. Just slower."

Anita gave her a familiar, pitying nod.

Most of what she'd said was true. The "it's okay" part was a lie. Jess told herself she was fine, but she hated how weak she'd become and how much slower she was at everything, from typing, to simply opening a door. Worst of all, she hated the surge of grief that came every time she looked at her arms, and the guilt that arose every time she felt the cold ache of the rods beneath her skin.

Anita glanced around the room again after watching Wyatt and Floyd leave the lounge. The Red Badges in the corner were the last to get up, solemn and silent. Had they spoken at all over lunch? Maybe they were all the socially awkward supergenius type. That made Jess want to talk to them even more, to find out what they were working on—but she remembered the decapitation threat and surrendered that idea.

Anita dropped her voice to a whisper. "Hey, so … That's really exciting Floyd gave you a project already. It's advanced, what they're doing."

Jess smiled. Though Floyd hadn't exactly been enthusiastic about it, she decided not to mention that detail.

"If you need help with anything, or someone to talk to about—Floyd's team," said Anita, "don't be afraid to stop by, all right? I know Kit feels the same. We were both interns once and would be happy to mentor."

There was something about her tone, but Jess couldn't understand what. Did she expect Jess would need someone to talk to? About the algorithm, or about the Image Analytics Team? She brushed aside the mild unease.

"That's really nice of you. Thanks."

"My office is on Asgard."

"What?"

Anita stood. "Fourth floor. Left at the giant Thor hammer."

Jess could have pranced back to her office. She had a real engineering project. The world had opened before her through the eyes of the Aries 180 fleet. If today was any indication, this internship was going to be amazing.

Chapter 3
Halley Submits Her Resume

Halley pushed the gym doors open with enough force to earn glares from everyone inside. She kicked off her stilettos as she crossed the mats, leaving them where they landed. She dropped her coat and cuffed the sleeves of her button-down blouse.

The trainer, a wisp beneath a gym-issued sweater, trotted over. "Miss, you can't—"

Halley punched Bob, the body opponent bag, as hard as she could. The base tipped, catching air before crashing back down to the mat.

"Miss—"

"I – just – need" – said Halley between punches – "two – minutes."

"You need to sign in—"

Halley whirled around. *"I'm a member!"*

Her freshly straightened and highlighted hair fell over her eyes. She gritted her freshly whitened teeth.

"But you need … proper attire …" The trainer's voice faded beneath the peppy girl-power playlist and the thumps of the other women kickboxing in the circuit.

She hovered behind Halley, then seemed to decide it wasn't worth her hourly wage to argue and walked away.

Halley elbowed Bob in the ribs. She gave him an uppercut that made his head wobble.

Effing – system – isn't – fair.

She gave a roundhouse kick and felt the crotch of her pantsuit threaten to rip. She stopped, heaving, skin cooling with the beginnings of sweat. The others in the circuit were casting her nervous glances.

Why were interviews a thing, anyway? Why couldn't employers look at actual achievements instead of testing how well someone did under rapid-fire? Halley could solve any puzzle alone. She was more than prepared for the standard challenges, like 'reverse a linked list', and 'calculate the Fibonacci sequence'. But being forced to talk through the problem, to show her thought process on a whiteboard, ground her brain to a humiliating halt.

She unleashed another wave of punches. "Dammit!"

Her career plans were doomed. She didn't even look like a software developer or have the right interests. She barely knew what a mage was.

The trainer was now pretending not to notice her, loudly encouraging the other women.

"C'mon, Becky, you've got this! One, two, one, two."

The interviewer hadn't helped. It had been impossible to think with him staring at her across a table with his notebook and collared shirt, and—

And eyes the color of chocolate, and cologne that smelled like cherries.

"Halley … Like the comet? Beautiful," he'd said.

Panting, she stepped back from Bob, kicked her stilettos upright, and rammed her feet back into them.

Beautiful. The word had rung through her mind over and over, stalling her answers before they could reach her lips. Would it have been inappropriate to ask him to rip off her clothes in the interview room? Maybe, but it would have been the most exciting thing to happen to her in months.

That was the problem. Tony exuded excitement. He talked about Aries so passionately.

She kept imagining him outside the interview room— working in the computer lab together, finishing a project late one night. He would make her laugh the whole time.

"So an SQL query walks into a bar, goes up to two tables and asks, 'Can I join you?'"

"Oh, Tony, you're so funny!"

He would lean in to show her something on the screen, and there would be a moment when their eyes locked and they both became aware of how close they were sitting.

Halley sighed as she left the gym. She'd gone there wanting a job and came back wanting the interviewer. It was more than the failed interview that had her so disappointed. He'd represented something more than a job. He promised a new life—a fresh start—when she needed it most.

She eyed each storefront as she walked toward the bus stop. Now what? January term had started and she needed her summer internship lined up, like, yesterday. Other students were filling spots in all the good software companies.

What if she didn't find an internship? She should be applying for non-software jobs, too. But what? A barista? Ugh, so ordinary. Bartender? Ugh, drunk assholes. Either of those would end in her drowning a customer in his own drink.

Someone must want her computers experience. Sure, she was still a student, but she'd been coding since she learned to type.

She stopped in front of Tech Warehouse. Fixing old people's computers with the Nerd Herd in the back must pay more than minimum. They would probably take her without an interview. ("Wow, a girl wants to work here? Quick, don't let her escape!") Or, they would take pity and hire her for the position of, "Hello, would you like a flyer?"

She pulled her resume from her purse.

Halley Lovelace. UBC Undergraduate. B.Sc. Computer Science. Expected graduation: 2022.

Mom and Dad would tell her she should at least drop off her resume because it was better than unemployment.

A minute passed as Halley stared through the window, unable to walk through the door. A bank of televisions stood behind the glass, broadcasting the news.

"Global Nanosats hack prompts security investigations," read the ticker.

She shook her head and turned her back to the store. No, a job so plain was worse than unemployment. She would find something better. She had to.

As she headed for the bus, she tried to forget everything Aries had promised—the bleeding-edge technology, the chance to make a difference, and the fresh start.

When she got home, Mr. and Mrs. Basic across the street were returning from walking their golden retriever puppy. They didn't see her, or at least pretended not to. Newlyweds

25

in their mid-twenties, they'd moved in a few months back and had gotten their perfect puppy with its perfect pink collar and leash.

Halley didn't know the couple's names. They never spoke. But everything she needed to know about them was in their routine of jogging together every morning, their shared Mazda 3, and that puppy they took for walks hand-in-hand. Halley was sure she once saw them riding a Vespa together. Mrs. Basic always had her blonde hair perfectly styled, and her clothes always looked new—from the Lululemon pants she wore jogging, to the airy blouses she wore to whatever job she had. She was probably a social media manager. Mr. Basic had the perfect amount of stubble across his jaw and always wore collared shirts. Their life was a #blessed one.

Was that the life Halley should aspire to?

She couldn't picture it on herself. Though she came home to the same comfortable house she'd always nested in, with parents who commented endlessly on how smart their baby girl was and how amazing it was that she was in university, she wasn't destined for a life that perfect. She was a month away from turning twenty-one with only shame to show for it, from the better part of elementary school, to Brooke, to last summer.

She wished she could strip away her name, her face, her identity, and start her life over. With a past as irreparable as hers, that might be the only way to move forward. She wanted to find a world where nobody knew who she was and the choices she'd made.

She opened the door to the smell of garlic and the sound of a Jimmy Buffett track coming from the kitchen.

"How was it? What did they ask you?" said Mom.

"Did you impress them with big words like *nanotechnology*?" said Dad.

"It was fine. Yep." Halley sped upstairs, not ready to discuss her day.

"We're making your favorite," Mom called after her.

"It's your mom's specialty—spaghetti with burnt garlic toast."

Halley shut her door and threw her bag onto its usual spot on the bench, biting her lip against the surge of emotion in the back of her throat. If she could start a career and earn enough to get her own place, she could move on from everything. She could make new friends and build herself a new identity. She could stop clinging to the life she had before the summer, because it was clear nobody from that life wanted to be around her anymore. They'd cut her out, and rightly so. It was time for her to stop pining. Time did not mend what had broken. It put ugly scabs over the wounds.

She faced the unicorn poster on the back of the door. It was ridiculous she still had this thing up, but it covered the gash she'd once made by hurling scissors across the room—and besides, it reminded her of happy times. Like how the glowing stars stuck to the ceiling reminded her of a childhood dream to go to space. The rest of her room was a daily reminder that she'd always dreamed of being a professional science nerd: telescope pointing out the window, microscope on her shelf, gyroscope beside the pencil jar. Somewhere under her bed, she still had the stethoscope she got for her seventh birthday, alongside the half-dissected doll she operated on.

This place was a kangaroo pouch. It was time to climb out and find her place in the world.

Halley stripped out of her interview clothes and flopped on her bed, burying her face in the pink duvet. She inhaled a mix of perfume and hairspray. Downstairs, the volume of Jimmy Buffett grew louder. Dad sang along loudly—and terribly—to a song about a cheeseburger. Halley caught herself bobbing her foot and pulled a pillow over her ears.

But where would she go? She had no income, no job prospects. She could never afford to live in Vancouver on a minimum wage job. She needed someone to move in with.

And no, *not* Tony the Aries interviewer.

Someone as exciting as Tony must be out there, waiting for the perfect girl to sit next to them in Databases class—or, more realistically, to swipe right.

Halley grabbed her phone and opened Tinder.

The first profile was a muscular guy holding a dead fish. What was with guys and fishing pics? The description read, "Looking for someone less crazy than my ex haha. 6'5" wear ur heels".

Halley scoffed and swiped him away. The next profile was a pouting brunette, pretty, but with hair and makeup that suggested high maintenance. Halley browsed her photos, hoping for something less airbrushed so she could tell what the girl actually looked like—and then a picture of her with a dude appeared. Halley glanced to the description. "Fit couple looking for a third."

Halley groaned and threw her phone on the floor. Obvious '*no*'s aside, she never understood how it was possible to gauge attraction to someone based on photos. In her experience, attraction was chemical. In grade ten, something about Gregory Pace (she still drew mental hearts around his name) had hooked her immediately. It was his aura, the way he carried himself, how easy it was to flirt with him, the ease of their conversations.

Then there was Brooke.

Passion, yes. More than with Gregory Pace. But that situation was something she never needed again. Brooke's voice still rang in the back of her head like a gong. *Psycho. Bitch. Selfish.*

Halley dug her nails into her palms, making herself live in the pain. Tears sprang to her eyes. When it was enough to make her gasp, she kept pushing a moment longer, holding onto the remorse.

She sat up. She should go out and meet people in the real world. This would be the first step to a new Halley.

She grabbed her laptop from the bedside table and searched 'events in Vancouver'. There must be some concert or party going on.

Lots of clubs advertised girls got in free every Friday—which meant enduring a hundred pervy guys for every cute one, so no. The only event going on in Davie Village, Vancouver's gayborhood, was for men.

She stopped scrolling at 'Vancouver Tech Show'. *Interesting.* She clicked. It ran all week, with social events tonight and tomorrow at some fancy lounge in Coal Harbour.

Would she be a total dork for doing this on a Friday night?

Better than staying home and singing a melancholy song with Dad about wanting to be a pirate. Plus, this would serve multiple purposes. She could schmooze and find a job, *and* meet the attractive founder of a startup. She imagined a guy in a casual blazer and hipster glasses, and some adorable business plan that he'd pitched to hundreds of people since graduating university.

She stood. It was perfect: social, without having to endure nightclub creeps. And she wouldn't look out of place being there alone because she was job hunting.

Also, she could tell Mom she was going to a tech show. God knew how she would react if her baby girl was heading out to grind on some strangers in a club. She got anxious even when Halley took the bus by herself. Halley recalled with burning embarrassment how if she ever had to go somewhere alone as a kid, Mom would make her do it wearing her hapkido uniform with the black belt showing.

She pulled several outfits from her closet and threw them on the bed. The idea of going to an expo without friends for emotional support sent her pulse racing, but this was the perfect opportunity to bring new people into her life. This was a room of strangers who had no idea who she was and what she'd done, and who would decide upon first glance at her poise and smile that she radiated potential.

She vowed to talk to at least one person before the night was out. A new life was waiting for her, and in some way or another, tonight would be the start of it.

Chapter 4
Jess Gives a Demo

Floyd piled QA tasks onto Jess like she was a plate at a Thanksgiving feast. Thankfully, British Man and the tired-looking guy on her team, who both turned out to be named Steve, made her job easier with their meticulous programming skills. Quality-checking their code involved little more than applying routine tests and adding a comment to confirm she found no bugs.

The predictable work was a blessing since it gave Jess more time for the project that mattered. If she could get this algorithm done and into the Aries toolkit within the next few weeks, she would have plenty of time left in her internship to convince Floyd—or better, Doctor Ries—to nominate her for that scholarship.

By Friday, she adapted her code so she was able to apply it to arbitrary images from the Aries satellites, and so far it had stopped thinking dogs and cows were humans. Each species, it turned out, had unique infrared signatures she could use to distinguish them.

She was testing it on other animal species using satellite images from the San Diego Zoo when she heard Wyatt's voice down the hall.

"… playing frolf tomorrow, if anyone wants to come. I'll post it on Slack."

What the heck was *frolf*? She zoomed in on the monkey exhibits, wondering how her A.I. was supposed to make that particular distinction.

She heard a noise outside her door and looked up to find Wyatt there with the other two interns.

"Foosball break," said Grace. "I'm going to lose my shit if I have to spend another minute coding CSS this morning."

Grace's favorite pastime was swearing loudly in the hallways. Her 'fun fact about me' during orientation was that she'd been her high school's undefeated bloody knuckles champion.

Jess looked at her code, brain hung up on some combination of frolf and monkeys. A break would be nice.

"Let's go."

The games room was empty, once again. The novelty had clearly worn off for the permanent hires, which was ridiculous, because the place was basically a 1980s arcade. Retro video games and pinball machines covered a space the size of a classroom, while the newer systems stayed in the corner so as not to detract from the theme. It was geek heaven.

Jess and Ethan took one side of the foosball table (Grace dubbed them Team Four-Eyes because they both wore black-rimmed glasses), while Grace and Wyatt took the other.

Jess had been hesitant the first day they'd asked her to play foosball, unsure how much dexterity the game would demand from her fingers and forearms. She would have rather been left out than be the subject of pitying glances. But they all turned out to suck at it, so they were an even match.

"What did you guys work on this week?" said Jess. *No scholarship-worthy projects, I hope?*

"I made the webpage for the upcoming webinar," said Ethan, who was interning on the Marketing Team. "I'm still trying to think of a catchy description."

A straightforward project. Good.

Grace pushed the ball onto the foosball table and they began to play. "What's the webinar about?"

"Our image analytics toolkit."

"Sweet, that's our team!" said Wyatt.

Abandoning the play, he raised a hand. It hovered awkwardly for a moment before Jess clued in. She met his high-five across the table.

"All I could come up with is, *see how our algorithms put the anal in analysis*," said Ethan.

Wyatt stared, letting Ethan score a goal. Ethan looked up, smug.

"Keep thinking," said Grace.

"You should angle toward deep learning," said Jess. "Teaching the computer to understand the world. We're processing images more efficiently than anything humans are capable of."

Ethan turned to Jess. "I like that. You should write the webinar description."

"Stop pawning off your work on other people," said Grace.

"I'm leveraging my available resources."

Wyatt had his tongue between his teeth, slamming his players into the wall to try and jostle the ball out of the corner. It rolled out slowly, skimming past his players and into Ethan's control.

Ethan scored again. He and Jess fist-bumped.

"I'm refreshing the interface for the Aries image portal," said Grace. "Some dinosaur implemented the original version and then quit, and now nobody can maintain it."

Okay, this was a bit more impressive. Threateningly so.

Jess was about to ask for details when Wyatt said, "Floyd gave me a project."

She looked up at him. "He did?"

"Yeah. Chris is mentoring me."

His shot flew past Jess's players and into her goal.

Wait. Jess had to fight for a project, and now Floyd handed one to Wyatt *and* gave him a mentor to guide him through it? A twisting sensation tightened her gut.

"It's so cool," said Wyatt. "It tracks volcanic activity. I call it 'Project Pompeii'."

"You're a dork," said Grace.

Wyatt pulled a face at her. "We're presenting what we have at the Developer Demos this afternoon."

"This afternoon? Already?" said Jess, voice rising a pitch.

She'd heard about Developer Demos in orientation. They happened every month, a chance for the engineers to show what they'd completed recently so the whole company was aware of what everyone else was doing. Everyone important came to watch. It was an amazing opportunity for visibility within the company.

Okay, no need to panic. If Jess got a mentor, she could present next time.

"Did you ask for a mentor or did Floyd offer?" said Jess.

"He just told me Chris was gonna help me. Why, you want a mentor too?"

"Maybe."

Wyatt spun his players violently, whipping the ball at Jess's goal. By fluke, she saved it.

"Cool. You should talk to Floyd," said Wyatt.

"I will." She spun her goalie so hard that the ball shot right through all the players and into the opposing goal. She raised her arms in victory.

Team Four-Eyes cleaned up the game 10-3. Afterward, Jess headed straight to Floyd's office.

He was at his desk, sitting very upright on a gray yoga ball. Rock music played softly from his speakers. The walls were bare, not a poster or photo in sight. A single bamboo plant sat on his desk, and even that looked pale and colorless.

Jess knocked on the open door. "Hey, Floyd?"

He faced her with a pointed 'I'm all ears' expression.

"Wyatt was telling me he and Chris are presenting at Developer Demos this afternoon."

"They're at three. You should come watch. It's good to know what everyone else is working on."

"Yeah. Hey, so, my human detection algorithm is 95% done."

Floyd raised an eyebrow. "Already?"

"Yeah. I was wondering if I could present at the next one. Maybe … with a mentor?" she said, trailing off at Floyd's expression.

"Have a seat, Jessica." He motioned to the chair in the corner. "I think we need to talk about your time management."

She hesitated, then sat. The chair put them awkwardly far away from each other.

"I get the impression you're spending a bit too much time on this project," said Floyd with a little grimace, as if to convey 'oopsie'.

"Oh. I'm not. I completed all my QA this week and my queue is empty."

"That's good. But I don't want you to spend more than four hours a week on this project, okay?"

"Four hours? But—that's less than an hour a day. I won't be able to get anything finished in that time."

"It's not about getting things finished. It's about time management and learning opportunities."

Jess bit back her argument. Four hours a week was hardly a learning opportunity. Besides, this project would be profitable for Aries. She studied Floyd, with his wispy side-comb and that inflated sense of importance. Was it detrimental if she spent time on non-QA tasks?

"It'll be plenty of time to complete the project by the end of your internship," said Floyd, picking up the silence.

"Is that the amount of time Wyatt gets to spend on his project?"

Floyd hesitated. "I'll make the restriction clear to him."

"Okay." He at least had to level the playing field if he was going to be an assface about it.

"You understand, Jessica, that I gave Wyatt a project to give both of you the same opportunity."

She searched for polite words to express that giving Wyatt a mentor and a chance to demo today wasn't exactly the same opportunity.

"So you're best to congratulate him on the project. No one likes an upstager."

"I … Wait, what?" *Did he just imply no one likes me?*

"Anyway, if your project is 95% done, that's more progress than Wyatt and Chris have made, so why don't you demo it today?"

The conversation had derailed. At the idea of presenting something, Jess thought she might vomit. "Today? Like, in a few hours?"

Floyd leaned back on his yoga ball and rested an elbow on his desk. "Sure. It sounds ready enough."

Jess took a deep breath. Could she get up there in front of all those important people? Was she confident enough in her code? This was a good opportunity—but it was too soon.

Floyd checked the time and grabbed his notebook. "I have a meeting. Go ahead and sign up on the spreadsheet."

Jess returned to her office feeling like the floor was moving beneath her feet. She'd wanted a mentor. How had she come out of that office with no mentor and an appointment with the public speaking gallows?

Well, if Wyatt was good enough to present, so was she. She'd worked hard on her project this week and deserved the opportunity to show it off.

Strong, confident, independent. You're a woman of science. You can handle anything.

Screw time management. She spent the next few hours practicing the demo, skipping lunch with Kit, Anita, and Omar.

At five minutes to three, Jess and the Image Analytics Team descended to the demo room on the first floor—a lecture hall with sixty seats, a drop-down screen at the front, and dim lighting. The room had seemed cute on orientation day, but now it felt like a chamber on the Titanic.

Team leads and full-time developers filled at least half the seats. Ethan, Grace, and the Cloud Team had come, too. Some dev guy was pulling up the demo list on the screen at the front of the room, with the order of demos apparently random. Jess's heart thrummed when she saw her name listed fourth out of nineteen.

"Doctor Ries isn't here," the guy said. "He's stuck at the Tech Show. He says to go ahead."

Jess relaxed her grip on her sleeves a little.

She sweated her way through the first three presentations, taking mental notes on how they were delivered. She would start by introducing herself, the project, and then get into showing it. Five, ten minutes tops. She could do this. Right?

When it was her turn, she had a moment of panic thinking she forgot how to walk. Somehow, her legs carried her to the front of the room. She stepped up to the demo computer. Sweat prickled beneath her hair, which felt too thick. Her forehead felt clammy, though she resisted reaching up to wipe it because she was pretty sure it had nothing on her sweaty pits.

"Hi, um, I'm Jessica Curie. I'm going to be demoing a new algorithm for human detection," she said, very aware of how high her voice had become.

She opened the Remote Desktop application. The room full of eyes watched her and the screen behind her. Floyd sat at the front, mere feet away.

Her trembling fingers left greasy marks on the keyboard as she entered the name of her machine, IVY, and then her username and password. She cursed her forearms. She'd gotten used to the slower speed when she was alone, but having a room full of engineers watching her type did nothing to quell the growing urge to vomit. Should she explain why she was typing so slowly? Did they care?

The dialog rejected her credentials. Heart beating in her throat, she tried again. How was it possible for a room to be this *silent?*

"You need to enter the domain," said Jesus Chris from beside Floyd. *"Aries-slash-machine name."*

The silence resumed. Jess followed his instruction without looking at him, typing ARIES/IVY. The computer registered the domain and let her in.

God, the demo hadn't even started and already she wanted to die.

Weren't desk jobs supposed to minimize public speaking?

Classmates and teachers liked to point out that she must *love* public speaking since she was *so extroverted.* Well, they could piss off. Just because she was social didn't mean she enjoyed whatever circle of hell she was currently roasting in.

Jess opened the Aries image portal. She pushed her glasses back up her sweaty nose.

"So, uh, I'll show you how it looks on a given area of interest."

"Will this be offered with the standard license?" said someone who was probably also named Steve. She would call him Steve 3.

She looked imploringly at Floyd. How was she supposed to know?

"Professional license," said Floyd.

Jess looked back at the computer, finding her thread. "So, like, for example, here's a query of Queen Elizabeth Park."

Cringing at her word choice, she ran the query and got an image mosaic of the park, taken half an hour ago. Her tool went to work, picking out the humans and making them glow brighter in the mosaic.

"The polygons and metadata for each human are copied to the SQLite database so the user can do more processing."

Floyd raised his hand. "What metadata do you save?"

"Um, location, timestamp, satellite info, percentage of certainty."

Floyd raised his eyebrows and nodded. Jess couldn't tell if it was a 'that's good' expression or a 'that's an interesting choice' one.

"How's the initial performance?" said Steve 3.

"Um ... good?"

Gah! Stop it, Jess. A bit of nerves and she was reverting to a vocabulary of *likes* and *ums*. Worse, had she really ended a statement like it was a question? This was Professionalism 101.

"The performance is good," she said more boldly.

"Can we see an area you haven't tested yet?"

Jess shifted. This demo was stressful enough without having to go off-roading.

"Sure!" she said, like it was a great idea.

Under everyone's stares, Jess picked a random area in Cairo. There was a long, long pause in the room while her tool went to work. Her glasses slid down her nose again. The sweat on the back of her neck ran down her shirt. She prayed her long hair would hide the dampness from view.

What came out was a perfect rendering of a few city blocks, with every human in the photo glowing brighter. Flawless. She let out a tiny breath of relief.

"Wait," said a curly-haired guy she christened Steve 4. "What's going on near the top, there?"

Jess's heart jumped. She zoomed in. Sure enough, a square in the mosaic appeared starkly different than the rest. It was dark and gray, showing what looked like machinery instead of a city block.

"Uh." Jess clicked the tile to see its attributes. The information meant nothing to her.

A second passed that felt like a thousand.

"We haven't code-reviewed yet," said Floyd. "Probably a little bug."

A bug? In her code? In front of all these people? In an instant, the rest of Jess's life flashed before her eyes. She would get fired. She would go back to school, a failure, and the UBC advisor would tell her she wouldn't be able to complete another internship after having been let go from the previous one. And without proper work experience, she would never be able to land a job again. She would follow in her sister's footsteps and spend her evenings as a cam girl.

"What data is it getting, then?" said Steve 4.

"Looks industrial," said Steve 5. "Airfield?"

"Shipyard?" said Steve 6.

Who cares? thought Jess, wanting to sink into the floor. She needed to go back to her office and fix this. Better yet, she needed to go back in time and fix it before this disaster happened.

Afterward, Jess stared at the space-themed carpet and let her hair shield her clammy face as she slouched in her seat. She suffered through the remaining demos, one of which was Wyatt's. He, of course, had Jesus Chris standing next to him to answer questions. Their code had no glaring mistakes— although another guy, Marco, had his demo crash. Everyone seemed to find this hilarious, while Jess found herself sweating all over again on his behalf.

The demos wrapped up with a polite round of applause.

On the way back upstairs, Jess caught up with Floyd.

"I'll fix it," she said. "Give me until Monday. I'll figure out what happened."

"Sure," he said, seeming indifferent.

She would. This internship was worth working through the weekend.

She let Floyd continue ahead of her, watching the back of that stupid side-comb disappear around the corner. She hated him. Two weeks into the job and she wanted her team lead to get sneezed on by a dragon. He'd set her up for failure. If he was anywhere near being a decent manager, he would have offered her a mentor and told her she could demo her project next month. Instead, he'd thrown her into it without any time to prepare, without any guidance.

Before, she'd wanted to do well on this project to avoid letting him down. Now, she wanted to prove him wrong. Whatever he wanted from her—if he expected her to crumble and beg him for help—she wouldn't give him the satisfaction.

Jess fumed during her entire commute home. By the time she stomped through the door, she was ready to get to work.

The ancient, one-bedroom, unfurnished basement suite she shared with Mandeep was an hour from downtown Vancouver and a short walk to transit. It was central enough to get Jess to work and Mandeep to UBC, so the location-to-price ratio was worth it. The quality-to-price ratio was questionable. Anywhere else, this place would have cost a third of what they dished out each month. But they loved it. The bare, peeling walls were a canvas ready to be filled with pictures from their future travels. Their pantry, sparsely stocked with cheap crackers and noodles, sat waiting for the day they could afford all the overpriced snacks from the organic section of the grocery store.

At the kitchen table—a plastic patio set from the 90s inherited from her parents—Jess sat in front of her laptop, debugging her code.

"The Steves, Anita, Kit, Omar, Chris, Stanley ..." she mumbled.

When Mandeep bumped through the door, laden with cloth bags, Jess greeted her briefly and went back to reciting.

"What are you doing?" said Mandeep, heaving the bags onto the table.

"Trying to remember everyone I met this week."

"Well, you sound like Arya Stark chanting her hit list." She sat across from Jess with her arms on the table, looking toned and refreshed after her spin class. Her short, black hair was soaked with rain. When Jess kept mumbling, she added, "You know, it's okay to forget people's names sometimes."

"I need to make a good impression!"

"Don't get me wrong. I like this new, career-driven Jess."

Jess inwardly cringed. Why did Mandeep insist on comparing the old Jess to the new one? She made it hard to forget about the former.

"I've always been career driven," said Jess.

"Your party-to-study ratio suggests otherwise."

"Ha."

Party. Desi plummeted through her mind's eye—taken from this world because of the recklessness that went hand-in-hand with a party. There was no fixing that mistake. The regret was forever.

Her forearms twinged. She pulled her sleeves down.

Maybe Mandeep noticed a shift in Jess's expression, because she said, "Did you eat lunch with the Cloud Team again?"

"They'll be initiating me into their fight club soon."

"What about the other interns?"

"What about them?"

"You're still friends with them, too?"

Jess considered telling her how Floyd had made her feel like an ass for sitting with them at lunch, but didn't know how to put it into words without sounding petty.

"Sure, we get along. Unless you count the argument we had over which Doctor is the best."

"Oh, god. Did you deliver your Tenth Doctor disquisition?"

"You know it."

Jess dropped her gaze, keen to get off the topic of new friends. That wound was fresh, the mourning period not over. It was then she noticed Mandeep had brought home takeout from Dragonmeat—a nerd cafe with exceptional burgers.

"Holy crap. Have I told you I love you today?"

"You're welcome."

Feeling guilty over being so on edge, Jess reached across the table to squeeze her girlfriend's hand before unwrapping her Wizard Burger (beef patty with cheese, avocado, and magic sauce).

"What are you working on?" said Mandeep, digging into the green vegetable stack called the Ogre Burger.

"I did something dumb at work."

"I'm sure it's not as dumb as you think."

Jess opened the output map and turned her laptop around. "This is supposed to be part of a city block in Cairo."

"Looks like the inside of a warehouse," said Mandeep through a mouthful.

Jess leaned back, squinting. "Maybe."

"Any idea what it is?"

"It doesn't matter. It's wrong, and I want to fix it by Monday."

"Don't work over the weekend."

"I need to."

"You need to watch your stress levels and take care of yourself—"

"I have to fix this, Mandy."

Mandeep huffed. They ate in silence while Jess returned to debugging, and then Mandeep moved to the couch to study. She pulled out her chemistry textbook, which was so thick that Jess had used it as a step stool last week when she couldn't reach the mixing bowl on the top shelf.

Jess set a bunch of breakpoints so she could inspect each value as it passed through her code.

She pushed her bangs out of her eyes and leaned closer. So, she determined which satellites she needed based on the location of interest. That was all fine. Then she sent the request to the Aries matrix to retrieve the satellite imagery for that area. That looked fine, too. Then—

She groaned.

"Find the mistake, Mr. Holmes?" said Mandeep.

"An off-by-one error! I made a freaking off-by-one error."

"Hey, at least that's a simple fix—"

"How could I have made such a basic mistake? This is mortifying."

"It's fine. I'm sure no one will care."

She frantically changed the call to the Aries matrix to the correct values.

Un-freaking-believable.

Where she was supposed to get an image from Aries 180, her code was trying to get one from Aries 181. There was, of course, no Aries 181. There were 180 satellites, so trying to get the 181st was giving her this stupid random tile.

"I can't believe I made such a newbie mistake," said Jess. "How embarrassing."

"You *are* a newbie," said Mandeep. "That's the whole point of an internship, remember?"

"This isn't just any internship!"

Jess ran a few more tests on her code to make sure she'd fixed it. How frustrating that calling Aries 181 returned an image instead of an out-of-bounds error. Whoever made the application programming interface, or API, had overlooked something. Her query must have pulled whatever was cached, or looped back and pulled an image from Aries 1.

Whatever. It didn't matter what the bad code was doing. It was wrong, and now it was fixed.

Jess felt herself being watched. From the couch, Mandeep seemed to gauge her mood before saying tentatively, "I got you a present for your new job."

"Oh?"

"You can have it if you promise to stop working for the night."

"Come on. You're over there studying!"

Mandeep snapped the textbook shut.

Jess narrowed her eyes. Now that she fixed the bug, she supposed she could take a break—and she did have ample time to work on the fine-tuning part.

"Okay."

Mandeep walked over and held out a superhero action figure.

"A placeholder until I can afford the real thing."

Jess examined it. "You're going to buy me Scarlett Johansson?"

"You know what I mean. The statues."

She melted a little as she planted a kiss on Mandeep. "Thank you. You know I don't expect you to fund my ridiculous obsession."

Mandeep leaned back and grinned. "Blake says hi."

They liked to go to the comic store once a week—not to buy anything, but to say hi to Mandeep's former coworkers and to look at whatever new stock they had. Also, it was Jess's weekly opportunity to gaze at the Marvel statues locked on the other side of the display, hand pressed against it, singing 'Over the Rainbow' softly to herself.

She kept the top shelf of her bookcase empty, ready for her heroes to assemble there someday.

Though Mandeep had to quit the comic store when university became too demanding, Blake still gave her a 10% discount on anything. Even so, nobody with a student loan should be buying toys that expensive.

Jess tried to downplay how much she wanted her childhood heroes. She never expected her girlfriend to buy them for her, but that was Mandeep. She would buy Jess statues spanning the entire Marvel universe if she could.

Someday, Jess would earn enough for the both of them. She could buy herself these statues and get Mandeep the road bike she secretly wanted but would never admit. She would pay off their student debts, and they would buy a townhouse together.

She could move on with life—and if she was lucky, make new friends that were half as good as the ones she'd lost.

Chapter 5
Halley Goes to a Tech Show

This. This was better than any nightclub.

Beneath the chandelier of the hotel's massive ballroom, hundreds of people wound shoulder-to-shoulder through the exhibitor booths. Halley was one of them, head on a swivel, dazzled by all the technology. The companies had brought their flashiest prototypes, priciest equipment, and most charismatic staff—a smorgasbord of the most cutting-edge tech the world had to offer.

The number of exhibitors filling the ballroom injected hope into Halley. Maybe she didn't have to be a "hello, would you like a flyer?" girl.

Phone ready, she took notes on what companies to apply for. She was determined to find a solid job prospect before the night was out.

A 3D printing booth brought her to a stop. One of the employees in front had a white prosthetic arm that looked like something out of a sci-fi movie, which he was using to solve a Rubik's Cube. Intrigued though Halley was, the booth was surrounded by viewers trying to get a better look, and she continued on, letting the flow of the crowd guide her.

She stopped at another cluster of people who were wearing headsets, looking around and waving their arms. Augmented reality, no doubt. One guy was making an odd gesture akin to milking a cow.

Okay, humanity had either reached a peak, or it was officially doomed.

"Want to try?" said a twenty-something employee, catching her staring.

Halley summoned some extrovert powers and stepped closer. She took the device from the girl's outstretched hand.

"Are you hiring software developers?"

"We are. Are you looking for full time?" said the girl, helping her tighten the headset.

A 3D dreidel appeared on the booth. Halley reached out and spun it by closing her fingers over the air where the augmented object appeared.

"Internship. I'm a Computer Science undergrad at UBC."

"Great! I'd watch our job listings online to see if anything comes up."

So ... is that a soft rejection?

Halley let the girl show off a 3D tap dancer and a kettle she could pour—but the graphics were terrible. She had seen better dancing hot dogs and twerking rabbits in Snapchat.

"You should try augmenting information about the surroundings—maybe the pipe network beneath the floor—instead of a tap dancer." She handed back the headset. "Show prospects the potential for real-world applications. Military. Architecture. Construction. You know."

The girl stared at her blankly. Halley moved on.

The next booths had robotics, drones, and sensors for self-driving cars—engineering that was tragically beyond her skill set. She stopped at a company that made wearable GPS devices. The guy showed her a web interface where he'd tracked his cat's day-to-day journeys using a GPS collar. Halley refrained from pointing out that tracking a cat wouldn't stop it from getting run over.

"We've got two internships open," he said, handing her a business card.

"Excellent. What's the position?"

"Are you comfortable wearing a GPS collar?"

"Yes. Wait, what?"

The guy flashed her a charming smile. "Kidding. We're hiring devs."

Halley's cheeks warmed. She gave a weak laugh and dropped her gaze to the business card. "Thanks."

This, she was qualified for and interested in. She made a note in her phone to send them her resume.

One prospect in the bag. A couple of others would be nice, and then she could go home, roll herself into a blanket burrito, and call the night a success.

Past the GPS booth, two girls struck a *Charlie's Angels* pose in what looked like an airport security scanner. They held still while it whirred around them, rendering their shape on a computer screen. A 3D scanner. Halley entertained the idea of becoming immortalized as a 3D model, posing like she'd died dramatically in someone's arms. But that would mean finding a willing stranger. Besides, the queue of geeks waiting their turn stretched out of sight.

She continued on, contemplating how to start her cover letter to the GPS company.

I made an idiot of myself when I met you at the Vancouver Tech Show … Your useless cat demo was intriguing.

A spacey-looking car rotated in the middle of the room, which must have been self-driving. Beyond that was the aerospace section, marked by a massive rocket standing in the midst. Halley smirked. Funny how competitive men got about rockets. This particular eight-foot phallus stood erect in the middle of the booths, showing everyone how much bigger it was than all the other exhibitors' products.

Then Halley saw the logo on the side, and her heart skipped a beat. Heat rushed to her face, making her lips tingle.

This was an Aries rocket.

In front of it stood a vertical banner explaining a launch vehicle concept. The booth had stacks of flyers and a bowl of miniature satellites.

And there, standing beside it, talking animatedly to a young man wearing a backpack, was Tony, her interviewer. He was more handsome than she remembered, dressed for the occasion with his thick hair gelled back. He wore a charcoal suit with the jacket open, revealing a white collared shirt underneath.

Before Halley could stop herself, she imagined what it would be like to unbutton that shirt.

Then he looked up. She flinched and turned away.

Dammit. Their gazes had definitely connected. Should she go over to him? What would she say? He probably didn't remember her, and she'd look pathetic for thinking otherwise.

"Hey, there!" A guy with a *Volunteer* badge appeared out of nowhere, motioning in the opposite direction of Tony. "I'm Tim. Would you be interested in—?"

"Yes." She bolted in that direction.

Tim jogged beside her. "Love the enthusiasm! This way."

She brought a hand to her face, trying to calm the charbroiled tomato feeling in her cheeks.

They excused their way through the crowd, Tim checking to make sure she was following. Perplexed, Halley stayed close behind.

They arrived at a circle of computers and gaming chairs. Five of the six chairs were already occupied. A banner advertised a Guavasoft-sponsored hackathon.

Halley's mouth dried up. *Shit.* What did she agree to?

Cheers erupted behind her, mostly from women.

"Go, girl! Represent!"

The other computers were occupied by dudes, who all appeared older than she was.

"Winner gets five hundred bucks and an interview with Guavasoft," said Tim, the total asshole who tricked her into this.

Halley stood immobile, stage fright ready to come out in the form of projectile vomit.

Why? Why did she think going out tonight was a good idea?

The crowd cheered. The other participants were looking at her. Tim grinned, motioning to the vacant seat.

Five hundred bucks. Interview with Guavasoft.

Halley weighed which was the more embarrassing choice: running out of the building, or staying.

Tim picked up a megaphone. "Let's hear it for our final participant!"

Never had a round of applause sounded so sinister. She glanced around as if searching for the place from which the hungry lions would emerge.

"Um—" said Halley.

"Hands off the keyboard until I say *go*," said Tim, making eye contact with each of the six hackers. "On my word, open the doc on your computer to read your challenge. You have one hour."

The empty chair waited. Halley had been looking for an opportunity, and the universe had shoved her straight into one. She could do this. She *should* do this.

Pretending she wasn't at the center of a crowd full of geniuses, Halley sat.

A new PC lay before her, Visual Studio installed as the programming environment, a Word document titled *Challenge.docx* ready to open.

"Hackers ready!" said Tim.

Halley grabbed the mouse.

"Go!"

The noise of the crowd faded. She opened the document to find a half-page essay outlining the problem.

Explore how a rat can be conditioned to reach the end of a maze as quickly as possible. At each junction, the rat picks which direction to go based on the best choice value. Every choice at every junction starts with a value of zero. Use the following learning formula to update the choice values …

Halley re-read the problem a few times. Hey, this wasn't so bad. The formula was complex, but all she had to do was code it. The computer would handle the calculation part. The real focus was on how to write the loop.

So, the first time the rat reached the end of the maze, the choice value at the last junction should be updated. That meant the solution would involve iterating through the maze many times, building up the choice values.

Ah. This was machine learning. Halley would output graphs and matrices so she could visualize the improved steps the rat took to reach the end of the maze.

She got to work coding a virtual maze and a set number of iterations. She named her virtual rat Peter. She would make Peter walk through the maze until he reached the end, choosing a direction based on the learning formula and updating the choice values at each junction. Then he would loop through again, and based on what he'd learned, do better next time.

The crowd bought Halley and the other hackers drinks and snacks. She left the alcohol untouched in favor of stuffing her face with peanut butter cups.

Forty minutes in, she'd coded a working solution with consistent improvement in Peter's ability to learn the maze.

She analyzed the results and frowned. Not good enough. Sometimes, random chance would send Peter down an incorrect path and her code would increase the wrong choice values.

But how to fix it? She glanced up from the screen as her mind worked and regretted it immediately. So many eyes on her, judging her. She could jump up and run away before anyone knew what was happening.

No, she almost had this. She just needed to tweak the algorithm.

Her gaze fell to the hackathon banner, then to the eager students and candidates around her, all of them looking for their perfect job in a shiny new office with the best perks and the greatest benefits.

She thought of Tony the Aries interviewer. She wondered what kind of office life she could have had at Aries. Maybe it was the same as all other tech companies. Maybe it wasn't as exciting and unconventional as she'd built it up to be.

It came to her. Little Peter needed a sense of adventure. To help him reach the end more quickly, she would have to adapt her algorithm so he would make surprising choices occasionally, taking a less favorable path to test if it would yield a better result.

This called for an epsilon value. She implemented a factor of 0.05 for occasional exploration.

"Ten minutes left!" Tim said into the megaphone.

The countdown felt like she was on one of those competitive cooking shows her dad always watched, Halley's mind running in circles as she finalized her solution. The stress did nothing for her productivity, the last two minutes mere key-smashing.

"Time's up!"

She stuffed her face with another peanut butter cup.

The noise of the crowd came back to her. Everyone was applauding.

That wasn't so hard. She had a functional output, at least, and the graph looked more efficient with the added epsilon value.

Tim came around to check everyone's solutions.

Halley's stomach sank as she saw the screen of the guy to her left. He'd generated a gorgeous visual interface, with an image of a rat actually moving through the maze.

"Nice GUI," said Tim.

This earned applause.

At the next hacker, he hummed over the solution before saying, "Probability?" in a tone that suggested it was an impressive strategy.

More applause.

Tim got to Halley's computer and checked her code. Her pulse quickened while he looked at her output.

Impossibly, he said, "Good. Very smart."

Halley let out a breath as he moved on to the others. She hadn't made a fool of herself, after all.

Now, how quickly could she get out of there?

A few long minutes passed as Tim and his colleagues studied everyone's solutions. They compared the outputs, whispering among themselves.

Finally, Tim faced the crowd.

"We had some nice graphical interfaces," he said into the megaphone. "While we like to see some pizzazz, the primary goal was functionality. In terms of this, we had just *two* complete solutions."

He paused dramatically, smiling at the crowd. Everyone cheered.

Hurry up.

"One hacker showed ingenuity beyond a formula. The solution was adaptive and even implemented artificial intelligence techniques. And so, with unanimous agreement, we – have – our –"

He raised an arm and pointed.

His finger aimed straight at Halley.

"—winner!"

Cheers exploded.

Halley gaped, checking to make sure he wasn't pointing at someone behind her.

"Are you serious?"

Tim laughed, but she'd been asking a real question. How was that possible? Was he trying to make her feel better, or were the other hackers idiots?

"Good job," said the guys to either side of her—older, better, more qualified contestants.

This made no sense. This was a set-up. Someone was playing a joke on her.

She stood. "I'm going to get a drink."

Tim said something about her resume and the prize money, but she kept going, her need to escape outweighing all else. She considered sitting in a bathroom stall for a few minutes, like she had to do at parties when the sensory overload sucked her social well dry.

People clapped her on the shoulders as she passed, congratulating her. She pushed through the crowd until she found an exit in the form of double doors. She flung herself through them. The noise dropped as the doors swung shut.

It was a lounge. The staff was setting up for cocktail hour. The room glittered with crystal chandeliers, shiny snack bars, and an impressive pool table. At the far end, a live band was quietly unpacking their instruments. Her pulse slowed.

Smoothing her blouse, she crossed the room toward the bar. She needed something cold. And a napkin to discreetly dab her armpits.

Breathe.

Now that she had some distance and space to think, it seemed obvious nothing sinister was going on. She really had coded the best solution. Maybe she wasn't a totally dysfunctional human being. Had she just run off on a real opportunity? She would have to go back and give Guavasoft her resume. Plus, wasn't there a mention of five hundred bucks?

As people trickled into the lounge, the mob beyond the swinging doors churned like wasps in a hive.

Later.

A dozen or so men occupied the lounge, most of them older, with expensive suits and graying hair. A few gazes lingered on her as she approached the bar. Were they here for the tech show, or … ?

Not a bad way to pay your tuition, she told herself, hiding a smirk. Her friends would have been all for it. Amusement turned to wistfulness at the thought.

As she flagged down the bartender, someone tapped her shoulder. Halley turned to see a guy she recognized from a robotics booth.

"Hey, wanted to give you my card. Send me your resume and I'll pass it to my team lead. Get you in for an interview."

She blinked at him. *Resume? Interview?*

"I'm Ernest," he said, still holding out his business card.

She took it. "Um. Yeah. Thanks."

There was an awkward pause, and then he said, "Well, see ya."

He left.

"Nice work in there," said another voice, and Halley looked over to see a guy her age giving her a thumbs-up.

She returned the gesture and looked away.

Slowly, a smile pulled at her lips. Earlier today, she'd been desperate to find anywhere she could send her resume. Now, she had employers *asking her* for it.

Unable to stop herself, she glanced back to the doors. As someone pushed through, she could see Tony still at his booth, chatting to a pair of young women who were laughing too much and listening too closely.

She ordered a cranberry soda. Why was she bothering to stay? She'd seen all the booths had to offer. She'd talked to recruiters and found at least a couple of job prospects. She'd even been sucked into a contest she had no intention of entering. She should go back to the Guavasoft booth, give them her information, and go home.

But she didn't want to leave, knowing Tony was here. She couldn't decide if she was hoping to get a second chance at an interview, or to flirt with him. Or both.

The band started, sending waves of upbeat jazz through the lounge. The room gradually filled with more people. Halley sipped her drink, leaning against the bar. Men walked past, a few of them less than subtle about trying to catch her eye, but her attention was on the doors.

Finally, Tony walked in, still chatting with his two fangirls.

Halley turned away.

Her eyes landed on an expensive three-piece suit, filled out by a broad chest and biceps, over at the pool table. Halley lifted her gaze and found herself making eye contact with a middle-aged man. He gave a nod to invite her over.

He was with two friends, a pair of silver foxes with the same 'rich businessman' look. Halley hesitated, shifting her weight on her stilettos and curling her fingers around her purse. She reminded herself of the business card in there. No need to be shy. She was on a roll tonight.

The three men were casting grins at her as they spoke to each other over the pool table. Steeling herself, she strode over to them, determined not to look in Tony's direction. Maybe he would see her talking to these guys.

Mr. Sugar Daddy looked smug as Halley approached.

"Hey, mister," she said over the music.

He was actually nice to look at. He definitely put some effort into lifting heavy things.

"Only one reason legs like yours would be walking around a tech show," said the man, giving her a once-over.

Halley considered using one of said legs to kick him in the balls. Instead—because Tony might have been watching—she tilted her head and kept smiling.

"I'm Theo," said the man, stepping uncomfortably close.

Theo? Like, Theodore? God, she should introduce these men to her dad's golf team.

"Halley," she said.

"What are you drinking, Halley?"

"I'm good for now, thanks." She swirled her cranberry soda.

61

"We're headed to the bar," said Theo's friend. "We'll grab you another. What is it, vodka?"

"No, thanks." She wasn't going to drink anything these guys bought her.

"Get her a cosmopolitan," said Theo, leaning over the pool table to line up his shot. Halley slammed her hand down over two of the balls. He faltered, glancing up at her with crystal blue eyes.

"I said I don't want one."

He stared at her, then cleared his throat. "Just a scotch."

His friends left and she removed her hand from the table. She observed Theo's pressed suit and groomed eyebrows. He wasn't wearing a ring, but that didn't say much.

Theo rolled his shoulders and took the shot, sinking a ball.

"So, Halley, you here for a girls' night out?"

"Looking for a job at one of the companies out there. I'm a student."

He raised an eyebrow. "Marketing?"

"Computer Science."

He looked her up and down. "No, you're not."

Halley was finding it harder to keep smiling. Was this guy for real?

The salt-and-pepper hair and chiseled jaw were wasted on him, she thought, entertaining the idea that he would be more useful stuffed and mounted on a wall.

Homo Sapiens Misogynist, the plaque would say. *Ensnared in his natural habitat.*

"You don't need to try and impress me," he said. "I already like what I ..."

He peeled his gaze away and raised his perfect eyebrows. An impossibly seductive scent, familiar, with a hint of cherries, met Halley's nose.

The hairs on the back of her neck prickled.

"That's my girl you're sweet-talking," said a low voice.

An arm slid around Halley's waist. Her breath hitched as Tony pulled her to him, their hips touching.

Theo opened his mouth. Halley braced for him to call bullshit. He had several inches on Tony in every direction. But he stepped back, sneering.

"Funny how that works."

Halley met Tony's dark brown eyes. They glimmered with amusement.

Theo caught sight of his friends—or pretended to—and glared at Halley before walking away into the thickening crowd.

"With all the offers you'll be getting after that hackathon performance, I wonder what made you decide to pursue that one," said Tony, lips curling into a wry smile.

Hackathon? He'd seen it?

His breath tickled her cheek, leaving her lightheaded.

"You often call a stranger your 'girl' without asking?"

"You looked like you needed a fast exit."

"I'm not the type of girl who needs rescuing."

He took his hand away. "My mistake."

Her waist tingled. She wanted him to put his hand back.

"But I can't say I'm much of a pool person."

Tony grinned, sending blood rushing to Halley's face, and motioned for her to follow.

Halley fluffed her hair while his back was turned. Her heart was still pounding from the feel of his hand on her waist.

Tony stopped at the bar and turned to face her. Halley leaned against it, sucking on her straw. She looked up at him through her lashes.

He leaned in. "I was supposed to be here for just the morning, but it turns out Vancouver has more geeks than I anticipated. Been schmoozing since breakfast, waiting for the right prospect to catch my eye."

The feel of Tony's breath on her neck dizzied her. "And no one has?"

He shrugged. "A few. Anyway, this gets me out of going to a mind-numbing social event."

Halley glanced around. "If this isn't a social event, I'd like to see your calendar."

"It's better than a birthday party."

Theo shoved past them as he was leaving the bar, not missing the opportunity to give Halley another nasty glare. Tony watched him go with narrowed eyes.

Unfazed, Halley said, "We can still play pin the tail on the jackass, if you want."

Tony laughed. Oh, that sound. She wanted to save his laugh in a bottle, like people did with tiny ships, and she could open that bottle whenever she felt sad and listen to it over and over.

The bartender placed a glass of scotch before Tony. "Anything for the lady, Doctor Ries?"

Tony's eyes flicked to Halley's full glass. "Not yet. Thanks, Harold."

"Ohmygod," said Halley, nearly dropping her drink. *Doctor Ries?* "You're Anthony Ries?"

He made a tiny bow. "How d'you do, Halley Lovelace?"

Looking pleased with Halley's revelation, Tony—or rather, Doctor Ries—sipped his scotch. During her interview she had thought he was handsome, charming, and funny, but it had never occurred to her that he would also be a genius billionaire, much less the *founder of Aries* itself. And he remembered her name.

Willing herself to form coherent words, she said, "You saw the hackathon?"

"Caught a bit of the finale. Your solution was what I would have done."

"Oh," she said, her voice feeling disproportionately small compared to the blood rushing in her ears.

"What do you plan to do with it?"

"If they send it to me, I—I guess I could put it on Github."

Not that Guavasoft had her contact info, or even her name. She ought to go back and give them her resume.

Doctor Ries studied her. "You want to open source your work?"

"What's the point in keeping it to myself? It'll be more useful out in the world where people can collaborate on it and make it better. Code should always be open source."

He stared at her until her face felt like a charbroiled tomato again. Ugh, was she really babbling to this handsome stranger about open source code?

"I make my interview questions a bit suffocating on purpose," said Doctor Ries. "I like to test whether pressure transforms a person into a diamond or a pile of dust."

"I've heard that about tech interviews." She'd also heard companies liked to ask stupid-ass questions like *why are manhole covers round?*. Thankfully, he hadn't gone there.

His lips curled, revealing that perfect row of teeth. Halley's inside squirmed pleasantly.

"And how did you think I performed under pressure, Doctor Ries?"

"Like a diamond. You showed me intelligence, good work ethic, eagerness … Everything I wanted to see."

She fiddled with her straw, watching the liquid swirl in the glass. "But?"

She knew the answer. She'd stammered like an idiot, and when he challenged her solution, she'd been too insecure in her logic to properly defend it.

There was a clink of ice as he downed his scotch.

"Refill? What are you having, Halley?"

"Oh. It's just cranberry soda. You know, the drink for those only pretending to drink."

He raised an eyebrow. "Is that your usual?"

She tended to consider the 'why don't you drink?' question to be rude, but didn't mind Doctor Ries asking it.

"I don't trust alcohol."

He searched her face. The lounge was getting busy, the public coming in for their usual weekend prowl. People pressed in on all sides, pushing the two of them closer. Halley let it happen, stepping in to let the guy behind her order.

Their hips pressed together, Doctor Ries' body firm against hers.

On the other side of the bar, Harold the bartender poured the guy a whiskey and turned to the next person, looking harried.

Halley cleared her throat. "It's unusual for the CEO of a company as big as yours to do interviews."

"If you owned a company, would you trust any random nitwit to decide who works for you?"

Halley opened her mouth. The answer was obviously supposed to be *no*, so she shook her head.

"Of course not," said Doctor Ries. "I interview all candidates and decide who I let in the door. That's what makes Aries what it is."

Halley tongued her straw, considering his words. She caught him watching and sipped the last of her drink before placing it on the bar.

He leaned in so his lips brushed her ear. "See the bottle of scotch behind the bar?"

She glanced sideways and nodded.

"Grab it."

There was that smile, again. His eyebrows arched in a mysterious, almost wicked way.

Glancing to confirm Harold was occupied, Halley snatched the bottle in one fluid motion.

Doctor Ries laughed. "Perfect score."

She reached for his glass. "May I?"

"Thank you."

Halley let their fingers brush as she took it. He watched her pour, the intensity of his gaze making her cheeks burn.

"If not drinks or pool," he said, "what can I interest you in?"

Feeling a rush of bravery, Halley said, "I can think of a few activities."

Doctor Ries' mouth twisted into a grin.

The music swelled, the jazz band playing an energetic tune that had a few people swinging on the dance floor. Halley backed toward it.

"How about a dance?"

She pretended not to notice the way Doctor Ries' eyes traced over her legs, waist, and chest.

He stepped closer and extended a hand. She took it. He pulled her toward him. She pressed close, inhaling scotch and that hint of something sweet.

"You weren't going to have sex with that man, were you?" he said in her ear.

Something fluttered in Halley's belly. "No."

"Do you have sex with strangers?"

"No. I never have."

"How old are you?"

"Twenty."

"Hm."

His warm hand slid around her waist and pressed against the small of her back.

"How old are you?" she said.

"Don't you know you should never ask a man his age?" said Doctor Ries. "God, can't this band do a cover song instead of overindulgent saxophone solos?"

"I can fix that," said Halley, pulling away.

Doctor Ries stopped her. "Where are you going?"

"What song do you want me to request?"

A strange smile played at his lips that made Halley desperately wonder what he was thinking.

After a lingering stare, he motioned toward the band. "Surprise me."

Halley pushed through the dancing crowd, missing his touch already. She took the moment to fluff her hair and adjust her cleavage.

What song could she request that would be sexy, upbeat, and cool, without making her seem too young? What did thirty-somethings listen to? Nineties music? Something told her this was not the time for the Spice Girls. Maybe she would ask for Michael Jackson.

She was waiting for the overindulgent saxophone solo to end so she could catch the band's attention when fingers clamped around her tush. She whirled around to see an expensive suit standing behind her. It was Theo.

Halley snarled. "Do that again and I'll break your fingers."

Theo grabbed Halley's waist, pulling her in so she was trapped against his stale breath.

"That guy isn't your boyfriend. Don't lie to me."

She pushed against his chest. "Get off me!"

He held on, trapping her. "Look, I promise I'm a nice guy. Let me show you."

"I said no!"

His arms were a vice, his chest a brick wall, rendering her small and powerless.

"Halley, I've got a nice suite upstairs—"

Halley punched him. His jaw popped beneath her knuckles. The nearby people stumbled as he fell into them.

A hand closed around Halley's arm. Theo's two friends were there, uncomfortably close on either side. An icy feeling plunged into her gut. Had they been waiting like a pack of hyenas? What exactly were they planning to do?

She felt a surge of relief for having refused a drink from these guys, and then kicked the closest one behind the knees. He cried out and buckled to the floor.

The throbbing in her knuckles was like a memory trigger. Years of elementary school flooded back, pounding in her ears. Kevin and his two goons leered in her mind's eye. She saw shoes flying toward her face, felt fists driving into her stomach, tasted blood on her tongue.

Gasping, she whipped around with her fists up, ready to take out the third guy. But Doctor Ries was there, looking angry, and he punched him in the face before she could do anything.

Though the band continued to play, the surrounding people were staring. Halley wiped her brow, breathing fast, trying to ground herself in the present. What had she done?

A pair of hands wrapped around her arms and she was lifted off her feet.

"Get out!"

It was a security guy, all muscle beneath a pretentious black cloak. He threw her away from the dance floor.

She stumbled away, raising her hands in surrender. "All right!"

Another security guy went to seize Doctor Ries by the arm but stopped, as though he'd touched an electric fence.

"Doctor Ries! My apologies—"

Halley missed whatever he was going to say because the first security guy advanced on her like a charging bull. She trotted backward, wobbling on her heels.

"I'm going! You don't need to chase me," she said, hands still raised.

He grabbed her arm and hauled her to a door at the back of the lounge. "Get lost before I call the cops."

Halley stumbled into the frigid, dark alley. The door slammed, plunging her into silence.

She stood in the empty lane, staring at the door, trembling. How had she let her temper get in the way of this? Could she not hold it in for one night?

She and Doctor Ries had definitely been getting along on more than a professional level. Now he would never want to see her again, after that public embarrassment.

And what about job prospects? She'd been so distracted by Doctor Ries that she forgot the main reason she'd come here. God, the other recruiters might have seen. Even if they hadn't, there would be gossip. *'Did you see what the hackathon girl did?'*

Halley crossed her arms against the icy January air. Her jacket was still in the coat check. What about her hackathon prize? What about winning an interview for the perfect job?

No way was she going back in.

Her throat constricted. Even without a drop of alcohol, she was still the mess of the party. She dug her nails into her palms and let the pain frisson through her until it blocked out the anger and all she felt was numbness. She didn't deserve that interview. Tonight should be proof enough of that.

Swallowing, she was about to turn away when the door flew open and Doctor Ries burst out, hair scruffy.

"You can fight," he said. "Properly!"

Halley stared at him. What was he doing out here?

She smoothed her hair and stood taller. "Yeah. I do kickboxing."

"Why didn't you put that on your resume?"

"My resume? I … I didn't think that was relevant."

He looked down, eyes darting as though reading something on the pavement. "No, I guess you wouldn't have put that on a developer application."

Why is this relevant now?

Something telling her this wasn't the time for modesty, she said, "I grew up doing hapkido and taekwondo, too. I'm good. I've won almost every tournament I've entered."

She would've beat the shit out of Kevin and his goons, too, if her parents hadn't made her switch schools in grade six. But she pushed those memories aside.

Doctor Ries ran his fingers through his dark hair, taming it. He held out his hand.

"Come here," he said.

She stepped closer, heart beating fast.

He grabbed her hand, giving her an appraising look, and then pulled her down the dark alley. "Let's go."

He reached into his pocket and typed something on his phone as they walked, Halley taking small steps in her stilettos. She stayed a step behind him, watching the back of his neck. The feel of his palm against hers did nothing to calm her pulse. He gripped tightly enough to numb her fingers.

A Bentley pulled up outside the alley. Doctor Ries opened the back door. Halley hesitated for a fraction before climbing in. The car smelled like leather. The seats were frigid against her already cold skin, sending shivers through her body.

The driver, a ridiculously attractive woman a few years older than she was, said nothing. Halley adjusted her skirt and crossed her legs, composing herself. The silence was thick and ringing after the noisy lounge.

When Doctor Ries climbed in beside her and faced her, her heart leapt into triple-time.

Would he kiss her? Push her against the seat, pull her onto his lap? She'd never had sex in a car before.

"Where are we going, Doctor Ries?" she said, only managing a whisper.

He cast her a sly grin, then turned to look out the window.

"Call me Tony, darling."

"Tony."

Okay, so he was waiting until they got to his place. Much classier. Besides, the driver was like, an arm's length away.

They pulled up outside a Yaletown high-rise and the driver let them out.

"Do you live here?" said Halley.

He flashed a key over the black box beside the door, and the lock clicked.

"Top two floors."

He opened the door and Halley trotted in after him. There were four elevators, one of which stood apart from the rest and had its own call button. He swiped his key and jabbed it. The doors opened immediately. They stepped inside.

As the doors closed, Tony faced her. She waited for him to close the gap, to push her against the back of the elevator. The breath was high in her chest, coming hitched and shallow.

Tony smiled. The elevator rose.

Kiss me, Halley thought, willing him to step closer.

She could, of course, go to him.

Amazing how enormous an elevator could feel.

"I take it you're not involved with anyone, Halley?"

"No," she said, heart thudding. "Single."

"Kids?"

"No."

"Big family? Close friends?"

"I have my parents." She hesitated, the weight of the words hitting her. "That's it."

Ding. The elevator opened.

"How did the other four hackathon entrants do?" said Tony.

There was only one door across from the elevator. They entered his suite, and she took it in with her jaw unhinged. The decor was dazzling, all creamy white and pale blue, leather and crystal, with a huge wall of windows. This was a place of unsmudged reputation, everything meticulous and orderly.

"Fine, I think," she said. "There were actually six of us."

Was that a river of pebbles running through the floor?

"No, there were five. Did you see their results?"

She tore her eyes from the raindrop chandelier and thought back. Maybe there were only five hackers. She had been under stress. "One of them had a nice GUI. The other three had graphs. They looked different from mine."

"Less accurate?"

"I guess."

Tony nodded solemnly, staring across the room for a long moment. Was he doubting whether she really won?

Before she could ask, he said, "I want you to do some things for me, Halley. Things I wouldn't trust just anyone with."

"Like what?"

"Business endeavors."

Business. This sounded like employment. She didn't dare believe it. "Are you offering me a job?"

"Not the one you applied for. A better one. Your salary will be twice as much."

Halley forced down a roar of triumph. A job! A salary!

"What's the position?"

"I want you to be my live-in assistant," he said. "I need someone to be available at all hours. Someone fully dedicated. Can you handle it?"

Live-in? Like, move out of her parents' place? Sleep in a foreign bed and leave behind the one with the Halley-shaped imprint? Abandon her nighttime Beanie Baby companions?

She drew a steadying breath. This was exactly what she'd wanted. She'd planned to move out on an intern's salary, which would have afforded her a moldy basement suite in the suburbs.

This was more than a job offer. This was a career opportunity with one of the most successful businessmen in the world. This was life changing.

"It would be a new start for you, Miss Lovelace," said Tony. "I hope you're okay with that."

A human-sized rat maze sprawled before Halley. She could follow any path, applying to work anywhere she wanted. Only the universe knew where each junction would lead.

She could choose a career based on job security, benefits, and a pension. She could have her own office with a company-issued laptop, and lunch at noon, and play ping-pong with her newfound geek friends on Casual Friday.

Or she could add an epsilon value to her life. She could embrace her sense of adventure and explore, taking the less conventional path. To become the personal assistant of Doctor Anthony Ries, founder of one of the best aerospace companies in the world, was to seize a one-of-a-kind opportunity. What he was offering was uncharted territory in her own maze.

"I have classes until May, but then I'll be available full-time—"

"You can continue your studies while you work for me."

Halley nodded.

"So you accept?" he said.

A new start.

This job, more than an ordinary Aries internship, was a worthy achievement. She hadn't dreamed this big.

"Yes, sir."

Exhilaration swept through her like a blast of radiation. Finally, her life was coming together. She could look ahead with excitement, instead of behind with regret.

"You'll start on Monday. In the meantime, send me a void check for direct deposits, and your measurements. You'll need a new wardrobe. That shirt is unacceptable. The clothes you wore to the interview won't do, either. I'll arrange everything new for your arrival."

Halley crossed her arms as though to shield her clothes from his words. *Fair enough.* She'd gotten the shirt on sale. Maybe he could smell the cheapness.

"I'll wear whatever you want me to wear," she said. If that was part of the job, then fine.

Halley would be a better version of herself during this internship. She would make sure he knew he'd made the right choice by hiring her.

He stepped toward her. Anticipation swooped through her body. Then he walked past her and opened the front door.

"I'm looking forward to this partnership, Halley. See you on Monday."

Chapter 6
Jess and the CSA

Jess tried to be productive on her daily commutes. She'd tried books, podcasts, world news, meditating. No matter her efforts, she always found herself browsing social media. One minute, she was looking at an article on the Kenyan political landscape, and the next, a video of a bat eating a waffle.

She compromised by browsing Reddit. It was a nice balance, giving her an equal sampling of scholarly and not-so-scholarly.

Monday morning, it was with a sense of achievement that she expanded a video of a penguin chasing a butterfly. She'd had a busy weekend fine-tuning her code and was at the point where she could set the algorithm free. Free like a house cat bolting through an open front door.

Go forth, my artificial intelligence. Do your deep learning.

Like a declawed house cat wearing a bell collar, her code would probably be ripped to shreds as soon as it hit the open world. It would need to endure a bunch of testing before going public. But for now, she could tell Floyd she was done.

The penguin video fulfilled its promise, and Jess was about to search for another dose of adorable when the next post drew her attention.

Multispectral imaging telescope disappears from the Canadian Space Agency.

It was the 'multispectral imaging' that caught her eye, given the satellite data she'd spent the last week working with. She clicked the link. The CBC article reported that CSA employees turned up to work this morning to discover one of their research projects missing. Nobody knew how, but surveillance footage had been silently cut at 7 PM on Saturday night. There were no witnesses and no leads.

Jess imagined the look on the first employee's face as he entered the lab—coffee in hand, serious case of bedhead, gazing around blankly while wondering if someone was playing the kind of joke only science nerds find funny.

The article had no details on what exactly the telescope did. There had to be something special about it. Jess returned to Reddit to read the comments. People speculated about corrupt employees, competition from NASA and Roscosmos, and aliens. One person suggested it was the same cosmic force that had interfered with the 2009 start-up of the Large Hadron Collider, which was thought to have traveled back in time to prevent itself from launching. Nobody said anything about the function of the telescope and why someone would want to steal it.

Jess had heard about other break-ins at tech companies and space agencies lately. Was Aries on the hit list? She would be in no danger as a software developer on the third floor with nothing but posters and an action figure in her office, but the idea of her workplace being broken into was unsettling. Given the lab's security level, Aries had valuable research hidden inside. Jess might not know anything about it, but she was part of the Aries team, and by extension, part of whatever amazing work the researchers were doing inside there. She had a duty to protect it.

She went to the CSA webpage and clicked through their current activities. Nothing. She searched for 'multispectral imaging telescope' on Google and found a paper published by Canadian researchers last year. The abstract said the telescope was being developed for asteroid surveying. Similar to how the Aries 180 fleet had been launched to get multispectral images of the earth, this telescope was attempting the same thing for Near-Earth objects, or NEOs. It looked like the goal had been to make technology that would inspect the surfaces of asteroids and comets.

Jess added a Reddit comment to explain her findings. Nothing like a bunch of upvotes from strangers to make her feel validated. She would have to keep an eye on this story and hope the culprit was caught.

When she got to her office, she opened a chat with Floyd.

Jess: *I fixed the bug in my algorithm. It's ready to go.*

Less than a month into her internship and already she'd made a significant contribution to the Aries toolkit. Surely someone had to care.

Floyd didn't reply, so she started on her unread Slack messages. An hour passed before he responded.

Floyd: *What was the issue?*

Jess hesitated, wanting to downplay her lame off-by-one error.

Jess: *I was trying to query a satellite that doesn't exist.*

Floyd: *So the Aries API gave you whatever images happened to be cached?*

Jess: *I guess so.*

Floyd: *Ok. I'll be by for a code review in a few.*

Jess: *Great, thanks.*

Jess considered again why she'd gotten back an actual image. The Aries API should have returned an error when she tried to query the 181st satellite. Was she really getting random, cached data?

Indulging her curiosity, she coded a manual query for a few tiles in the 181st satellite. The same gray palette came back. This was definitely a warehouse. She clicked a tile to see its attributes. The images were taken that morning.

Jess put the images into the earth viewer so she could see where they were located.

"Huh."

She rested her chin on her hand. This was Metro Vancouver. To be precise, it was the location of the Aries office.

But she'd seen the satellite images of the Aries office, and they looked nothing like this. Did these images have the wrong coordinates attached? Maybe the location of the Aries office was the default.

Jess entered a query for the latest images of the Aries office. What came back was a building surrounded by a forest.

Right. That seemed normal. Building, parking lot, forest, roads.

So what were these warehouse images?

Jess requested all data stored in the 181st matrix element, just to see what was going on. This wasn't a cache thing. She was getting real images when she queried a non-existent satellite.

She let the query run in the background while she returned to her work. Such a big request could take a while.

She checked her phone. Someone had replied to her on Reddit.

sexymage24816: *Someone at NASA did a project on this in 2017. The idea was to launch telescopes on CubeSats to identify what asteroids are made of and basically start a gold rush in space.*

Floyd appeared in Jess's door. She tossed her phone away from her like it had transformed into a ball of spiders. It slid across her desk, knocking a few pens and some sticky notes to the floor.

Subtle.

"Morning, Floyd," she said peppily.

He was wearing a Monday-morning face. Or maybe that was just his face.

"Ready?"

"Yep!" She invited him in and opened her code.

The code review, like her demo, was full of awful silences and questions she couldn't answer. She powered through as though she wasn't fantasizing about ripping that side-comb off his head.

After a grueling hour, Floyd approved everything, and she committed her first addition to the Aries code branch.

She hoped to hear something congratulatory from him, or at least the assurance that her code would be valuable to customers.

All she got was, "I'll need you on QA for the next while. I'll let you know if another project comes up."

He said it in a friendly enough tone—so why did she feel so terrible? She wondered if Wyatt had gotten another project. Her throat was too tight to ask.

She opened her list of QA tasks.

The shot at winning that scholarship, at being highly recommended and earning a six-figure salary, was slipping further away each day. Sure, Jess had been in the top 5% of the bell curve in her classes, but everyone knew school hardly reflected the real world. Apparently, her programming skills had been artificial. How did she end up here? Did her inflated confidence come off as actual skill during the interview?

Her phone buzzed. Her heart lightened a little when she saw her girlfriend's name.

Mandeep: *How's your day going?*

Jess: *Ugh. I need a win tonight. Want to play Sonic the Hedgehog?*

Mandeep: *That's not even a real game.*

Jess: *You only say that because you suck.*

Mandeep: *Fine. You're on. But next time it's Donkey Kong.*

She took off her glasses and rubbed her face. No moping. She could fix this.

She opened the chat window to Anita. It was blank, having never seen a conversation between them. Their only interactions had been at lunch. Had Anita just been trying to be polite?

She thought of Floyd being a passive-aggressive asshole. She thought of Wyatt being handed a project and a mentor without having to fight for it like she had. She put her glasses back on and began typing.

Jess: *Hey Anita. I'd like to take you up on that mentoring offer, if you're game.*

There was a long pause. She stared at the chat window, heart thumping. Anita could be in a meeting. Or she was cursing at her computer screen, wondering why she ever offered—

The indicator showed she was typing.

Anita: *I'd love to! Do you want to meet today? My afternoon is open.*

Jess: *Awesome. Yes please.*

The prospect got Jess through the morning, even during her team's weekly check-in, when she was again the scribe while Wyatt fished marshmallows from his mug and updated the team on his volcanic activity project.

After lunch, Anita came with Jess back to her office and they walked through the QA tests she was working on for Shy Stanley.

"Nice work," said Anita. "You've covered every boundary case I can think of."

"Yay."

Finally, some positive feedback. As ridiculous and needy as it seemed, the simple 'nice work' gave her life.

"Have you considered cases with null queries?"

"Oh." Right—the all-important test for what would happen if the input was empty. This was often a source of crashes.

"It's easy to add. We have a custom type for it. Here." She showed Jess how to add it. "And what about performance tests?"

"I added … one," said Jess lamely.

"You'll want to check for failures, too. Did you try your hardest to make it crash?"

Jess covered her face. "I'm sorry. I'm still learning."

"You're doing great!"

"I feel like Floyd wonders why the company hired me."

Anita gave a knowing grimace. "You're a good programmer, Jess. Floyd is … well, a dick."

Hearing it said aloud by someone else—someone like Anita, who had been here a while and who had authority—was a weight lifted. Maybe Jess's good grades did mean something.

"But I keep making mistakes," she said.

"Jess," said Anita. "Programming is just a big series of mistakes. Floyd is making you feel this way. It's him, not you."

She let out a breath. "This morning in our code review, he literally told me what keyboard shortcuts to use. Apparently I couldn't even type correctly. I thought he was going to grab my fingers and start moving them for me."

Anita laughed. "See? Micromanager, and more."

"Your team lead isn't like that?"

"Chuck tends to use terms like *ubiquitous* and *push the envelope* and *low-hanging fruit*. It's a harmless sort of douchebaggery. But Floyd? You're not the first woman to want to pepper-grind his neck."

"Does HR not care?"

"What HR?"

Jess grimaced. "Right."

She found out after being hired that her scary-intense interviewer had been Doctor Anthony Ries, the actual founder of this place. She hoped never to have a one-on-one with him again. Something about those intense, dark eyes, that strange smile, and those long, thin fingers had creeped her out for days afterward.

"Anyway, don't worry about Floyd," said Anita.

"It's hard when he's my team lead. He won't let me start a new project. I have to stay on QA."

Anita scoffed. "Seriously? The point of internships is to give students learning experience. You should be able to do something innovative while you're here."

"I know. And the thing is, I was hoping to be nominated for that Canadian Junior Engineering Scholarship."

Anita's face lit up. "You'd be great for that!"

"Not if I don't get decent projects."

"Floyd's being a moron. I'm going to talk to him."

Anita made to go, but Jess grabbed her arm.

"No, don't. He'll hate me even more."

Anita huffed. "If he hasn't let you work on anything new in another two weeks, come see me."

"Deal."

"If it makes you feel better, me and Kit and a few other girls have nicknamed him Double-F. You can guess what the additional F stands for."

Jess smiled. It did make her feel better.

Her spirits were significantly higher by the time Anita left, and she powered through several more tasks before the day drew to a close.

Let's see you downplay this light-speed productivity, FF.

She was about to shut her laptop when she remembered the query to Aries 181 she'd left running.

She opened the window to find it had returned millions of images, a mosaic of tiles collected over time.

"Whoa."

The query was still running, pulling more from further back in time. Jess killed the process before it filled her entire cloud drive.

The images definitely weren't being pulled from a cache. If that were the case, she would have seen a patchwork quilt of random image tiles. This was a complete, connected landscape.

When she stitched together the images with today's date, the mosaic showed the inside of a warehouse. She opened it on a world map and let the application detect its geolocation.

That couldn't be right. The map placed it behind the Aries office. But there was just forest behind the office.

Unless the building secretly extended—?

She brought her hands to her forehead, clutching her bangs. "Oh my god."

This was the Aries research lab. The top-secret, don't-ask-questions research lab they'd been warned about during orientation. Ordinary satellite images showed a forest. Jess was seeing *the inside of the lab* hidden underground.

It was dark, rectangular, big enough for ten thousand people. A wasteland of equipment was packed inside— rockets, satellites, vats and barrels, solar panels, and more— leaving a maze of narrow walkways. A balcony along the perimeter created a second level to overlook the operations. Several staircases led up to it.

At the entrance, a wall separated a white, classroom-sized lab from the rest of the warehouse. A handful of people were in the white room, wearing lab coats and working around a surface. Jess zoomed in on one person, but the resolution was too low to identify who he was. Red Badges, for sure.

Then she noticed the item on the surface. She stared at it. Slowly, an icy feeling plunged into her gut, and she wished she could unsee everything.

It was too late.

She recognized it without ever having seen it. It was a large telescope, gray, cylindrical, with several lenses on the end. Stamped on the side, blurry but recognizable, was the logo of the Canadian Space Agency.

She was looking at the inside of the Aries research lab, and they had the stolen telescope.

Chapter 7
Halley Gets a Project

Halley stepped into her new life carrying her phone and a one-way Skytrain ticket. Tony had emailed to remind her that he had a new wardrobe waiting, and she shouldn't bring anything with her—not even her wallet.

He was giving off a bit of a serial killer vibe, but okay, Doctor Billionaire could make whatever demands he wanted. He hadn't specified not to bring her phone, so like hell was she leaving that behind. As for her schoolwork, she hadn't bought her textbooks yet this term, and all her notes were in the cloud.

With nothing to pack or prepare, Halley's only tasks over the weekend were to email back the signed job offer (that $8,000/month salary, though!), and to tell her parents.

She'd awoken on Saturday to find them in the living room reading. There was no Jimmy Buffett playing, no smell of garlic toast—just her parents, and the house she grew up in, and a silence waiting to be filled.

Halley stood there for a long minute before they sensed her hesitation and looked up.

"Uh oh," said Dad. "What'd you do?"

She cracked a smile.

"Um, I got a job offer from Aries. I'm going to be Doctor Ries' personal assistant."

"The founder?" said Dad.

"The billionaire?" said Mom.

Halley nodded. "I start Monday."

They ambushed her with a group hug and cheers of, "'atta girl!" and "proud of you, kid!"

"Thanks," she said into Dad's armpit.

"Bet he hired you to help him with all the smart stuff. *Angular momentum* and *thermodynamics.*"

"Good job, Dad. No, I'm not sure what I'll be doing, but ..." She pulled back, suffocating in their embrace. "It's a live-in job. So I'll have to live there."

It occurred to her that Tony hadn't specified how long the internship was. They usually lasted one or two terms, but this one wasn't exactly conventional. She would have to clarify.

"Can't say I'm surprised," said Mom, voice thick. "The founder's personal assistant!"

"Since you were this big," said Dad, motioning by his knees, "you always reached for the stars."

"It's fate we named you Halley."

"Halley's Comet isn't a star," said Halley. "It's a—"

"Oh, stop it," said Mom.

Halley didn't let the praise go to her head. Her parents looked for any excuse to hug and kiss her and tell her how wonderful she was—overcompensating for all that Kevin bullshit. The way they saw her through rose-colored glasses only filled her with guilt. The praise was undeserved, and that made it suffocating.

When they dropped her off at the Skytrain on Monday morning, Halley left feeling afraid, yet free—a baby kangaroo emerging from its pouch.

By the time she stepped into the streets of downtown Vancouver with the other commuters, her heart fluttered in anticipation of something new. Whatever Tony assigned her, she vowed to get the job done perfectly. The opportunity was too big to screw up.

She arrived at his building at 6:45 AM and waited around the corner until 6:59. He'd said 7:00 AM, so she would be there at exactly 7:00 AM.

When she reached the penthouse, Tony opened his door looking as good in casual jeans and a t-shirt as he had in business attire. His hair wasn't gelled back, but soft, messy, and sticking up in the back.

"Pleasure to see you, Miss Lovelace."

He led Halley through the living room, which was as dazzling as she recalled, and down the stairs. "Your suite."

"Oh – my – god," said Halley.

Hers? She was looking at the whole lower floor of his penthouse. The living area had a leather sectional couch and huge TV, a workspace, and a kitchenette. Through the open door to her right was an exercise room with a punching bag.

He walked her to the bedroom, which had a king-sized bed and a walk-in closet full of new clothes and shoes.

Yup, she had officially adopted a billionaire lifestyle.

Be cool, Hal. You can jump on the bed later.

As much as she wanted to snoop in every corner and cupboard, the workday had begun. Tony led her to a white, plant-adorned desk where a tiny laptop waited.

He began clicking and typing on it. "Would you mind plugging this in, Halley? Charger's under here."

She retrieved the charger from the desk drawer and plugged the laptop into the outlet for him.

"And get rid of this." He motioned to the empty laptop box on the desk chair.

Halley put it in the recycling bin that she found under the kitchen sink. She returned to find his dark gaze on her, that peculiar smile pulling at his lips.

"What do classical conditioning and penicillin have in common, Halley?"

She hesitated, calling upon her limited knowledge of Pavlov's dogs. "They were both accidental discoveries?"

"Smart girl. The theory of gravity, microwaves, X-rays … I'd say accidents and luck have to do with most discoveries."

"I agree," said Halley, remembering the time she discovered that taking a picture of the crook of an elbow looked like a picture of a butt.

"Sadly, people hoard knowledge for financial gain, and for this, progress suffers. Do you know who created the periodic table?"

She racked her brain, feeling like she should know this. When she came up with nothing, Tony said, "Mendeleev!"

"Right."

"Are you aware, Halley, that someone else invented a periodic table around the same time, completely separately? His name was Meyer. To this, I say, what a *colossal – waste – of – effort.*"

He had a point. She'd also heard two men invented the jet engine at the same time on the opposite sides of World War II.

"I don't want to wait for an accident in order to do something great," said Tony. "I want collaboration. Imagine how science would hurtle onwards if humanity's best minds worked together."

Halley nodded eagerly. People were so concerned about protecting intellectual property and making money off discoveries they believed were 'theirs'. What would happen if the world's top minds worked together instead of being recruited by competitors and forced to sign NDAs?

"I want to unite aerospace knowledge," said Tony. "I want to create a world more advanced than if every discovery was left in its patent-pending silo."

"It's a good idea."

"I'm tickled you think so." He turned the laptop to face her. "Your first assignment."

She was looking at the website for Global Nanosats. Specifically, she was looking at a page titled *'What's Next?'* with an image of one of their nanosatellites hovering in space.

"GN is keeping secrets," said Tony. "Of course, Aries slays them at 99% of what they do—data quality, satellite-to-satellite communication, computational systems ..." He placed a hand over his heart.

"And the one percent?" said Halley.

"Propulsion. I need to know how they do it."

She stepped closer to the laptop. Okay, a research project. She could do this.

"Try hunting down conference notes, message boards, archives," he said. "They were at a trade show a couple of weeks ago and might have revealed prototypes. Look for social media posts by partners and clients who've let confidential info slip. Dig into their help forum. Sometimes support staff tries to be helpful by telling customers what's in development."

"Okay." Halley made mental notes of everything. *Archives. Social media. Forums.*

This wasn't so much 'collaboration' as an aggressive form of competitive analysis. But she liked his style.

A faint buzz sounded. Tony looked at his watch.

"I'll check on you at the end of the workday." He pulled his phone from his pocket and made for the stairs. "And, Halley ..."

"Yes, sir."

"I think they're doing more than satellites and propulsion. I want you to find out what they're hiding."

The door shut behind him with a click, leaving Halley staring after him in the abrupt silence.

At least her parameters were well defined. Propulsion and a mysterious project. Before the end of the day, she was going to find out all of GN's secrets.

She spent the next hours digging into everything Tony had suggested. She left the desk alone, preferring the bench beneath the window so she could look up from her screen to gaze across the unaffordable expanse of downtown Vancouver.

Tony worked upstairs, his voice and footsteps pulling periodically at Halley's attention. What she wouldn't give to skip up there, throw herself onto the couch, and ask him about his life and family and favorite flavor of Ben & Jerry's.

After spending the morning following Tony's research suggestions, Halley had a few notes on GN's roadmap and breakthroughs, but everything was frustratingly vague and coated in marketing language. This wasn't good enough. She needed secrets, formulas, data. She had to try more creative research tactics.

Her stomach grumbled fiercely.

Food. In her excitement, she'd forgotten about lunch. Pleased to find the kitchenette fully stocked, she made her favorite: pancakes smothered in peanut butter and maple syrup.

She got back to work fueled by this nutritional grand slam.

LinkedIn revealed who worked at GN, their resumes, and what topics they posted about. There, Halley learned that someone named Brody Campbell had completed his thesis on propulsion two years ago and was hired by GN immediately after. His research must have caught their attention.

She searched for Brody Campbell's thesis and found a PDF on the Caltech website called 'Experimental Techniques for High-Energy Liquid Tetrapropellant'.

Experimental propellant!

Ninety-eight pages of analysis, tables, and formulas. Finally, a trail worth going down. She saved the document.

The next search result was titled, 'Campbell – High-Energy Liquid Tetrapropellant (Amended)'. Halley's heart leapt. The URL was a subdomain of the Global Nanosats website. She clicked and found herself looking at a login page.

"Damn."

She'd hit the internal GN network.

The word 'amended' in the title was tantalizing. GN must have had data beyond what was in the thesis. Two years' worth of newer information, in fact, lived behind that login screen.

Halley scoured the remaining search results and stalked more GN employees on LinkedIn but found nothing else useful. She moved on to Glassdoor. In the last two years, six anonymous employees reported salaries between $105k and $120k. All of them worked on propulsion.

One of them rated the company one star and wrote, "Applied for the propulsion engineer job and ended up on the Campbell project. The guy's a dickwad. If you get a job offer from his team, do yourself a favor and look elsewhere."

The Campbell project. Yes, that thesis was definitely an active area of interest at GN.

The sun approached the horizon, darkening Halley's suite. She stretched, spine aching after being hunched like a Neanderthal all day. She was so close. Brody "Dickwad" Campbell's thesis was a start, but this amended document was the real gold mine. Now, how to get it?

She returned to the GN login page. The cursor blinked in the Username text box, every tick bringing to mind something hidden behind the company's firewall. *Equations. Formulas. Trade secrets. Proprietary data.*

A knock sounded at the door of her suite. She jumped up from the bench with her laptop, and only then realized how badly her feet had fallen asleep. Blood rushed back into them, prickly and painful.

"Well?" said Tony, letting himself in.

Her door didn't lock. She would have to remember that.

"I found a thesis on liquid—um—tetrapropellant," she said, dancing from foot to foot. "They've been working on it at GN for a couple of years."

Tony's eyes widened. "You found—already?"

She beckoned him over and put the laptop on the desk, opening the saved PDF. A minute passed as he scrolled through the pages in silence. Halley's heart pounded. *Please, be useful.*

Finally, he said, "Good, Halley. My boys will be able to use this."

Halley pursed her lips so he wouldn't see the manic grin fighting its way to her face.

"Is this the only document on the subject?" said Tony. "Any more experiments, adaptations, results?"

She hesitated. "GN has more in their internal network, I think. I couldn't access it."

There was a silence. She tried not to squirm.

"This is impressive, what you were able to find for me." He motioned to the laptop. "You show above-average research skills. I wonder if your technical skills match. It's a shame a login page stopped you."

Halley cringed. Her technical skills *did* match. In fact, they were better than her research skills. She needed Tony to know this. She needed him to know she was smart enough to find what he wanted.

He made the roadblock sound so insignificant—a minor inconvenience.

"I could—" She hesitated. This was her chance to do something worthy. If she handed Tony the most up-to-date research from GN, she would help Aries catch up in that final 1%. It wasn't exactly ethical, but it was possible. "I can get into their network."

Tony raised an eyebrow. "Can you?"

She nodded. She'd spent all day hunting for useful information, and she'd come too damn close to give in.

"You are a brilliant thing, aren't you?" said Tony.

Her belly gave a swoop, the praise soothing her like a hand stroking her hair. Doctor Anthony Ries thought she was brilliant! Those were words for her resume.

Relying on the sketchier places of the internet for technical help, she spent the evening setting up a VPN, which would act as a tunnel to Global Nanosats' internal network. It would give her access to their entire system. She would be able to give Tony whatever he wanted.

It was a stretch from the 'collaboration' he'd talked about, but it wasn't that bad. Nearly everyone pirated something at one point or another, and Halley had downloaded her share of music and movies. What harm was pirating scientific information? It wasn't real stealing. Nothing physical would be lost.

Whatever you need to tell yourself, said a voice in her head.

Okay, fine, it was hacking. But she refused to accept defeat.

As she finished configuring the infrastructure and launching a decryption script, her phone buzzed. It was a text from Mom. Below that was an email from UBC reminding her about tuition and a missed call from Guavasoft.

Interesting. They'd found out who she was.

Well, she already had a job. *Look at me now, nerds!*

She opened the text.

Mom: *Hope irks fun call me and fill mean*

Halley whispered the text out loud to decipher it. Mom was terrible with technology, her texts constant products of Siri misinterpretations. This sounded like she was meant to call Mom to fill her in.

Halley grinned. *Oh, hacking into an aerospace company, no biggie.* She would have to use technical jargon so her parents would get confused and not ask questions.

Finally, she was doing something worthy of their praise. After one day working for Tony, she was already contributing to space exploration. She wished she could jump back in time and tell Brooke she wasn't pathetic and selfish. She was brilliant, and Doctor Anthony Ries said so. She was good enough to help him build his aerospace empire—and that was something to be proud of.

In the morning, Halley spent five minutes taking a celebratory jump on her king-sized bed. She'd done it. During the night, her script had broken through GN's firewall.

Her first order of business was to save the document behind the login page. It was loaded with formulas she didn't understand and words like fluorine-diborane and ammonia-nitrogen tetroxide, which boded well. To her dismay, there was a note at the top: 'To be used with Specification 4059.'

Ugh. Now she had to find whatever that was.

After her morning cereal, she settled on her bench and tracked down Brody's computer, emails, chat history, and cloud drive. She ran a search on all of it for '4059' and 'propellant' and a few other keywords. While that churned, she reviewed the company's internal site and found an organizational chart showing all the employees who worked in the physics department. She searched their files, too.

They'd done a lot of work in propulsion. A *lot* of work. A startup growing this quickly probably had all kinds of structural chaos and poor organization. All the better, if their security systems couldn't keep up.

If Halley was honest with herself, she enjoyed having Global Nanosats at her mercy like this. From a comfy seat in a penthouse, she was in control of their enterprise. And that felt pretty good.

In emails and chats, Specification 4059 came up a few times. But it was all talk—no data. A few people mentioned 'chemical firearms' development. Maybe this was the mysterious project Tony was talking about. She would have to come back to it. For now, she had to figure out what the hell 4059 was. Was the amended thesis useless without it?

The sun touched the horizon by the time she found a clue in the form of a chat.

Brody: *We're trying the propellant with the prototype tomorrow. Can you send me 4059?*

Tyrel: *They're on a hard drive. Luyten b. Come grab it from the server room – just bring it back when you're done.*

Halley searched Tyrel's files for anything that might relate. She went through his temp folders and trash. Zilch.

Her spirits sank. That was it, then. The final piece was not accessible on the network. It was on a hard drive, disconnected from everything.

What would she tell Tony? He wouldn't be satisfied with this.

Neither was she. Her two days of work were useless without that specification.

Before she could hurl her laptop across the suite, she opened GN's IT portal and accessed their surveillance images. She searched for the server room—304B.

The most recent photo, taken minutes ago, was a JPEG taken from what must have been a security camera above the door. Dozens of servers lined the walls, and in the middle of the room sat a gray folding table covered in cables, packaging, manuals, and USB keys.

And there, atop the table, was a black, rectangular object. A hard drive. Relative to the cables, it looked to be the size of a pocket romance novel, with a single USB cord coming out the back. The white label on top was too grainy to read—but the shape of the letters might very well have said *Luyten b*.

"You little ..."

A knock sounded. Halley sat taller on her bench as Tony came through the door.

"How did we do?" he said.

"They do have more data. I got some amended formulas."

Tony must have sensed her dismay, because he said, "But?"

She turned the laptop to show him the photo of the server room. "There are associated specs, and that part isn't connected to the network. Someone used it last week but he didn't save it to his machine."

Tony came over to the bench. He stared at the image for so long that Halley had the urge to poke him. She couldn't read his expression. Was he disappointed? Angry? Confused?

"You're so good," he murmured, and his husky tone, his closeness, and the way he stood over her sent a tendril of heat snaking through her abdomen.

But she wasn't good. She'd been thwarted before she got something useful for him.

Tony pulled out his phone and opened the calendar app, brow furrowed. She watched him scroll down a long list of appointments.

"I need it," he said, his voice strained.

"I know. I'll keep a watch on it. Next time someone connects it to a computer—"

"No." His jaw worked as if he was physically chewing on his thoughts. He tore his gaze from his phone. "I need you to go get it, Halley."

Halley looked at him sharply. What, she was supposed to waltz on over to Global Nanosats and *break into their office building?* What the actual hell?

"You want me to break-and-enter?"

"You've already hacked into their system intending to steal. This is hardly any different. You'll just be there physically instead of digitally."

"But—" She spluttered. Yeah, stealing was stealing. She'd crossed that line hours ago. But breaking into an aerospace lab?!

She opened the amended thesis and pointed to the first formula. "Look. Maybe you don't need the specs. You're a genius. You can figure out how to fill in the gap."

Tony smiled down at her. "Honey, there's only so much one man can know. My education is in business and psychology. All that rocket science goes past my zone of specialty and into the land of don't-give-a-flying-fuck."

Last term at UBC, Halley had taken to hanging out in the Computer Science Student Society lounge between classes, where students from the business faculty were infamous for popping in. They always had the same message: "Hey, nerds, I've got an idea for an app. Want to build it for me and I'll give you 3% of the profits?"

The response was always some form of, "Pass us the business plan. We know just where to stick it."

Halley was on the point of hoping Tony wasn't one of these douche bags when he said, "My engineers are kings. I do back flips to give them what they need. They need what another company is working on? I'll skip away and get it for them. They need someone else's prototype? Done."

"And they need this propellant data."

Tony made a finger gun at her.

Her heart beat faster. Hacking was one thing, but this? Tony was asking her to become a criminal!

"What if you offer to buy it? Or you could poach their engineers. If you offer to double their salaries …"

"I won't take the risk. Besides, why blow money on something you can just take?" He extended a hand, composed and confident. She took it and let him pull her to her feet. "There are other career paths, Halley, if that's what you prefer. But I see promise in you. Your dedication to science, your passion, your skills … Don't let them go to waste. You were brilliant enough to get past Global Nanosats once today. You can do it again."

Halley curled her toes, feet cold on the expensive stone floor. She opened her mouth, but no words came out.

"Back in a jif," said Tony, and he disappeared up the stairs.

Halley brought her hands to her face. *Ohmygod, ohmygod, ohmygod.*

Hacking was morally questionable, sure, but this was all-caps-ILLEGAL. If she got caught, she would spend her life living out *Orange Is the New Black*.

Would that be so bad? Sharing a cell with someone who looked like Alex …

She shook her head. No! God, it would be life ruining!

Working for Tony was the career of her dreams. But how could she do what he was asking of her? She'd broken rules before. She'd even broken the law when she and her friends were being particularly rotten—but never something like this.

She had to get out of here. She went to grab her purse, making it halfway across the suite before remembering she hadn't brought it with her. She hadn't brought anything. She ran in a little circle before stopping where she'd started. Her breaths were coming fast.

If she could slip out the front door while Tony wasn't looking, she could be down the elevator and back on the street before he realized she'd gone. She could go home and send her resume to Guavasoft.

She strode back across the room and had one foot on the bottom stair when Tony appeared in the doorway at the top.

He was holding a black backpack, the outdoorsy kind with a bungee cord criss-crossed over it.

"You'll want a scarf and hat for your face—"

Halley let out a squeak, stepping back.

He raised an eyebrow. They stared at each other, Tony towering above her, the silence heavy.

"Tony, I—I can't."

"Halley—" His watch lit up with a notification. He looked at it, shoulders tensing. "Look, I know this is fast, but I really need you to do this."

"But Tony, the law."

"Oh, pish. Every revolutionary act in history has been in opposition to the law."

Halley eyed him. "Are you telling me this would make Gandhi proud?"

Tony came down the stairs and stopped in front of her. "Galileo was put on trial. Einstein was exiled."

"Galileo was convicted of heresy—"

"The law, back in that time."

Okay, laws changed, and a lot of important moments in history fell on the wrong side of the law. In fact, maybe most of them did. Did Tony believe this was one of them? Was he enlisting Halley in a scientific revolution?

He winked at her. "Every great company has to take morally fuzzy steps to reach the top. Surely you've followed the scandals, seen the movies, read the biographies. No CEO is a saint. If you want to change the world, you have to bend the rules."

There was no denying Aries was a great company. She'd seen the headlines. Tony's satellite fleet supplied imagery that saved lives during rescue efforts after natural disasters. It kept a protective eye on glaciers, rivers, reefs, oil fields, even international military activity.

Tony had more vision than almost anyone in the world. He had the potential to change the aerospace industry—and he was begging *her* to help him.

"Have you done this before?" said Halley, recalling a news story about a security breach at GN.

"I'll be able to equip you with everything you need," he said without looking at her, sending a few texts. "You'll have my business jet to yourself. GN is in Colorado, but you won't have to worry about getting probed by airport security, flight tracking, any of that crap. I've got enough connections to set you up for a perfect entry and exit."

"But—I can't—"

"Halley, you already broke into GN today."

"I know." He'd said that already.

But his tone had cooled, something hard gleaming behind his dark eyes.

You already broke in …

Oh. He wasn't reassuring her. He was threatening her. She'd done all of that on his laptop, which he'd probably rigged to track every step she took, linking her to the crime she'd committed.

If she double-crossed him, he had all the proof he needed to have her put in handcuffs.

She could try to weasel out of it, yes. As her parents and relatives spent her life telling her, her blue eyes and blonde hair and smooth skin made her look like "an angel fallen from heaven". She could plead innocence, saying Tony forced her into it and she was a victim. But who would the authorities believe—Doctor Anthony Ries, billionaire and esteemed member of a zillion societies, or Halley Lovelace, a student who had already been linked to criminal activity months ago?

Her stomach churned. She had no honor worth defending, and besides her parents, no one to defend her. She dug her nails into her palms.

She could quit, give up the opportunities this job presented, and go back to her kangaroo pouch. She imagined calling her parents and saying she wasn't up for the job. They would pick her up from the Skytrain and pull her into another one of those suffocating hugs, and they would tell Halley she was wonderful, and they were so proud of her.

Or she could keep going. She could do something that had the potential to impact the entire course of space exploration.

The promise of adventure coursed through her, as if she had leaped off a rope swing.

"I'm not trained for this," she said. "My expertise involves sitting in front of a computer."

"Baby, you underestimate yourself. I wouldn't be asking you to do this if I didn't think you were capable."

Her mouth opened. Despite everything, the word 'baby' morphed her into the heart-eyes emoji.

"You've shown me all I need to know," he said. "If I can do it, you can do it. Your physical training is better than mine."

Wait, was this why he was so impressed with her kickboxing? Did he know it would come to this?

His eyes roved over her, dark and deep-set, a little baggy from overwork. "You've never bent the rules?"

"Sure, but—"

"Were you naughty in high school? Did you ever take anything that wasn't yours, vandalize someone's property, sleep with someone you weren't supposed to?"

She'd been as naughty as a good student could be. That was to say, high school had been a time of giggling through sex-ed class, using spare blocks to get Starbucks, and reenacting various musicals at slumber parties while 'drunk' on half a shot of vodka. Post-high school had been the shitshow. Post-high school, she'd learned things about herself she wished she could bury. *Psycho. Bitch. Selfish.*

Tony didn't think she was any of those things. He believed she could do this assignment.

"What if the police come?"

"They will. Getting around them is a simple matter of planning. Don't worry, I have experience to share. You won't fail. Cross my heart."

They held each other's gaze, the moments ticking by to the beat of Halley's pounding pulse. Slowly, Tony grinned. His eyes narrowed like a cat's. Halley nodded once.

He motioned for her to follow him upstairs, and she went.

This is fine. This is fine. Tony had a point. She'd spent so much time and effort studying computers, getting fit, honing her reflexes. This was her chance to put those skills to use. It was as though her whole life had led her to this moment— even the hours spent pretending to be a spy as a kid. If she stopped being so modest about her abilities, she knew she could do this.

He led her to the coat closet by the front door, which had a deadbolt in place of a knob. He pulled a key from his jeans pocket and unlocked it.

"Which one are you comfortable with?" said Tony.

Halley's jaw fell open. Six guns were on the wall inside, from a palm-sized handgun, to a machine gun half as big as she was.

None of the above.

"The second one," she said, feigning confidence. She'd shot a pellet gun once at her aunt and uncle's ranch, and it looked similar. Back then, a line of dolls had been the target.

"Good choice," he said. "A pistol will be easy to conceal. And it'll look nice in manicured little hands like yours."

As he placed the weapon and ammo into the backpack, she assured herself that Tony knew what he was doing. Of course she would need to arm herself. She wouldn't need to shoot anyone—just threaten them into letting her through the building.

Tony looked her over with the intensity of a drug detection dog, as if he could smell her doubt.

Trapped between Tony and the wall, between stone floor and vaulted ceiling, between unemployment and the life of her dreams, Halley saw only one path ahead. The choice wasn't whether or not she should accept the assignment; it was whether she should face it like a cowering little girl, or dive into it head on like she was born to do this.

She felt a swoop of excitement. This was the adventure she'd been waiting for. She just had one condition.

"I want training first. A few days, at least. Show me everything you know."

If she was going to do this, then she was going to do it properly.

Tony looked at his watch. His jaw worked. He hesitated, shifting from foot to foot.

Halley squared her shoulders, unwavering.

He met her eye, that peculiar smile on his lips. "Deal."

Chapter 8
Jess Plays the Game

Jess exploded through the door so violently that Mandeep dumped the bowl of tortilla chips she was holding.

"Seriously?" Mandeep looked down at the corn-based confetti explosion. "I just vacuumed!"

"Aries is running an illegal operation."

Mandeep stared at her from the couch. On the TV across from her was Sonic the Hedgehog. She'd been practicing.

"What do you mean?"

"A telescope went missing from the CSA, and Aries has it. I saw it on surveillance images."

"What were you doing looking at surveillance images?"

"It's complicated. That's not the point. They stole a telescope, Mandy!"

Jess struggled out of her coat, shoes, and gloves, feeling like she was trying to disentangle herself from a straitjacket. Mandeep waited in silence until Jess tossed them by the door and spun back around.

"You're sure it was the same one?"

"It had the CSA logo on it."

Mandeep combed her fingers through her short hair. "Maybe they're doing something for the government."

"The CSA *is* the government! Why would they report it missing?" She took a deep breath, hearing herself growing high-pitched.

When Jess and her sister were little, they tattled on each other for everything. Swearing, hitting, sneaking an extra cookie. Any rule breaking was cause for retribution. A strict moral code had been so firmly ingrained in them that it sent six-year-old Jess running to her mom when her big sister used the word 'crotch', insisting that justice be served to Millie for using such foul language. Little Jess always trusted authority to stop the world from crumbling.

Now, to have authority break the laws put in place by authority? Was society caving in on itself?

Mandeep stood, brushing stray chips to the floor. She approached Jess sideways, as though trying not to set off an anxious dog.

"Whatever you saw, Jessie, I don't think Aries would let a random intern witness an illegal operation like that."

"That's the thing. I wasn't supposed to see it. Maybe whoever dishes out the API keys forgot to restrict my permissions. I'm supposed to have access to imagery of Aries 1 through 180, but I also have access to 181, which gives me the Aries research lab."

Mandeep's brown eyes narrowed in bewilderment. "And the stolen CSA telescope is in there?"

"Plus loads of other equipment. Do you think more of it is stolen?" Jess raced back through time, thinking of other instances where technology had gone missing recently.

"Remember the CubeSat that went missing from that California startup last year? What if it's there?"

She paced, making a path between the kitchen and living area. The 8-bit Sonic the Hedgehog tune looped relentlessly in the background.

"Is 181 a secret satellite?" said Mandeep.

"I think it's drone imagery. It's underground, taken from inside the lab. The whole point of 181 seems to be to show this landscape of ..." She waved her arms. "Stolen things? Who knows what else could be in there! I bet Doctor Ries is monitoring it to make sure nobody without a security clearance trespasses."

How many people knew about it? The Red Badges did, but what about management? Suddenly, the entire office staff seemed untrustworthy.

Floyd had seemed oblivious to her out-of-bounds query, so he probably didn't know. Ordinary employees like the Cloud Team certainly didn't. They were too happy and fresh-faced for such a dark secret.

"Why is he storing this in the same database as the other imagery?" said Mandeep.

"Why not? He's paying for the storage. Might as well add another set of images to it. There's no way he intended to let me access those. Oh, god, what do I do?!"

Mandeep stepped closer, trying to stop her from pacing. "Jessie, calm down."

"My employer is a thief! Does this make me a criminal?"

"No. If it's that serious, why don't you report Aries and quit?"

Jess rounded on her. "This is exactly the problem!"

"What is?"

"Quitting will ruin everything I've worked for. Plus, you know we can't afford it. We need the income and that scholarship. We're a step away from living in a cardboard box."

She gestured to the plastic table and peeling walls. Never mind saving up for tuition—she wouldn't be able to afford rent or food. Mandeep didn't have enough saved to carry both of them. Jess would have to submit her resume to a cafe or something tomorrow. And what good would that job do for her resume?

"We've got each other, and that's enough," said Mandeep.

"Aren't those the lyrics to 'Livin' On a Prayer'?"

"I'm saying don't worry about money."

Jess shook her head. Reporting Aries to the authorities was out of the question. It would sabotage her chance to earn work experience, to get a glowing reference, and even to put Aries on her resume. She might get blacklisted for future job opportunities. No one would hire a girl who betrayed her employer. Plus, everyone else at the company, like Anita, would be out of work if Aries got busted.

"Jess, think of your stress levels. You're not doing yourself any favors by worrying about this."

Stress levels. How many times had Mandeep shamed her about that? Jess had listened, dammit, ditching the friends who caused more harm than good, avoiding activities that could make her injuries worse. Where did it end? With every reminder, she felt more and more helpless and fragile.

She rolled her wrists, working out the tension in her forearms.

"My stress levels are fine."

"If you still want to get paid and get the work experience, just stay quiet," said Mandeep. "Pretend you saw nothing."

Jess grimaced. "But Aries *stole* things. They stole from—" She stopped, facing Mandeep. "Maybe it's not that bad."

Mandeep stood with her hands in her pockets, waiting for Jess to continue. Sonic's 8-bit soundtrack kept looping, seeming to get louder and more frantic.

"I saw a picture with no context. There could be more to it. Plus, even if it is stolen, it's not like they're stealing money from an orphan. We're talking multi-million dollar corporations losing, what, a million? It's pocket change to them."

When Mandeep continued to stare at her, she said, "Say something!"

"There is a possibility you saw something criminal," said Mandeep with exaggerated calmness. "But you're only on contract for four months, and your work has nothing to do with the lab."

True. If this was something sketchy, it might take ages to blow open, and by then, she would be gone.

She paced some more, rubbing her aching forearms.

"Okay. I'll shut my mouth and keep my job."

And I'll win that scholarship.

"Good," said Mandeep, sinking back onto the couch. "Now, want to play?"

Jess crossed her arms, hardly in the mood for a video game.

"Hun, I'm serious. You need to pretend you saw nothing. It's better for your health and your career. It's not like anyone got hurt. It's a telescope."

Jess exhaled. Okay, it wasn't like she'd discovered a bomb waiting to explode.

She sat beside Mandeep. Knowing her, it was best to agree now and let the subject drop.

"All right. Let's play."

But her arms were throbbing from tension, the agility in her fingers worse than usual. She could usually beat Mandeep no problem, even with the titanium slowing her down. Today, she couldn't focus—physically or mentally.

Mandeep paused the game as Jess was about to plummet to her death again. She kissed her and stood. "I've got an 8 AM lab tomorrow."

"Night."

Jess waited until the bedroom door shut, then got out her laptop. A bit of investigating couldn't hurt. She opened her web browser and typed 'Anthony Ries'.

Hundreds of millions of hits came back. She started with his Wikipedia page, scanning for a 'Controversy' subheading. There was nothing like that, so she scrolled to the next best thing: 'Personal life'. She found no hints of a criminal record, but that meant little. He might have thrown money at it to make it go away, or he hid his activities well. She did find a short section on his family. Apparently, his mom left when he was a kid, passing away a few years later and leaving his dad to raise him alone. He was an only child, and his dad owned a software company and a vineyard in Kelowna, BC. There was also a brief section on relationships, which said he'd been engaged to the CEO of a solar photovoltaics company from July 2015 to May 2016.

There were no photos on the page, so Jess backtracked to the search results. She found no headshots, pictures from speaking engagements, or anything other than blurry paparazzi-type shots. Was he keeping his identity hidden for a reason?

She browsed the search results for something more substantial. She tried searching for Anthony Ries crimes, theft, and lawsuit. Nothing. So much for finding out his dirty secrets.

Keep quiet, she told herself, the voice in her head sounding like Mandeep's.

She would—but that didn't stop the feeling that Doctor Anthony Ries was hiding something.

Chapter 9
Halley Goes on a Business Trip

The ridiculously attractive woman who had picked Tony and Halley up from the tech show turned out to also be a pilot. Reah lived on the fifth floor of Tony's building, apparently earning a living by taking Tony wherever he wanted to go.

"Help yourself to whatever you want," she said before entering the cockpit of Tony's private jet. "There are caramel snickerdoodles and gummy worms at the bar. Also carrots, but let's be real."

Halley, after embarrassing herself by squealing like a fangirl when she saw the inside of the jet, thanked Reah calmly. Then she flung herself on the nearest couch. Complete with plush leather seating, glossy tables, a bar, and a TV, the jet's furnishings were worth more than her entire UBC tuition.

She wondered how much Tony had told Reah about her assignment. Did others know Tony stole knowledge? There was a certain thrill about being in Doctor Anthony Ries' inner circle.

Donning a pair of noise-canceling headphones, Halley opened her laptop. She had three hours between here and

Colorado to review the plan she and Tony had come up with for her Global Nanosats assignment. Over the last week, she'd learned everything she could from Tony—from simple tips like how to avoid leaving DNA evidence to more seasoned strategies like calculating how much time she had before she needed to get out. Confidence, he'd said, was the key ingredient. She'd taken pages of notes. His final instruction had been to "get this hard drive by any means necessary. Creativity is crucial, baby."

Halley opened the most recent security images of the GN server room.

Target acquired.

The hard drive was in the same spot Tyrel had left it in. The plan also included how to get it, what to bring, how much time she had, and how she would safely exit the building once she got the hard drive. She ought to have a checklist.

Target, Tactic, Tools, Time, Exit.

No, that wouldn't do. She needed something that started with a *T*. Then she could call her heist plan the Five T's. T for thief. T for Tony.

Target, Tactic, Tools, Time … Takeoff.

She was a pro already.

GN's security camera archive, along with employee chats and emails, had revealed a few things about the company. They had the occasional board game night. Amber and Ravi liked to hook up in the fifth floor washroom. Most pertinently, a few engineers were under a tight deadline and would still be there when she arrived at around 8 PM. At least four people would be having a pizza-fueled coding jam on the second floor.

Getting through the gate and into the building would be tough, but she could do it. She'd decided to Trojan horse this shit. Creativity, baby.

The floor plan showed the server room, 304B, in the middle of level three. It would be locked, but zooming in on those grainy security images told her every employee had a badge. She would get one of those badges from the coding jam participants.

By the time she got into the server room and took the hard drive, someone in the building would have called the police. A quick takeoff would be important. The room had a window, but it was likely suicide proof, so she would need to break it. Then she would use a rope to descend from the third floor.

Given the proximity of the police station, she gave herself eight minutes to get out.

Reah said something from the cockpit. Halley pulled back her headphones, letting the full volume of the engine assault her eardrums.

"We're landing, hon, if you could put your seatbelt on."

Halley drew a deep breath. She had this.

"Roger, Charlie Delta Sierra descending eight thousand, cleared for an approach," said Reah into her headset.

Halley completed her checklist.

Target: hard drive, room 304B.

Tactic: Trojan horse.

Tools: pistol, rope, pizza.

Time: eight minutes.

Takeoff: third-floor window.

Her heart was pounding so hard she could feel it outside her chest. Did she know enough? What was she missing? She checked her notes from Tony's lessons.

There was a whine as the jet's wheels descended.

Hands trembling, Halley opened her backpack. While the jet landed and taxied, she rummaged through everything inside: rope, digital watch, temporary phone, cash, Swiss Army knife, pistol, silencer ... Yep, all the equipment of an ordinary bag. She braided her hair and folded it under a toque. She wrapped a scarf around her mouth and nose and pulled on gloves to prevent fingerprints, doing her best to achieve a 'bundled against the cold' look and not an 'about to put a gun to your head' look.

She put on the watch and prepared it with a silent eight-minute timer.

Finally, she fit the silencer on her gun. Or rather, the *suppressor.* Apparently, that was the proper term for it. New vocabulary word of the week.

"Ready, Freddy?" said Reah.

Halley put her laptop inside her backpack with everything else.

It was dark and snowy when they landed. A rented SUV waited across the tarmac, and Reah hopped out of one vehicle and into the other. Halley had to admire her gusto.

"I'm going to a conference social nearby," she said, meeting Halley's eye through the rearview mirror. "That's the *reason*—" Halley heard the air-quotes. "—we're here. Call me when you're done."

Halley nodded. So, Reah knew what was going on. This was oddly reassuring. Halley considered asking for advice, but couldn't bring herself to do it. She got the impression Reah had a long resume and more intense qualifications than Halley assumed.

She had Reah drop her off a block away in front of a food stand called Cheesy Dick's Pizza. The inside smelled like chemically enhanced dough and ethically questionable pepperoni. She used the cash to get a medium of whatever was ready.

It was snowing peacefully, a few inches of fresh powder on the sidewalk. Pizza box in hand, Halley trudged around the corner and across the street, where GN's logo stamped the top of a five-story brick building. The front gate was shut and required a badge to pass through—or someone on the inside to open it.

Halley pulled out her laptop and tethered to her phone's hotspot. She logged into GN's network. Her research indicated that Albert White was away on vacation, so she dialed his extension. She answered her own call via GN's virtual phone service, logged in as Mr. White. She pushed 9. The gate slid open.

Feeling smug, Halley slipped her laptop into her backpack. She picked up the pizza box and walked through the gate toward the building entrance.

In the two-foot blind spot between security cameras, she aimed her pistol at the camera above the door. Though she'd disguised herself, she couldn't be too careful.

She scrunched her face in preparation for the shot and pulled the trigger. At least, she tried to. Her finger wouldn't move.

Right, the safety. She turned it off and tried again. The bullet hit the wall beside the camera with a *thwang!*

"Oopsie."

She fired again, gripping harder to protect her wrist from the recoil. Her few days of practice hadn't been enough to accustom her to how different this thing was from a pellet gun.

Who came up with the term 'silencer', anyway? Halley sneezed more quietly than this. Maybe this was why the proper term was 'suppressor'.

After several shots cratered the wall around the camera, she hit it. It burst like a glitter bomb.

She would have stored the pistol in the waistband of her yoga pants, but she'd heard that was a sure way to shoot yourself in the ass. Instead, she opened the pizza box, placed the gun on the pizza, and closed the lid.

With the box balancing on her palm, she stepped up to the door. Her heart raced. She thought of that time in grade six when she and her friends had knocked on their teacher's front door and run away. There would be no running away, now.

But before she could knock, the door flew open, and she found herself facing a scruffy man in jeans and a faded black tee.

"What the hell was—?"

"Delivery!" sang Halley.

For effect, she jutted her hip like a sassy waitress at a fifties diner.

The guy blinked. He looked from her face, buried in a scarf, to the pizza box. "Uh, lemme check who ordered ..."

"They said third floor. Don't worry, I'll take it to them."

"Hold on." He glanced over his shoulder.

Halley inched over the threshold. "If you let me through, I'll find—"

"I'll get them. What's the name?"

Halley pursed her lips. He had to make this difficult.

"Mister, can you please let me in?"

His eyes narrowed.

Damn.

Before his suspicion could grow, Halley kicked him in the groin. He curled over, lining himself up for a perfect TKO.

"I'm sorry about this," she said—and meant it—before she delivered an uppercut to his jaw.

He crumpled, unconscious before he hit the ground. The pizza box landed next to him with a cardboardy thump.

"Oh, Hal." She looked down at her work. "You know how to take a man's breath away."

A scream filled the room.

Halley snapped her gaze up to find a startled woman around her mom's age standing across the lobby. She wore high-waisted jeans, a pink collared shirt, and held a flowery handbag, which she dropped as she pulled out her phone.

"Um, hey!" said Halley, tugging the scarf so it still covered everything below her eyes.

The woman was dialing, backing away.

Halley kicked open the fallen pizza box. "Put that down, please."

She didn't listen.

Halley kept her eyes on the woman as she squatted and rummaged for the pistol, getting cheese on her gloves.

"I'm going – to ask you – ah." She wrapped her fingers around the gun and aimed.

The woman squeaked, dropping her phone and raising her hands.

"Get on the floor," said Halley, in her best 'I'm Batman' voice.

A clump of cheese dripped from the muzzle and hit the floor with a *plop*.

The woman sank to her knees.

"Good. Please stay here, and don't call anyone."

Halley strode past the front desk, pistol trained on the woman, shoes squeaking on the tiled floor.

She paused and pulled out a printed map. According to the office floor plan, four elevators were on the far side of the lounge.

304B. Eight minutes.

She checked her watch. She'd forgotten to start the timer.

Okay, seven minutes.

The office was a try-hard place, probably business casual since the 80s, until management decided they needed to look hip to attract millennials. The lounge had drink refrigerators, circles of colorful bean bag chairs, board games stacked in the corner, and a big TV on the wall. The room was empty.

On her way to the elevators, she changed her mind.

"Actually, can you follow me, please?" She couldn't leave this woman here. She would go right back to phoning the cops.

The woman sidled into the lounge, trembling. Losing patience, Halley marched over and grabbed her by the elbow. The woman gave a terrified squeak.

"Relax, would you?" Halley dragged her to the elevators and pushed the call button.

The doors opened with a soft *ding*.

"Going up," said the elevator serenely.

Halley made an 'after you' motion. The woman shuffled in, sobbing quietly.

Halley pushed the third floor button. Her nerves had steadied—or reached a peak and flatlined—but either way, her adrenaline level was under control.

The doors closed. Halley's stomach swooped as they rose.

"It's only experimental," said the woman through her tears. "That leak was misleading."

Halley looked at her. Interesting. Something else was happening on the third floor?

With all her focus on the hard drive, she'd forgotten she was supposed to check out whatever else the lab was working on. This was her chance to investigate beyond 304B.

The woman's badge identified her as Sherry Franklin.

Experimental, she'd said. Experimental and confidential, perhaps? In the name of research, this was a detour worth making.

"Take me there, anyway, Sherry." For emphasis, she pointed the gun at Sherry's head. The woman nodded, lips trembling.

"Third floor," said the elevator, and the doors opened. Sherry edged out, eyes fixed on the pistol.

"Oh, just walk," said Halley, the wasted time ratcheting up her anxiety. Eight minutes never felt so short.

Sherry led her down the empty hall and stopped in front of a closed door. On the sign were the words 'Chemical Firearms'.

"Yes, please," breathed Halley.

Exhilarated, she seized the door handle.

"Hey, what do you do with a dead chemist?"

Sherry looked back blankly. "Um ..."

"You barium."

Not even a hint of a smile. Halley shrugged and turned the handle.

The room was locked.

There was a black box beside the knob.

"Open it," said Halley, pushing Sherry forward.

Sherry pushed her badge against the box and an LED light blinked red.

"Oh no," she said tearfully, "they lock it after six."

Halley looked around. 304B was on the other side of the building and she had already lost a couple of precious minutes. She had to hurry.

Sherry was repeatedly flashing her badge, desperately trying to open the door.

"Shit!"

"My thoughts exactly," said Halley, shoving her out of the way.

She aimed her pistol and squeezed. The bullets ricocheted off the handle, the noise thundering in the hallway. Sherry screamed. Halley fired in the same place until the pistol gave a disheartening *click click click.*

No time to reload. She clubbed the bullet-ridden door handle until it snapped off.

An alarm filled the hallway.

If the police hadn't known she was there before, they would know now. Her heart rate sped up. *Work faster. Get out.*

Halley drew a breath, reining in her emotions, and checked her watch. Four minutes left.

She kicked the door open.

"Show me which one—" Her eyes widened. "Jesus mother of Pete."

Rifles and handguns sprawled across worktables in varying degrees of completion, raw and matte, their parts scattered as if picked over by crows. Test tubes, tools, and bottles lay strewn between the pieces.

More guns hung on the far left wall that looked like functioning prototypes. Sparkling like gemstones, every weapon seemed to be coated in a semi-transparent resin. Halley was overcome by the urge to touch all of them.

"Which ones work the best?" she shouted over the alarm, throat constricting.

Sherry said nothing. Halley turned her gun on the woman.

"The pistols have been in development the longest," said Sherry.

God, even without bullets, the power of this thing was disgusting. Time for an upgrade.

Halley swept along the wall and plucked a sleek, silvery pistol from its rack. It was lighter than she expected. The grip fit her hand like it had been custom made for her.

She glanced around for a target. Nothing suited, so she aimed for a blank space of wall at the back of the room.

Using two hands to brace against the recoil, she squeezed the trigger.

A continuous stream of bullets left the barrel. It happened smoothly, almost unnoticeably, as though she had been watering plants in a garden.

She gaped at the wall, which had turned to Swiss cheese. Each hole was black around the edges, like the bullets had burned through them.

"How does it work?"

Sherry furrowed her brow as if surprised by the question. She pointed to the stock, which had *Global Nanosats* engraved in block letters. "The compression chamber converts the liquid solution to bullets."

Halley nodded, impressed. She dropped her old pistol into her backpack, adopting the new weapon. Now to take a chemical firearm for Tony, and then skip off to 304B. This wasn't so bad.

"How do the bigger ones perform?"

"Hands off," someone said behind them.

Halley and Sherry whirled around. A girl Halley's age stood in the doorway, trembling hands closed over a gun.

"The police will be here any second," she said over the screaming alarm. "If you come quietly, you won't be charged for stealing."

Halley stepped closer, her new pistol raised. No. This chick was not about to ruin her first assignment.

"You know, puss, you're missing a good party downstairs. I brought pizza."

"I saw."

"Then you know I'd be charged for a bit more than stealing."

"I can't let you take these," she said, quavering.

"I just need one more," said Halley. "Sherry here was about to tell me which rifle is closest to being finished."

The girl's eyes flicked to the wall—a tiny act that betrayed everything.

Halley reached out, hovering over one with a telescopic sight on top. Sniper or something? Russian … carbine … Kalashnikov-47? Whatever. Halley didn't know her guns.

When the girl kept her aim steady, Halley moved to the simpler-looking one next to it. The girl tensed, her fear palpable.

Halley clicked her tongue. "I hope you don't play poker."

She plucked the weapon off the rack.

"Stop!"

The girl pulled the trigger.

Several tables and pieces of equipment exploded. Halley was launched into the air. There was a cloud of smoke and a car-sized hole in the wall where the rifles had been. Then her back collided with a table, and she dropped to the floor.

She gasped at the pain, the breath knocked out of her.

Smoke. Something was burning.

She couldn't breathe. She had to get away from the smell, the heat, the sting. *Not again.*

Then she saw the flames. Her gloves were on fire. She screamed, clawing at the material, trying to get them off.

Anything but fire. Drown me, bury me alive, just please, not fire.

A flaming balcony surged to the front of her memory, and for a moment, she heard Brooke shrieking, and Desirae's body lay on the floor before her.

She ripped the gloves off and threw them across the room, then smacked at the flames on her sleeves until they went out.

Small fires were peppered around the room, consuming the walls and spreading across the worktables. She scrambled away from them, scanning her singed clothes for danger.

With a hiss, the sprinkler system turned on. Halley gasped as water doused her.

In the doorway, the girl who'd pulled the trigger was on all fours, coughing. Sherry lay a short distance from her, groaning as she cradled her leg.

Halley's scarf had fallen, revealing too much of her face. She fixed it hastily then balled her hands into fists, swallowing a surge of dread. She was exposed. She had to get out before she left fingerprints everywhere.

Why hadn't she brought extra gloves? It would have been easy to pocket a second pair.

The alarm was still wailing, filling her head, the flames growing and roaring closer. Explosions punctuated the din as the fire ate the fallen prototypes and scattered parts. The sprinklers rained over everything, making little difference.

Halley forced the fear down. This wasn't the time to give in to panic.

The pistol and one unharmed rifle lay beside her. She snatched them up, stuffed the rifle in her backpack with trembling hands, and dashed into the hallway.

She had to get out.

Wait. What about 304B? Could she get to the other side and grab the hard drive before—?

At the end of the hall, two police officers burst from the stairwell door, guns raised.

Halley swore and spun back to the room. She could see a small window at the other end through the flames.

There was no time for anything else. She might have been able to knock out the engineering nerd who answered the door, but she didn't have the guts to take on the cops.

Shouts rang out behind her. "Freeze!"

Halley ran back into the flaming room and raised the GN pistol. She aimed at the window, shattering the glass with a barrage of bullets. She raced down the corridor between the flames and leaned out into the darkness. Shards flaked away and fell down, down, down. It was too high.

Did she have a choice?

The shouts grew closer.

She hesitated. She wouldn't have time to uncoil her rope, tie it to something, and lower herself. They would shoot her through the top of the head before she could remember the difference between a square knot and a clove hitch.

A pine tree rose beside the window, its snow-dusted branches out of reach.

Halley stuffed the pistol into her bag and wiped sprinkler water from her eyes. She pulled herself through the window, shirt tearing on the glass.

Kneeling on the window sill, she stretched for the tree. Her fingers brushed the outermost pine needles. With an index and middle finger, she pinched a twig and eased the branch toward her. She wobbled on the window sill, knees protesting.

Footsteps sounded behind her.

"Cannonball," she whispered.

She got her feet under her and jumped, holding the pine branch for dear life.

Her stomach swooped at the free fall. The branch carried her into the trunk and she landed with a snowy explosion, pine needles stabbing her everywhere. She tumbled through the branches and to the ground.

Knees and wrists protesting from the impact, she hobbled to her feet and limped across the snowy lawn toward the gate. It was open. A cop car was at the building entrance with its lights flashing. Employees ran out the front door, shouting to each other over the alarm.

Weapons rattling in her backpack, she sprinted along the fence, through the open gate, and down the dark street. The snow slowed her pace, thick and slippery, like a nightmare. Sirens wailed in the distance.

She ran until she was past Cheesy Dick's and an alley opened beside her. She leapt into the darkness and sank behind a dumpster.

Reah. She needed to get out of here. She pulled the phone from her backpack and dialed the only stored number.

"Where?" said Reah.

"Alley. West of the pizza place. Need my GPS?"

"Got it."

Catching her breath was excruciating. She crouched behind the dumpster for several long minutes, praying no one would follow her footsteps in the snow. She shivered as the water covering her turned frosty.

Her watch showed a big fat zero, the expired timer blinking to the rhythm of *"you suck, you suck, neener neener neeeeeener"*. She reset it aggressively.

In the distance, they cut the building alarm, plunging the snowy night into silence.

An SUV pulled up and stopped beside the alley. Halley leapt into the back seat.

"Go!"

Reah drove away calmly, obeying the speed limit.

Cop cars screamed past them, heading toward the Global Nanosats building. Halley sank lower in the backseat.

In the rearview mirror, Reah looked back toward GN. Halley shut her eyes. She didn't want to know how bad the flames were.

Tears leaked from beneath her closed eyelids.

How had she failed so spectacularly? She'd been distracted by these stupid weapons and failed to get what Tony had sent her for.

The explosion in the firearms room replayed in her mind, tightening her throat and pushing her closer to a panic attack.

Breathe. The flames are far behind.

With a jolt, she remembered her scarf had slipped when she hit the floor. She grabbed her laptop, tethered to her phone's hotspot, and entered GN's system. She located the surveillance images from the last few minutes. *Shit.* Her face had been exposed for three entire pictures.

She scrolled back and deleted all images from the last hour, praying no one had consulted the surveillance archive yet. She should've put more effort into cutting off the CCTV before she entered the building.

And what about hair and fingerprints? Nothing she could do about that, now. She had to hope any evidence was burning with the room.

She threw the laptop on the seat next to her and buried her face in her hands. One week on the job and she'd failed Tony. She didn't know him well enough to know how he would react. Would he be angry? Would he ask her to leave?

The chemical firearms were her only hope. She prayed they would be enough.

Midnight tolled by the time she got back to Tony's place.

Reah pushed the button for the regular elevators. As Halley stepped into the one dedicated to Tony's penthouse, she said, "You did well, Halley."

It was the first time she acknowledged the assignment since they'd left Colorado. Maybe she'd been instructed not to talk about it, but knew Halley was doomed and these were her words of consolation.

Halley considered thanking her, but didn't trust herself to speak without the waterworks starting again. She'd cried the entire flight home. Her face resembled a red balloon.

The elevator closed, taking Halley to the top.

When she walked through the door, Tony emerged from his bedroom looking freshly showered and wrapped in a bathrobe. He stopped dead, gaping at Halley, who was singed, dirty, and trying not to wince from the pain all over her body.

Before he could comment, she said, "You were right. They were working on something besides nanosats."

Tony stepped closer, looking greedily at her backpack as she unzipped it, hands icy and trembling. She took out the rifle and pistol and placed them on the counter.

"What's special about them?" said Tony.

She picked up the pistol, tapping the stock with an index finger. "Chemicals. They've got compression chambers. They convert some kind of solution into bullets."

Tony studied the rifle, arms crossed, as though examining whether a new coffee table would look nice in his living room.

"I haven't tested that one," said Halley, "so you probably want to have someone look at it first."

"And the pistol?"

"Works a million times better than that ordinary one."

Tony stepped closer so they were inches apart. He didn't take the pistol, but raised Halley's wrist gently, examining the weapon and her hand like they were a single entity.

He ran a thumb over the stock. "We were experimenting with something like this. Couldn't get the chemicals to play nice."

Halley was too distracted by his breath on her cheek and his fingers brushing hers to register his words.

"And the hard drive?" he said, letting her hand drop.

She lowered her gaze. So much for a good-news decoy.

"Um—" Dammit, she was blinking a lot. The waterworks were returning. It was all over. "I'm sorry. The cops came. I didn't have time to …"

She took a breath, furious with herself for crying at work. This was so unprofessional.

"I know exactly where it is, Tony. I ran out of time. I should have gone straight there instead of—"

"Yes. You should have."

There was a long, terrible silence. Halley swallowed hard.

Tony motioned to the rifle. "Did you get more bullet solution for these?"

Everything seemed to drain from Halley's head. She hadn't even gotten that. She'd stolen guns, but no extra bullets. She'd created chaos and terrorized the GN staff, but for what? Of all the opportunities behind the doors of GN, all she got were two weapons that would be useless once their ammo ran dry.

Tony's expression darkened. Halley had the urge to step back from him, but she was too numb, too shocked by her utter failure, to move.

"I'll have my boys open up the assault rifle and study the chemicals," he said. "I'm sure they'll be able to replicate it. I'm ... disappointed."

He backed away, studying Halley up and down with his dark eyes. Halley's insides ached. She never wanted to be the cause of the word 'disappointed' passing his lips again.

"I'm sorry," she whispered. "I can do better."

She wouldn't be able to live with getting fired. As disastrous as tonight was, it had been the most exciting day of her life. She had been doing something big, something important. Returning to her old life would be unbearable.

Tony nodded. He glanced to the time on the kitchen stove. "Get some sleep. Tomorrow, we'll take a jaunt to the office."

137

"The office?"

"Yes, Halley. Consider this a learning process. You'll do better on your next task, won't you?"

She stood taller. "Yes, sir."

Next task. Could he really be giving her a second chance?

"Of course you will. And for now, you need to understand what I'm trying to accomplish. You might be less inclined to get distracted while on assignment."

Halley nodded, a glimmer of hope easing her pain. He was prepared to trust her. She could fix this.

Tony clamped a hand over her shoulder, making her wince, and guided her to the stairs.

"Tomorrow, we're going to explore what I'm working on in the Aries lab."

Chapter 10
Jess Swears a Bit

"Well, fartbuckets."

Scrolling through social media on the way to work, Jess's eyes drew to a trending story about Global Nanosats.

It wasn't *necessarily* a red flag that one of Aries' competitors had been broken into last night, right?

She tapped the story, looking for an indication of whether anything was stolen. The article didn't specify. She clicked through several stories, but the only details were that a woman had broken in with a gun, and her identity had not been determined. They had a single, blurry surveillance image of her stopping at a place called Cheesy Dick's Pizza. She'd covered her face.

What, they don't have surveillance cameras around the GN building? Useless turds.

Her stomach churned as she studied the photo. Yes, the culprit was female, but Doctor Ries could have sent her on his behalf. Was this another CSA ordeal? Was a GN satellite now sitting in the Aries lab?

She put her phone away and rolled her wrists, letting out a slow breath that fogged up her glasses and the window. Why was this bus so freaking cold? She crossed her arms, sinking lower in her seat. On days like this, she could feel the titanium in her arms, cold and sharp, pressing beneath her skin and reminding her how broken she was.

Mandeep's voice rose in the back of her mind, scolding her for letting herself become stressed.

Drop it. This is outside your control.

But if her employer was committing a serious crime, she had a moral obligation to report him.

She skipped her usual start by the coffee machine and headed straight to her office, where she woke her computer with frantic keyboard taps and mouse jiggles.

Maybe the world was oblivious to Doctor Ries' crimes, but Jess wasn't—and despite what she told Mandeep, she was unconvinced the best course of action was to let them keep happening.

She queried the latest Aries 181 images and scanned the lab's contents for anything new, feeling like she was playing *Where's Waldo.*

After several minutes spent scanning every pixel, she was sure the lab had no new equipment—just employees, laptops, and piles of junk. She slumped in relief.

Still, stolen equipment could arrive at any time, and if that happened, she wanted to know about it. She opened the Aries Knowledge Base and searched for 'alerts tutorial'. In another tab, she opened the Aries portal. Between the moral obligation to report Aries and her personal desire to not sabotage her career, she had a third option: stay quiet while keeping a digital eye on the lab.

It couldn't be that hard. People set up alerts all the time to monitor satellite images for changes—usually for ship traffic or deforestation activity. Why couldn't she configure the server to notify her if something significant happened in the Aries lab? Using artificial intelligence to detect changes would also save her from this *Where's Waldo* hunt, because the computer could scan the pixels better than her inferior human eyes.

She would have to do trial and error to determine what the algorithm deemed a significant change. She didn't want an alert every time an employee moved around, but she did want to know if a new piece of equipment arrived. She could configure it to treat the employees as noise.

With the tutorial open on one half of her screen and the server interface on the other, she set to work.

Setting up the lab activity alert took half the morning, leaving Jess feeling guilty over neglecting her actual job.

Nothing an espresso couldn't fix. She would have to make up for lost hours by tackling her QA tasks double-speed.

The first Slack message to greet her was her group chat with the Cloud Team, where Kit had shared an *Arrested Development* gif depicting her mood today. Jess reacted with the laugh-cry emoji and moved to her next unread message— an automated note from the compiler. Some code she'd checked in yesterday broke the build. That meant the entire Aries codebase was unable to compile because of something she did.

"Fffuuudge …"

Jess dropped her head on her desk, fighting a surge of nausea.

But she'd had a code review! Floyd said it was okay!

Reluctantly, she typed a message to Floyd asking for help. She was about to hit *Send* when it occurred to her that Floyd might ask why it took her more than two hours to address the compiler issue this morning.

There had to be a less painful way to fix this.

She opened her chat with Anita.

Jess*: Help, something I did broke the build.*

Anita responded immediately.

Anita*: Don't worry, happens to everyone. Probably missing some dependencies. Want me to come by?*

Jess: *Yes please. Would rather avoid a FF attack this morning.*

She tried to analyze the issue before Anita got to her office, but had absolutely no idea where to start. So she waited to be rescued, helpless, like a cat waiting for its owner to come pry it out of the blinds.

Anita was right: before checking in some new tests yesterday, Jess should have compiled them with the rest of the code tree.

"Floyd's fault," Anita insisted. "You had no way of knowing. He should've told you."

Jess made a face. His fault or not, her name was still on the build failure.

Anita showed her how to build the proper dependencies. Jess watched closely, taking notes so she could avoid calling for help again.

As they waited for the code tree to compile, Anita turned to Jess.

"Feel better?"

Jess nodded, relaxing under Anita's calm vibe.

"Good. Last thing you should always do is update the XML files." She tucked back a lock of her long, black hair, and the sleeve of her blouse fell to reveal a tattoo Jess had noticed at lunch last week. It was a swirl of vines and flowers, an intricate pattern that must have taken hours.

"Does it mean something?" said Jess, motioning to it.

Anita pulled back her sleeve to show the whole thing. "Nah, I just liked the design. My sister did it."

"Your sister's a tattoo artist?"

"Not exactly. We bought a tattoo gun."

Jess raised an eyebrow before she could stop herself.

Anita laughed. "She's a good artist. I'm an artist, too, but I didn't want to tattoo myself so I did the next best thing and got my twin to do it."

Just when Anita couldn't get any cooler.

"What kind of art do you do?"

"Manga. My sis and I are trying to be comic artists, actually. It's a bit of a side job."

"I love comics! Can I see?"

Anita flushed. "I don't usually show people."

"But you want to get published?"

"I know. I'm hopeless. Call it self-esteem issues. Here, this is the metadata folder." She pointed to the screen, and Jess embarked on a riveting tour of XML data structures.

"What about you, Jess?"

"What?"

"Aspirations?"

Jess shook her head. She'd given up volleyball, bouldering, and piano after high school—and then the accident happened, so she couldn't go back to those hobbies even if she wanted to. "Two feet into engineering."

Anita hummed. "I recommend doing something artsy. It's good for the brain to change focus."

"So I hear."

She was artistically challenged, but she did enjoy D&D for the social and creative aspects. *Maybe someday.* For now, she was determined to launch her career. It would set her up for everything she wanted in life, including social and creative hobbies, and so that had to come first.

The code compiled without error. Anita beamed at her. The process of fixing the build had been simple, but Jess would never have gotten there without help. She thanked Anita profusely.

"You'll still need Floyd to code review," said Anita, "but it should be quick."

It was not quick.

Floyd insisted on going through every step she and Anita had taken.

"Why was Anita helping you?"

"She offered."

"She's on the Cloud Team."

Jess took a breath. She had to address this. "Wyatt has a mentor. I thought it might be helpful if I had one, too."

Floyd furrowed his brow. "Jessica, you need to go through me for something like this. I can't have you going around me and leaving me in the dark."

"I didn't think it would be an issue to ask—"

"It's okay," said Floyd, in a tone that indicated it was not okay. "Just make sure you check with me next time. It's unprofessional to undermine your team lead."

Jess's face grew hot. "I wasn't trying to undermine you."

He winked. "Just a bit of constructive feedback."

Constructive feedback? How the hell was this constructive feedback? 'Constructive' implied he would also tell her what she did well, which he hadn't done once. She silently cursed him.

"Sorry," she said, the word taking a tremendous effort to spit out.

A message appeared in the corner of Jess's screen.

Aries Server activity alert.

Something was happening inside the Aries lab.

"I'm going to send you some resources on teamwork," said Floyd. "I want you to read them and think about how you can apply those tips."

"Sure."

Her mind had turned elsewhere. Was this activity related to last night's GN break-in?

"In the meantime, I'll talk to Chuck and make sure Anita has the bandwidth to mentor you."

"Okay." *Pretty sure Anita can manage her own bloody time.*

But if the lab activity did turn out to be stolen GN tech, what could she do about it?

"I'll also schedule one-on-one check-ins between us so I can provide help where you're struggling."

"Right."

When Floyd left, Jess cursed him under her breath.

Down the hall, Wyatt and Jesus Chris were having a loud meeting. Apparently, R-trees were a hilarious data structure. Jess shut her door, hoping they would hear the click and get the hint.

She'd set the server to copy new images into her cloud drive when activity was detected on Aries 181. She opened the drive and found a new folder with a dozen JPEGs already. A new image appeared every ten seconds.

She hesitated. Her inner Mandeep voice was telling her to mind her own business, watch her stress levels, blah, blah, blah …

She opened the first image.

Two people were entering the lab carrying some kind of large case. With her algorithm trained to ignore the employees, the case must have been what set off the alert.

Jess discerned enough from the blurry faces to know it was a man and a woman. The six Red Badges in lab coats turned to greet them.

The pair opened the case and put something on a table— a rifle, by the looks of it. Her pulse quickened. Was this from Global Nanosats? She zoomed in, searching for a logo, but the weapon became pixelated before she could get close enough.

Maybe this wasn't from GN. They built satellites, not weapons.

Then again, wouldn't other aerospace companies have secret operations like Aries? Jess was willing to bet a lot of them developed defense weapons, whether privately or for the government.

Wyatt and Jesus Chris burst into laughter again, the sound traveling through her closed door. *Honestly.*

She flipped through the other images, speeding up. They were coming in faster than she was scrolling.

The pair left the rifle with the engineers and moved toward the warehouse door. Then they were gone. The server didn't deem their movement significant, so rather than track them into the warehouse, it kept feeding her images of the engineers and the rifle.

A knock at the door made her jump like a cat beside a cucumber.

She peeked through the blinds beside her desk to see Floyd standing in the hall. Biting back an outburst of frustration, she forced a smile and opened the door.

"By the way, did Stanley touch base with you?"

"I haven't seen him yet today."

"All right. He's got a few tasks lined up for you, so check in with him."

"Will do."

He didn't turn away. Jess willed him out the door, finger over the mouse like a fangirl waiting for concert tickets to go on sale.

"I'm also going to ask you not to shut your door," he said. "We have an open-door culture here. You don't want to send the wrong message."

Jess couldn't force a smile, this time. What were the chances she could shove him into the TARDIS poster and lose him somewhere in the space-time continuum? She watched him go with a clenched jaw, then turned back to her screen, blinking it into focus.

"Look at this one I found yesterday," said Wyatt loudly, while Jesus Chris roared with laughter.

Jess caught up to the most recent image. The six engineers were still gathered around the rifle.

Hoping for some indication of what was going on, Jess kept opening each new image as it appeared. The ten second intervals were agonizing. She wanted to see the man and the woman return from the warehouse. She wanted to know what they were going to do with that rifle.

Finally, one of the engineers picked it up and aimed it at a blank whiteboard.

She clicked on the next image. There was a smoking black hole in the wall.

"Holy ..." whispered Jess.

The other engineers had gathered around the one holding the rifle. Then he appeared to be moving toward the door. Images of the stark white lab were replaced by the dim warehouse.

Jess leaned closer to her screen.

There were the man and the woman! The engineer met up with them at the base of a metal staircase. He passed off the weapon.

And then—

Jess's jaw fell open. No.

The next image came in, and she recoiled from her screen.

"Oh, f—"

Chapter 11
Halley's Worst Nightmare

Sneaking the pair of firearms to the Aries office gave Halley a thrill not unlike the time she and her friends hopped a park fence so they could skinny dip in the public pool.

"I think this is a bucket list item for me," she said.

"What is?"

"Concealing weapons inside a guitar case."

Tony raised an eyebrow at her from the driver's seat of the Bentley. "That's a strange goal to have."

"And your ambitions aren't totally nuts?"

A dimple formed in Tony's cheek as he suppressed a smile. His disappointment seemed to have abated since last night, leaving Halley hopeful for another chance to prove herself. Her GN blunder had been a rookie mistake. Today, she would make Tony realize he couldn't live without her.

"What else is on your bucket list?"

Halley mulled this over as she watched passing traffic. "Part of me secretly always wanted to hack into something."

"Ahh, you were holding out on me."

"Well, it's scary, when you actually get the chance. And don't say *do one thing a day that scares you.*"

He pursed his lips.

After a pause, Halley added, "I used to want to star in a school play. I was painfully shy, but I had this fantasy that I would shock everyone and burst onto center stage with all this hidden talent."

"You don't strike me as painfully shy."

The fact that he noticed and thought about her behavior sent a flutter through her belly.

"Introverted, then." Halley shrugged. She could barely figure herself out. Was it possible to be an outgoing introvert?

"And the hidden talent?" said Tony.

"I couldn't even bring myself to audition."

"That's too bad. You never gave yourself a chance."

"Maybe I'll join a theatre club," said Halley defiantly.

Tony smiled at her, a glimmer in his eyes reminiscent of when they'd danced at the tech show.

Halley turned back to the road ahead. "Also I want a unicorn."

They arrived at the Aries office and parked in a reserved spot out front—the only spot out front. Everyone else had to park in the rear lot.

"My engineers will do some of their hocus pocus for us," said Tony as they left the Bentley. "We'll leave it with them while we take a tour."

Halley prayed the engineers would find they could easily replicate the bullet solution and announce that the assault rifle was a gold mine and Halley was a total queen and Tony should promote her to Vice President of Aries.

"Will your employees know where we got these weapons from?" said Halley.

"The engineers who work in the lab know what's in it. But don't worry. I vet personalities before I hire them, plus they receive special training and very specific instructions—" He gave her a meaningful look. "—on how to navigate the sensitivities of the lab."

Halley didn't ask how threatening said instructions were.

They entered through pristine glass doors that led into a lobby, the vast floor of which was emblazoned with the Aries logo. A massive satellite hung from the ceiling. Halley had a flash of anxiety as the place brought to mind her interview with Tony—which maybe hadn't been so disastrous, after all.

They approached the receptionist, whose workspace was decorated with an admirable number of Harry Potter figurines.

"Good morning, Doctor Ries."

"Good morning, Beth," said Tony. "I'd like a red badge for Miss Halley Lovelace."

Halley gave her address, phone number, and birthday, and smiled for a photo. Tony went around the desk to authorize the badge's security clearance.

Minutes later, they passed through a door near the elevators and wound down a concrete staircase, leaving behind the sunlight that streamed into the lobby for the glow of fluorescent bulbs. There was a steel door at the bottom of the stairs.

"After you," said Tony, motioning to the black box beside it.

Halley flashed her badge, pushing aside the memory of Sherry and the fire. The indicator light turned green and they stepped inside.

The lab was a white room about the size of Halley's old high school gym. Rows of long tables reminded her of a poorly attended science fair. Six people in lab coats labored over half-dissected equipment, test tubes, Bunsen burners, and laptops.

Everyone greeted Tony as he walked by.

"Hello, Doctor Ries."

"Morning, Doctor Ries."

Halley's stomach swooped. *Call me Tony,* he'd told her.

Their eyes fell onto Halley. No doubt they wondered why this twenty-year-old chick was granted the same level of clearance as them.

It was a valid question. She dropped her gaze, face growing hot.

"Scott," said Tony, leaning against a table covered in exciting-looking test tubes.

"Yes, Doctor Ries."

"I've got a little project for you."

Halley placed the guitar case on the table. Scott opened it to reveal the rifle and pistol.

"GN's chemical firearms," said Tony. "The only bullet solution we have is the teacupful inside. Take a sample and see if we can replicate it."

"They work, then?"

"The pistol does. We haven't tried the rifle. Take her for a spin and let me know."

"Yes, sir."

If Scott was worried about firing a mysterious weapon, he didn't show it. Halley had the urge to whisper in his ear and beg him to tell Tony how valuable the firearms were, but he didn't so much as make eye contact with her.

Tony led her to a set of double doors at the far wall. They left behind the relative quiet of the lab and entered a vast warehouse filled with whirring fans. Halley's stomach churned at the smell—toxic and suffocating, like burning plastic. She could taste the air's impurity. Weren't there any windows down here?

No, of course not. They were underground. She blinked as the dim room came into focus and she took in the sheer amount of *stuff* that surrounded them. There were piles upon piles of it, starting with the old satellite prototype mounted on a podium in the entrance. There were rockets, containers, tools, countless objects whose purpose Halley had no idea. She half expected to find a robot with rabbit ear antennas. Maybe a homemade Tesla coil? A potato cannon? Oh, god, was Tony about to reveal this was all a giant Rube Goldberg machine?

"You remember what my goal is, Halley?"

"Advancing science through collaboration."

Tony placed a hand on her lower back, sending a pleasant tingle through her middle, and guided her along the warehouse perimeter. Her gaze drew to the logos and symbols on everything they passed. There were private companies, NASA, CSA, ESA ... A sampling of the world's most advanced aerospace technology. The room was an endless supply of it.

"The aerospace world is full of sky-high goals," said Tony. "Everyone's going for speed, distance, power—we've even got tycoons trying to turn outer space into a vacation destination.

With what's in this lab, I have the potential to do all of that. I want to be the world's largest aerospace company. I've already become the best at imaging the earth with the Aries 180 fleet. It's time for the next escapade."

"And what will that be?"

Flashing that wide grin, Tony motioned ahead.

The room grew darker as they walked deeper into the warehouse, lights casting dim halos every thirty feet or so. Green LEDs flecked the ceiling, like stars from another universe winking in the night sky. Security cameras, maybe. Judging by their movement, they were connected to drones.

The temperature increased until sweat began to pearl on her forehead. She was about to question Tony on the heat when they came to the base of a steel mesh staircase and he motioned upward.

Halley climbed the steps, her flats echoing on the metal. At the top was a balcony that overlooked the entire room, disappearing into darkness as it extended in either direction. Below, a vat of something red, orange, and black churned like lava. Heat billowed up at them.

"*More – powerful – rockets,*" said Tony.

He pulled her to the railing, like they were at a zoo overlooking the gorilla exhibit.

But the suffocating heat and fiery glow from below was too much—the balcony, the flames, the feeling of falling. Her chest constricted. Her vision went black at the edges.

Her knees weakened and she stumbled back. She should have listened to her racing pulse the moment the temperature rose. She wasn't ready for this.

Arms wrapped around her waist, and she found herself leaning against Tony.

"I know. Overwhelming, isn't it?"

It took Halley a moment to choke out, "What is it?"

Tony regarded her, their faces close. His breath was cool and minty on her face. Was he wondering how much he should tell her? This room represented his life's work.

A thrill went through her at the thought that he'd chosen to bring her here. She'd won his trust. Something she had done—or something in her personality—was good enough for him. If only she could stop letting him down.

With an arm cinched around her waist, he said, "What do you know about rockets?"

"Physics 101," she admitted.

"So you understand that a rocket's power depends on how forcefully particles are expelled."

She nodded.

"To increase thrust, we need particles to combust with maximum gusto," he said. "Powerful fuels and oxidizers are out there, but the best ones are too toxic and unstable—especially for rockets carrying astronauts."

Again, he pulled her closer to the railing, wrapping his free hand over it so he could gaze down at the vat. Wisps of smoke and particles spat upward, like the contents were trying to taste them.

"This propellant has potential to be an order of magnitude more powerful than standard rocket propellant—and safe enough to touch," said Tony.

Halley averted her gaze from the molten substance, but found herself studying a human-sized dent in the concrete floor, charred and rippled, suggesting a massive explosion.

"It's safe?"

"Not yet. We're close. If only it would stabilize. The compound is continuously reacting with itself."

Hence the heat. Halley inhaled deeply. Tony was the only thing keeping her from descending into panic. She studied each bead of sweat on his face, each dark hair on his jaw line, the shape of his Adam's apple.

"What's the vat made of? Tungsten?"

"Hafnium, nitrogen, carbon." He waved a hand. "It's the only compound that wouldn't melt."

Halley wiped the sweat running down her face, unsure how much was from the propellant and how much was from anxiety. It was hard to breathe. But this lab was everything to Tony, so she would have to get over it if she wanted to work for him. She couldn't lose this opportunity to start a new life. Plus, as much as she wanted to get away from the hellfire in the vat, being in Tony's arms was every bit as blissful as she'd hoped.

"The power is there," said Tony, "but if I want this to be adopted as the standard propellant for space missions, it has to do its job combusting one element while preserving everything else. In other words, the propellant has to keep organic matter and every part of the rocket intact, but still react with the substance it's meant to combust."

There was a whirring sound overhead. A drone coasted by like an oversized bumble bee. Halley chewed her lip. This warehouse was giving her the creeps, in the sort of way only warehouses were capable of. She was ready for the tour to be over.

"What does it combust?" she said.

"That's what we're trying to isolate. We're modifying its chemistry and hitting some teensy snags. Metals are proving to combust the most forcefully, but unpredictably."

"I guess that's why you wanted to know about GN's propellant," said Halley sadly.

Tony squeezed her shoulders. "Right you are. Their data will help us understand some key chemical reactions."

"You'll figure this out," said Halley. "I know you will."

She meant it. Tony's refusal to accept defeat was all too recognizable.

"Once I have the best rockets, I'll be able to launch space missions more ambitious than anyone's dreamed."

He gazed across the lab like a lion overlooking his kingdom. He'd worked so hard to bring everything together.

"Tony, why did you—?" Her throat constricted. She wasn't sure if she wanted the answer. But she had to know. "Why me?"

It had been prodding at her. Why was she here with him and not Reah, Scott, or any other Aries employee?

Tony turned to face her, eyes burning with intensity. He pushed a sweaty blonde lock from her eyes, and she looked up at him clearly.

"I knew, someday, work would demand too much of me, and I would need more than an ordinary assistant. It had to be someone who would share my values and dedicate herself to science, the way I have."

Halley studied his clammy face, trying to understand. "And you think I'm that person?"

"Your personality ..." His eyes flicked away, as if searching for a word. "Fits. You only need practice to harness your abilities. I've combed the earth for candidates. Trust me when I say you are—perfection."

Halley hadn't been fishing for compliments, but she could have floated into the warehouse ceiling.

Breathless, she said, "So I'm here to help realize your vision. You think I can help you grow Aries."

"With your intelligence, skills, and passion—I see myself in you. I see someone who will go to any length for science. This is what I need in a partner."

Tony's *partner*. It was a big role to fill. She needed it. This was everything she'd been waiting for, and more.

Holding both of her hands in his, he said, "You think you can commit to this life, Halley?"

"I do."

The vision Tony described would make him king of the aerospace world. So what would that make her?

Tony looked at his watch.

"The news I wanted to hear," he said, reading a message. "The rifle is mine."

"It works?"

"Like a flamethrower in an oxygen tank. Come."

He pulled Halley down the stairs, their sweaty palms pressed together.

Halley hardly dared to believe it as they descended. The rifle worked. She'd done something right. Tony's pleasure radiated off of him, blending with the heat of the propellant.

Reveling in victory, she wanted to tug him back up to the balcony, to pull him in and kiss him.

No. He's Doctor Anthony Ries. He's your boss.

At the bottom of the steps, he faced her once more. "I'm trusting you, Halley. I know you'll never let me down."

"Never."

"Good girl." His cool breath tickled her cheek.

"We've tested the shot, Doctor Ries." Scott was approaching them holding the rifle. "Destructive power of a grenade with sniper precision. We extracted a sample and will work on producing more ammunition."

Tony smiled—not at Scott, but at Halley.

Halley smiled back.

Keeping his gaze on her, Tony held out a hand. Scott placed the assault rifle in it.

"And the pistol," said Scott.

Tony nodded to Halley. "This one is yours, baby."

She broke Tony's gaze to take it.

Mine.

She wrapped her fingers around the grip, exhilarated. She had her own pistol—and not just any pistol. This was one of the best weapons science had to offer.

The contents inside the vat hissed as smoke curled into the rafters, a haze settling around them like a curtain. Flecks spat out the top like ash from a campfire.

Scott left the two of them at the base of the vat, facing each other with their new weapons.

"Shoot it," whispered Halley.

He had to see its power. He had to know the magnitude of the gift she'd given him.

Something in the way he looked at her changed. His eyes softened as they bore into her. They seemed lighter, somehow.

"This one's for you, baby." Tony aimed the rifle across the room, into darkness.

Several things happened at once.

Scott shouted, "Tony, wait!" just as Tony squeezed the trigger.

A fleck of something—was it condensation? A spark?—fell between them. It was so small, so insignificant, but Halley understood. This was rocket propellant. Tony was firing a chemical weapon near something highly combustible.

There was an earth-shattering explosion. Halley caught a glimpse of flames. Her back collided with the staircase, and she gasped, crumpling as she lost feeling in her limbs.

The room became black with smoke. Everything was numb. Had the impact paralyzed her? No. Pain came surging up her spine like a jolt of electricity.

She lay there for what seemed an eternity, coughing through the smoke as it gradually cleared. The balcony had torn in the explosion. Half the railing melted off the staircase, leaving it tilted as if they were inside a funhouse. Scott was slumped against the base, semi-conscious.

There was a groan of metal. *The vat.*

Eight feet from the ground, a dent scarred the smooth material—but it was changing, warping. The contents pushed the blemish outwards until it was swollen and red, like a zit ready to pop.

The vat was going to burst.

She scrambled away from it as an ear-splitting roar filled the warehouse.

"Tony?!"

A blazing light caught her attention and she twisted around to see where it had come from.

He was on fire. Flames engulfed his forearms, traveling inward. He shrieked, smacking his arms, but it was out of control.

Halley stumbled to her feet and raced for him.

Fire extinguisher.

She cast around desperately for signs of one. "Tony, where's—?"

"Scott," shouted Tony. "Close the barrier! Halley, help him."

Halley whirled around. Close *what?*

Scott heaved himself up, swaying, then lumbered up the tilting stairs. At the top, he grabbed a chain and pulled. Slowly, noisily, a wall began to slide over a rusty track in the floor, closing around the vat.

Halley turned back to Tony. How could he be concerned about protecting the rocket propellant right now?

She wanted to run. Sweat soaked through her clothes.

Tony was thrashing and screaming, bits of clothing hitting the ground like embers. Halley stepped back, a sob escaping.

"Halley, help him!" Tony roared.

Scott labored over the chain, grinding the heavy wall into place. Would the wall be enough to stop the flood of chemicals?

All she wanted was to get out and leave all of this behind. But the bulge in the vat continued to grow, threatening to burst. Tony was feet away from it.

Scott roared as he heaved the chain, leaning all his weight on it. The wall had stopped moving. The track in the floor was warped and broken—maybe from the same explosion that left the dent in the concrete.

She had to help. They were going to die.

With the heat smothering her, Halley ran to the vat. She seized the wall and pulled. It inched over the broken track.

In the growing bulge, a slit tore open. The contents of the vat oozed through and splashed onto the concrete. Halley shrieked, leaping out of the way.

"Tony, I can't ..." She choked back a sob.

The slit widened.

Run, said a voice in the back of her head. *You can save yourself.*

But to run would be to betray the man who made her feel alive after months of misery. He'd promised her a kingdom. She could have everything with him—a career, a home, adventure, maybe love.

Family, friends, school? said the voice.

Mom and Dad. The programming assignment waiting for her. Her old group of friends, shattered though they were. Deep down, she'd hoped they would reunite someday, when the scars had healed and the mistakes were forgotten.

God, what was she doing? She couldn't die like this! Her life had only begun. Yes, there was so much missing—the start of which was the black hole left by her friends—but an entire lifetime of adventure lay ahead of her, if only she would run.

With a tremendous effort, she took another step back.

She turned to Tony. His body was in flames, his clothes disappearing, his skin blackened. Through it all, his dark eyes found hers.

"Halley, please, stay with—"

The vat burst. A flood of propellant sprayed out.

It was too late. Halley had made her choice the moment she entered Tony's penthouse, and she would take that choice to hell with her. She held Tony's gaze, catching a last glimpse of his wide, terrified eyes, before the molten chemical swallowed them up.

Chapter 12
Jess Discovers Hell

When Jess and her friends were seventeen, they got drunk at one of their slumber parties and had a fashion show. It began with a clothing line inspired by Desi's box of Halloween costumes. Then the alcohol kicked in. Their outfits degenerated to wigs and scarves, and eventually, just paint and sharpies in place of clothing. They found it hilarious, until they discovered the next day over pancakes that they'd taken pictures.

They pinky swore to delete them and never discuss it again. They were the most horrifying photos Jess had ever seen. Until now.

Oh, sweet, young, innocent Jessica.

She sat in front of her computer watching the tragedy unfold onto her cloud drive. In all likelihood, she was the only witness to it. She alone had to decide what to do.

For a long moment she stared at her screen, frozen by a feeling of unreality. Beside her, the *Game of Thrones* map she'd pinned up slipped from its hold and swung dangling by one corner.

Summoning movement into her body, she flipped back a few images.

The two people stood next to a massive container of what looked like lava.

Jess zoomed in on their faces, but the container's shadow masked their features in darkness. She wanted to smack whoever was in charge of lighting the place. Since when did an evil laboratory need mood lighting?

She kept clicking.

They were on the ground, smoke billowing, the man engulfed in flames. They stayed like this for two more images, the woman seeming at a loss—until the vat opened like a dam, sending the contents cascading out. The man and woman disappeared beneath it, along with every piece of equipment in its path.

Another image appeared in the folder. Jess clicked. The river darkened as it spread across the floor. The bottom half of the vat stayed intact, the remaining contents churning inside it.

"Oh my god," she said into her hand.

Those people had died, and she was sitting here watching it happen. She had to tell someone. Her boss.

And the police! An ambulance! A Hazmat team? Where should she start?

Another image appeared in the folder.

Jess clicked it, stomach clenching as she prepared to see the same river of liquid. This couldn't possibly get any worse.

Somehow, it did.

Chapter 13
Halley Doesn't Like Rocket Propellant

Pain roared through her body, piercing her flesh, peeling it, eating it away. It flooded her mouth and nose.

She gagged. Her vision was dark, tinted red as if her eyes had filled with blood.

A desperate need for air consumed her. She was still alive.

Swim. Find the surface.

She couldn't tell which way was up.

Her shoulder banged into something hard. She tumbled along, helpless. White spots bloomed in her vision.

Then the movement slowed. She got a hand under her and pushed.

Her head broke into the open and she gasped, choking back air.

I'm alive. I'm alive. The miracle of it was overwhelming.

But where was Tony? Halley tried to yell for him but couldn't feel her tongue.

She moved blindly, consumed by the agony.

With a great effort, she rose to her hands and knees. She slid across the floor, slimy and slippery, as if wrapped in a placenta. The liquid fell behind and she sprawled on the floor in a loose heap.

God, her skin burned!

She kept her eyes shut. She must have been sizzling, like bacon in a pan.

Please, don't let me be on fire.

Nothing would be left of her. She would become a pile of ash.

She turned over and threw up.

An eternity passed. The blinding pain receded to something like a bad sunburn.

Her breaths came to her awareness, fast and panicked, rough like gravel. She pried her eyes open. The dim warehouse yawned before her with its heaps of junk. Behind her was a steel wall and crooked steps rising to the balcony.

A river of propellant led from the vat, blackening as it cooled. The top half of the vat had been destroyed, red liquid dripping from the tear in the side.

No one should have been allowed near this thing without a Hazmat suit. She should never have agreed to this.

Where was Tony? And what happened to Scott?

Halley braced herself and looked down at her body. Her breath accelerated, coming in panicked bursts.

Hole-filled, frayed rags hung from her limbs. Beneath the rags … She stared, processing what she was seeing. Was that her skin?

It was charred, peeling, like a chemical burn across her whole body. She raised a scorched hand to her head and let out a sob. Fingers met raw scalp. Her hair was gone. Thin wisps remained, strands clinging to roots in sparse patches.

A retching noise came from nearby.

Halley cast around, frantic. Her eyes locked onto someone, dripping in red liquid, skin charred and blistered. She knew the shape of him beneath the disintegrated rags that were once a button-down shirt and suit pants.

Tony was on all fours, throwing up onto the concrete. The rifle that did this was beside him. Halley's pistol lay beyond it. The flow of liquid had missed the weapons.

As she traced her gaze along the blackening river, it dawned on her: the propellant was a success. Tony had described a substance that should have killed them, and his goal to make it preserve everything except one compound. This river of propellant had been unleashed, yet it failed to destroy anything.

Halley tried to ask Tony if he was okay. The words lodged in her throat.

He turned his hands over. "My skin!"

Trembling, she crawled a step closer and managed to croak, "It's okay."

"It's not! I can't spend my life looking like this."

"But we're both alive—"

Tony let out an agonized scream. He was hyperventilating, clutching the rags that were once clothes.

"Tony, please … calm …" But Halley heard in her voice that she wasn't calm. Her heart slammed into her ribs, trying to escape this body, to find a new one that didn't look like this.

They were alive, but they'd been boiled past recognition. Her identity was gone.

Her brain fired impulses too fast to process.

Fight. Flee. Escape the pain.

She couldn't. There was no way out. The torture was part of her.

She shouldn't have told Tony to shoot that rifle. She should have paid more attention to everything around them, and not been so absorbed in herself that she failed to notice urgent warning signs. She could have prevented this disaster. Why couldn't she learn from her mistakes?

She covered her ears, trying to block everything out. Her worst fear and memory, all over again, a hundred times more terrifying than her nightmares. Months of fearing it, months of flame-triggered panic attacks, months of telling herself to calm down because Brooke was out of her life and something like that would never, ever happen again.

It had happened again. She would never be the same.

Tony's screams filled her head, his panic adding to hers. Even with ears covered and eyes closed, the room battered her from all directions. Her exposed nerves quivered in the air blowing through and around the alleys of junk. Every bump in the cement floor, every breath, every minute gust, raked her raw flesh like sandpaper.

She had to get a hold of herself and take Tony away from this vat. They needed somewhere quiet where she could calm him down.

Breathing deeply, she focused her senses, trying to do a grounding meditation. But shouts tore through it, and the smell of burning hair and flesh, and the taste of blood where she'd bit her tongue. Tony's sharp breaths pounded her exposed nerves like a meat tenderizer.

"Doctor Ries!"

A man was shouting.

Footsteps. Halley felt as much as heard them, the movement sending rushes of air at her. She clenched her jaw.

Scott knelt in front of Tony. The propellant had missed him, and he was fine except for some singed hair and char marks across his skin and lab coat. He was trying to calm Tony, who was curled in the fetal position, ears covered, eyes shut.

Scott was shouting. "Doctor Ries. Say something!"

Rage filled Halley at the sight of him unharmed, touching Tony like he could help him. He was the one who'd handed Tony that weapon. He knew they were standing in a dangerous area.

"Doctor Ries! Christ. I'm calling 9-1-1."

He pulled out a phone.

9-1-1? As in, bringing people in here? Exposing everything Tony insisted on keeping secret?

"No!" said Halley, standing.

Her voice came out strong. Scott looked at her sharply.

As Tony's assistant, or partner, or whatever she was, she had a duty to protect this lab's secrets. Tony was going through too much without also losing his life's work.

"Tony made it clear. No one is to enter the lab."

Scott rose from where he was crouched. "I know this place's priorities, honey."

"Apparently not. Put the phone away."

"I'm not taking orders from some intern."

"I'm not *some intern*."

"Whoever the fuck you are, then. You both need a hospital."

Halley stepped closer. Scott scanned her up and down—and shrank a little.

Halley took courage from this. "A hospital can't fix this. Bringing medics in here will sacrifice all of Tony's intellectual property. Everything he's worked for."

Scott squared his shoulders. "None of this intellectual property will matter if the CEO of Aries is dead. I'm calling for help."

He opened his phone's keypad. Halley made to grab it, but Scott backed away.

"Does he look dead to you?" shouted Halley.

Scott dialed and raised the phone to his ear. "He will be, if you—"

A sound ripped through the room. The lash of air sucked the breath from Halley's lungs.

Scott's eyes widened.

Halley stared numbly at the splotch that had appeared on his white lab coat, blooming larger, turning bright red. Scott's hand came up to touch it. His knees buckled.

Tony was standing, a pistol in his fist. Her pistol.

Scott crumpled, taking a last, ragged breath. The stench of burning flesh became stronger, like the GN bullet had burned through him.

It hit her like a punch to the stomach. *Scott was dead.* Tony had murdered him—and he'd done it by shooting another chemical weapon right next to the propellant. Maybe he thought he had nothing to lose.

Their eyes locked. Halley didn't know whether to be scared.

Her body chose a different reaction, a tingling that started in her belly and moved lower. Scott's death was a moment she and Tony shared. A secret. No deeper connection could exist between two people.

"You did it, Tony," said Halley softly. "Your propellant preserved our bodies."

Tony was still, chest rising and falling with quick breaths. She tried to read his expression. With his skin peeled and distorted, a mass of charred muscle and nerves in its place, she had no clue what he was thinking.

But he was calmer, his attention fixed on her. Like he'd done before they fell, he really looked at her.

"I did it," he whispered.

"Are you still ... ?" She knew the answer before she finished. His pain would be the same as hers. The burning had subsided, but the ache lingered as her nerves adjusted to the exposure. It was as if the propellant had cauterized the damage on its own.

"I ... feel," he said, wincing as he brought a palm to his face.

Yes. She felt, too. The propellant had done something to her. Everything in the room had its own effect on the circulating air, combining to batter her senses with shapes and chemicals.

She flinched. She didn't know why. Her brain told her to. Something inside her head was warning her of the pain.

The danger is gone, she told herself.

Her brain responded by telling her to fight, to escape whatever was causing this torment.

"I can't," she whispered to herself.

Fight. Flee. Stop the pain—

Halley covered her ears and squeezed her eyes shut. Impulses were firing too fast, responding to a threat she could do nothing about.

"Halley!"

She opened her eyes. Tony was in front of her, fingers around her wrists.

She felt for his presence, trying to isolate him from the sensory storm coming at her from everywhere.

His breath moved across her face, soft and gentle. His fingers were firm and comforting. His whole body radiated energy.

"We're okay," he whispered. The words carried on his breath, brushing over her cheeks and lips.

"We're okay," she echoed.

She kept all her focus on Tony, letting him ground her, blocking everything else out.

He closed the gap between them. She felt his lips before they touched hers.

He kissed her, pushing her backward until she hit the steel wall. One hand slid around the back of her head, fingers moving through the wisps that were once hair. The other went to her waist, where a frayed scrap of material hung.

Halley let her hands travel to his hips, pulling his body closer. The sensation was at once a battery of pain and pleasure.

She knew it. All along, he'd wanted her. He'd been suppressing it for the sake of business, and now he'd come to a near-death epiphany.

Or did he just hit his head really hard?

No. Something about their relationship had changed before the vat burst. They were together. He promised her a kingdom.

Tony pulled back, leaving her gasping. She stared into his dark eyes, the only part of him that remained unchanged.

"You're mine," he said. "You won't leave me."

Halley nodded, her breaths coming fast.

"Say it." He shook her so the steel behind her gave a *pop* that echoed through the warehouse.

He was as scared as she was. Nobody else could love someone so damaged as this. Just like Scott had shrunk away from Halley, the world, too, would cower.

The propellant exposed what had been festering inside Halley. Her singed nerves, unable to experience the world like normal, embodied what she'd been feeling for so long. Her distorted flesh revealed the damage inside her. This was who she was—repulsive, unlovable, blistered. If Tony was no different—if this was the manifestation of him as much as Halley—then they belonged together.

"I'm yours," she said.

His mouth found hers again, his body pressing closer. She was his. She would be his forever.

Chapter 14
Jess Works Through Lunch

Jess picked up her office phone and stared at the keypad. *Floyd.* This was a team lead situation. What was his extension?

"Damn."

She'd never used her office phone and had no idea how to dial internally.

She slammed the phone in its cradle and speed-walked down the hall toward Floyd's office. Most people were eating lunch, leaving empty offices with action figures and spacey posters to witness her panic.

What she'd seen couldn't be real. She'd get to Floyd's office and he'd say, "Oh, yeah, they're filming a movie down there."

A movie. Fake blood. She didn't *really* see a man get shot.

The bile creeping up her throat told her otherwise. She'd looked into the real Aries lab, and something terrible had happened.

The image of those two people emerging from the liquid was totally going to haunt her—like the girl emerging from the well in *The Ring* had done for way too many years. In the dimly lit images, Jess could tell the pair's skin had been seared raw. How had they survived?

No, the *how* was hardly important. What mattered was that they'd shot someone.

She pounced through the doorway of Floyd's office.

"Floyd, something just happened—"

He wasn't there.

Jess spun in place, wondering who else to talk to. She balled her sleeves in her fists, the panic a memory that sent throbbing pains down her forearms.

Stay present.

Anita. She would know what to do.

She was about to run to Asgard when she heard, "Jess!" from behind.

She whirled to find the other interns approaching.

"Rumor has it there's a Japadog truck down the road," said Grace. "Wanna come?"

The thought of eating anything right now, never mind an extreme hot dog, nearly made Jess dry heave.

"I can't, I … I'm waiting for Floyd."

"Oh, you two having lunch?" said Wyatt.

"What? No." She looked past them.

"Oh. I'm having lunch with him tomorrow. Want to join us?"

"Um." Should she hunt down Floyd in the lounge? Or was he in a late-running meeting? "No, thanks."

"Why not?"

"I don't think my presence would be much appreciated."

"What do you mean?"

She met Wyatt's earnest gaze. She hadn't really meant to say that aloud, but she was too panicked to filter anything right now.

"I always appreciate your presence," said Wyatt.

"She's talking about Floyd, fuckhead," said Grace.

Jess glanced around at the empty offices, wishing she hadn't said anything. A life-sized Spock was staring at them through someone's window, giving her the Vulcan salute.

"Why wouldn't Floyd want you there?" said Wyatt, looking genuinely surprised.

"Oh, Wyatt," said Jess, exasperated. "Haven't you noticed he's never said a single nice thing about me?"

Wyatt looked thoughtful. Grace looked like she was ready to enjoy this exchange with a bag of Maltesers.

"He has, too," said Wyatt. "You came up the other day over lunch."

Jess squinted at him. Floyd had talked about her?

"I did?"

"Yeah, and he said we should have a cute face like yours doing more customer-facing work—"

"*What?*" said Jess and Grace together.

Wyatt looked between them, expression falling. "Well, he meant like, you're really personable, you know?"

"No," said Jess, "that's not what you said."

Wyatt looked to Ethan for help.

"He was probably pointing out the obvious fact that attractive faces are for marketing," said Ethan. He took off his glasses with a flourish and made a Vogue gesture.

When Jess and Grace continued to stare, Ethan said, "I'm sure Floyd doesn't have a problem with you. He's just

177

awkward. I bet the company he enjoys most is the Microsoft Paperclip."

Floyd rounded the corner, then, and everyone jumped.

"Uh," said Grace.

"And that's why it's important for you to get your vision checked on a regular basis," said Ethan, putting his glasses back on.

"To the Japadogs!" said Wyatt.

Jess turned her attention back to the matter at hand, frantically waving Floyd down. "Floyd!"

"Hi, Jessica. I have a meeting—"

"This is important." She glanced past him to make sure the others were out of earshot. "I think something bad happened in the lab."

Floyd raised an eyebrow. "What, like downstairs?"

"Yes." Jess dropped her voice, grateful everyone had left. This was not a conversation for prying ears.

"How do you know what's going on in there?"

"Surveillance imagery. I, uh, got access to it."

"And you saw inside the lab?"

Never had Floyd given Jess such rapt attention. Was he as curious as everyone else was about what went on inside? Or did he already know what was in there?

"Two people went inside," said Jess. "They—"

Floyd pulled his phone from his pocket. "Were they authorized?"

"I ... don't know."

"Were they wearing lab coats?"

"No."

178

Floyd scrolled through his contacts. "You were right to tell me this. No one is supposed to be in there, and if you have access to the images, that means other unauthorized—"

"Floyd! There was an accident. They—"

She choked on the words. Floyd looked at her sharply. In his hand, the phone's screen dimmed as he waited for her to finish.

"They killed someone," she said, hearing how ridiculous it sounded. People didn't get *killed* at a software company—they got carpal tunnel syndrome and Vitamin D deficiency.

Floyd blinked. Without changing his expression, he tapped something on his phone and raised it to his ear. "I'll let Doctor Ries know."

"Him?"

Floyd gave her a *WTF* look. Jess opened her mouth, couldn't think of a sufficient argument, and closed it. Of course Floyd should tell the company owner about this. But after discovering Doctor Ries' criminal activity, Jess didn't like or trust the man.

She crossed her arms to stop her hands trembling.

Floyd returned his attention to his phone, dropping his gaze to his square-toed shoes. Jess hoped his exaggerated calm was simply from shock. Did he believe her?

They waited, and waited, for an agonizing minute. Jess heard the automated voicemail pick up.

Floyd lowered the phone. "I'll try again in a few. Don't worry, Jessica. I'll find out what's going on."

"And the police?"

"Doctor Ries will take care of it. He has to be involved before anyone else. Intellectual property. You know how it is."

Jess tried to think of a polite way to say, *Are you freaking kidding me?*

"Will you send me the surveillance images?"

"Sure." Her tone was flat.

Getting the vibe that the conversation was over, she turned to leave.

"How did you access the imagery?" said Floyd.

Jess answered without turning around. "My API key. The data's stored in Aries 181."

Back in her office, she shut the door. She ought to cry, after having witnessed a murder.

Floyd needed to get a hold of someone quickly. A Red Badge, at least. What if the pair had already escaped? She should have called the police right away instead of going to Floyd.

She picked up her phone. Was it too late? Floyd had specifically said *no.* Then she remembered her promise to send him the images and opened her cloud drive. The last one had been from several minutes ago. Her stomach churned at the thought of the man in the lab coat lying dead on the concrete floor.

That meant the duo was gone. Had they run back up the stairs?

Needing to know, she opened the last few images.

"Ugh!"

They'd kissed! Beside a dead body! What kind of psychos were they?

Then they'd sprinted hand-in-hand for the far corner of the warehouse, taking the guns on the floor with them.

That was it. No activity had been detected in the lab since then. Where were they now?

A message appeared at the top of her screen.

Anita: *We missed you at lunch! All good?*

Jess glanced at the time. Everyone would be back to work soon. She had a meeting with British Steve this afternoon to go over his latest code changes.

She copied the link to the cloud folder and sent it to Floyd, then opened her chat with Anita. What should she tell her? She didn't want to be the source of this kind of information. Besides, she had no desire to relive it to Anita.

Jess: *Hibernating. Not feeling the greatest.*

Anita: *Aw, sorry to hear. Head home if you want – you're allowed to take a sick day.*

Jess considered, but the idea of being at home alone right now was discomforting. Besides, she wanted to stay in the office to hear what Floyd came back with.

Another notification appeared.

Aries server error.

She furrowed her brow.

The message had a text attachment with the error log. She opened it and scrolled through.

12:46 ERROR: Invalid Aries API key.

Invalid? How? She'd been using the same key since—

"Oh," she breathed.

She'd told Floyd she had access to restricted surveillance imagery through her API key. He must have revoked it.

She opened her cloud drive. She would have to copy the saved images to another location before—

"No ..."

It was gone. Her entire cloud drive had been wiped clean.

Staring open-mouthed at the place where all the proof had been, Jess thought, *Message received.*

Apparently, this cute face of hers shouldn't fuss over whatever Aries had to hide. It was none of her business, and the company would make sure it stayed that way.

Chapter 15
Halley's New Skin

Halley raised the whirring hair trimmer to eye level, squinting at the clippers. The blades were moving too fast to see, but she could feel the divots they made in the air as they jolted back and forth. The movement raked her exposed nerves like an itch. If she focused, she could feel the current of each moving prong.

She adjusted her grip on the plastic handle, where its chemical makeup told a story on her fingertips. The molecules reacted with her nerves like flavors on taste buds. Plastic was smooth but artificial, like sour candy. Metal had a sharp kick to it, like salt and vinegar chips. Rubber felt like an overcooked pork loin smothered in expired barbecue sauce.

Halley looked past the blade at her reflection in Tony's bathroom mirror. She raised the trimmers to the wispy remains of hair and began shaving. Bald was better than this parasite-eaten look.

She hadn't looked back as they left Aries. Scott was beyond saving. She'd felt it when air stopped flowing through him—like his very presence had vanished. In the far corner of the warehouse, Tony had installed an emergency exit that emerged into the forest behind the building. Bursting through the trapdoor and into the January rain felt like being dumped in the middle of a tornado, complete with swirling cows and wood splinters.

As Tony drove them home at triple the speed limit, she'd bravely pulled down the sun visor to look at her reflection. The first glimpse made her gag. She would have thrown up if she hadn't already emptied her guts in the warehouse.

Tony made no comment about her nearly vomiting in his fancy car. He just said, "I shouldn't have shot him. He was my chemical engineer. Now I can't reproduce the bullet solution."

Ah. The bullets.

"No shit, you shouldn't have committed murder," she snapped. Her heart accelerated, jumping wildly as she took in the charred face in the mirror.

In her periphery, Tony fired her a glare.

"I didn't know what I was doing. My head was—it told me to—" He waved a hand.

Fight. Flee. The panic response, rocketing around the brain like a firecracker. She knew what he meant, but that didn't make what he'd done any better.

"Well, how are you going to explain it?" she said. "To his family? To *forensics*? Who, by the way, will *want access to your lab.*"

"Nobody's coming into the lab. I'll make it look like he was in a car crash on the way home."

Halley hesitated. Staging an accident might work, but the whole situation worried her.

"What about me? I'm as good as missing. I can't show my face like this." She raised a shaking hand to her cheek, but couldn't bring herself to touch it, not wanting to feel the texture.

"You won't be missing. Keep talking to your parents on the phone. Just—don't video chat anyone."

Halley crossed her arms. "Fine. You'd better hope none of your engineers get hurt cleaning up that mess. People are going to ask questions if anything happens to another Aries employee."

Tony made a face.

"What?" said Halley.

When he stayed silent, she turned in the passenger's seat to face him. "Someone died in there before, didn't they?"

"It's not my fault."

"Tony! People are going to connect the dots if Aries employees keep dying in car crashes."

"I'm aware," he growled.

The conversation ended. Halley huffed and looked out the window as they blew through a red light. She'd done all she could to warn him. It was up to Tony to make sure he didn't open the doors of his lab to police investigation.

In the bathroom, with her singed clothes in a heap on the floor, she moved the trimmer over her scalp. As she reached the crown of her head, the cord slipped off the stone counter and a gust of air swooped up her body. She cringed.

Would she ever get used to this? Every movement, every opening door and turn of a fan scraped across her flesh like someone had turned on the jets in a hot tub.

She couldn't shake the feeling that something inside her had been damaged, too. Her brain worked overtime, leaving her constantly frazzled, like when she crammed for an exam. Were her neurons trying to understand where this constant, dull ache came from? Or did the propellant singe her insides, too? She envisioned a short circuit in her brain, the neurotransmitters hitting dead ends as they struggled to find their way around.

At least she'd subdued the rising panic for now—as much as she wanted to claw at her new face, to rip it off and search for her real skin beneath it.

Panicking will accomplish nothing. You're fine. You're alive. Looks mean nothing.

Nothing, except that her own mother probably wouldn't recognize her—if she ever did see Mom again.

She inhaled deeply. *This is how you look now. No going back.*

She thought about Lady Gaga.

Halley, too, could buy wigs in every color and style she wanted. She could own this charred scalp thing. She wasn't a real blonde, anyway. Since she was seventeen she'd attacked her hair with chemicals every two months, but her natural color was potato-brown.

"Time for a change," she breathed, willing herself to believe she was sick of being an attractive blonde.

She leaned closer to the mirror, concentrating on getting every last strand.

Footsteps. Left leg, right leg, cutting through the air. Tony was coming.

How interesting that the way Tony walked was so unique. Without seeing or hearing him, she could probably identify his walk from across a field by the way the air curled around his legs.

She turned off the hair trimmer, letting the mechanical whine and itchy air current die.

So strange. Maybe the effect of the propellant—this overwhelming heightened sense—had a purpose. Maybe it didn't have to be torturous.

Something was bubbling to the surface of her mind.

The pistol lay on the counter. The chemical solution inside was running low. Like Tony had said, with Scott gone, so was their hope of making more of it. But what if ...?

"Dammit! God, dammit!"

Halley jumped and spun around. "What's wrong?"

"Phone's dead. Just saw an email from work." He appeared in the doorway, white teeth stark against his charred skin, so he looked like a jaguar ready to pounce. He'd stripped down to a tattered, singed pair of briefs. "It's the surveillance images."

Halley recalled the winking green lights in the warehouse ceiling.

Tony roared, fists balled by his temples.

Her heart pounded. She didn't like this Tony.

"I won't be ratted on by an intern," he said. "The bitch was never supposed to ... How did she get access?"

He wasn't making sense. Halley wanted to move closer and calm him down, but his temper paralyzed her. So she stood across the pristine bathroom, with its glossy white floors and the stone counter covered in her hair, watching Tony throw a fit.

She needed to give him a win. He needed to feel like he was on top again, instead of like this helpless victim.

He'd wanted GN's intellectual property. If she got it, she could still set this day right.

She would need a rope, extra gloves this time, and a hat. Except …

That bubbling thought came back to the surface.

She ran her fingers over her bare head. She studied her hands, free of fingerprints. Not to mention her face, free of the old Halley's identity.

She looked up at him. "I was thinking I should go back to GN. I'll get the bullet solution and the hard drive."

Tony hesitated. Halley waited for him to make the connection, to agree that this would make everything better.

He nodded. "Hard drive first, bullet solution second. Those are your priorities. Understand?"

"Yes, sir."

"I'll arrange your flight. Don't let anyone see you between here and the airport."

He looked at his watch, tapped the dead screen aggressively, and clenched his fists. He stormed to the closet and rifled through his clothes. Halley felt his movement on the air as much as she saw it. He gingerly pulled sweatpants and a sweater over his disfigured flesh, then put on a toque and sunglasses and began wrapping his face in a scarf.

"There's something I need to do," he said, voice muffled beneath the material.

She slipped past him and hurried downstairs to get ready. The carpet was like wasabi under her feet.

She turned her hands over and smiled. The propellant had done more than keep her and Tony alive. It had *made* them alive. It had gifted her with a new sense, giving her impossible power.

When the old Halley burned away on the warehouse floor, a new Halley had been unleashed. She could feel the world in a way that no one else could. Between the currents flowing through the room, she understood her place better than ever. She was tuned into her environment. She was in control.

If only Brooke could see her now. She would be the one cowering, not Halley. *Tell me I'm a doormat now, B.*

She thought back further, to Kevin in elementary school, hating her because she was smart. *Try to bruise my ribs now, boys.*

This version of Halley wouldn't have let any of that happen. The propellant had stripped away the smothering sense of powerlessness she'd carried around for her whole life.

Nobody would look at this face and call her a little angel. Her innards had been exposed, and if anyone crossed her, she would show them what a devil she could be.

And with that empowering thought, she was ready to take on GN properly.

Chapter 16
Jess is so Over this Fucking Tuesday

Jess's productivity that afternoon was about O(n!) in terms of algorithmic efficiency. That was to say, it sucked, and was getting worse with each passing minute.

When she tried to read about a feature she was supposed to be testing, she stared at the same line for minutes without processing what it did. When she tried to type, her fingers trembled over the keyboard.

A *murder*. She'd witnessed a *murder*.

It had been two hours. Floyd should have gotten back to her by now. Was he following some questionable and mysterious protocol set out by Doctor Ries?

With each second, the culprits—whoever they were—got further away. Doctor Ries would be making sure of it. God, they were probably special agents hired to steal technology from competitors.

She couldn't even check what was happening in the lab, with her API key revoked. Her imagination leapt from a full SWAT team barging into the warehouse, to a camera crew appearing in her office and Doctor Ries laughing because he'd pulled such an epic prank on a stupid intern.

A shadow appeared in the doorway.

"I'm dying," said Wyatt, and apparently noticing how Jess had spooked like a nervous horse, added, "Oh, sorry."

"S'okay." Jess grabbed the tube of lip balm on her desk and fiddled with it. "What happened?"

"Japadog. I ate way too much."

There was a pause while Wyatt seemed to wait for her to continue the conversation, but her mind was several floors beneath her office, hovering outside the doors to the warehouse.

"Um, so I've been QA-ing your human detection code," said Wyatt. "I found a couple of minor things. Can I show you?"

Jess scooted her chair so Wyatt could share her screen. She'd had the same window open for two hours. He walked her through a couple of error cases, while Jess inwardly cursed him for finding bugs in her code.

"Anyway," he said, stepping back. "I wanted to show you in person before I report the bugs. Give you a chance to fix them."

Jess blinked up at his Justin Bieber bowl cut and round, earnest face. If she fixed these issues before he reported the QA results, it would look like she had committed flawless code on the first try. He was making her look good in front of the rest of development.

"Thanks, Wyatt."

He was a decent guy. Floyd was the one pushing him unfairly ahead—the blazing sun in her solar system of frustration.

"No worries. Hey, you okay?"

"Yep," she said, too quickly. She adjusted her bangs over her clammy forehead.

He squinted at her. "All right. Have you got a lot in the queue?"

Jess shrugged. "Normal amount."

"Do you mind if I hand off a few bugs? Chris and I are working on a new agriculture project and it's taking up a lot of time."

Ah, there it was. "Sure," she said tightly.

"Cool. Thanks."

As he left, Jess inhaled deeply, trying to calm the bubbling rage. How was this fair?

She turned back to her screen, tapping the lip balm on her desk. Her hands shook worse than ever.

Was Floyd talking to Doctor Ries while a forensics team swept the warehouse? Or was he, too, having a crisis? If he didn't know what was in the Aries lab before, he did now. She wondered if he'd made the connection to the stolen items, or if he was preoccupied by—she shuddered—that situation lying on the ground.

There were only a couple of hours left in the workday. She should tell British Steve she was sick, go home early, and make up the time later. At this rate, if she tried to get through their meeting this afternoon she might accidentally explode and send her brains all over the wall. Or worse, start crying at work.

She glanced to the door. How bad would it be to take the stairs a floor deeper while she was on the way out? Not that she'd be able to get inside the lab, but she might hear what was happening or see if anyone was coming or going.

It would be a bold move, and if any of the Red Badges saw her she would get in trouble, but the situation was getting desperate.

A message appeared from Floyd. She seized her mouse so fast that she accidentally dragged a bunch of code across the screen and lost it inside another text editor. Whatever. She'd fix it later.

Floyd: *Heard back from Doctor Ries. He says not to worry. What you saw was nothing.*

Jess stared at the message for a long minute, her mouth open.

It took her several tries to form a reply that wasn't littered with typos.

Jess: *Did he say what it was?*

Her heart was pounding. She had half a mind to run down the hall to Floyd's office. Then he started typing.

Floyd: *No. He sounded calm about it. Don't worry, Jessica. It's nothing to be concerned about. We'll get you a new API key. In the meantime, please keep focusing on your work.*

Jess ground her teeth. Gee, a new API key! Just what she needed to make all of this better!

Her fingers hovered over the keyboard. She wanted to rage at him for thinking this answer would satisfy her. Doctor Ries was lying. He was hiding the murder, same as he'd hidden all of his other crimes.

As much as she wanted justice, she also wanted to just say, "thanks," and move on and pretend she saw nothing. This was a messy situation, to say the least, that had absolutely nothing to do with her. She didn't owe anything to the victim. Did she?

A message from Steve 2 appeared.

Steve: *I need help with something and Floyd said I should ask you. That ok?*

Jess drew a breath, trying not to spiral.

Jess: *Sure, send it my way.*

Steve: *Thanks. Just copying the river detection documentation over to the new template. I'll send you the link.*

Jess stared at his message. Did he seriously ask her to copy and paste documentation? Her ten-year-old cousin could have done that. Was this what her engineering skills were worth?

She looked forward to the day she was in the position to manage others—and could make a point of *not* being a dick about it.

She went back to her chat with Floyd and re-read their exchange. She wanted to pry him for information. How could he think she would accept that kind of answer?

Abruptly, the office went dark. The building seemed to exhale as all the lights, fans, and desktop machines turned off.

Jess's screen dimmed as her laptop reverted to battery power. Slack turned yellow, notifying her there was no internet connection.

Down the hall, someone said, "Nooo! I didn't save!"

Well, if she was waiting for the nail in the coffin to tell her she should go home for the day, this was it. Fuck this Tuesday and all its fucking fuckery.

In the glow of the emergency lights and the fading daylight reaching through the windows, she packed up her bag and put on her jacket.

She stuffed her mug in the dishwasher, amid poorly loaded bowls and sideways plates with food stuck to them, and passed British Steve's office on the way to the stairs.

"Hey, I'm going to work the rest of the day from home." Lie. She was going to wrap herself in a blanket like a human sushi roll and watch *Paw Patrol*. "Can we meet tomorrow?"

He cast her a sly grin. "Skiving off, are we?"

"No, I—"

"Only joking. Of course. Take it easy."

Jess turned away before he could see her flush. Not in the mood to be chipper, she hurried to the stairs without saying goodbye to anyone else.

The stairwell was dark, lit by a few emergency lights. She moved cautiously, using the handrail to guide her. The clunk of her boots echoed off the concrete.

When she emerged into the lobby, the place was empty. She had been the first to pack up. She suppressed the immediate surge of guilt. No one else had watched a man die today. She had every right to blow this joint.

At reception, Beth was on her cell phone. "Did a car hit a powerline?"

Jess passed her and approached the glass doors. A swanky car was parked in the only space in front of the building. She knew nothing of cars, but recognized the grille enough to know it was a Bentley.

Wondering which coworker was earning enough to afford that, Jess pushed on the glass door and almost crashed into it. It was locked.

"You have to go out the emergency exit, honey," said Beth. "Security measures. I'm having trouble overriding the lock." She pointed toward a long corridor.

Jess glanced back to the Bentley. Something that expensive had to belong to Doctor Ries. Had he come to the office in the wake of what happened? Again, Jess entertained heading down to the lab to snoop. But the halls were so dark, she'd probably fall on her face.

Plus, sneaking down a black stairwell into a cold basement full of science experiments sounded about as fun as getting hit by a waterfall of toxic waste.

She shivered.

Right now, she needed home. She needed a fleece blanket and Mandeep's company.

She thanked Beth and went down the windowless corridor in search of the side door. It really was very dark.

There was a soft tinkling ahead.

Jess rounded a corner and stopped. Between here and the red *Exit* sign, it was pitch black. The emergency light overhead had shattered. Glass littered the floor beneath it.

Had that been the sound she heard? The bulb must have overheated and burst.

She pressed on, speed-walking through the blackness.

Something rustled behind her. She whirled around, heart leaping. No one was there. She scolded herself for being so jumpy. This was an office building, not a broken-down fairground full of starving clowns.

She turned back around and—

He was clothed head to toe, a scarf around his face. In person, under a mask of darkness, the man from the warehouse was a nightmare a hundred times worse. His skin was charred, rotten even, like he'd been decaying for years.

He held a gun with a fat silencer on the end.

"All you had to do was keep your mouth shut and do your work—"

Jess kicked him in the groin.

He folded over, letting out a startled, "Oomph!"

She ran. The door was steps away. She pushed it open and sprinted through, into the blinding daylight. The front of the building would be safe. She needed people. Traffic.

"Someone help—!"

A force hit her from behind so hard that it sent her sprawling across the pavement.

I'm shot!

But the pain was in her forearms, which she'd thrust out to break her fall. She gritted her teeth as they throbbed in agony, balling her fists.

Footsteps pounded behind her. She tried to stand.

The man grabbed her by the hair, pulling her to a sitting position. She gasped. The cold barrel of the gun pressed into her temple with bruising force.

"Don't shoot me—"

"Shush, and I won't make this mess any bigger." He sank into a squat, face level with hers. He was panting. Through a haze that told her she'd lost her glasses, his dark eyes were wild, his teeth bared. "I know what you saw, Jessica Curie. I know what you did. If you speak a word to anyone, I will come after you. Understand?"

She nodded.

"I want you to ignore anything you—" His head snapped up and he looked across the parking lot. A shiver seemed to pass over him.

She could hear voices in the distance.

He cast her one last glare—a warning—and let her go.

"I know where your office is, your home, your parents, and your sister," he whispered.

Jess scrambled back from that mutilated face.

His shoes ground over the pavement as he turned and sprinted away.

Jess waited until he disappeared around the building before trying to move. She reached a trembling hand to her temple, and then her knees, checking for blood. She was fine, except for her throbbing forearms.

"Jess!"

The blurred figures of Anita, Omar, and Kit were running toward her.

"Did you fall?" said Omar, reaching her first and helping her up.

"I'm fine."

It seemed the only response she was capable of. Did that seriously just happen? The weak January sun reflected off remnants of snow. Cars blew by in the distance.

Kit passed Jess her glasses, which had skidded across the pavement. She put them on with shaking hands.

"You sure you're okay?" said Anita, and then to the others, "She told me she wasn't feeling well."

"Yeah, I—slipped—"

Anita put her hand on Jess's forehead. "You're like a million degrees and all clammy!"

"You're allowed to take sick days, babe," said Kit. "Just stay home if you're feeling off."

"Right," said Jess.

They walked with her to the bus, Omar sticking close like he was helping an old lady cross the street.

I will come after you.

The initial shock left Jess's body and the truth of the event sank in. Was the man serious? Was her life in danger after what she saw? Based on the gun he'd waved in her face, she had one choice, and that was to do what he said.

While they stood at the bus stop, Kit said, "Anyway, Omar, I think it's a pretty tough question with a lot of parameters."

"Oh, come on. There's no contest," said Omar. "Gandalf is immortal."

"But if he was human."

"But he's not."

The bus came, and they climbed on. They insisted Jess take the only empty seat. She obliged, staying mute because she was sure her voice would tremble.

Your home. Your parents. Your sister.

She thought she'd done the right thing by reporting what she had witnessed. Instead, she had made herself a target. If she'd listened to Mandeep, her biggest worry would still be whether she had a project to qualify her for a scholarship.

"Okay, say the fight was fair and they were both human," said Anita. "Dumbledore has a broader skill set."

"Skill set, maybe. But overall, he's way less powerful than Gandalf," said Omar.

Jess took off her backpack and placed it between her feet. She tried to blink the bus back into focus but everything was blurry. She pulled off her glasses, which were smudged with dirty snow, and reached into her backpack for the case.

She froze. A bullet hole tore through her bag from one side to the other. She ran her fingers over it, nausea climbing up her throat.

"What about the Elder Wand?" said Kit.

He'd shot at her. The bullet had torn through her bag and pitched her off balance, missing her by an inch. Had he intended to kill her?

No. If he wanted to, he would have. Like he said—it would have made a mess. Too many people around. A murder in the Aries parking lot would invite investigation. It was a can of worms he probably wanted to keep closed, especially in light of what happened in the warehouse.

She rummaged for her case and began cleaning her glasses.

Jess had told Floyd everything she saw, and Floyd told the man willing to do anything to prevent Aries' secrets from escaping. He'd come to the Aries research lab with full security clearance and stolen technology. He was informed that Jess had seen his crimes and the murder.

"It makes a difference whether we're talking about Gandalf the Grey or Gandalf the White," said Anita.

The man from the warehouse was no ordinary employee, nor was he a contracted agent. He was more central to Aries than that—and thinking back, the surveillance images had given Jess an odd feeling of familiarity, like she knew him.

She put her glasses back on, seeing the world with clarity. Doctor Anthony Ries certainly did have a lot to hide.

Chapter 17
Halley Crashes Board Game Night

Tuesday at Global Nanosats was board game night. A pizza delivery might work, but if anyone was in the office, they would be extra cautious after last time.

Yesterday, Halley reminded herself. Her last attempt had been yesterday. How could so much have changed in twenty-four hours?

Sitting behind Reah on the way to the airport, Halley set her jaw. Failing again was not an option. She would do whatever it took.

She flinched. Her brain was zipping around again, telling her to take action, to do *something* to fix its state of distress.

The symptom would have concerned her, but knowing Tony was going through the same thing was comforting. She wasn't alone, as long as he was there for her to come home to.

She ran through her Five T's.

Target: hard drive in 304B and chemical bullets.

Tactic: forced entry.

Tools: GN pistol, rope.

Time: eight minutes.

Takeoff: third-floor window.

A boost of confidence came with her new skin. The constant pain had dulled and she'd spent the last few hours relishing the ability to feel every whirl in the air, knowing a room's layout without looking at it. She could even discern distant traffic by focusing on the air flowing through an open window. With this ability, her exposed nerves would prove more valuable than any other sense.

She'd gone so far as to wear less than usual, because clothes muffled the sensitivity. Her heist getup consisted of a sports bra and black yoga shorts, like she was a California girl going for a jog on a hot summer's day. Sure, it was cold out, but—

"*The cold doesn't bother me, anyway,*" Halley sang to herself, prancing over the snowy tarmac toward the jet. The wind blasting from the engine was more bothersome than the temperature.

With a new sense to help her navigate the world, she'd never felt more fluid and athletic.

What was it people said? *Beauty is only skin deep.* Well, if the person in question barely had skin, that meant Halley's beauty was boundless.

Yes, she'd decided to disconnect her self-worth from being blonde and soft-skinned. With a universe of opportunity yawning before her, she had much more to offer.

Reah said nothing about the new look, but averted her gaze. Conversation between the two of them was even more minimal than it had been before. Best to keep it that way.

On the flight, Halley checked GN's security cameras and discovered they'd hired a couple of security guards. Nothing she couldn't handle.

She checked the internal chat logs. Human Resources had sent a mass message to all employees.

Lorie: *By now you've heard about last night's break-and-enter. The police are investigating, but we suspect this was a petty robbery attempt by a troubled youth. We want to assure you this is nothing to worry about and you can resume your regular work. The security guards are a temporary measure for everyone's peace-of-mind. If you have concerns, don't hesitate to speak to your manager.*

Halley's mouth twisted into a smirk. So, they were downplaying what happened. They didn't want the public to know their office was worth breaking into. Good.

Next, she poked around for info on GN's alarm.

Hacking the alarm system from their network proved impossible, but they did have a number to call and a password to relay to the security company if the alarm went off. *Proxima Centauri.* Simple enough.

When Reah dropped her off, Halley let herself through the gate and strode across the parking lot with resolve. Time to get this done properly.

The security camera she'd shot out had already been replaced, a bulletproof case enclosing it.

She hesitated, but only on instinct. Without a face, there was nothing to recognize. Without fingerprints or hair, there was nothing to trace. She didn't need to hide her identity.

Halley stepped into the camera's line of sight and waggled her fingers at it, wishing godspeed to whoever went through the footage.

"Na, na, naaaa ..." she whispered, singing herself a theme song. "Halley's got a gun ..."

She aimed her stolen pistol at the door handle and pulled the trigger. Bullets peppered the lock, burning holes into the metal until—

Pop.

The door opened a crack. The building alarm began blaring.

She started the countdown on her watch. Eight minutes.

"Ohh, Halley's got a gun ... blah blah something undone ..."

Air pulsed through the opening. Someone had heard the gunshots and was running over.

After taking a moment to relish the sensation in her nerve endings, Halley front-kicked the door, putting the force of years of martial arts training behind it. It flew open and smashed into the person on the other side.

She stepped through, pistol ready, and found a security guard regaining his balance. He raised a handgun—and blanched when he saw her face.

The hesitation was enough. Halley smacked the gun out of his hand and drove her knee into him. Jab-*crack!* She clubbed him in the head and he fell.

Keeping her eyes on the guard, she gave the lobby a quick feel for danger. The air curled steadily around her. Nobody was there.

She felt it coming before she saw it coming. The guard kicked out. She jumped, his leg swooping beneath her. He grabbed for her. Again, she felt it coming and dodged him.

She pointed the pistol at his head. "Quit your flailing."

He tensed, about to disobey—but met her gaze and froze.

Halley couldn't help smiling. She'd always been small, blonde, with a diamond face and a compliant personality. Nobody feared her. Though she'd been able to kick anyone's ass since she was a kid, everyone assumed her hands were made for manicures, not punching.

The security guard looked from her to the pistol. He sank back to the floor, hands raised. Halley wished she had his expression on camera so she could look at it over and over again.

She pulled out the temporary phone she'd brought from Tony's and dialed the security company. Making her voice go a notch higher, she said, "Hello? This is Sherry Franklin at Global Nanosats. I accidentally set off the alarm."

The guard looked on in horror while Halley giggled her way through the phone call.

"Proxima Centauri," she told the nice man on the other end. "Thank you."

The alarm went silent.

Holding the guard down with the threat of the pistol, Halley put the phone away and rummaged through his belt. He was heavily armed.

"Wow, they were really serious about protecting this place! Mind if I borrow these?"

She plucked off the handcuffs and used them to attach the guard to the door handle. She removed the key and anything he might use to call for help and threw them across the lobby.

Catching her breath, she straightened. The front door had been a tad more difficult to pass through than last time, but she got there in the end.

Unfortunately for the board game nerds, the elevators were across the lounge. Halley crashed their party by firing shots into the ceiling. The dozen or so people, approaching the door after hearing the alarm, shrieked and scattered and hurled themselves to the floor.

"Ooh, good choice. I love *Catan*." Halley snatched someone's badge from beside a pile of sheep and ore.

Nobody tried to fight her as she crossed the lounge. They stayed down, silent, watching her with identical expressions of terror.

"I expect all of you to stay here," she said, pushing the elevator call button. "Or your next game will end with Miss Scarlet in the elevator with a pistol."

She blew on the end of the weapon. The elevator doors shut, and she swooped up to level three. First stop: server room.

She jogged down the hall toward 304B, pulse racing. A few late-working employees stirred the air in the rooms branching off the hallway. Would they have heard all the noise?

Either way, best to assume the cops had been called and move quickly.

She swiped the borrowed badge over 304B's lock pad. The LED turned green, and she pushed the door open.

Finally, the server room.

Dozens of computers whirred, their fans pushing air at her with irritating force. She scanned the room, orienting herself to where the surveillance images had been taken. The fans made it hard to focus. There was the gray folding table, littered with cables, manuals, and packaging ...

"Ha!"

The hard drive sat exactly where it had been in the images.

Halley strode in. She imagined the hard drive screaming in a tiny little robot voice, begging her, reasoning with her.

"No, Halley! Please, Halley! Don't take me! I'm too young to go!"

She snatched it up and dropped it in her backpack.

Time to find those chemical bullets.

She stepped into the hall, and the tiniest hitch of air came from the far end. Someone was moving slowly, creeping toward her without making a sound.

She retreated inside the server room and put her back to the wall beside the open door, hidden from view.

Beside her, plastic shelves and four steel table legs leaned against the wall. She wrapped her hand around a steel leg. She closed her eyes, mustering all her energy to block out the whirring fans.

The person came closer, moving with caution. *Left, right, left, right.*

Large build. No artificial bulk surrounded him as it had with the security guard, which meant he was in ordinary clothes. His arms were outstretched, wrapped around a handgun.

Ah, a 'right to bear arms' bro who thought he could be the hero who saves everyone.

Halley's lips twisted into a smile. This was getting fun.

She gripped the steel rod tighter. Mr. Office Hero drew closer, his breaths coming fast.

As a kid, Halley's parents had put her in softball for a few years. All her friends were on the same team, so some of her fondest memories were from the dugout, singing cheers and spitting sunflower seeds and heckling the other team. She'd never been particularly good at the throwing and catching part. When she was up to bat, on the other hand ...

The man appeared at the server room door, pale, mid-forties, plump around the middle. Halley swung the steel rod with perfect form, extending her arms and twisting on her back toe like she'd been taught. The rod slammed into him with so much force that he flew backward. His breath exploded from his mouth, tingling all over Halley's flesh.

She leapt out after him, striking his wrist with the rod. He dropped the handgun and she kicked it away.

"The police will be here any second," he wheezed—as if the threat was supposed to make her give up.

"Then you understand what a hurry I'm in."

With a twinge of guilt, she wound back with the steel rod.

"Bases are loaded," she breathed.

"Don't!"

"Bottom of the ninth ..."

He made to stand, and Halley swung. She clubbed him in the jaw, sending him crumpling back to the floor. Her conscience made her pull the swing a bit, so she failed to make a KO—but he was stunned, lying flat and spluttering.

"What – a – *swing!*"

She glanced at her watch. Two minutes left. Chemical Firearms room, and she was out of there.

Grabbing her stuff, she left the steel rod behind and raced down the hall. She arrived at the Chemical Firearms room to find caution tape forming an X across the door. It was ajar, the lock still peppered with bullet holes. Halley pushed it further open with her foot.

The room had been vacated. Empty racks lined the walls. Broken tables were scattered. Craters and scorch marks covered every surface.

Halley backed away, nauseated by the remaining signs of the fire.

A door opened down the hall. She raised the pistol just as a man in a lab coat stepped out.

When he saw her, his face turned to horror so quickly that Halley laughed. The man raised his hands and retreated back into the room.

Halley ran after him. She kicked the door open before he could lock it.

"I'm wondering if you can help me with something."

"Please!" said the man.

Halley took in her surroundings. Test tubes, labeled bottles, laptops, and notebooks cluttered every table and counter. The walls and surfaces were worn, blemished, like all the chemicals were eroding everything in the room.

The man, also looking worn and blemished, lowered his arms—reaching, it seemed, for his pocket.

"Nope!" Halley lunged for him.

She dug into his pocket, grabbed his phone, and threw it across the room.

"Okay! Okay!" said the man, close to tears.

Halley pulled out a chair from the table beside them and motioned with her pistol. "Sit."

She seized a laptop charging cord from the table and used it to tie his wrists to the back of the chair.

"I'm looking for something. Can you help me?"

He shook his head.

Seriously?

Halley grabbed the lanyard around his neck and yanked him closer.

"George," she read off his badge. "You're a chemist, are you, Georgie?"

He nodded, lips trembling.

"I learned a rhyme, once. Do you want to hear it?" She plucked a test tube off the table, clear liquid sloshing inside as she held it in front of his face. Sweat beaded on his forehead.

"It's about you, Georgie," she said, straddling his lap.

George turned his head, as though ignoring her would make her go away.

Bringing the test tube closer to his lips, Halley recited, "Georgie was a chemist, but Georgie is no more. What Georgie thought was H_2O, was H_2SO_4."

Sweat poured off him, making little streams down his cheeks and neck.

"Do you think this is H_2O?" said Halley.

The air changed. Halley looked to the door, listening. Somewhere close, an elevator had opened.

Halley slid off George's lap and placed the test tube back on its rack. She crept to the door, pistol by her ear.

George was breathing too hard.

"Quiet!" whispered Halley.

He pursed his lips, holding his breath.

Several people were moving down the hall with trained stealth. Police.

It was time for takeoff.

She returned to Georgie in a few swift steps. Pressing her face close to his, she whispered, "Where's the solution that goes inside this gun?"

George looked at the gun, and back to Halley.

"Don't make me," said Halley, pressing the gun to his knee.

"Top c-cupboard over there." He nodded toward the corner of the lab.

Halley hesitated. "I'm going to go over there. If you yell for help, I will shoot you."

He nodded, the sweat now forming rivers down his face, and she crossed the room and opened the cupboard. It was jammed full of bottles.

"God, you guys need some organizational help, in here."

The police were steps from the door. Abandoning caution, she rifled through the bottles, sending several crashing to the floor.

There. A two-liter bottle of gray liquid with the label 'CF Solution'. A piece of paper was wrapped around the bottle that had formulas scrawled across it, held in place by a rubber band.

"Chemical Firearms?" she said, turning to him.

He nodded.

"Police! Freeze!"

Two officers leapt into the room, ready to shoot.

Halley dove to the floor, cradling the bottle, and shielded herself behind a table.

"What the hell is that?" said the female officer. "Did you see that?"

Halley would have shouted, "Your worst nightmare!" and thrown in an evil cackle, if it wouldn't have put her life in danger.

She had to get to a window—one that wasn't so high. She might not have a tree to break her fall this time.

She stuffed the CF Solution in her backpack and zipped it up, trying not to think of how combustible the stuff was and what would happen if a bullet pierced it.

The two cops hesitated in the doorway. Halley aimed her pistol through the tables and equipment. The door was a fair distance away, but she could hit them.

Their eyes were locked onto George, who sat there looking like a startled rabbit.

For a terrible moment, the cops stood in the doorway, and Halley aimed her pistol at the woman's abdomen—below where her bulletproof vest ended.

It would be fatal if she pulled the trigger.

She had agreed to commit crimes for Tony. Her job was to get whatever he asked her to, by any means necessary. But to take a person's life …

Tony would do it. This, she knew.

But her finger stayed frozen over the trigger. Her eyes fell on the test tube she'd left on the table beside George.

She adjusted her aim and squeezed. Bullets left the pistol in an explosion of sound, whizzing so close to George's face that he screamed and jerked backward, his chair toppling over.

After the stream of bullets burned a hole in the wall and table, one finally hit the test tube. It exploded, sending a cloud of smoke into the ceiling. The two officers hit the floor.

Halley sprang up and bolted for the exit, leaping over them before they could react and landing in the hallway outside the door. She sprinted toward the nearest stairwell and flew down several steps at a time, hopping the railing at the turn. The cops weren't far behind.

She located an emergency exit on the second floor and burst out of it onto a fire escape. The snow-covered lawn below seemed bright through the darkness.

She let herself fall, crumpling on impact, ankles throbbing. The wind-hardened snow was a thousand paper cuts against her flesh.

No time to sit there in pain. She gritted her teeth, got her feet under her, and ran.

Multiple police cars blocked the gate, their blue and red lights piercing the sky. A German Shepherd barked wildly. Halley stopped. She would never make it past them. Like hell was she going to shoot a dog.

She spun. The chain link fence surrounding the property was topped with barbed wire. If she couldn't go over, under, or around ...

She ran to the back of the building, as far from the parking lot as she could manage. An alley was on the other side of the fence, the wall across the way covered in graffiti.

Halley raised her pistol and squeezed the trigger. Nothing happened. She shook it, hearing a small amount of liquid slosh around inside. She squeezed again, and a last hurrah of bullets came out. She traced a hole in the fence.

"Come on, honey. Just a bit more," she whispered.

More bullets passed through the links than hit the metal, but slowly, it broke. The wall across the alley grew black with smoke from all the bullets.

A lot of shouts were coming from the front of the building, everyone probably trying to figure out where Halley had gone and how to get her.

The pistol stopped firing again. She shook it, but no solution was left inside. She kicked at the circle she had burned into the fence, the chain links rattling and snapping where she'd scorched the metal. She kicked several more times. The circle popped free and crashed into the alley.

She'd done it. The hard drive was hers. She had bullet solution. She might have even gotten the formula for it.

She stepped through the opening like a Looney Tunes character with a portable hole.

"Beep beep!" she said, nearly hysterical with glee, and sprinted down the street.

Tony was on the couch holding a glass of whiskey when she came in the door. A new phone and smartwatch were on the coffee table in front of him alongside their opened boxes.

He stood. "Did you do it?"

Wordlessly, she passed him the hard drive, unable to keep the grin from her face. He set his glass down before taking it from her. She half expected him to whisper, *"Precioussss,"* the way he cradled it in his raw palms.

"And—" She pulled out the bottle labeled *CF Solution* and the formulas that went with it. "Bullets!"

His eyes lit up as they fell upon the gray liquid.

"You're welcome," said Halley.

"You got all this? No one saw you?"

"Loads of people saw me," said Halley. "But look at me!"

She twirled, letting him take in her new skin.

"Tony, we're untraceable. We don't have fingerprints or hair. Our faces are a mess. It's the perfect disguise. The only way we're going to jail is if they physically catch us."

Tony stared at her.

"We can pull off perfect heists," she said.

He was silent as he processed this, eyes darting over the floor. She waited for him to react, holding her breath.

"And the feel?" he said at last.

"Feel?"

"The air. Your nerves."

"I felt the cops coming before they left the elevator."

Tony closed the distance between them. He stopped near enough that she could feel the blood pulsing through his veins. With a gentle hand, he brushed a finger over her bottom lip. The sensation sent a shiver through her.

"Get some sleep," he said. "We're leaving first thing."

"Where are we going?"

He planted a soft kiss on her lips. "Every business model needs testing. Let's play with how effective this one is."

Chapter 18
Jess Plays it Cool

Jess locked and bolted the door. She turned on every light in her and Mandeep's suite, plus the TV, and found a kids' channel where cartoon kittens were baking muffins.

She curled up on the armchair in the corner (an inheritance from her great aunt, which they'd covered with a dinosaur blanket so the asparagus-green velour wouldn't offend anyone). With her back safely to the wall, she dropped her head into her hands.

Though Jess wanted nothing more than to be wrapped in a pair of arms, it was better that Mandeep wasn't home yet. Jess needed to calm down before her girlfriend came through the door. She'd promised she would forget about the Aries 181 images. How was she supposed to bring this up?

By the way, I kept snooping around, saw two people murder someone, and then one of them came after me with a gun.

The kittens on TV began singing. "Sugar, butter, eggs, and flour! We'll be done in half an hour!"

No, this would make Mandeep worry, and then Jess would feel worse than she already did. She had escaped, and there was no use causing further issues.

"Put it together and blend, blend, blend! Baking muffins with friends, friends, friends!"

It would help if Jess could prove whether the man from the lab was Doctor Ries. If only Floyd hadn't deleted everything in her cloud drive. She needed those pictures to investigate.

"However bad I feel, it's nothing friends can't heal! Everybody needs friends, friends, friends!"

The kittens put the muffins in the oven, and that was enough of this show. It had served its purpose: exasperation took over any fear Jess had. She turned off the TV.

What could she do about it? She'd thought, before, that reporting Aries' stolen items would be career suicide. Now, it was actual suicide.

The lock clicked on the front door. Jess jumped to her feet. The knob turned, but the bolt stopped it from opening.

"Jessie? You in there?"

Jess ran over.

"Sorry. Weird noises outside." She let Mandeep in and threw her arms around her. "I missed you today."

"Oh—" Mandeep squeezed her back. "I missed you, too?"

Jess leaned over her and bolted the door again. "What are you up to tonight?"

Mandeep waved an arm to her backpack. "The usual ..."

Her gaze lingered on Jess. Either she knew something was off, or she was gauging whether Jess was feeling extra affectionate tonight.

Jess turned to the kitchen. "I'm making stir fry."

"Sounds good to me."

Mandeep retreated to the couch and opened the step stool she called a chemistry textbook.

Jess put on rice and pulled vegetables from the fridge. The reckless part of her wanted to talk to Mandeep about what happened. She needed someone else's opinion on what to do.

She cut up the vegetables, mind working rapidly.

Was it more dangerous to report Aries, or to let this crime spree keep happening? What—or who—would be next on the hit list?

It would be her own life if she reported Aries. But it might be someone else's if she didn't. She added the vegetables to the skillet and pushed them around.

God, she needed someone else to talk to. Her girlfriend was too strong-willed for this. Jess knew from experience that she would have no choice but to go along with whatever Mandeep decided. She would try to force Jess to run away from the problem, all the while pummeling her with a guilt trip about the mess she'd gotten herself into.

Jess paused, staring at the sizzling pan. Actually, if Mandeep's opinion was that she should go back to work and dig deeper, that would be fine.

There was her answer. She didn't want someone to tell her she was stupid for wanting to figure out what was going on. She wanted someone to agree that she should return to the office and investigate.

Today was nothing she couldn't handle. She'd been through worse.

"Bring yourself online, Jess," said Mandeep, appearing beside her with a phone charger. She stuck the end in Jess's ear, as though to recharge her.

Jess smiled and shoved her hand away.

"What are you thinking about so hard?"

"I was wondering if this carving knife would be a good thing to put in our zombie survival kit."

"I'd go for the cleaver."

"Hm, good idea."

Yes, this was her plan. She would return to work and prove whether that man was Doctor Ries. After identifying him, she could make an informed decision about what to do.

In the morning, she felt relatively calm about everything. The whole threatened-at-gunpoint situation seemed distant, like it had been a dream. She said hello to everyone on her way in and grabbed her latte as usual, and was pleased to find a mound of cookies in the lounge.

She recalled what Omar had once advised her: *If it's on the counter, it's free.*

Score. Jess downed a double-chocolate fudge cookie for second-breakfast while she caught up on messages, emails, social media, and RSS feeds.

The peachy morning went to shit around 10 AM, when her eyes drew to a trending story on Twitter, *#OttawaRobbery.*

She clicked it—and let out a squeak.

It was him.

Jess scrolled, finding pictures of the familiar pair storming through some hipster-looking office holding firearms.

"Eyewitnesses claim the burned appearance is not a disguise, but their actual skin," said one news outlet.

"Same woman who stole chemicals from Global Nanosats," said another, sharing a chilling photo of her waving up at a security camera, face half-melted, hair completely gone.

Jess paused at the mention of Global Nanosats. This was not looking good.

Tweets were coming in fast, the top of the feed notifying her of dozens of updates.

She expanded them to see a flood of photos and videos.

Her heart sank. This #OttawaRobbery was happening live, and they were inside a company called Boopify. Jess had never heard of it. She did a quick search and found it was a startup, but she wasn't clear on what exactly they did. Their webpage was a picture of a beagle's face, and their business model seemed to start and end at "for those times when you just need to boop something."

She went back to the Twitter feed. Pictures taken by phones led her to believe twenty or so employees were hiding under their desks while the man and woman held them at gunpoint.

Apparently, they were taking everyone's wallets.

Jess leaned back. *Wallets?* After stealing priceless technology from Global Nanosats—and presumably they were also responsible for the Canadian Space Agency telescope—they had downgraded to *wallets?*

Jess rubbed her temples, feeling a headache forming. This made no sense. Boopify had nothing to do with Aries, or any aspect of aerospace. What could the pair possibly want with this company?

She kept scrolling. Someone tweeted a photo of a piece of paper titled 'Feedback Form'.

The tweet read, *"Bitch throwing these around telling everyone to fill them out. #boopify #ottawarobbery"*.

Jess expanded the photo.

Feedback Form
Company name: _____
On a scale from 1-10, how competent would you say your armed robbers are?
On a scale from 1-10, how terrified are you?
On a scale from 1-10, how likely are you to surrender anything we ask for?
Do you have any thoughts/comments on how we can be more efficient in the future?

Jess stared at the screen. This was insane. Were they terrorizing all these people for kicks? Like a test heist?

There was only one thing for it. She needed to call the police. Aries was involved in all of this, and Anthony Ries was front and center. If she could get the police to search the warehouse downstairs, they would find the stolen items, and from there, they could track down these two people.

Jess picked up her phone. She should have done this long ago. This was about more than just stolen things, now. This was about a dead person, and these people had broken into places where they might leave more dead people.

She had to protect the public, and she had to trust the police to keep her safe.

Heart thumping, she called the non-emergency number for the Vancouver police.

A bored-sounding woman answered. Before Jess could chicken out, she explained the stolen technology she saw on the Aries 181 images, how the pair had come to look like they did, the murder of the employee in the lab coat, and how the man had come back to threaten her.

"You watched all of this on a satellite?" said the woman on the other end.

"Sort of. I think it's drones or something. It takes proper remote sensing imagery, with infrared data and—anyway, that part's not important."

"Do you have the images?"

"Well … no," said Jess. "They got deleted."

A long pause.

"I understand your concern, miss, but these crimes aren't happening in Vancouver, so there isn't much we can do about it."

"I know, but I'm telling you they originated here in Vancouver."

There was another long, aggravating silence on the other end.

"I think the man is Doctor Anthony Ries," said Jess boldly. "Everything points back to him."

"You're telling me the one and only Doctor Anthony Ries is the creepy-ass man I'm looking at on Twitter right now?"

"Yes."

"Doctor Ries, the man responsible for stopping all that illegal logging in Bolivia? The one who found that missing oil tanker with his fancy computer systems?"

Jess deflated, recalling her own opinion of Doctor Ries before all of this happened—Nobel Prize candidate, international hero, philanthropist. From the government to PETA, everyone found something in him worthy of praising.

"If you come investigate the Aries lab, you'll find the evidence," she said with a note of pleading.

"Miss, we can't barge into Anthony Ries' research facility without a warrant."

"So get one!"

The woman sighed. "Can you see why I'm having a hard time believing your story that these people walked into a fire pit and came out alive?"

"It wasn't a fire. And they didn't *walk* in, they—"

"When the girl emerged from the flames," said the woman, "did she have a couple of baby dragons on her shoulders?"

Jess said nothing, mouth agape. Was this woman *laughing* at her?

"They threatened my life!" said Jess, temper flaring. "Did that detail not get through to you?"

"Of course. And now they're robbing banks, right?"

Jess closed her eyes, feeling close to tears.

"Honey, we get a lot of conspiracy theories," said the woman. "If you want to share your ideas, you can find a forum or make a blog."

"Conspiracy—? Excuse me, but I'm not some crazy person!"

"Do you have any evidence?"

"I told you, it got deleted!"

"Right. Well, I'll make a note. Can I have your information?"

"I'll get back to you with proof," said Jess, snarling.

She threw her phone down, fighting the urge to kick her desk. How was she supposed to convince the authorities of

223

any of this? Somehow, she had to prove Aries was doing something very illegal—without putting a target on her head.

"Proof," she breathed. She needed proof.

She grabbed the mouse and scoured her history and trash for any images that might have survived the purge. Even a single photo would help.

She found nothing.

Maybe she didn't have access to Aries 181 anymore, but the public satellites might have something. What if she could get a shot of the pair running from the Aries building?

Jess navigated to the satellite portal to search for images, but stalled upon realizing she no longer had an API key. Floyd still hadn't given her a new one.

She leaned over until her forehead hit the desk and her glasses smushed into her face.

Okay. Minor setback. Could she borrow someone else's key? Or generate her own?

She browsed the code tree and found the place where they generated API keys.

Ha.

With a line of code, she could call the method herself and get one.

She did.

It wasn't *hacking*, per se—just getting the job done when a certain FF was being a dumbass.

With the birth of her new API key, she first tried to query the 181st satellite. The query was rejected, which she figured would happen. Undeterred, she began searching the Aries portal, starting with what was going on right now at Boopify.

With the satellites taking images every hour, success depended on timing. There was an image of the police cars, but going back in time, Jess couldn't find anything showing the pair entering the building.

She went back further and looked at the Global Nanosats robbery.

Darkness. This one had happened at night, so while the satellites had taken multispectral data, Jess couldn't see anyone with the naked eye.

Growing anxious, she went back to her remaining hope: lunchtime at the Aries office.

She moved the timeline again and gasped, leaning closer to her screen. There! Two people sprinting from the forest behind the building.

It was them! They were charred from the spill, clothes hanging like rags.

She moved the timeline a step further. They were gone, and so was the Bentley that had been in front of the building.

Jess's mouth fell open. *That was their car!* Well, she didn't have an image of them climbing in, but come on. This had to be proof enough.

Her heart skipped into double-time.

She sent a chat to Anita.

Jess: *What kind of car does Anthony Ries drive?*

She couldn't zoom in on the image enough to see the license plate. She closed her eyes and envisioned what she'd seen through the glass. Any numbers at all.

Nope, no Leo da Vinci memory for her.

Anita: *Something expensive. A Bentley I think. Why, did you see him drive by?*

Jess backed away from the computer like it was ready to detonate. Hypothesis confirmed. Her own boss had threatened to kill her.

Okay, breathe, she told herself. *He's not here. He's in Ottawa.*

Hands shaking, Jess saved the image of the two people fleeing the forest behind the Aries building. Then she emailed it to her personal account and saved it on her phone. Floyd wouldn't get this one away from her.

Now to decide what to do with the photo.

Jess returned to the Twitter feed. Hundreds of new #OttawaRobbery tweets had come in. She expanded them and scrolled through. Photos and videos showed the girl skipping—yes, *skipping*—through the cowering Boopify employees, gathering their completed feedback forms. Meanwhile, the man—Doctor Ries—was standing by with that scary-looking rifle. There was that sickening feeling of familiarity again.

Jess had to act before they hurt or killed anyone else.

Her phone lit up with a notification. She grabbed for it, but it was only Reddit. Someone had replied to a comment she made this morning in r/books.

She scrolled through the wall of information blasting through her Twitter feed. After a moment, she tapped her phone where the notification was still waiting to be viewed. Her Reddit comment had impacted a total stranger enough that they took time out of their day to respond.

"Huh …"

Maybe she didn't have enough proof to convince the authorities that they should investigate Aries—but she did have the internet. And with that, Jess had a plan.

Chapter 19
Halley Learns About Intellectual Property

Target: data and prototypes.

Tactic: ka-boom.

Tools: chemical firearms, empty luggage, and a surprise.

Time: six minutes.

Takeoff: east door.

Their entrance was more dramatic than Halley expected, but Tony did have style. With the force of a bazooka, the assault rifle disintegrated the glass doors and the walls beside them in a deafening crash.

Halley bounded into the convention center, dragging two empty suitcases through the glass. Screams echoed in the lobby. The hall became a blur of collared shirts, lanyards, and conference-issued backpacks. Someone knocked over the 'Los Angeles Aerospace Con' banner, which marked the entrance to the main hall. Halley's flesh tingled pleasantly in the chaos.

"Ladies and gentlemen," she said, opening her arms. "Please welcome your keynote speaker!"

The sight of Tony stepping over the threshold—assault rifle in hand, dust swirling around him, dressed in his most expensive suit pants—set her heart aflutter.

"Thank you, my little comet," he said, giving her a wink that turned her knees to jelly.

Four security guards ran at them, bellowing. "Drop your weapons! Get down!"

Tony fired at the ground between them, clearing the path like a parting sea. The guards soared, hitting walls and railings and slumping to the floor.

Tony's aim had become smooth and precise over the last few days. Halley, herself, felt confident and ready to prove her value as his partner. Together, they were a well-oiled Large Hadron Collider.

Save for the ringing in her ears, the lobby fell silent. She scanned the unconscious victims by the entrance—all that damage caused by Tony's weapon. Her heart raced a little.

"We're going to kick off this conference with an interactive activity," said Tony, making a show of waving the rifle. "If everyone could please lie on the floor and put your faces on the ground. That's it."

Rolling the luggage behind her, Halley pranced to the exhibition booths lining the lobby. The place was all corporate banners, flyers, useless free swag like pins and erasers, and most importantly, laptops and prototypes.

Weaving through the couple-hundred people lying between the booths, she stuffed everything she deemed interesting into the suitcases—new flame-retardant materials, adhesives, sensors, capacitors, scale model engine designs ... The innovation was enough to wet her panties.

Tony strode a few booths ahead, collecting everyone's electronics.

He'd explained it to her. "Nobody takes enough security precautions at these exhibitions. They let their staff take their ordinary work laptops. And you know what's on them?"

"Intellectual property," Halley had replied.

Halley stacked this intellectual property haphazardly in her luggage, collecting as much as possible before their six minutes were up. She stuffed in a few marketing brochures, too. Who knew what Tony's researchers might find valuable?

To maximize her new sense, Halley had again worn a sports bra and yoga shorts. Tony wore only his suit pants. The conference-goers were either overtly staring or peeking sideways from their places on the floor.

"Hey, what's an aerospace engineer's favorite part of a computer?" Halley said as she swiped someone's tablet. "The space bar!"

Silence.

God, the fear was palpable.

"You don't think I'm funny?" She jammed her pistol into the spine of the nearest hostage, a thirty-something guy in a black overcoat. "Laugh."

He gave a pathetic whimper.

Satisfied, Halley continued on. She caught up to Tony, who picked up a mannequin head wearing an astronaut helmet prototype.

"Alas, poor Yorick!" he said dramatically, placing the mannequin head in her hand. "You're up."

"I don't know *Hamlet*."

Tony grabbed the head and tossed it over his shoulder. It hit the floor loudly. "What would you prefer?"

Halley giggled. He embraced her and dipped her low, sending a swooping sensation through her belly. "But, soft! What light through yonder window breaks?"

Halley reached into her memory for something from *Romeo and Juliet*. "Good night, good night. Parting is such sweet sorrow," she said breathily.

Tony laughed, that sweet sound she wanted to bottle up and keep. He planted a kiss on her lips before standing her up again.

"You feeling okay?" she teased.

"You said you wanted to star in a play. I give you—" He motioned around them. "—your captive audience."

Halley thought she might melt into a puddle on the convention center floor.

Tony opened his arms to the room and gestured to her with a flourish. "Round of applause for our prima donna!"

This was met with silence until Tony picked up his rifle. Halley curtsied to a smattering of applause.

Tony winked and continued along the booths.

Halley watched him, the breath high in her chest. He'd remembered what she said about wanting to star in a play.

Tony had seemed more pleased with her than ever over the last few days. Thanks to her efforts at GN, his boys had made headway with the rocket propellant as well as with explosive devices based on the bullet solution. But something more than that was warming his expression.

Halley couldn't remember the last time she was so happy she wanted to skip instead of walk. *Euphoric* wasn't a strong enough word.

There was a deafening gunshot. Halley ducked. A bullet whizzed past from a booth behind her and tore a hole in the wall.

"Whoa! Time for target practice, is it?" said Tony.

Halley hit the floor and plugged her ears.

Tony's retaliating shot whipped by like a hit from a sand blaster. The room shook, sending dust flying. She looked back to find a hole in the floor in place of a booth of military drones. The guy that had shot at her threw himself onto the floor, flames dancing across his collared shirt.

Halley took a steadying breath and climbed to her feet. Okay, close call. She was getting distracted. This was America—of course some of these science geeks were armed. She should have kept a feel on the room's circulation so she would know if anyone was drawing their weapon.

Tony strode over to her and cupped her face. "Did it get you?"

She shook her head. His shoulders slumped in relief.

"Next idiot to exercise his right to bear arms gets turned into a black hole," he shouted to the room, teeth bared.

The lobby fell back into silence. The smell of mass-produced swag and poorly masked sweat had been replaced by the stench of burning wood and plastic.

Halley continued to wind through the booths with the two suitcases. She swiped the laptop and a brochure from Duncan Laboratories and checked her watch. The countdown showed just over a minute. One or two more booths and it was time to blow out of here. Literally.

The middle-aged man at the next booth was not lying on the floor like everyone else. He was sitting behind his table, hands over his laptop, glowering at Halley.

"Thought you people were supposed to be smart," she said.

"Smart enough that I don't need to steal what I know."

She glanced to his banner, twirling her pistol. "Lidar Systems, eh? You want to join us on stage to share your wisdom, Mr. Smarty Pants?"

"I've spent my life building this software," he said. "You psychos will have to try a little harder to pry it from me."

The insult jolted through Halley like lightning. She stopped it, channeling the feeling, remembering her promise to herself. No one was allowed to talk to her like that. Not anymore.

She sat on the booth and swung her legs over so she was nose-to-nose with Mr. Lidar Systems.

"Call us psychos again."

The man snarled. "Hits a little close to home, honey?"

Somewhere in the distance, a siren wailed. The heist was reaching its expiry.

The man tilted his head, a grin tugging at his lips.

"You seem smug for someone who's about to get his ass kicked," said Halley.

His grin fell. She grabbed him by his salt-and-pepper hair. He pulled back his fist to punch her and she caught it mid-swing, bent her knees to her chest, and kicked him. His chair flew backward. The woman at the neighboring booth screamed.

Halley hopped off the table. Mr. Lidar Systems made to get up, so she shot a hole in the floor beside his face. It sizzled like a cigarette burn. She leaned over his terrified face.

"First of all, my *psycho* partner happens to be a genius. Tell him he's smart."

The man kept his jaw clenched. She leaned her pistol against the side of his face, the barrel adjacent to his ear. It wouldn't kill him, but it would prove a point about listening.

"Go on. Tell him," she said, catching a satisfying glimpse of fear in his widening eyes.

A hand wrapped around her arm. "Let's go." Tony pulled her upright, gripping so hard that she gasped.

Outside, the sirens grew louder. The police were here.

"Sorry," she said. Her arm tingled below his grip. She liked the firmness of it—like he was making sure she was his.

Tony let go, offering a little smile, and the blood flowed back into her arm. "Never apologize for having passion in your work. You did spectacularly."

The praise melted over her like a hot shower. She stood on her toes and kissed his cheek.

As she snatched the guy's laptop from the floor and stuffed it in the suitcase, the rising unrest in the air told her the cops were closing in. They must have been visible to the crowd, perhaps steps from the entrance.

Tony beamed at Halley. Excitement radiated from him and into her.

A universe of potential lay within their suitcases. All of this knowledge belonged to Tony now—and in time, it would push Aries to the top of the aerospace industry.

With their newfound intellectual property in tow, the two of them sprinted across the lobby. A gust of air hit Halley as the cops entered through the front doors.

Tony glanced at his watch. Halley braced herself.

The room shook as a bomb exploded in the main hall, sending a hurricane across her skin. "Guess you can tell your boys the new explosives work."

"Of course they work."

Tony aimed his rifle at the east door and they blasted through it. Reah had rented an SUV under a fake identity, and it was waiting for them.

"I was thinking," said Halley, panting as they ran. "That Vancouver tech show—there were 3D printers."

"Yeah?"

"Why don't we get one? Think what kind of stuff we can mass produce."

Tony cast her a sideways smile. She twirled the pistol around her finger.

"Baby, you're brilliant," he said.

Halley giggled, unable to contain her elation. She and Tony were unparalleled, unidentifiable, unstoppable—and together, they would conquer the tech world.

Chapter 20
Jess and the Pancake-Generated Idea

The internet responded in the way the internet does.

panda339: Illuminati.

iamsmeerp: Faaaaake

lawl00: Relationship goals!

hamboorgurz: It's like Bonnie and Clyde fell into a fire pit.

Comments aside, the number of upvotes on Jess's post pleasantly surprised her. Hours after she posted it on Thursday, it climbed to the front page of r/worldnews. It got more upvotes than the time she found a puddle shaped like Samuel L. Jackson and posted it in r/mildlyinteresting.

She'd spent all week checking the Aries database for new images of the duo. The timing hadn't been right during the robberies in Los Angeles, Chicago, Montréal, or New Mexico, but she did find a shot of them about to climb into the upper floor window of a software company in San Francisco.

Her post included that photo and the one of them running out of the forest behind the Aries building. She challenged people to find more using whatever surveillance or aerial imagery they had access to, and proposed that the pair originated from Vancouver since it was the first known image of them. Hopefully, people would make the connection to the Aries building and the authorities would take it from there.

Jess took every step she could think of to ensure her anonymity, but even then, she couldn't bring herself to be the one to name Anthony Ries. The feel of the gun against her skin was too fresh to brush aside, so she relied on the masses to do the incriminating. The internet had banded together many times before, proving there was power in numbers. The numbers just had to be pointed in the right direction.

Only one user, cdn_pirate, found another photo. Impressively, he'd managed to capture a drone image of them creeping hand-in-hand across the roof of a defense corporation in Chicago moments after robbing it.

cdn_pirate's discovery was the top-voted comment. The second top-voted comment was a dissertation by someone named tyl3r_69 on the implications of using satellite imagery to track people, and questioning whether Jess's call-to-action was ethical.

Jess made a face at the comment. The guy had totally missed the mark. What was so bad about using technology to track wanted criminals? Also, the satellites technically couldn't be used to track people since the resolution was hardly crisp enough to differentiate faces. These two were just so distinct that they were literally recognizable from space.

Jess wasn't about to engage in an internet argument. Trolls gonna troll.

To her chagrin, the post lost steam by Friday morning. She refreshed the page compulsively on the bus ride to work, willing the numbers to climb, considering making a bunch of fake accounts for the purpose of upvoting it.

By the time she got to the office, her post had fallen into the Reddit abyss.

That's it? thought Jess, staring at her phone. *No one cares?*

Fifteen minutes of viral fame wasn't enough. She needed a lasting legacy, like the ermahgerd girl. It had to go viral enough for the authorities to see it, make the connection to Aries, and use the evidence to get a warrant to search the warehouse.

The media certainly cared enough about them to get people to click their articles and watch their coverage. After the L.A. convention, a story popped up noting the man had called the woman 'Comet', and the nickname had appeared in a few headlines since then. News outlets made them sound like the horsemen of the apocalypse, describing them using words like 'paranormal' and 'transcendental'.

It was unsettling how the duo seemed to have a sixth sense. A video circulated of the man throwing Comet a hard drive, and she caught it without turning—like she didn't need eyes.

Between that, their steel-melting firearms, and Comet's ass-kicking skills, the media's sole advice to the public was to stay low and obey their demands.

Insight on their real identities and how to stop them, apparently, was the lesser priority.

Jess made her morning latte and got to her desk feeling like a rage monster ready to smash. She had to do more than watch news stories pop up. That dick had threatened her, and now he was holding innocent nerds at gunpoint.

How dumb would it be to try and get into the lab? She could take pictures of all the stolen items and send them to the police. A high-quality photo of the CSA telescope in the Aries lab would get their attention.

Dumber than a Yosemite buffalo selfie, was the answer. She'd known since the first day on the job that she was never getting into the lab. She hadn't taken the orientation-day threat that 'Doctor Ries will have your head' literally, until now.

When she turned on her laptop, a message from Floyd was waiting.

Floyd: *I've emailed you a new API key.*

Jess sighed and gave the message a thumbs-up emoji.

All morning, in between every QA test she created, she went back to her saved images and tried to find something that would incriminate Anthony Ries and this *Comet* girl. She opened the Aries Viewer to poke around the multispectral data. She might find fresh perspective in the values beyond the visible spectrum.

She clicked through them all, analyzing the images from various perspectives, and paused on the infrared view.

Whoa.

Normally, the infrared image of a person showed up in rainbows of red, green, blue, and yellow. Jess had never seen anything like these people. The values were ridiculously high, making them glow like red beacons.

She cross-checked this on all three images—the original, the one from San Francisco, and the Chicago drone photo. All of them depicted the same off-the-charts infrared signatures around Anthony Ries and Comet's bodies.

What could she do with this information? She had a human detection algorithm already, designed for picking out any human in any image. Could she adapt it to find these two in particular? Surely no one else in the world gave off infrared signatures like this.

Jess opened her human detection code, scanning the logic. Picking out these two based on their unique spectral signatures would be easy. Then she could automatically find this pair of criminals in the continuous stream of new Aries satellite images coming in. She would have to set up a server. Whenever new satellite images were taken, the server could send them through her algorithm, and if the algorithm detected Anthony Ries and Comet, Jess would know exactly where they were.

She squirmed in her chair at a little thrill of victory. No matter where they were, if the satellites could see them, Jess could find them.

The algorithm would need to be fast. It would need to run continuously, scanning tens of thousands of images per hour. She could make it happen.

But then what? Manually post each new image to Reddit and hope people cared enough to upvote? She needed a plan for what to do with the images. Saving them to her personal laptop would accomplish nothing.

A new message popped up.

Anita: *All-you-can-eat pancakes across the street. You in?*

Okay, she was starving. Even Sherlock Holmes needed to take lunch breaks.

Jess: *Um YES.*

With a rush of affection for the Cloud Team, she bundled up and met them at the front doors. Anyone who deemed pancakes a good lunch was a worthy friend. It brought to mind the summer after high school, when Jess and her friends had gone for pancakes every Saturday. It was a pivotal time in their friendship. After all, if their entire group agreed pancakes were the best possible breakfast, they were obviously soulmates.

Jess, Anita, Omar, and Kit sat down and ordered (Kit went a healthier route and got an omelette instead of pancakes, a poor life choice that Jess failed to talk her out of). While the others launched into a discussion about various clubs they wanted to start at work, Jess's brain floated back to the office, thinking about infrared signatures. It took her a moment to realize Omar was speaking to her.

"… ever want to go with me, Marco, and Steve, if we started a climbing group?"

"Um. I can't really—" She pulled her sleeves over her fists, conscious about the scars on her palms. "I mean, I used to be into climbing and bouldering, but I kind of had to give everything up to focus on university. And then I …"

"Would you join a D&D group?" said Omar, bypassing her self-conscious rambling either out of kindness or obliviousness.

"Yeah! I used to play all the time with my girlfriend and her friends. Then we stopped on account of university."

"I hate that about school," said Kit. "It's all suffering in the hopes of being rewarded later."

Anita's brow furrowed. "But now that school's done until September, you have your weekends, right Jess?"

"Well, I was trying to get that human detection algorithm done. Floyd wouldn't let me spend more time on it at work, so I did it at home."

Anita and Kit exchanged a dark look.

"Okay, first of all," said Anita, leaning across the table, "focusing on your career is important, but don't spend so much time working toward your perfect life that you forget to enjoy it in the meantime."

Jess met her eyes across the table. Anita had a point—but she also didn't understand how important this scholarship was. Fun and games could wait. The present was about goals.

Their food arrived, smelling like everything wonderful about the world.

"And speaking of people not enjoying life," said Anita, picking up her fork, "has Double-F given you anything new to work on yet?"

Jess impaled her stack of pancakes with a bit too much force. "No."

Kit scoffed. "That bastard is unbelievable."

"I'm going to talk to him on Monday," said Jess. "Wyatt's still working with Chris. It's only fair."

"Good," said Kit. "Don't be afraid to get bitchy."

Jess smirked. But ugh, she didn't want to confront Floyd about this again. He already seemed to hate her. What if she got herself in trouble, or fired for being so defiant? Then there was his silent decision to kill her API key and cloud drive.

"What are you guys working on?" she asked, keen to steer the subject away from herself.

"At the eleventh hour, Doctor Ries asked for a GIS component on the open data portal," said Omar, already half-done his first pancake stack.

"Apparently, letting people download our images isn't good enough," said Kit. "We need to let them overlay geographic information."

"Sounds like a lot of extra work," said Jess.

"It is!" said Anita. "He's another one who takes himself too seriously. I barely ever see the guy."

"The only time I hear from him is when a request like this trickles down from above," said Omar. "He only talks to senior managers."

"Pompous ass," said Kit.

"I'm sure he shows his face in the lab a lot," mumbled Jess.

They all looked at her. She swallowed. Did anyone ever discuss what went on in the Aries basement?

Kit snorted. "Probably. Bet he's got his creepy long fingers all in their work."

"Do you guys, uh, know anything about the lab?" said Jess, taking a casual sip of her coffee.

"Oh, so many rumors about that place," said Kit. "Organ farm, grow-op, underground cathedral for religious sacrifices …"

"There are booby traps if you try to get inside," said Omar.

"All the Red Badges are trained ninjas," said Anita.

"If authorities show up, the lab closes like a bat cave," said Kit. "Pass the ketchup?"

Jess slid it over to her. So much for that. Those rumors sounded about as likely as the one about Marilyn Manson having his ribs surgically removed.

"Anyway," said Anita. "Doctor Ries could put his creepy long fingers into our work more often. Like, it would've been nice to get this request ages ago—not when we're about to ship."

"We should still ship," said Omar. "We can do it in phases. We'll add the GIS component later."

Anita rubbed her forehead. "True. We can't postpone again. Marketing will kill us."

As the team discussed the plan for their portal, an idea occurred to Jess. She put down her fork.

Open data portals.

If she automatically saved all satellite images containing Doctor Ries and Comet, she could make a data portal to share those images with the world. She could make a webpage and put the images on a map with a timeline to show their known locations. She could crowdsource the effort of catching them!

She'd been looking for power in numbers—a reason for the authorities to lock onto Doctor Ries and get a warrant to investigate him and his lab. A data portal would provide an almost real-time map of where he and Comet were located. Anyone in the world could track their location. With a virtual beacon over their heads, their crime spree would lead them straight into handcuffs—and Jess could remain anonymous through it all.

"Jess? You okay?" said Kit.

She stood abruptly. "Yeah. I need to go."

"What? Why?"

"I've just thought of something. I have to go adapt some code."

She slapped $6 on the table to cover her pancakes and bolted for the door.

"This is how we know she's a genius," she heard Kit say. "She exhibits all the signs of a mad scientist."

Chapter 21
Halley Takes a Selfie

Saturday night, Tony took Halley on a romantic heist in northern Manitoba. After dumping the business jet and switching to a Cessna for a more discreet approach, Reah circled them over Hudson Bay for landing. Halley pressed her nose to the window and took in the sparkling view of the water.

"The Hudson Research Centre is more of a defense lab," Tony explained. "Their security is no fudge sundae, but the data they have on fission-fragment rocket design is some of the most advanced in the world."

"Sounds like a worthy business opportunity," said Halley, using her reflection to apply lipstick. "Need me to do any prep?"

"Got it under control, baby."

Of course he did.

Halley put away the lipstick. Without hair or any real complexion, there was little to do in terms of preening. She watched the passing landscape out the window instead, admiring the patterns in the broken ice floes.

"I've never been anywhere else in Canada. Flights are so expensive that if I'm going to spend that much on a trip, I'd rather go to Mexico. Know what I mean?"

"Hm," said Tony, focused on his laptop.

"I can see a pod of beluga whales," said Halley. "Look how pretty they are."

Tony didn't look. Halley shot him a glare he didn't see and admired them alone.

This was probably the type of place people visited to take polar bear safaris and see the Northern Lights. She would have liked to extend this trip to take a couple of days to explore the wilderness with Tony, but she had a suspicion of what he would say to that idea.

She pulled out her phone and snapped a picture through the windshield. She unlocked her phone with the passcode (thumbprint recognition no longer worked) and texted the picture to her parents.

Halley: *Landing in Hudson Bay on a business trip. So amazing. Love and miss you both xo*

She'd been putting off coming up with any kind of disguise. Visiting her parents posed so many risks. They would wonder why she showed up wearing unusually thick makeup and wildly different hair, for starters.

"It's worth seeing Nova Scotia, one day," said Reah.

Halley looked at her, with her aviators and white collared shirt and tie.

Reah smiled. "It's a nice place. Not a beach vacation like Mexico, but you should do it. Try a bike tour."

"Thanks," said Halley, and she meant it.

She looked at Tony. Would it kill him to show any interest? This was supposed to be date night.

Her phone buzzed.

Dad: *Proud of you, peanut. Can't wait to hear all about it.*

She smirked, wondering what she would tell her parents if they asked for details. She'd have to say her projects were confidential.

Her phone buzzed again.

Mom: *Wow are those wheels looks beautiful you're not missing much over here love you*

Halley blinked at it for a minute before deciding it was supposed to say 'are those whales'.

"Roger, Tango Whiskey Mike descending three thousand, cleared for an approach," said Reah, and then to Halley, "Turn your phone back to airplane mode, hon."

"Sorry."

They touched down at a tiny airport made up of a few rows of hangars and little Cessnas. Apparently, this wasn't the time of year for hobbyists to be out with their toys, because no one was around to stop them.

They broke open half a dozen hangars before finding a vehicle to borrow: a classic Ford V8 that looked like it was from the 1930s. It was uninsured, perhaps stored for the winter by rich people who owned more motorized things than was healthy. Their hangar was better furnished than the average person's house, with mahogany tables, animal furs and antlers on the walls, a bar, an air hockey table, and a dart board (Halley tested her aim with the pistol but couldn't tell how well she did because it disintegrated the whole target).

The Ford started after a few tries. As they puttered away, Halley slid across the bench to lean against Tony. He smiled down at her. She hoped the ride was a long one so she could stay like this for a while.

When they were a few minutes from the Hudson Research Centre, Tony said, "Grab my laptop and tether to my phone. Get ready to pull the trigger on all the tabs I've got open."

She pulled the laptop from his bag. "What's our timeframe?"

"Five minutes until the security company notices the building's alarm is cut off, two for them to realize we're having a luau inside, twelve minimum for the Mountie squad to arrive."

"Nineteen minutes total," said Halley. "Bless. We should do heists in rural areas more often."

"Well, there will be people working—"

"On a Saturday?"

"Science never rests, baby. We'll try to threaten them out of calling 9-1-1, but you know how it is. I give it fourteen minutes from the time someone calls for help."

Target, Tactic, Tools, Time, Takeoff. Halley reviewed the building layout and completed her Five T's.

The Hudson Research Centre was a boxy, glass-front building with a modest sign out front. An iron fence marked the perimeter.

Tony accelerated toward the closed gate. Halley cut the building's security system, internet, and phones, then tossed the laptop aside and reached for the assault rifle.

Even in the old Ford, they approached the gate fast. Halley leaned out the window and blasted a hole in the iron. She held the trigger down, tearing as big an entrance as possible before they plowed through.

In the time it took them to cross the parking lot and stop at the front doors, the building alarm started wailing. Metal barricades descended behind the glass.

The building's security efforts were fruitless. No connection to the security company existed, so only the empty tundra around the building could hear it scream.

Halley passed Tony the rifle and grabbed their stuff.

Tony blew open the entrance.

Employees had trickled into the lobby, confused by the alarm. Screams erupted at the sight of their intruders.

Halley grinned. "Congratulations, Hudson employees! You've qualified for government funding! Would you please direct us to your manager?"

They kept screaming, scattering in all directions.

Tony seized Halley's pistol and shot a stream of bullets into the ceiling. "Get on the floor!"

Half the people in the lobby dove onto the sleek gray tiles. The other half disappeared down the halls or behind potted plants, garbage cans, and the reception desk.

Halley wiped her shoes on the blue rug embroidered with *Hudson Research Centre*. She looked around for the source of the alarm, found a siren over the entrance, and shot it. The noise quieted a little, though it continued to wail from the hallways.

The lobby smelled faintly sterile, like bleach. Glossy blue and gray surfaces shimmered everywhere, *Hudson* emblazoned in random places as though the employees needed reminding of where they were.

As Halley and Tony crossed the lobby, heads peeked around corners and up from their hiding places like gophers.

While Tony went behind the reception desk, Halley waved her pistol in the air and said, "If I find any one of you with your phone out, you'll have thirty bullets in your head before you can enter your passcode."

"Comet," someone whispered, and then others. "Those are the ones. Look. It's them."

On the floor, a blonde girl Halley's age raised her phone. The click of her camera was amplified in the silence.

Halley was over to her in three steps. She snatched the phone from the girl's manicured hands.

"Wait!" The girl reached for it. "Can I post it first?"

Halley leaned back, appraising her. Blondie had nerves. Halley appreciated that.

"At least take a good one." She handed the phone back. She and Tony would be out of here before any of the girl's followers could send in the cavalry, anyway.

The girl made a doe-eyed face and held the phone out for a selfie. Halley pressed her gun to the girl's temple and stuck out her tongue.

The girl took the photo, posted it to Instagram (#cometselfie #goals), and passed Halley the phone, looking pleased. Halley tossed the phone in a planter.

The alarm stopped. Everyone looked around. Tony straightened from behind the reception desk, having silenced it from the computer.

"Our treasure awaits, my little comet," he said.

She grinned. The genius had managed to unlock the fission lab.

Halley threw her arms around him and kissed him.

Somewhere across the lobby, there was the click of a camera. She peeled away from Tony. "I swear to god——"

"Priorities," said Tony, pulling her by the hand. "Twelve minutes from here."

They ran.

The lab they needed was in the basement. Two doors led in and out, so they would have to stay inside the time limit to avoid getting trapped by the cops.

Tony kicked the logo-emblazoned door open. "H marks the spot."

The lab was a dimly lit pod of computer screens and geeky toys. A rocket hung from the ceiling by thick cables. Whiteboards covered the walls, full of ridiculously complicated physics.

Two employees whirled around and raised their hands.

"On your knees, lady and gent," said Halley, pistol up. She scanned the rows of computers. "Boss, do you know which machine I need?"

"I got it. Stay there," said Tony.

"I can get in quick if I know what——"

"Stay there!"

Halley's teeth clacked as she shut her mouth. *You're the boss, Mr. Huffypants.*

She strode over to the kneeling hostages while Tony beelined for the computers.

The pair looked like they were in their mid-twenties. The girl was all lips and eyelashes, hair swept sideways with an undercut.

"Mamacita," said Halley, pulling the girl's hair back. "This one puts the *hot* in *photon*."

The girl flinched away from her. Halley motioned the guy forward. He shuffled on his knees until he was beside the girl.

"Now," said Halley, putting her hands on her thighs. "My boyfriend's going to need your help."

They both avoided her eyes. Sweat was beading on the man's forehead.

Tony jumped from computer to computer, looking for one that was unlocked.

"Ha." He grabbed a mouse. "All right. Daddy needs a login for the fileshare."

Halley leaned closer to the girl's face. "Well?"

No response. She turned her pistol on the guy. "One of you is going to start talking. Whose computer is that?"

Nothing. She was about to turn up the aggression when she spotted the collection of Funko toys beside the computer.

She gasped. "Oh my god, are those Clarke and Lexa?"

The girl finally met Halley's eyes. Confusion flickered across her face. Maybe it occurred to her that the criminal at the other end of the pistol was an ordinary fangirl like herself.

"I love *The 100!*" said Halley. "Did you read the books?"

"Um," said the girl, barely audible.

Halley lowered her gun. "What's your name?"

She hesitated. "Mae."

"You like working here?"

"Can't say today's particularly fun."

Halley laughed. Mae returned the tiniest of smiles.

Tony shot them a glare. Halley took a moment to bask in his jealousy. If he wouldn't play with her, she'd find someone who would.

"Mae, honey. If you give me a password, I'll put away the gun," she said.

Mae glanced to her coworker, who grimaced and gave a little nod.

"Okay. Username is MBartik. Password is snoopy1314."

While Tony typed that in, Halley deposited the pistol into her bag. Then she bent to check Mae's pockets for anything valuable or helpful.

"You must have a smarty-pants degree, eh?"

"Masters in Engineering," said Mae.

Halley nodded, pulling out the girl's phone. "I'm going for Computer Science. Any career tips?"

The guy beside her said, "Choose your job opportunities more carefully."

"I wasn't asking you," Halley snapped.

Mae glanced to Tony, looking lost for words. "Um."

"Hey, what's it called when a person is attracted to intelligence?" said Halley to Tony. "That's a thing, right?"

Tony ignored this, continuing to type.

What happened next was what Halley had come to know as Gay Eye Contact. She and Mae looked at one another lingeringly, a flirty moment passing between them that said, *I get you.*

Halley smiled, breaking the gaze with a small twinge of guilt. She was only playing. Plus, she had read enough about Stockholm Syndrome to know that Mae's interest was just an irrational psychological response. However that worked. Tony was the psychology expert, not her.

Outside this situation, Halley and Mae would have never crossed paths. Mae Bartik, Masters in Engineering, hot enough to send blood rushing to Halley's face, would never take an interest in someone as broken as her.

"I need the design models," said Tony. "Where are they?"

"D drive," said Mae, still looking at Halley.

Halley wondered what kind of life this girl had outside Hudson, and what kind of social circle she'd ran in high school. Did her looks gain her popularity? Did those brains get her into the advanced program? Maybe both. Maybe neither. Maybe she'd been rebellious. Halley could picture her wearing heavy eyeliner and black lipstick.

Halley and her friends had floated in a nebulous, undefined space during school, not part of any particular group. They were outcasts, but not with each other.

Thinking of them put an ache in her chest. She began checking the guy's pockets. Her fingers closed over a key fob. He winced as she pulled out the key to an Elion.

"Boy, you must earn a good salary here!" she said. "You, too, honey?"

Mae tilted her head modestly.

Halley squatted so they were eye level. "Beauty, brains, money ... What else you got going on?"

That little half-smile returned. "Care to find out?"

Okay, in another life, the two of them would have gotten on spectacularly.

Tony rose from the computer so fast his chair toppled. He strode over and shoved Halley aside. She stumbled, catching herself on a desk.

"Tony, don't—"

He clubbed Mae across the face with his rifle. She made a noise between a sob and a gasp, a spurt of blood flying from her mouth and hitting her colleague.

"Hey!" said the guy, reaching in vain to protect Mae.

Tony thumped him in the temple, knocking him out. He turned his focus back to Mae.

"This isn't a trade. I take your data, but you don't get my girl. Got it?"

Mae nodded, eyes downcast. She brought a trembling hand to her jaw.

Halley's playfulness evaporated. She was only having fun, flirting, teasing, making Tony jealous. She hadn't meant for this to happen.

"Help us out, *Mae*," said Tony. "What else do you have on fission beyond the corporate share data and design files?"

Mae hesitated. Blood trickled down her chin.

Tony drew his arm back to strike again. Halley was about to shout for him to stop when the air changed. They both looked to the door they'd come through. People were creeping down the stairs, silent and in trained formation.

"We gotta go," said Tony, grabbing the USB key from the computer.

Halley abandoned everything she'd taken from Mae's pockets. What use would she have with the girl's phone, anyway? She pulled the pistol back out of her bag.

They failed to make it to the door before the police flooded in, guns raised, shouting at them to freeze and drop their weapons.

Halley's eyes darted around the room—computers, desks, whiteboards. The rocket hanging from the ceiling. She aimed for the cables suspending it and squeezed the trigger.

Snap, snap, snap! The rocket crashed onto the desks, sending bits of monitors and toys flying.

Everyone ducked and covered. Halley and Tony used the moment of confusion to flee.

Wishing godspeed to Mae the hot engineer, Halley fired blindly over her shoulder. Tony cleared the path ahead, blowing holes in everything he could.

They sprinted up the stairs.

On the ground floor, the lobby door burst open as two more officers came running inside. Halley tackled the nearest one, using her arms and back to send him rolling over her shoulder. He hit the stairs and tumbled down. Tony used his rifle to smash the other one in the shins.

Before he could go through the door, she grabbed his arm. "Wait."

She motioned to an exit door on their right.

Emergency exit. Do not open. Alarm will sound.

They burst through. No alarm sounded after Tony's meddling with the system, but their ears were blasted with police sirens coming from the front of the building. They ran the other way.

"Did you get the data?" said Halley, panting.

"Hope so. Damn Mounties got here too fast."

They had. By her watch, they were at eleven minutes. She hoped Tony had gotten everything he was after, for both their sakes.

As they sprinted across the parking lot, she clicked the alarm on the Elion fob repeatedly until their ride home beckoned. They followed the noise and skidded to a stop in front of the vehicle.

"Oh my," breathed Halley. The car was sleek and geometric, glossy red, with vents in the side. An orgasm on wheels. Her eyes were drawn to the emblem on the hood. "Tony, do you think the Elion logo is intentionally shaped like the female reproductive system?"

Gunshots sounded behind them. The pavement exploded at her feet.

Tony flung open the driver's side door. "Get in. We can discuss subliminal marketing later."

She slid into the passenger's seat and dropped her bag and pistol at her feet. Tony passed her the rifle. She stuffed it between her legs.

Tony caressed the steering wheel and moaned. "I've been meaning to test drive one of these."

Excitement constricted Halley's lungs. The material was soft and clean beneath her skin, a tactile version of the 'new car' smell that had her running her palms obsessively over the seat.

Words twinkled serenely across the dash. "Good morning, Joseph!"

"Here we go," said Tony.

Nothing happened.

He pumped the pedal.

"Please fasten your seatbelt," said the words on the dash.

They put on their seatbelts.

Gunshots continued. There was a *clink* like a rock chip hitting the car.

Tony frowned at the dash, foot pulsing. Halley's heart lurched. Oh, god, was this a security feature?

"Please choose your destination," said the Elion in large, twinkly letters.

"Don't tell me the nerd got a self-driving one," said Tony.

Halley considered searching the glove box for a manual. The clinking gunshots told her there wasn't time. She scanned the dash.

"Driver assist!" She slammed the button, turning off the indicator light.

"Autopilot deactivated," said the Elion.

Tony hit the pedal. Tires squealed. Halley braced against the door, laughing.

Joseph's satellite radio kicked in, and Halley found her ears bombarded by *Love Shack*.

They zoomed through the gate, clipping the fence and a cop car as they squeezed through, skidding out onto the road. Tony held back nothing. The building disappeared behind them, along with any threat of the police catching them. Then it was just Halley and Tony, flying down the highway.

Tony whooped, excitement radiating off of him. "I'm getting myself one of these, baby."

"Whatever you say," she gasped.

They tripled the speed limit, dodging traffic at a pace that sucked the breath from Halley's lungs. Accelerating felt like taking a plunge on a roller coaster. Thank god she'd put on her seatbelt. The car jerked whenever Tony switched lanes, like it was trying to help him stay inside the lines. He fiddled with the controls, and the air conditioning, heated seats, and interior lighting assaulted her at varying intervals. At one point, the whole seat constricted around her, and the dash helpfully told her they'd entered sport mode.

Still, it was fast. It got them to the airport in a quarter the time it had taken them to get to the research center.

They dumped the car in a dead-end street ("Goodbye, Joseph!" said the Elion) and cut through a bush to their pick-up spot. Reah was waiting for them in a nondescript sedan.

"Cessna's already running," she said as they climbed in the back seat.

Tony pressed his palm against the sedan's window in a silent goodbye to the Elion. He was probably going to order one the moment they got home.

Halley watched him, savoring his exhilaration. The chase had awoken something fiery in Tony that hadn't been there on the flight over.

Reah flew them back to Tony's jet in record time, and then they were soaring over western Canada back to Vancouver.

Across from Halley on the plush leather couch, Tony pulled out the USB key and plugged it into his laptop. His brow was wrinkled, gaze darting around the screen. Was this a face of concentration or concern?

Slowly, a lopsided grin appeared on his lips, and something fluttered deep inside her.

"Looks good?"

"Unprecedented."

He put the laptop down, letting the data transfer. Halley slid forward in her seat for a kiss, unable to wipe the smile from her face.

In a husky voice, she said, "How does it feel to own the world's sexiest fission-fragment technology?"

She expected him to pull away and return to his work, but he curled a hand around her neck and kissed her.

Halley responded eagerly, arching into him. They moved against each other until Tony pushed her away, breathing hard.

He glanced over his shoulder. Reah was humming to herself in the cockpit.

Tony kissed Halley again, pulling her firmly against him.

They were so close. Halley was ready, straddling him on the seat. Would he let her?

One hand on his neck, she reached down with the other and hesitantly removed her shorts. His breath caught. He ran his fingers over her shoulders, down her back. She shivered, every part of her ultrasensitive skin tingling.

She unzipped his suit pants. His hands tightened over her hips, pressing her down.

He was as ready as she was.

She lowered herself onto him, unable to stop the moan escaping.

Reah stopped humming. Halley was too fired up to care. A moment later, a door clicked shut.

Tony moved against her, kissing her deeply, sounding breathless. He broke away from her lips to kiss her neck, and then her collarbone. Halley whimpered, the sensation almost unbearable.

She wouldn't say it, but three words whispered in her mind as they moved against each other, faster and deeper. She was hopelessly falling for him.

Curled next to Tony in his enormous bed, Halley felt his chest rise and fall. They'd had sex several times since the plane as though making up for lost time. She could hardly believe the turn of events and had spent the past few minutes considering ways she could keep him in this bed forever—bribing him with food and sex, or tying him to the mattress.

"Tony, do you think we should go away somewhere together?"

"What, you want a suntan?" he said coldly.

"I thought a break from all this hard work would be nice." With a little pang in her chest, she thought of her family vacations to Orlando. "Did you ever go on holidays growing up?"

He snorted and rolled out of bed. "That would have meant my father taking time off work."

"What did your father do?" she said, watching him put on his robe and leave the room.

No answer. She felt the gust of the fridge opening and closing. After a minute, she rolled onto her back and stared at the ceiling. Yes, Tony put work before romance, but that didn't stop her from hoping for more.

She grabbed her laptop.

Before she could get to Buzzfeed, a trending story on her homepage caught her eye. *Comet and Blitzen: Duo continues to rob tech companies across North America.*

What even?

She clicked and was greeted by a picture of her own charred face. The featured image was the selfie she'd taken earlier with the blonde girl, pistol pressed to her head, tongue sticking out.

Halley swallowed the shock at seeing her face looking like that and giggled.

"Tony, we're trending!"

He stormed into the room with the force of a tornado, holding a block of cheese. "What?"

Halley shrank a little on the bed. She turned the laptop so he could see, unable to read his expression.

"What the hell is that?" said Tony.

Halley shrugged. "Some girl wanted a picture."

Tony said nothing. Halley watched him, sensing danger.

"It's not like anyone will identify me," she said. "They already know what we look like."

"Why does it say *Comet and Blitzen?*" Tony's voice was low, excessively calm.

Halley turned the laptop back around, wondering the same. She clicked the featured article.

"It says … it talks about our appearances, and people noticed that you call me Comet."

Apparently, the top comment on a Huffington Post article had been, *Comet? What, like the reindeer?*

To which some smart-ass named Dave replied, *Then by the order of Saint Nicholas on this 30th day of January, the man's name shall be Blitzen.*

Tara: *Blitz also means lightning in German. I mean, he does look like he got struck by lightning.*

Yuvan: *Anyone want to write the story of Comet and Blitzen, two reindeer who got struck by lightning on their way back to the North Pole, fell to earth, and decided the only way they could earn a living without Santa was by pilfering aerospace conventions?*

Tony put the block of cheese on the nightstand and sat next to her. Halley clicked the Back button before he could see the comments.

"*Blitzen,* though," he said.

She hesitated. Not for the first time, she wondered if Tony had experienced a childhood in which things like Santa Claus existed.

"Like … like based on the German word for lightning," she said.

"Hm."

She kept scrolling through the article. "I think it's badass. They could say your victims got struck by lightning."

Embedded social media posts included a blurry picture of her planting the kiss on Tony at Hudson, and more from their other heists. People and their damned phones. As much as she and Tony threatened their hostages, they couldn't stop people from sneaking photos.

She checked Twitter, where #CometAndBlitzen was trending. There was the selfie again, with thirteen thousand retweets and twice as many likes.

The second top tweet was a distant photo from a few days ago. '*Robbed by #CometAndBlitzen. Laptop gone with all my work, but #grateful to be alive. Photo does no justice… they look 100x worse in person.*'

Halley ignored the jab at her appearance and smiled.

"Tony, we're famous."

A swoop of air came at her. She flinched as Tony slapped the laptop shut.

"We're not supposed to be famous, Halley."

"I know. It's a side effect of the way we look—"

He stood. "It's your doing. You think I hired you so you could run around taking selfies?"

"It was just for fun."

"Fun? This is the problem with you! You're treating this job like a Vegas trip."

Halley sat up. "I gave up everything for this job!"

Tony jabbed a finger at her. "Not emotionally. Get into this life with two feet, or stop wasting my time. Because right now, you're making us out to be a circus show for public enjoyment."

His raised voice sent Halley's heart beating double-time. Her instinct was to sink further into the bed. Instead, she pulled back the sheets and stood.

"Who got us those firearms, Tony? Who's gotten countless terabytes of data, prototypes, everything you ask for? I want Aries on top as much as you do. I'm the perfect partner, and you know it."

Tony moved forward so abruptly that she flinched. He grabbed her face, gripping her jaw between thumb and fingers. "Raise your voice at me again, Halley Lovelace, and I'll do more than just fire you."

He threw her backward. Her legs hit the bed and she fell onto it. Without another word, he stormed from the room.

Halley waited a minute, sitting on the bed, heart pounding. Once she'd caught her breath, she collected her scattered clothes and raced downstairs to her suite.

Not for the first time, she wished the door had a lock.

She clenched her trembling fists, breathing deeply. He'd been scared of the spotlight put on them by the trending stories. That was all. He was angry at the public and he took it out on her. She should sympathize with where he was coming from. She should pay attention to his needs.

Her room brought the smallest of comforts. She'd ordered décor for herself using stolen credit cards and a few proxies— but while the stuffies on her bed were cute, they had no sentimental value. The beach painting she had hung above the sofa was pretty, but it was just a space-filler. She wanted her old unicorn poster and worn-out Beanie Babies back.

But what did Tony want from her? The man was a P versus NP problem. That was to say, unsolvable. Halley was sure they could be happy together, if only she knew how to go about this relationship.

Her jaw throbbed where he'd pinched it. She rubbed her palm over it, mulling their argument over in her head. She shouldn't have shouted at him. He was her boss, and he could fire her whenever he wanted. She was lucky he'd only given her a warning.

He was right: she had to do better. No more playing on the job and no more gun selfies. Unfortunately, "it sounded fun at the time" seemed a common theme in Halley's life. She had to stop doing that.

If she wanted commitment from him, she had to show Tony she was dedicated to the job. She would have to work harder to prove herself.

Chapter 22
Jess's Guide to Crowdsourcing Heroism

Catching these asswipes was going to take a lot of work. Thankfully, work was what Jess did best.

Over the weekend, she adapted her algorithm to locate Comet and Blitzen. She coded it to search for human-like objects that emitted the pair's weirdly high infrared signatures and tag the images that contained them with 'TRUE'.

Late Sunday night, wearing her favorite flannel jammies and panda bathrobe, Jess tested her work on the few images she had.

"Boom!" She threw her fists in the air.

"Done?" said Mandeep from the couch. "Bedtime?"

"Ha. That was only phase one."

Mandeep furrowed her brow. "Why are you working so hard on that?"

Because if I don't, it's a matter of time before someone else gets killed.

Jess shrugged. "You said yourself you like it when I'm career-driven. Would you rather I was out drinking?"

Mandeep shot her a glare.

Okay, she was being difficult, but Mandeep was making a hobby of telling Jess how to spend her time.

"We can go snowshoeing next weekend," said Jess. "How's that?"

"Sure." Mandeep kissed her head on the way to the bedroom.

Jess plowed into the workweek already exhausted, having stayed up too late coding. Her subconscious never rested, tackling problems even when she wasn't at her computer. She kept finding herself lying in bed with code flashing across the inside of her eyelids, as though all the additional computer time had turned her into a fembot.

But seeing code beneath her closed eyelids came as a relief compared to the usual visions of Desi that filled her mind at night, and the screams as the flames rose up the balcony.

With all her focus on building her web portal, work was less frustrating, which meant she was less motivated to punch Floyd in the balls. In their Monday catch-up meeting, when she was again the scribe and Wyatt delivered an update on his and Jesus Chris' project, she sipped her latte and thought about how to optimize her algorithm. It would need to be a lot faster if it was to keep up with the number of satellite images coming in.

At noon, she was on her way out for sushi when Floyd poked his head out of his office.

"Going out for lunch?"

"Yeah. With the Cloud Team."

"I see. Just make sure you're not cutting into your work time. I noticed you disappeared pretty quickly after the power went out a couple of weeks ago."

"After—you mean the day I told you what I saw in the lab and you told me it was nothing?"

Floyd dropped his gaze to the stupid tiny sandwich clutched between his sausagey fingers. He gave a little shrug. "Maybe that day. Can't remember."

"I'll watch my time management," she said flatly.

"You should have a chat with Wyatt. You might be able to glean some things from him. I've been really impressed with the way he's taken initiative on his projects."

"Sure," she said, and thought meditatively of a bottleneck in her code and how she might be able to leverage more processing cores.

By the end of Tuesday night, after two evenings of toiling over her algorithm, her code was leaps and magical bounds more efficient. She celebrated by going to bed at a reasonable hour.

On Wednesday, she spent lunch defending the fact that she hadn't talked to Floyd about getting a new project.

"I've been busy with QA," she assured the Cloud Team. "I will."

Lies. She was fine, really. She was obviously not getting any scholarships, and at this point, the best thing she could do for her resume was cooperate with her team lead. Being an annoyance to Floyd would do her no favors when it came time for him to give her a reference. *'Team players'* and *'hard workers'* weren't complainers.

"Okay, we won't pester you about it," said Kit, "but we're here if you need a support team."

Jess did appreciate it. Dare she call them … New Friends?

"Chuck and I have a call with Doctor Ries tomorrow to talk about the cloud portal," said Anita. "I'll casually mention what a great job you're doing—"

"No!" said Jess, so forcefully that the other three froze mid-eating.

Jess cleared her throat and put down her sandwich, lowering her voice to a more casual tone. "Don't mention me to Doctor Ries, I—" She scrambled for an excuse. "Floyd—said he would. Yeah, he's going to talk about what I've been doing when they meet this week. It's better, uh, coming from him. My team lead. You know."

For the love of space and time, keep me off that man's radar.

"Sure," said Anita, her gaze lingering on Jess. "Makes sense. Let me know if you change your mind."

Avoiding her eye, Jess looked down and fiddled with her napkin. "Thanks."

Wednesday night, she set up a few servers using the Aries development account. The team had access to a service for launching virtual servers to run intensive processes, like testing and development projects. The service launched as many servers as needed to complete a task—like a pack of lions sent to take down a giraffe. For Jess's project, the giraffe was all the imagery that needed analyzing. The lions were the servers sent to tackle the task.

Jess frowned. That was a sad image. Okay, it was like a swarm of bumble bees sent into a meadow. The flowers needing pollination were the images needing to be analyzed. The swarm of servers provided the power Jess needed to automatically run her code on every new image taken by the Aries 180 fleet. Images that tested TRUE for the duo would be forwarded to a cloud drive she'd set up under the name of Lucy McGillicuddy.

Jess took Thursday evening as her Day of Rest—because it happened to be the premiere of the latest Marvel masterpiece. She almost cancelled on Mandeep to keep working, but they'd bought tickets weeks ago. Also, Marvel.

Unfortunately, she was too distracted to do her usual fangirling throughout the movie, and Mandeep asked her the whole way home whether she liked it or not.

"Of course I liked it," snapped Jess. "How could I not? The MCU is only the best goddamn movie franchise of the century."

"Oookay," said Mandeep, raising her hands. "Jeez."

They walked in silence the rest of the way.

When she got back to her laptop, she was ecstatic to find several new photos that had tested TRUE sitting in her Lucy McGillicuddy folder. Apparently, Comet and Blitzen had spent time searching for a car to jack at a small outdoor airport in Manitoba, and their infrared signatures had been exposed the whole time.

Holy crap, that little plane on the tarmac must have been theirs. The authorities could track its registration number!

Jess hugged her laptop.

On Friday night, with tremendous bags under her eyes and the complexion of a toilet bowl, Jess set to work on the next step: dealing with the images containing the duo. She would have to build a webpage to serve as a data portal. While Mandeep went out with her spin class friends, Jess looked up tutorials on how to embed a map and a timeline.

Through the weekend, every news story of a robbery urged her onwards. Recent heists seemed to involve less skipping and sassy feedback forms, and more shouted demands and unconscious victims. She couldn't stomach one video that had a group of blood-soaked hostages tied together in an elevator. Apparently, the office hadn't had the information Comet and Blitzen came for.

It was too rainy and windy for her and Mandeep to go snowshoeing, which suited Jess fine. She added the map, timeline, and a feed that gathered any post mentioning 'Comet and Blitzen' or #CometAndBlitzen. She put geotagged pictures from social media onto the map.

Monday was Family Day holiday, giving Jess a full extra day to keep working. By that evening, the webpage was a complete portal dedicated to tracking down these criminals. Anyone who landed on the page would see every picture, location, and post about Comet and Blitzen.

Jess sat back, staring at her work. She'd done it. She made a working web portal. And unless she'd slipped up somewhere—she avoided thinking what would happen if she had—she'd set it all up anonymously.

Removing her glasses, she rubbed her eyes, a familiar burning sensation telling her she'd been staring at the screen for several hours too long.

The ceiling didn't open and release balloons on account of her achievement, of course, and when Jess announced she was done working, Mandeep gave a half-hearted, "Yay," from the couch. Jess took the celebration into her own hands and made a traditional Nine-o-cake (a sprinkle cake made at 9 PM—something she and her old friends used to do).

Jess had done all she could to make the webpage function. It was time to see what the world would do with it. Would people monitor the duo's last-known location and help catch them? Would they contribute to the feed by sharing their own photos of Comet and Blitzen on social media? Anyone could be the hero, here.

After her Nine-o-cake, she made fake accounts and drafted posts on a dozen social networks and forums. She included the link to the web portal and encouraged people to contribute their geotagged pictures.

If this didn't get people's attention, nothing would.

For good measure, she also drafted emails to news outlets and the Vancouver Police Department. With all her tabs open and the posts ready to go, she hovered over the 'Share' button on the first page. What were the chances she'd slipped up and someone at Aries could trace it back to her?

She got another piece of cake.

If someone from Aries did find out it was her, that shouldn't stop her. This was bigger than her career. Lives were at stake every time these guys targeted a new building.

Her phone beeped.

Exercising self-control, she put down her forkful of icing.

Millie: *Are you alive?*

Jess furrowed her brow at the text. This had to be unrelated to Aries.

Jess: *Was there an earthquake I don't know about?*

Millie: *Mom and dad are sad you haven't visited in a while.*

Ah, a family guilt trip. Well, she supposed it was Family Day, and she'd chosen to stay here and work on her project.

Mandeep, at least, had spent brunch with her parents and siblings.

Jess: *I've just been busy. I'll call them tomorrow.*

She wasn't trying to avoid her family. She really was busy. But yes, it had been a few weeks since she'd made the commute to the suburbs.

Millie: *I thought you were supposed to have free time now that you don't have homework or studying.*

She hesitated. Her sister would call her a dork if she said she was working weekends when she was only being paid for forty hours a week—and no way was she telling her about her "catch the nation's most notorious criminals" project.

Before she could form a reply, another message came in.

Millie: *Remember, all work and no play makes Jess a total nerd with no social skills.*

Jess: *Ha*

Millie: *Have you talked to your friends lately?*

Gah. Knife to the gut. Jess swallowed down the sick feeling.

Jess: *They're not really my friends anymore.*

Millie: *:(*

Jess: *I've got friends at work now.*

Millie: *That's good. You doing ok?*

Jess: *Yeah. How's work? Still making more on one table than I make in a day?*

Millie: *You know it. Want me to get you a job?*

Jess: *It's ok. Mean customers would make me cry.*

Millie: *You've got the personality for it. A better bra and some less preppy clothes and you'll be living off tips.*

Jess: *Give me a few years and I'll double what you earn at both your jobs combined.*

Millie sent a flying money emoji. Jess sent back a peach. Millie sent a computer and a nerd face. Jess sent a computer and an eggplant.

They kept going, until Mandeep emerged from the bedroom and said, "What are you laughing at?"

"Chatting with my sister."

She stood behind Jess and looked over her shoulder. It didn't take keen intuition to know she disapproved of Millie. Mandeep denied it, of course, but she never quite relaxed at Jess's family gatherings. Unconventional career choices aside, Millie was the sort of person who encouraged Jess to lose all sense of dignity, like the time the two of them hid in a bush at the park and made farting noises with their armpits every time a pedestrian walked by.

"These are just emojis," said Mandeep.

"A picture's worth a thousand words, my love."

Mandeep returned to the bedroom, shaking her head. Jess and Millie said goodnight with a series of moon and Zzz emojis.

Jess turned back to her laptop and let out a slow breath.

Commencing countdown. All systems are go.

A dozen posts were ready. All she had to do was launch.

Summoning a bit of her sister's reckless nature, she swept through each tab and hit 'Share' and 'Tweet' and 'Post' and 'Send' before she could change her mind. Her pulse was racing, like she had sprinted the distance between each web host.

Done.

She sat back and picked up her unfinished (second) piece of cake.

Her webpage was out in the world. It represented all of the skills, knowledge, and energy she had to offer—and her last hope at exposing the truth about Aries.

Chapter 23
Halley in the Highest Tower

Halley curled her toes inside her new unicorn slippers. Tony had ordered them for her birthday, along with a virtual reality video game system, a stocked bookshelf (which included a copy of *Romeo and Juliet*), a gigantic stuffed bear, a new punching bag, and chocolates and roses, because it also happened to be Valentine's Day. She'd thanked him generously. The shower of gifts was heartfelt, right?

The slippers were her favorite. He'd left a note with them.

I couldn't find a real unicorn like you wanted, but I hope these will do.

Now her feet would be protected from the cold, hard floors of Tony's apartment, and she had adorable googly eyes looking up at her wherever she went. She named the slippers Jerry and Garth.

Her parents had tried to video call to wish her a happy birthday. As much as she desperately wanted to hit the green 'Accept' button, she'd made up a story about being in a high-security lab to get them to agree to a regular voice call. Mom insisted they try again soon, because she missed seeing Halley's face. Halley missed her parents' faces—and kind of her own face, too, if she was honest. She vowed to visit them in the next week or so. Yes, even through layers of makeup and a wig they would notice something off, but she was too homesick to care. Mom and Dad would love her no matter what.

She wrapped herself in a blanket and leaned against the giant bear, which was so soft and plush that she had the urge to knead it like a cat. Time for a cozy night in. Not that they ever went 'out', other than when they were on heists or Tony disappeared to the office—but she was looking forward to spending a quiet evening with a cup of tea and a few dozen stolen laptops.

Target: proprietary data.
Tactic: exploit weak security systems.
Tools: sheer brainpower.
Time: as long as it takes, baby.
Takeoff: destroy pilfered hard drives.

Halley pulled the first laptop toward her, determined to find something life-changing for Tony. While some password hacks would be necessary, most people made her job easy by failing to upgrade their systems and take proper security precautions.

They also had an overabundance of stolen cash and credit cards, but Halley left those alone. Tony had enough money. She considered buying him a present in return—a grenade launcher or a machine gun would be nice—but opted not to. Shipping that through customs might be a problem.

As she swooped through the laptops, exporting everything with potential, Tony came downstairs with a courier box. He pulled out something purple and hairy.

Halley tossed aside the laptop she was working on and bounded over. "That was quick!"

"What is this?"

"I ordered a wig and makeup so I can go out."

Tony looked around the room pointedly, making a sweeping motion with his hand. "Is this not enough for you?"

"I only—" She made to grab the wig, but he pulled it out of reach.

In truth, her homesickness was worsening by the minute. Her cozy night in wasn't the same without her own bed and Mom and Dad downstairs watching TV. She'd never gone this long without seeing them.

Thinking of that brought a lump to her throat.

"What am I missing?" said Tony, fist tightening over the wig. "Do you need more books? Better food?"

"There's nothing wrong—it's just—I want to visit my parents."

"No."

Though his response was unsurprising, the word hit her like a bullet. She'd been hoping he wouldn't open her mail. Truthfully, she had planned to slip off to her parents without telling him and deal with the consequences later.

"But my family, Tony."

"You're twenty-one years old. You don't need your parents anymore."

"I can't just never see them again!"

Tony snarled. "You'll have to part with them someday. Get it over with now."

Halley tried to understand. Tony had never once mentioned his mother. His father had come up only in passing.

"I'm sorry, Tony, if your parents—"

He stepped closer, expression blazing. "Don't!"

"I'm – not – leaving – you!" Whatever his past, wherever his family was, he needed to understand that Halley wasn't like that. She wouldn't walk out on him.

A muscle worked in Tony's jaw as he studied her. "This is about our safety."

Halley rolled her eyes. "Oh, please, Tony."

Of everything on his mind, safety was not one of them.

The sarcasm was a mistake. Tony threw the box across the room, scattering the wig and makeup. She flinched at the rush of air.

"For god's sake, Halley. Look at you. The risk you're—"

"We take risks for a living!" She waved at the mound of laptops behind her.

"Ones worth taking."

"What about employee benefits? Don't I get vacation time?"

"You signed the contract," said Tony. "You should know."

So, this was how it was going to go. She'd signed her life to Tony, end of discussion. He was paying her to stay here.

She made to walk past him—to where, she didn't know—but he grabbed her arm hard enough to make her gasp.

"I forbid you to leave, Halley. Not for family funday, not to scoot off to the bank, or the drug store, or some long overdue therapy appointment."

"Ouch! Tony, you're hurting me!"

He shook her. "If you're recognized and followed, we're fucked. All right?"

She gasped again at the firm grip—so different from the way he touched her earlier.

Looking into his dark, wild eyes, her anger faded. This was obviously of life-or-death importance to him.

"Have you considered," he whispered, "the amount of money and effort I've spent trying to keep us anonymous?"

She lowered her gaze to her slippered feet. Jerry and Garth's googly eyes looked back at her. She hadn't considered that at all. "I'm sorry."

Tony exhaled, releasing her arm. "Just … stay here unless I ask you to do something."

"Yes, sir."

He motioned to the wig and makeup scattered across the floor. "Throw it away."

When he left the suite, Halley swallowed a lump in her throat. She'd been naive to think she could leave. And why would she want to? Tony provided everything she could possibly need on these two floors. He'd made the apartment a haven.

She picked up the wig. The hair was real, the strands soft and pleasant as they slipped through her fingers. This was a version of herself that could never be. She'd made her choice, and now she was here. Mom and Dad were part of a different life, one she could never go back to. The only version of Halley was the one who'd signed up to be a professional criminal.

But couldn't she have both worlds?

If she was a good girl, and if she gave Tony enough wins, maybe he would trust her enough to give her her freedom. She had to be patient. There was no need to sneak out—she just had to earn her independence. She had to fully commit to Tony, like she'd promised. In time, he would let her out. He had to.

Halley awoke to a whirring sound from upstairs. She put on her silk robe and unicorn slippers and went up to investigate.

Tony was crouching at the front door. A moment passed before it dawned on her that he was installing a new lock. There was no keyhole, but instead an electronic plate.

As she slowly approached, he said without turning, "I want to make sure I'm the only one with in-out access."

He finished with the drill, took his phone from his pocket, and tapped the screen.

Click. The metal deadbolt jutted from the door, sending a tiny gust of air that raked across Halley's skin like a spike.

He tapped again.

Click. It retreated, sucking back into the door and taking Halley's breath with it.

He glanced over his shoulder, saw Halley's face, and gave her a sad smile.

"Go look outside, baby."

She obeyed him, Jerry and Garth taking her silently across the room to the large window. The sun hugged the horizon and wispy clouds stroked the blue sky. Snow-dusted mountains cascaded from east to west, sinking toward the Pacific Ocean. All of Vancouver's high-rises looked so small beneath the mountains. Few, if any, rose as high as Tony's penthouse.

Below, the city was bustling, everyone trying to get downtown in an endless traffic jam. And directly below their tower—

"Police," she said.

Lights and sirens were off, but several cars were parked below their tower as well as the neighboring ones.

"This part of town isn't normally such a popular party scene for the fuzz," said Tony.

Halley pressed her hands to the glass, heart pounding. "They found us?"

"No," said Tony. "But I think they know to keep an eye on this area. Somehow—and I don't know how, exactly—they suspect we live around here."

Halley felt the movement of Tony's legs taking him closer. When he stopped behind her, she tore her gaze from the street and turned.

Standing an inch away, he took her face in his hand. She tried to pull back. His grip didn't thrill her like before. This felt like he was trying to pry her jaw open to extract a tooth.

"You're mine," he said. "You understand that?"

She tried to nod.

"Say it."

"I'm yours."

He let her go. She stood there while he crossed the room and bundled himself head-to-toe.

"I'm going to the lab," he said, and shut the door. She flinched as the deadbolt snapped into place.

Halley spun back to the window and pressed her hands to it. The height made her knees wobble when she looked down.

This place that had been a refuge now felt like Rapunzel's tower—except Halley had no hair to throw down, and who would save an evil queen?

She knew every inch of the place, and the only exit was the front door. Unless she got access to the app on Tony's phone that controlled the lock, she would never be able to get out.

But did she want to get out? What life did she hope to lead? She had nowhere to go. If she went home to her parents, Tony would find her there. If she fled, she had no identity and nothing to her name, and would have to start a new life as a fugitive.

No, the outside world had nothing for her. Her life had led her to this tower, and here she would wait.

Of course, there was also Tony. Something about him pulled her in, like a dolphin caught in a net, spinning and thrashing, getting more deeply entangled, until the net was so tight and all-consuming she had no choice but to surrender to her fate.

The sad part was, she didn't want to leave that net. She loved him. He'd given her a more exciting life than she'd ever dreamed of. His mood swings were a small price to pay.

She brought her laptop upstairs. She hadn't gone to lectures over these past weeks, but there was still hope of passing if she could commit to studying. She would have to work out a way to write her midterms remotely. Tony could buy her some kind of doctor's note, right?

She worked by the door, feeling for Tony's return, like a dog waiting for its master to come home.

But her brain was functioning at half its usual speed. Across from where she sat, the firearms closet was as locked as ever. She searched for a video tutorial on how to pick a lock. It was all theory, of course. She wouldn't actually do it. Then she looked up the technology behind wireless locks and how the encryption worked.

All theory.

Her phone rang. She lunged for it. It was Mom.

Blinking back tears, she declined the call. As much as she missed her parents and the life she'd left behind, she knew that as soon as she heard Mom's voice she would burst into tears.

Her phone immediately rang again. She declined it. Besides, it was too dangerous to bring them into this.

With trembling fingers and a painful lump in her throat, she blocked both her parents' numbers.

An eternity passed. Darkness fell, and the living room clock kept ticking, and the ache inside Halley intensified. She wanted Tony to come home.

She fell asleep on the couch and awoke to the sun beaming in. Night had come and gone, and the apartment was still empty.

Had something happened to Tony? Had he been caught? The cops were still outside their building.

Sadness, fear, and anger battled inside her. She felt like a piece of her soul had been separated from her for too many hours. At the same time, she was furious with him. He'd left her trapped in here.

What if he never came back? What if the building caught fire and she couldn't—?

No! Don't think about that. You're safe.

But the idea took hold, and her pulse accelerated. She was stuck.

The apartment was too quiet. The living room clock filled her head like a chorus of voices. She paced until she could no longer stand the sound. She grabbed the clock off the mantle and threw it across the room. It hit the opposite wall and the glass face shattered. It kept ticking. She stomped on the clock, sending bits of it exploding across the stone floor, until it fell silent.

This wasn't right. She wanted her freedom.

"I'm not your pet," she screamed at the door, voice cracking.

The sun dipped toward the horizon again, and finally, there was a shift in the air.

Halley spun toward the door, heart pounding.

The lock clicked. The door opened. Tony stepped inside.

"Tony!" She reached for him. "I was so—"

Tony strode past her with a newspaper in his fist. He removed his scarf and hat and threw them on the floor, not sparing a glance at the smashed clock.

"Good work, Halley," he said through his teeth. "They've got a warrant for your arrest."

"Tony, where did you—?"

He snarled. "Look!"

On the front page, the largest of several photos, was the selfie of Halley and the doe-eyed receptionist from Hudson.

"They won't be able to identify me," said Halley, her shaking voice betraying her.

Tony read the caption. *"Leads have come in regarding the possible identity of the notorious criminals the public is calling Comet and Blitzen."*

"Burns or not—fingerprints or not—your features haven't changed, Miss Halley Lovelace."

She lifted her gaze to him, heart thumping.

"Think your parents saw this?" said Tony.

Oh, god.

Halley stared at the photo, seeing her old face beneath the deformity. They would recognize her. What parent wouldn't? And if that was true, and her parents had reported it … they would have said she was Tony's intern. Had they wanted to call her to confirm their fears?

A lump rose in her throat at the thought of how panicked Mom would be.

"They don't know you're Blitzen," said Halley.

He threw his arms up. "Not yet!"

"Calm down, Tony. It's not that bad."

"Do I need to remind you to *look down*? The cops haven't left. I had to come and go through the goddamn garbage room." He paced the apartment, kicking shards of glass over the floor. After a long moment, he said, "What was Duncan Laboratories working on?"

She glanced to the laptops scattered over the couch. Duncan Laboratories had been the only BC-based company in attendance at the L.A. aerospace convention. Was Tony after a quick win?

This wasn't the time for a heist. Neither of them was in the right headspace. The cops were literally right under them. He was being hasty and reactive.

"How are your boys doing with everything we've given them for the lab?" she asked, trying to distract him.

"Progress," said Tony. "I'm keeping quiet on a few things. Waiting for the right moment to launch."

"With all the stolen tech in the spotlight, maybe we—"

"Duncan Laboratories, Halley," he said dangerously.

"Um, they're experimenting with a linear artificial gravity concept. Creating gravity using centripetal force can give passengers nausea, so they're working on a linear design—"

"No. Was there anything related to remote sensing?"

Halley thought back to what she saw on the laptop. She had no recollection of anything like that, but she said, "I think so."

He stopped pacing. "The Canadian government is launching a satellite fleet."

Halley studied his expression, trying to get a read on his mood. "Not as high-resolution as Aries 180?"

"I don't know. They haven't released specs."

"When's it happening?"

"They're signing the contract with manufacturers on Wednesday."

Ah. Aries was supposed to be the best at remote sensing—but they weren't chosen as a manufacturer.

"And Duncan Laboratories?" said Halley.

"They're doing the sensors."

"I'll look into it," she said, grasping the silent question: What did they have that Aries didn't?

"Good. On Tuesday night we'll go borrow whatever it is they're working on."

Dammit.

Halley glanced to the window. "You sure you still want to go with—?"

"Of course," hissed Tony. "We aren't letting that stop us."

When she didn't move, he said, "If they go through with the contract, Duncan will get the publicity that should have been mine. What's good enough for the government will be good enough for anyone, and people will start looking to Duncan instead of Aries for their satellite data."

Halley went to find the Duncan Laboratories laptop. "I'll start on their security system."

They were a mid-sized company and nothing new, but she hadn't been this nervous for a heist in a while. Tony was getting overconfident, his mood unnerving and fueling his decisions.

She thought of the wig and makeup hidden in her bathroom inside empty tampon boxes.

On the coffee table, Tony's phone screen dimmed. As he strode to the kitchen, Halley peeked at the apps on the home screen.

eDen Smart Lock.

Maybe she would do a bit more research on the wireless lock—just in case.

Chapter 24
Jess's Old Friend

Jess startled awake at 4 AM, Desi's lifeless eyes lingering in her mind. She drew a few deep breaths while Mandeep's snores eased her back to the present. Then a strange feeling churned inside her. What day was it? Christmas morning? Oh, god, did she have a final exam?

She sat up. Her webpage. She'd set it free.

She crept out of the bedroom and made the most emotionally comforting breakfast she could think of: Pop-Tarts and Earl Grey tea.

It had been about five hours since she'd blasted the webpage all over the internet. Would anyone have seen it, given most people in North America were asleep?

She shouldn't get her hopes up. The page probably had no traction yet. Patience.

She put her plate on the table, her velociraptor mug beside it, and sat with a forced sense of calm.

Would people care? Comet and Blitzen might have gained a weird celebrity status, but that didn't necessarily mean the public was interested in stalking their every move.

Steeling herself, Jess opened her laptop and refreshed Twitter.

She froze with a Pop-Tart halfway to her mouth.

Comet and Blitzen were trending—and in the thick of it was her web portal.

"Jesus Murphy," she whispered.

She checked the post on each network, pulse accelerating as she found thousands of shares, comments flooding in everywhere, and a position on the Reddit front page. People were having arguments about politics in the comments sections.

She fist-pumped. When people started trolling each other in the comments section, that was definitive proof that a post had gone viral.

She felt a little pathetic for getting such a high over this, considering she was anonymous, but it was her hard work, and the masses were appreciating it!

She dove into the comments. People were excited about the map and timeline, discussing robbery locations and searching for patterns, trying to predict when and where the duo would go next. Some Reddit users were trying to calculate the next location with probability formulas—though in Jess's opinion, there was no predictable pattern.

New photos had already been added all over the map via the social media feed. At least one photo was tagged in every location Comet and Blitzen had pilfered. The photos from the little airport in Manitoba sparked the most excitement, because people realized that with the right timing, they might be the first to see where Comet and Blitzen were about to raid.

Jess got ready and went to work with a strut in her step, feeling like Miss Congeniality emerging from the warehouse.

Viral sensation coming through!

Arriving at the office was anticlimactic. In fact, the place was strangely quiet. Jess peered out the window to the parking lot, wondering if a lot of people were still away after the long weekend, but found the usual number of cars amid the February downpour.

She checked her social media posts compulsively, craving the high she felt when she had opened her laptop that morning. No amount of new likes and comments quite scratched the itch.

After what must have been the tenth time checking in ten minutes, she closed all her social media tabs and turned her attention on her work. This was pathetic. She was acting like a rat in a Skinner box. Was this what it felt like to be an addict?

Outside, the clouds thickened. Rain lashed against the windows fiercely enough that she heard it coming from every direction. She set to work on a tedious QA task from Steve 2's recent project and found herself slumping lower and lower in her chair.

The office really did feel like a ghost town today.

Her answer came at lunch, when she sat down with the Cloud Team. They were devoid of their usual enthusiasm, and it occurred to Jess she hadn't chatted with any of them on Slack yet that day.

"What's wrong?" said Jess with a sinking feeling.

"Chuck's breathing down our necks," said Kit quietly.

"Apparently," said Anita, "there've been like a hundred cloud instances deployed from the Aries account over the last week, but none of us know why."

Jess felt the blood drain from her face. "Servers?"

"Yeah."

"Uh, what are they doing, exactly?"

Kit stabbed her salad, sending a squirt of tomato juice across the table. "Something obnoxious. New ones are launching every hour."

"We sent a request to the cloud service provider to have all the instances killed," said Omar, "but that hasn't stopped the company credit card being charged at least ten grand."

"They can't fire all three of us at once, right?" whispered Anita.

Omar and Kit looked equally uncertain. Jess was quietly panicking, throat constricting. Her swarm of bees had cost *ten grand* to deploy? Why didn't she consider this? Of course computing power would cost money!

"Anyway," said Kit to Jess. "Chuck needs to justify the expense, and we've got nothing. He says if we don't figure out what happened we're going to get pulled into a meeting with Doctor Ries."

Panic must have shown on Jess's face, because Anita said, "What?"

Lie! Lie!

Jess covered her face, hiding the welling tears. Too late.

"I'm sorry."

She couldn't lie. She couldn't let them get in trouble—possibly fired—because of her. They'd become her friends, her mentors, a support team when she needed one. She owed them the truth.

Anita said, "Oh, no …"

"It was me," said Jess through her hands. "I didn't know it would cost the company money. I needed servers to—for a project—"

"For … QA?" said Omar, sounding like a deflating balloon.

"If Floyd gave you permission to launch them," said Anita, "we can justify—"

"No," said Jess. "It wasn't … I just did it."

The words were painful to get out. The following silence was even more painful.

Finally, she dropped her hands. All three of them were looking at her with such disappointment that she thought it might be better if they all just stabbed her with their utensils.

"Okay," said Omar, dropping his gaze to his untouched sandwich. "At least we know what happened. We can tell Chuck it was a testing error."

"I'm … I'm so sorry," said Jess, fighting the lump in her throat.

None of them would look at her. Why would they? She'd gotten them into serious trouble. She'd used them for this stupid obsession with serving justice. Of course cloud servers cost money to deploy. Of course those charges would come back to the Cloud Team. How could she be so thick as to not see that?

Now their team was responsible for justifying ten thousand dollars worth of fees.

"We won't rat you out," said Anita, but flatly, like she was saying it out of duty to be nice.

"It's fine," said Jess. "Tell Chuck I did it. You don't deserve to get in trouble for my stupidity."

"No, it's okay."

The other two didn't jump in with arguments.

After a terrible silence, Omar stood. "I'm going to do some work."

Before anyone could say more, he grabbed his sandwich and left.

Jess didn't wait for the other two to leave her. She stood, not meeting their eyes. She tried to think of something more to say. Should she apologize again? The lump in her throat ached too much to talk. She bolted from the lounge, wanting the isolation of her office.

Floyd was coming out of his office as she swept past. "No lunch for you?"

"Done already," she said, struggling to keep her eyes dry.

Before she made it a few steps past, he said, "Jessica."

She stopped, took a breath, and turned with the most forced of smiles. "Yeah?"

"Storming past someone without a bit of chit-chat comes across as rude. You should be polite and engage coworkers in conversation. That's how you make friends at the office."

She stared at him, with that stupid side-comb and that *I'm-such-a-helpful-mentor* expression.

"I'll remember that if there's someone I want to make friends with."

His eyes narrowed a little.

Before he could decide whether or not she had insulted him, Jess said, "Enjoy your lunch," and spun on her heel.

She meant, of course, she hoped he would choke on it.

She spent the afternoon with her door closed, giving zero fucks about Floyd's 'open-door culture'.

She crawled into bed at 8 o'clock that night, Himalayan salt lamp casting its pink glow around the room, laptop tilted sideways so she could type lying down. Mandeep wasn't home yet. Jess couldn't remember if she was at a lab or spin class.

Jess opened her web portal to find the servers still chugging, no doubt with mere hours left before the Cloud Team's request to kill them was received and executed. She imagined her little swarm of bees dropping dead in their meadow of satellite images.

People had started spamming the portal, sharing NSFW photos with the #CometAndBlitzen hashtag in some obscure location, just to get on the map. Clutter was forming rapidly, hiding the photos of real interest beneath the onslaught of dick pics.

She supposed it was a matter of time before that happened. She could go in and delete the irrelevant photos— but at this point, she hardly cared. Her bees were on death row.

Jess clicked through all the images, looking for new evidence. One of them featured a crowd of people walking down Robson Street in Vancouver. It looked like an ordinary stream of people going about their days. But the infrared signature proved otherwise. Blitzen was walking among them in full disguise.

A few people commented on this image, speculating that he and Comet lived somewhere in Vancouver.

Jess sighed. If only she had more time with the servers, she might get a picture of him coming or going from his home. This photo told her nothing except that he'd gone shopping on Robson.

She zoomed out to see the map as a whole. Vancouver had a few photos, but only of Blitzen. After that, the Hudson Research Centre heist had a notable cluster of images because of the time they'd spent at the little airport and the ones taken by the employees. That selfie of Comet and the blonde girl was still making the rounds, easily the most popular.

Jess had been refraining from looking closely at that one, on account of it being such a high-quality close-up of Comet's face. She'd gotten close enough when Blitzen held her at gunpoint.

Something needled at her every time she saw that image pop up. There was something almost familiar about it.

Curiosity eating her, she opened the picture to take a closer look. There was the girl, posing like she was taking a picture with Taylor Swift. Comet had the pistol pressed against the girl's temple, pulling a face, bearing an uncanny resemblance to—

Jess sat bolt upright. Her heart seemed to stop beating.

"No."

She stared at the picture, studying the girl's eyes and bone structure—every piece of her that would have looked the same before she ended up this way.

When Jess had stared so long that the picture swam in her eyes, she leapt off the bed, dropped on all fours, and pulled a shoebox from under the bed. She tossed the lid off and rifled through its contents. Notes passed in high school, concert tickets, photobooth prints, tiny theme park toys, and more spilled out.

She found what she was looking for: a picture of her and her best friend. Former best friend, technically. It was taken months ago, a week before the incident. They'd been playing with Kayla's new Polaroid printer.

Jess raised the picture and held it next to her laptop, hand trembling.

The facial expressions were almost identical.

How had she not seen it? She thought back to when she'd watched her in the Aries warehouse, and all of the satellite images that had come up since then. The resolution hadn't been precise enough. She didn't expect to recognize the girl, and so she'd never looked closely. She assumed any feelings of familiarity were because of Anthony Ries.

Comet—like Halley's Comet.

In the Polaroid, Jess was holding the camera. Halley stuck out her tongue. Her eyes were so bright. They'd always shone, like she was permanently on the verge of laughter. And she was. She was one of those people who laughed all the time. Not an annoying, forced guffaw, but the real thing, the kind that made you laugh with her. Everything was genuinely delightful, as if life was a game to her.

That had changed the day Desi died. Their friendship shattered like the bones in Jess's forearms. Now Halley was out there, a thief, an outlaw—the partner of the man who threatened Jess's life.

Chapter 25
Halley and a Series of Explosions

Halley cut the alarm system, froze the CCTV, and unlocked the hardware development wing in under two minutes.

"Hurry the fuck up, Halley."

"I'm going! Jesus, I'm not the Flash."

"Watch your tone—"

"Do you want my help or not?"

Tony snarled.

Halley shoved the laptop into his arms, took a running start, and pushed off the brick wall with her foot. Daylight was fading, but she felt her surroundings clearly in the breeze. She thrust a hand up and grabbed the ledge.

Pressing her feet against the wall, she used her arms to pull herself up.

She might pay for the snark later, but right now, Tony needed to shut up and let her work. While he waited below, Halley stood on the ledge and reached for the second-floor windowsill.

It was 6 PM, which meant only a couple of Duncan Laboratories employees were still inside—enough to help

Halley and Tony navigate the building, but not so many that they had to worry about paparazzi shots.

The street at this hour was too busy for them to go through the front entrance. Around back, the narrow alley hid them from view.

Tony's brand new Elion waited in the alley, glossy, black, as beautiful as a unicorn. Today would be its inaugural getaway job. Halley couldn't help wondering how it would look when they were done with it.

She pushed the overhead window. It creaked open, the disturbance tickling her flesh. No alarm sounded. She had done her job well.

It hadn't taken Halley long to learn that Duncan Laboratories was developing satellites that could do multispectral video. The Aries fleet did images only. This meant Tony needed to borrow the pieces comprising one of their sensors. Surely, Aries could do a superior job.

Inside, the lights were off, leaving the hall dim. Halley landed noiselessly and felt for movement. None in any direction. But that didn't ease her nerves.

The staircase was beside her. She removed the knotted rope from her backpack, tied it to the handrail, and threw the end out to Tony.

While he climbed, Halley oriented herself. They needed the sixth floor, east wing. Four flights up these stairs would do it.

Tony climbed through the window and looked around. "We've got ten minutes."

He'd given them thirteen total. Halley gave them eight. Already a voice in the back of her mind was telling her to *get out, get out, get out.*

Yes, winning a contract with the government was a titillating prospect for Aries. Tony wanted his company on top, and this would guarantee that position. Halley just wished they didn't have to do this *today.* They'd been going too hard, hitting too many companies. A better strategy would be to fall silent and let the world think they were done. Let the police get distracted with other things. Go hard again in a few weeks.

Tony refused to hear it. He made the plans, not Halley.

She stuffed the rope into their bag and followed Tony upstairs. The sixth floor required a key fob to gain access— but again, Halley had done her job, and it was deactivated. They pushed the door open and found what they were looking for: the hardware lab.

It was an open concept with at least forty workstations and a lot of wood and plants. The decor was eye-rollingly 'West Coast', complete with oars with pine trees on them, a cotton hammock hanging from a stand in the corner, and canoe-shaped pencil holders on the desks. Bits of hardware covered every surface, like an impossible puzzle. No one was around. The main lights were out, leaving the glow of the street lamps outside and a red emergency exit sign on the far wall.

Tony picked a computer that had been left on standby and began searching for CAD files. A design would help them find out which hardware pieces they needed to borrow. While he worked, Halley rifled through drawers, hoping some schmuck had written down their passwords. She tossed papers and notebooks aside, scattering them like confetti.

A terrible sound met her ears.

She and Tony froze.

Sirens.

It couldn't be. Already?

They wailed, growing louder—and stopped outside.

Halley spun. "How—?"

Tony stood. "I thought we had thirteen."

Halley checked her watch. It had been six minutes—and to the best of her knowledge, no alarm had been triggered. How could it be, when she'd cut the whole system?

Tony abandoned the computer and rummaged through the hardware on the nearest desk.

"I need someone who knows what all of this is. Get me some help."

"Shouldn't we go?"

"Do it!"

She hesitated for a fraction of time before sprinting into the hall. He wouldn't leave until he had the right hardware. The best she could do was finish the job as quickly as possible.

How had the cops shown up already? It was like they were waiting around the block, watching. But that was impossible. They had no way of knowing where she and Tony were off to. Sometimes, even Halley hardly knew.

She strode through the darkness, feeling the air for signs of life. People were still here. They'd shown up on the security cameras minutes ago.

"Here, kitty, kitty."

She stopped at each door and kicked it open, pistol ready, nerves wound tight. *Get out, get out, get out.*

The sirens were loud, blue and red lights splattering the walls around her.

She closed her eyes, meditating over the air currents. Someone was definitely up here.

"I feel you breathing. Come out and make this easy for both of us."

Further down the hall, something moved. She whipped her head up. A man sprinted away, making for the stairwell.

Halley ran—but he was too far ahead to catch.

Shit. He was their only hope at getting that data and blowing out of here.

She planted her feet and raised the pistol. She felt his movements—his velocity, his proximity to each wall, the way his arms and legs pumped. She honed in on the right leg.

Step. Step. Step.

It matched her frantic heartbeat.

Get out, get out, get out.

She pulled the trigger. The man screamed and fell, clutching his knee.

Halley closed on him. Burning flesh met her nose. She grabbed his hair and forced him to his feet.

"Come on." She took the hobbling, sobbing man back to the lab. "Got one. What do you need?"

Tony looked up, eyes wild.

Somewhere below, several floors down, there was a crash. The police were in the building.

"Which parts are for the new video sensors?" said Tony.

"I d-don't know," said the man.

Halley pulled his hair. "Try harder."

"I d-don't—I can't remember what—"

Tony snatched Halley's pistol from her hand and pressed it between the man's eyes.

"The CAD files are on the corporate server," said the man. "Fileshare4."

Tony dropped Halley's pistol and typed frantically.

Halley felt the air for danger. They had seconds. They should have been on their way out.

"Password?" said Tony.

"Boss, we need to—"

"Shut up!" He spat the words with the same venom he'd used on their hostage.

Halley glowered.

A thud sounded below. The police were in the stairwell. Would they check each floor on their way up?

Halley gripped the man harder. "He asked for the password."

"I c-can't—give that—I'll lose my j-job—"

She punched him in the stomach and the air from his lungs buffeted her like a strong wind.

"You're worried about your job right now?"

The guy mumbled something that sounded suspiciously like 'bitch'.

"I beg your pardon?"

Halley's eyes glazed over as a hot spike of anger went through her. Did he really think being difficult was going to help matters? She was making a simple request.

The air shifted as the man raised a fist. Before he could follow through with the punch, she kicked him in the knee, right where the bullets had hit. He crumpled like a rag doll. She stepped in with an uppercut, hook, and hammerfist, sending him sprawling on his stomach. He rolled onto his side with a pathetic moan.

"Password!" she said through her teeth.

"No."

She kicked him. He slid a couple of inches, trailing blood from his knee. She kicked again, rolling him on his back. God, this felt good. Frustration flew out her toes with each strike.

The man grabbed for her legs. She hopped out of the way and came down hard on his ribs with her elbow. The wind exploded from his mouth. It raked across her sensitive flesh, and any self-restraint she had left disappeared. The man transformed into Kevin, and the bloodthirsty look on his face as he beat her up every day before school. She gave his face a one-two punch and then straddled him to hold him down. He transformed into Kevin's friends, who held her arms back, laughing, throwing punches when Kevin let them. She struck him twice more. He transformed into Brooke telling her she was retarded, that she was too crazy to be taken seriously, that she was lucky she found Brooke to put up with her. One, two, *SNAP!* Everything that had built up over Halley's entire life surged from her core, pouring out through her muscles.

The man struck wildly with his fists, catching her in the jaw. She tasted blood. Adrenaline pumped faster, fueling her. She hit him again. Blood dribbled from her mouth onto his face.

I'm worth listening to. I'm strong enough.

The man gave up trying to hit her and protected his face with his arms.

"Hal—hey!"

No. This one is mine.

Blood poured from his nose, warm on her fingers. One, two, three—he was unconscious. She kept punching. Blood sprayed, and whether it was his or her own, she didn't know. It covered his face, her hands.

Someone was shouting. "Stop!"

Arms wrapped around her waist from behind and she was lifted into the air. She flailed until Tony set her down and spun her around to face him.

Footsteps pounded in the hallway.

Halley blinked her eyes back into focus. She was trembling. Everything was warm and sticky. She looked down at the blood soaking her front and pooling at their feet. The man was a pulp, unconscious. What had she done?

The police were at the door.

Halley and Tony spun around.

This wasn't an ordinary squad. These guys were armed to the tits.

They opened fire.

Halley and Tony hit the floor, clambering to get behind something. She used her unconscious victim as a shield as she reached for their bag. They crawled behind desks, backing away as fast as they could.

Tony balked. He looked at the weapon in his hand— Halley's pistol. His rifle was on the desk. She grabbed his arm before he could get up. His toy was out of reach, and right in firing range.

"We can't," she said, the words drowned beneath gunfire.

Tony grimaced, an expression of agony twisting his features.

The desk overhead exploded as bullets rained down on it. They kept crawling, scurrying like rats.

Crouching beneath the window, Halley wrenched the rope free from their bag. She passed it to Tony and went back to digging.

The device was a prototype, at best, meant for emergencies. If this situation didn't qualify as an emergency, she didn't know what did.

Her fingers closed around what she was looking for: a sort of hand grenade made from modified GN bullet solution.

If they couldn't steal the sensors Duncan Laboratories was working on, they could at least slow down their development. It would give Aries time to catch up—and the government time to reconsider the contract.

"Ready?" she said to Tony.

He had secured the rope to the nearest desk. "Bombs away."

With a silent prayer to the Norse god Loki (presumably the only god who wouldn't be thoroughly disgusted with her life choices), she bit the top of the grenade to break the barrier inside, igniting the fuse. She hurled it across the lab and plugged her ears as the advancing emergency responders scattered.

Nothing.

Whelp, they were dead.

Halley and Tony looked at each other with expressions of horror. They needed a new plan. But what? It wasn't like they could Hans Gruber this situation and pretend to be innocent hostages. They had to get out—

BOOM.

The grenade exploded with earth-rumbling force, sending hardware, papers, and shards of canoe-shaped pencil holders flying across the room like meteorites. Halley slapped her hands back over her ears and rolled into a fetal position. She heard glass shattering and looked up. Tony was using her pistol to smash the window.

She climbed to her feet, but he had thrown the rope out the window and was already making a rapid descent.

"What happened to *ladies first?*" she shouted after him.

As the dust from the explosion settled, the cops opened fire again. She threw herself back down to the floor. How was she supposed to escape, now? If she followed Tony through the window, they'd shoot her in the back. And the ass-face took her pistol, leaving her with the bag and an out-of-reach assault rifle.

She dug to the bottom of the bag, searching for the old pistol he had given her to take to her first heist at GN. Her fingers closed over the cool metal of the handgun. It seemed so pitiful, like a pellet gun, now that she'd been using the chemical weapon for so long.

She yanked it out and took aim, not at her attackers, but at the GN rifle.

She squeezed the trigger.

The rifle exploded, igniting everything around it.

Not wasting time, she threw herself toward the window.

"Yippee ki—shit."

The cops had the building surrounded. Tony had made it to the ground and was behind a pillar, shooting wildly as he retreated back into the building.

Were more cops waiting for him inside?

Turning away from the window, she had her own problems. The room was in engulfed, heat bearing down on her. The cops were still there, though they had been forced back by the flames.

Her eyes swam at the acrid smoke in the air, panic taking hold in her chest at the suffocating heat. She squeezed her eyes shut for a few seconds, forcing her mind to stay in the present.

The cops were driven further into a corner. She looked between them and the glowing exit sign at the back of the room before steeling herself and charging toward it. She snatched the cotton hammock from its stand on the way past.

She should have listened to her instincts. Before they'd even left home, she'd had a bad feeling about this heist. Tony was getting overconfident. No matter how skilled they were, they weren't invincible.

Halley leapt down the stairs several at a time and hopped the banister. She wished she knew what Tony was thinking. Was he inside the building, forming a plan? Would he try to find her?

She fumbled for her temporary phone and selected the contact for Blitzen. It rang and rang. He didn't answer. She hung up.

He wouldn't leave without her, would he? Her chest constricted.

She stopped at a landing and leaned against the wall, panting. What if the police had followed Tony inside? The heavy stairwell doors made it hard to feel what was going on beyond them. She had to act fast before she was cornered.

The landing had a small window. She pushed it open. Below, an engine revved.

Her breath caught. *Could it be—?*

She leaned out the window, following the sound of the engine, feeling the curve of the wind.

"Yes!"

He was in the Elion. Hail Loki, full of grace, the bastard had waited for her.

Two stairwell doors opened. Cops were closing on her from above and below.

She hooked the cotton hammock to the window latch and rappelled down the brick wall. When she ran out of hammock, she let go and fell two floors to the ground. The asphalt was like a bed of nails. Cursing, Halley sprang up and ran for the Elion.

The passenger door was closed, the window open. Tony sped away as she was still pulling herself through the window.

Gunshots rang behind them, peppering the car.

"Passenger, please put on your seatbelt," said the dash in helpful twinkly letters.

Halley untangled her limbs and buckled up.

Tony's disregard for human life got them through the narrow alleys and to the highway. They peeled away at a speed that would disintegrate both the car and their bodies if Tony lost control, seatbelts or not.

Blue and red lights bathed the inky sky behind them. Halley envisioned the next fifty years of her life behind bars.

"Tony, faster!"

He floored it. Halley twisted around in her seat. The cops were falling behind.

Dammit, tonight was a bad idea. Bad, bad, bad. She should have tried harder to make Tony listen to her. Her opinions should count for something.

They took back roads, guided by live traffic updates on the Elion's GPS. They wound the dark streets until it was clear no one was following and no helicopters were in pursuit.

When they burst through the door of Tony's apartment, they'd caught their breaths but not their composure. Like a bad hangover, Halley wondered if she would feel better if she went to the bathroom and forced herself to throw up.

Tony paced the length of the apartment while she vigorously scrubbed blood off her hands in the kitchen sink.

No, she was *not* having a Lady Macbeth moment—the blood was gross and she didn't want to get it on Tony's furniture.

Reality settled over her as she scrubbed. The rifle was gone. They had failed to get the data. At least they'd escaped that hellfire alive—but Tony would be seething.

She glanced to the open door of her suite. Downstairs, her laptop was running, waiting. Had her plan worked? She would have to find an opportunity to check.

Tony pressed his fists against his eye sockets. "What went wrong?"

"The cops got there way too fast," said Halley, drying her face on a tea towel. "We miscalculated."

Tony shook his head. "Something's off. That makes no sense." He grabbed his laptop and brought it to the couch. "The cops must have already been in the area. Another robbery. We should start checking for breaking news before we go."

His eyes darted back and forth as he scanned whatever was on his screen. She had to speak up before he got any ideas.

"Tony, we've gone too far. They're on to us."

"That's not it."

"No, listen. I was worried about this. We've hit so many aerospace companies by now. They might be predicting where you're planning to go next."

Tony met her eyes. "They're not that brilliant. They can't outsmart me."

"Okay, even if they can't predict our movements, don't you think they'll wonder why Aries is the only place that hasn't been broken into?"

He considered this. "We can stage a break-in at the office."

God, he was so stubborn!

"No. We need to back off. At least for a while."

"Don't tell me how to run my company. I'm losing to competitors."

"The government was one contract, and you haven't lost it yet! I bet they reconsider now that we destroyed half the Duncan—"

"Enough!"

She shut her mouth, teeth grinding, then flung open kitchen cupboards. She was famished.

Halley aggressively made herself a PB&J, tearing holes in the bread with the knife while Tony glared at his laptop. She was returning the jam to the fridge when he suddenly roared, making her jump and drop the jar. It shattered, sending the violently red jelly streaking across the stone floor.

"We're being tracked!" he shouted. "Some cocksucker set up a web portal to hunt us down. I don't know how, but that's why they've been dogging us. It's all over the frigging internet."

Halley stared at her mess, heart pounding. Someone was tracing their every move?

"Since when?"

"Looks like the images go as far back as the day we ..." He motioned down his body.

Standing in the kitchen, she listened to the flurry of his clicking and typing. Was she safer to go over there and comfort him, or to stay here and pretend she didn't exist? She waited, perfectly still, like a rabbit trying not to be seen.

After a long moment, Tony shouted, "It's my own fucking satellites! Look at the source. Those are Aries images."

Still, Halley said nothing, a sick feeling churning her gut.

Someone in Tony's own company was betraying him. Someone knew what he and Halley were doing. Did this person know their real identities, too?

Tony picked up his phone and tapped the screen. He raised it to his ear. "Steve. I need you to search everyone's browser history. Look up this URL."

Halley wasn't hungry anymore. She left the sandwich on the counter and used a cloth to wipe up the spilled jam. She moved slowly, ducking behind the counter and out of Tony's sight.

"I just want to know who's visited the site," said Tony. "Yeah. Anyone else? Give me a lis—wait. Jessica Curie?"

Halley snapped her head up, freezing in place. Thankfully, Tony was too focused on the call to notice her abrupt movement.

Jessica Curie.

"Christ. Okay. No, that's enough. Is she coming to work tomorrow? Not on vacation or anything?"

It had to be the same Jess, working somewhere like Aries. She'd been destined to become a professional nerd. In grade seven, she and Halley had formed a zoology club where they searched for animals in Jess's backyard and then researched everything's taxonomy and habitat.

Had Jess set up that portal?

It was just like her to do something like this. She was always on the right side of the law—and though she and Halley were a holy terror together, Jess was always the rational one. She was always the first member of their group to consider the consequences.

That was why Jess and Halley had clicked—instant friends from the day they were partnered for the grade six science fair. They were like the zinc and copper at either end of their potato battery, ordinary on their own, electric when together. They were like the opposite ends of the magnets on the table beside them, pulled toward each other by the forces of nature. They were like vinegar and baking soda on the table across from them, destined to be dumped in a papier-mâché volcano. And oh, what an eruption that had been.

314

"Book me a meeting with her at 9:30," Tony said into the phone. "Second-floor boardroom. And revoke her API key."

He lowered the phone.

The energy in the room changed dangerously. Halley stood up, still holding the damp cloth. Tony's anger prickled on her skin like static.

She cringed, her muscles tensing before he even threw the phone. It hit the wall, denting the cream-colored paint and shattering the screen.

"So," he spat, "not only did the bitch ignore my warning, but she's been tracking us. What happened today was her fault."

Anger sparked in Halley. She and Jess might not have talked in months, but hearing Tony call her a bitch made her want to smack him.

"We have to take her out," he said, striding into the kitchen. "Next time, everything will be back to normal."

His pupils were dilated. His body quivered.

Halley opened and closed her mouth. Take out Jess? Like, kill her?

Over her own dead body would she let Tony turn one of these filthy weapons on Jess.

Wait, *next time?*

Halley stood taller. "Tony, we need to stop. There shouldn't be a next time."

"Don't be stupid. We're not letting some kid with an inflated sense of justice ruin my plans."

"The cops shoot to kill. Have you not noticed? Think what could happen if we keep—"

"Quiet!"

He turned his back, gripping the edge of the counter. His temper was out of control, his breaths sharp.

Arguing would do nothing. Like before, he was scared and lashing out. Halley needed to show understanding, reassurance, sympathy.

She extended a hand. "It'll be okay, Tony."

He spun. In a blink, Halley was on the floor, a blinding pain in her collarbone.

"Now we're down a weapon," he shouted. "How can we do anything productive?"

The room darkened as he towered over her. His eyes were out of focus.

"We still have the pistol," Halley whimpered—though she wasn't sure why she said it. Maybe she hoped the remaining GN firearm would bring her forgiveness.

Tony turned to where it lay on the counter. He picked it up. "I'll use this next time. You can use the old one."

Sitting on the floor, Halley averted her eyes.

"Tomorrow night, we go back," he said. "I want those video sensors."

Though his temper sent a pulse of fear through her, telling her to escape, to hide, she had to protect him from himself. He wasn't thinking clearly.

"Tony, we can't. They'll have increased security, not to mention we blew up every bit of hardware they were working on."

"We can still get the CAD files. If we make sure the cops are occupied—"

"No." She stood, doing her best to ignore her trembling legs. "We're not going. This is getting too dangerous—"

He struck her across the face with the butt of the pistol. She gasped, stumbling back.

"We are not letting Aries lose deals because of this!"

She wanted to defend herself, to punch and kick him back, but survival instinct told her that would be a dangerous move. She took a steadying breath.

"Yes, sir," she said, all emotion removed from the words.

He stared at her for a moment, licked his lips, then dropped his gaze. A muscle in his jaw twitched.

"Be ready to leave for the office at 8:30."

With Halley's pistol clenched in his fist, he stormed into his bedroom and slammed the door. The gust hit her like a blast from a jet engine.

Halley looked down, shock numbing her. Blood covered her hands. She'd landed on the remains of the smashed jar. Pieces were embedded in her palms.

She finished cleaning up the mess and went downstairs to her bathroom. She used a tweezer to get the glass out of her palms, tears streaming down her cheeks. Her reflection lingered in her periphery but she refused to look at it.

When she was done, she rinsed her hands and pressed a towel between her palms to stop the bleeding. She looked up.

The girl in the mirror was not Halley. This was a mutilated, defiled version of her, burned alive and molded back together by Tony.

She leaned over the sink and dissolved into tears, her sobs echoing off the marble basin. Her collarbone hurt. Her cheek throbbed. There was a tender spot where she'd landed on her hip. Worst of all, her chest ached with an overwhelming sense of betrayal. If he loved her, he wouldn't have treated her like that.

Naive. She should have seen this coming long ago, when he'd made it clear that work meant more to him than she did.

She drew several deep breaths, gripping the edge of the counter. Then she threw the blood-stained towel on the floor and left the bathroom.

On her nightstand, her laptop whirred. She sat on the bed with it, wiping her eyes, and opened a folder in Downloads.

There was a new file. Her code had worked. When Tony's phone transmitted the password to the wireless lock earlier, Halley's laptop had been ready. It grabbed the packets out of the air and stored them. The file was an encrypted mess— and blurry through her swollen, teary eyes—but it was there. She had the password to Tony's wireless lock.

If there was ever a time to use it, it was now.

She picked up her phone and scrolled through her contacts. It wasn't quite 10 PM. Not too late to call.

She looked at her closed bedroom door, fingers hovering over her phone. Everything she'd done over these last weeks seemed a million times worse now that she thought about confessing all of it.

Living guilt-free came easily when her only companion was a person more dishonorable than she was. To rebuild that connection with the outside world made everything too real, too shameful.

Her parents had been so proud of her. They'd raised her with so much love, giving her everything she needed. She'd had amazing friends and every open door in life. She didn't deserve to be that fortunate. She didn't deserve anything more than what Tony had done to her. She had never been a good person.

Halley grabbed her pillow and pushed her face into it to force the tears back in.

The old Halley was good, a small voice said. *You were good, once.*

She wanted it to be true. She wanted to stop thinking she deserved to be punished. Since the summer, she'd been blaming herself for what her ex-girlfriend did. She could have prevented the whole incident if she'd been more compassionate to Brooke. But she'd been too drunk to notice the warning signs, and too cold to care.

She deserved to have her friends cut ties with her. They'd seen her arguing with Brooke before it happened. They had every right to blame her for it.

Even now, carrying out her sentence, Brooke maintained that the fire was an accident. Halley never knew whether she believed it. Either way, the intent didn't matter. Brooke had been crying for help for months. The point was that it happened, and Halley hadn't stopped it, and Desi was dead.

"It wasn't my fault." Halley cried the words into her pillow, willing them to be true. She never wanted it to happen. That had to mean something.

For the first time, she wanted the old Halley back. The old Halley went to parties and got drunk and broke a few rules. The Halley that had surfaced over the past weeks was a hundred times worse. She'd made the decision to work for Tony, and she had seen the consequences. She knew evil, now.

Trapped in Tony's apartment, aching both inside and out, she needed her best friend.

She had always been Halley's ray of sunshine. She had a purity about her that Halley never did. Maybe she would forgive her, after all this time.

We have to take her out, Tony had said.

Like hell, he would.

Halley would rather die at the end of the GN pistol than let Tony hurt that ray of sunshine.

Summoning every bit of her courage, she hit the call button.

It rang, and rang, and rang.

Maybe she had blocked her number, or maybe—

"Hello?"

Halley took a moment to spit the words out. When she did, her voice was thick with tears.

"Jess. I've done something terrible."

Chapter 26
Jess and Mandeep

"I know," said Jess.

It seemed the only response. She'd had mere hours to process that her former bestie was the continent's most notorious criminal. She had no game plan for how to navigate such a conversation.

Her heart thudded wildly after seeing the name and picture show up on her phone. *Halley's voice.* She was hearing Halley's voice again. And god, if it didn't bring forward devastation and fear and joy all at once.

"What?" The other end of the phone was all sniffles and hitched breaths—a girl trying not to cry.

"I saw you trending on, like, every social network in existence," said Jess.

Halley drew a shaky breath. "I'm surprised you recognized me."

"I'd know your face anywhere, Hal." *Even this version of it.*

Halley said nothing. Jess flopped onto her pillow, struggling to find words. Her heart pounded like she'd climbed a mountain.

How did this happen? Halley had been smart, ambitious, beautiful. Her grade six life aspiration was to make a YouTube series to teach people science. She could have had anything in the world.

"Hal, who did this to you?"

"No one." She hesitated. "The appearance is part of our cover."

"You're telling me you signed up for this?"

"He offered me an internship."

This was a *job*? And Jess thought her internship was bad.

"I know it's Anthony Ries." Her throat constricted over the name. Halley was silent for so long that Jess said, "Hal."

"I only just found out you were interning there. I didn't know he threatened you."

"He's horrible. Why has nobody seen that?" She said it to herself as much as to Halley. Had no one else at the office been exposed to what kind of person he really was? He'd murdered, maimed, and held people hostage. It took a special kind of psychopath to do everything he'd done.

"He was afraid of being caught," said Halley. "He's not all bad—"

"Excuse me?!"

"I mean, underneath all of it, sometimes I've thought ..."

"Hal, he's manipulating you."

Silence. A distant sniffle.

Of course, this was more than a job and a business venture. Jess had seen proof in the photo of them kissing. Halley and Doctor Ries were a couple.

Did Halley love him?

"I'm sorry," said Jess with a pang of guilt. "That was harsh."

"He takes care of me, here. He feeds me and buys me everything I need to be comfortable."

Jess gripped the phone tighter. "Like a pet kitty?"

"He says he's protecting me. I think he has a hard time expressing emotions."

"All emotions? Or just the good ones?"

Halley faltered. She whispered, "This was supposed to be a career move, J. An adventure. It's not fun anymore. I can't believe the things I've done."

Jess wanted to reassure her friend, to tell her it was okay— but nothing about what she'd learned of Halley's last few weeks was okay.

As if reading her thoughts, Halley said, "I've never killed anyone."

"I saw the guy in the lab get shot."

"I didn't want that. I might have injured people and stolen from them, but I've never killed."

That hardly seemed better. On a scale from Oops to Royally Fucked Up, the situation was a solid nine.

Jess put a hand over her eyes, sighing. "People have gotten seriously hurt."

"I know. He's got such a temper. I mean … I guess I'm no better."

A sick feeling rose in Jess's stomach. "Has he hurt you?"

"That's not what I—" Halley swallowed audibly. "I'm fine."

Jess clenched her jaw so hard that pain shot through her temples. "I'm coming over there. Where are you?"

Halley let out a breath that might have been an attempt at a laugh. "You can't come here."

"Did you report the assault?"

"Uh, to the police?"

"Oh." She considered how she could find this guy and cut off his testicles.

"J, this is why I called. To warn you about him."

"Consider me warned."

"No, I mean—we almost got caught tonight because of your web portal."

They almost got caught? Her plan worked? Had Jess found out in any other way that her portal was working, she would have jumped for joy. But she'd nearly gotten her best friend arrested—or worse.

"Wait. How did you know it was me?"

"He just called the office to track everyone's history."

Jess sat up in bed. She'd developed the portal anonymously and at home, but she did check the URL a couple of times at work. Visiting the site from the office network was incriminating enough. Anthony Ries would know she created it the moment he saw her name near anything to do with that portal.

"Is he coming for me?"

"Not yet," said Halley.

Jess glanced to the bedroom door, no more reassured. Had she bolted the front door when she came home? She contemplated dragging the fridge over to hold it closed. Not that it would stop that cannon he toted around.

"When?"

"Tomorrow morning, he's going to come to the office. You'll see he's booked a meeting with you at 9:30."

9:30. The gravity of it sank in. Doctor Ries wouldn't stop at a warning this time. He would finish her off.

God, what if Halley hadn't called? She would have had mere hours left to live. She would have gone into a meeting room and never come out. Would there have been innocent bystanders? What about Anita, Kit, Omar, the other interns?

Jess shook her head, stopping herself from skipping down Hypothetical Lane. The point was that Halley *had* called so Jess could avoid such a fate. Obviously, she would never return to the Aries office.

She let the concept sink in. Everything she'd strived for was represented in this internship: the opportunity to work for a world-class aerospace company, the splash of glitter on her resume, the references she would get, and the scholarship. None of that was possible anymore. In fact, she'd failed her internship so miserably that her boss literally wanted to murder her.

"I won't be there," said Jess.

"No. You need to go in."

"What? Why?"

"Because if you're not at work, he'll come to your house, and that's worse. Go. I'll make sure the cops are ready for him."

"Will they be able to arrest him?" said Jess, considering how poorly all the previous attempts to catch him had gone.

"I'll have to restrain him. He'll put a hundred bullets in anyone who gets close."

"And what about you?"

"I can handle a nasty temper. I've – handled one before." Halley choked on the words.

Jess's insides went icy.

Before she could say anything, Halley went on. "I need to protect people from him."

Jess thought of all the crimes Doctor Ries had committed, the people he'd hurt and stolen from. Everyone at work would be innocent bystanders tomorrow. If he came to the office with intent to kill, everyone in his way was vulnerable. Anita, Omar, Kit, Wyatt … she had to protect them.

"I'll help you."

"Um, no," said Halley.

"I'll be useful. We can lure him into a trap with the promise that you've caught me."

"I don't want you—"

"Come on. Together, we'll crush him," said Jess, and the venom in her own voice surprised her. "Like, metaphorically. I don't mean turning him into one of Mrs. Lovett's Meat Pies. Maybe a semi-crush, under a bookshelf full of heavy encyclopedias that won't kill him but will hold him there long enough for the cops to cuff him. Know what I mean?"

Halley gave a small laugh. "Sounds like a job for Team Jelley."

Jess smiled. They'd named themselves that when they were about thirteen.

"Team Jelley, makin' 'em jelly."

"We were so cool."

"Still are, apparently. So we're doing this?"

"Okay," said Halley. "We'll lure him into a trap, like you say, and bring the cops in."

"Somewhere away from everyone else."

They paused.

Halley said, "Gee, if only Aries had an isolated area that not many people have access to."

"Ha. It'd work, but I don't have a red badge."

"I do."

"Of course you do." Jess's pulse quickened at the thought of entering the lab. "This will also expose everything inside. All the stolen stuff. The cops will see it when they come arrest him."

Halley hesitated before giving a weak, "Yeah."

"What? Your hard work, gone to waste?"

"It was a lot of effort, taking all of it!"

"Other people's work, you mean."

"I know," said Halley in a *whatever, Mom* voice.

"Anyway, I'll take care of that part."

Jess would expose Anthony Ries as Blitzen. She had a plan. There was just one massive flaw.

"Hal, after restraining Doctor Ries—Tony—and before the cops arrive, we have to get you out of there."

"Don't worry about me."

"I will *too* worry. We're not getting you arrested along with him."

"It wouldn't be undeserved." Halley's voice was flat.

Jess was not about to let Halley get hurt again. She hadn't been there to help her friend before, when Halley needed her most, but she could be there now.

"Halley Lovelace, listen to me. You're going to be far away from Tony by the time the cops arrive tomorrow. They're not taking you both."

Halley hesitated. "There's a trapdoor I can use at the back corner of the warehouse."

"Good."

This was it, then. They were going to lure Tony into handcuffs tomorrow morning—or else Jess was going to find herself at the end of one of those freaky weapons.

All this time Jess had spent building a web portal and trying to get other people to deal with Comet and Blitzen, and it all fell onto her, in the end. She was the only one close enough to the problem to fix it. Together, she and Halley had the power to get Tony arrested.

She would do it to save her own life, yes, but even if he wasn't planning to kill her—if his only crime was hurting her best friend—she would still do it. She would save Halley.

But was this the same Halley she'd grown up with? Physically, the girl had irrevocably changed. Mentally ... there was no telling. They hadn't seen each other for the better part of a year. Could a few months of trauma and abuse erase the friendship they'd spent a decade building? What if Halley was repressing anger at Jess for abandoning her and would use this opportunity to get revenge?

No. She scolded herself for letting it cross her mind. Halley wouldn't do that. She'd been a victim of awful relationships, and she deserved better than this. She needed Jess—and this time, Jess would be there for her.

They discussed the details of their plan, but without knowing exactly what the warehouse contained, a few questions remained unanswered.

"Will you be okay until morning?" said Jess.

"Don't worry."

"Solid advice."

She wished it were that easy. Months apart from Halley hadn't diminished the way she felt about her friend.

She opened her mouth but couldn't find the right words. Should she bring up what happened all those months ago, or was that a sure way to make Halley angry? Jess had abandoned her after the incident. At Mandeep's urging—or shaming, more like—she'd backed away from everything relating to it, including friendships.

Maybe Halley was thinking the same thing, because the other end of the phone was silent—not a busy silence, like she was searching for a tissue, but a stiff one. It was the kind of silence that thought too hard, that mourned the past, that stressed over what to say next.

The decision was supposed to be best for Jess's mental health. It was supposed to heal her, and yet it was her greatest regret. She had to explain.

"Hal, I never should have—"

The front door opened. Mandeep's keys jingled. Her bag and coat rustled as she dropped them on the floor.

"I have to go," Jess whispered.

"See you in the morning. Shut your office door. I'll do our secret knock."

"We don't have a secret knock."

"Ask me for the password, then."

"Cheese puffs," they whispered together.

Jess stifled a laugh. "Just open the door. It doesn't lock."

"'Kay."

Jess plugged in her phone and lay back down with her laptop just as Mandeep walked in the room.

"Right where I left you."

Jess couldn't shake the vision of her friend on the other end of the phone, with her charred and melted skin, tears running down her face, stuck in Doctor Ries' house.

Though she could have burst into tears, she forced herself to smile.

In the morning, as Jess was staring into the cupboard debating whether or not she should try eating, Mandeep walked into the kitchen holding up the Polaroid of her and Halley. "Why was this out?"

Blarg. Jess looked away, deciding how to answer in a way that would keep the peace.

"Just reminiscing."

"Why?"

"She ... called me last night."

"You're talking to her again?"

Jess gave a half-shrug.

"Why?" said Mandeep again.

God, this was not going to be easy.

"She's going through something with her boyfriend. I said I'd help her get away from him."

Mandeep's face darkened.

Time to leave before this got messy. Jess crossed the room and put on her coat. She made to grab her keys and phone from the counter, but Mandeep blocked her path, hands up.

"Mandy, she's my best friend, and she's in trouble."

"Former best friend."

"We stopped talking, but it was never a falling-out."

"Don't forget everything you've said and felt, Jess. You're better off without that group."

"Without Brooke, maybe. But not Halley. Halley's different."

"She was dating Brooke," said Mandeep, voice rising.

Jess raised an eyebrow.

Mandeep clenched her fists in front of her. "Jess, you're reacting emotionally right now. Give it a day, and come back at the problem tomorrow."

"I don't have time to wait until then. Halley needs me right now."

That 9:30 meeting loomed. She needed Halley as much as Halley needed her.

Jess reached again for her things, but Mandeep caught her hand.

"Mandeep, let me have my keys."

"I can't let you go."

"I'm going to work!"

They stared at each other. Mandeep's eyes narrowed, jaw tight. Jess wondered if her girlfriend could see the agony battling inside her, or if she thought it was raw emotion and these were the actions of a delicate girl who couldn't put logic behind her feelings.

She stepped back, glaring.

"Do you forget what happened?" said Mandeep.

"How could I?" Jess opened her palms, exposing the scars.

In fact, she was willing to bet she recalled the incident more often than Mandeep knew. The scene haunted her dreams—Jess, Halley, Kayla, and Desirae, the four of them inseparable since high school. The party had been too loud, with too much drinking.

Jess remembered that feeling of being way past intoxicated, justifying it because her friends had crossed that line, too. They all planned to crash at Desi's that night—a slumber party, like the ones they had all through grade school.

That, itself, was enough to wring her with guilt. She should have been responsible. She should have cared about what was going on with Halley in the yard below while she was crammed on the crowded balcony with the others.

None of them had said it, but looks were enough, and they all knew Halley and Brooke's relationship was coming to an end. They'd been fighting for weeks, and there was something unstable about Brooke. She'd found a way to manipulate Halley with constant, hidden insults, complimenting Halley on her makeup by pointing out how it made her blotchy skin more tan, or admiring a shirt because of the way it hid the fat in Halley's stomach.

They were having a screaming match in the yard. Brooke called Halley nasty things, a few words rising above the crowd like wisps of smoke.

"You don't care about my feelings, you bitch … You don't give a shit about anyone … You're not even normal … The traits of a psychopath."

Jess didn't know what to do, and so she did nothing. She watched the orange flames from the campfire cast a glow across her friends' crying faces. When they screamed themselves into silence, Halley came up to the balcony, and Brooke vanished into the crowd below.

Jess heard later that Brooke claimed she intended to cause a scene without putting anyone in danger. If that was true, she'd failed. Witnesses saw her holding a flaming piece of wood. One moment, she had it, and the next …

Jess remembered the campfire smell, and then the too-close stench of burning plastic and chemicals. She remembered the music, shouted conversations, and beer pong inside the door—and then screams, and crackling and spitting wood.

Something was obviously wrong when people near the door started running inside.

Flames whooshed to life. Black smoke rose on all sides.

Those nearest the door escaped through the house. Those furthest didn't have time. Jess, Halley, Kayla, and Desi were forced to jump.

The balcony was so high. The fall was an eternity.

Halley and Kayla landed in the bushes. Jess and Desi landed on concrete. Jess remembered the pain of her arms shattering. She'd stopped herself from hitting her head, and would take shattered forearms over the alternative—but oh, the pain. She hardly remembered what happened between landing and being in the ambulance. Screaming. Being unable to move her arms. Looking over and finding Desi on the concrete beside her—that empty stare.

"Halley was a victim, same as me," said Jess, chest heaving. "Same as Desi."

Mandeep crossed her arms. "You were all there together."

"It was Brooke's doing."

"You were all drunk. You girls always got way too drunk. Something was bound to happen."

"What, you think we deserved that?"

"No! God, Jess!"

"Then, what? Karma? Fate?"

"That was never the real you."

"Don't tell me who I am, Mandy."

They stood at arm's length from each other, fuming, the distance between them feeling wider by the second.

"Remember what you told me afterwards?" said Mandeep.

"I remember agreeing to sever ties with them after you begged me." She would never forget the ache in her chest when she told Halley not to come visit her in the hospital.

"You agreed it was the right thing to do."

"I thought I needed time away from them. I'm thinking clearly now, and I know I need Halley in my life."

"You need to think about what's best for yourself, not some girl you used to—"

"Halley was my best friend! Of all the girls, she and I had something—"

"Something special? What, you've still got feelings for her?"

"Are you—? Oh my god, Mandeep. We kissed like, twice, in grade nine."

"It's not even about that. Jess, you can't hang out with her again."

Jess's vision swam as anger boiled inside her. "You forbid me?"

"I don't like who you are with those girls."

"You liked me enough to fall in love with me while they were still my friends."

"I fell in love with you despite all of that. I knew who you really were underneath."

"What if that's who I really am? Maybe I haven't been myself since all of that happened."

A muscle worked in Mandeep's jaw. "Then you aren't who I thought you were."

Ditto.

Jess pulled her sleeves over her fists. "You don't have to worry about me going back to that, because Desi's dead, Brooke's in jail, and I have no clue where Kayla is since I basically told her to piss off. So congratulations, Mandeep, you win."

"That's not what I meant. I wanted you away from them; I didn't wish any of them dead. And I liked Desi."

"Everyone liked Desi."

They fell silent. Guilt squeezed her lungs and crawled up the back of her throat.

"But you don't like Halley," she said.

"She turns you into a different person."

"What the hell does that even mean?"

"You get, like ... crazy, Jess! I don't know!"

Jess's fists tightened. Pain throbbed in her arms and temples, and she just wanted to get out of this house. Did Mandeep hate the outgoing part of her that much?

"I don't want you reconnecting with Halley, all right? She's bad news, and you know this."

"Don't tell me who I can and can't spend time with."

"It's her, or me."

Jess stepped back as if she'd been punched. An ultimatum? Seriously? She had to choose between the woman she loved most in the world, and the best friend who desperately needed her?

Jess was breathing hard. She'd been so blind. She thought Mandeep loved her for who she was. But she only loved a part of Jess. She loved Jess without friends, without that spark of wildness and spontaneity. But Jess loved that spark. It had been extinguished for too long.

She thought of Halley, burned and beaten, afraid for her life.

She considered the woman across from her—who'd been there for her for over a year, who could always make her smile, whom she'd pictured herself marrying some day.

"I'm protecting you, Jess."

Protecting. There it was, again. It was a less sinister version than what Tony was doing to Halley—but it was still about power.

"I don't need protecting."

"You do. You obviously can't recognize what's harmful to you."

"And that's exactly it. You're not protecting me, you're controlling me."

"Someone needs to stop you from hurting yourself even more. You don't seem to realize you're not as strong as you used to—"

"I'm not weak! Stop treating me like I am!" The words exploded from Jess, months of anger reaching the point of eruption.

She was sick of people thinking she needed help. She was sick of them assuming the disability in her arms was a weakness. She was as smart as she always was. She was capable of standing up for herself and getting everything she wanted in life.

She was done with the coddling—from others, and from herself. The insecurities were over. Her friend needed help and Doctor Ries needed to be taken down, and Jess had the power to do it.

She opened her fists, letting her hands out of her sleeves.

She crossed the room to Mandeep, whose eyes were watery, face flushed with rage.

"I don't need protecting, and I don't need pity," said Jess. "I need support."

Mandeep set her jaw. "I can't support you if this is your decision."

Jess nodded. "If you're going to forbid me from seeing my best friend, you aren't the woman I thought you were."

She reached past Mandeep, grabbed her phone and keys from the counter, and left their unfurnished basement suite.

Chapter 27
Halley Drives an Elion

Halley's eyes snapped open at 2:27 AM, her subconscious waking her before her alarm could.

She slid out of bed, went into the bathroom, and found a few bobby pins at the bottom of a drawer—useful accessories back when she had hair.

She crept upstairs, moving as cautiously as she could. If Tony was in anything other than a deep sleep, he would feel her movements and wonder what she was up to. Could she feign a hankering for a bowl of Cap'n Crunch?

She stopped at the firearms closet by the door. Tony had taken the GN pistol, but she still had whatever firearms lay inside.

Recalling the video tutorial, she slid the looped end of a bobby pin into the bottom of the keyhole. With a second pin, she fiddled inside the top part. It didn't catch on anything. There was supposed to be a row of pins that needed to be pushed up in a specific way.

Halley closed her eyes, feeling the room's circulation, focusing on the keyhole. The chemicals in the metal reacted with her fingers. She honed in on the lock's insides, searching for a clue.

Her gut clenched in frustration. The hole was so tiny. She'd been used to feeling the air for large movements, like a person sprinting toward her.

Experimentally, she blew into the keyhole. What came back and grazed her cheeks was a pattern mirroring the row of pins inside the lock.

Congratulating herself, she blew again until she understood how the pins were positioned. She pushed lightly on the lower bobby pin and raked the top one along the inside.

After a tense minute, she was able to turn the bobby pins.

She held her breath, trying not to let the deadbolt click.

It was impossible. The sound of it sliding back ricocheted through the apartment like gunfire.

Heart in her throat, she flung open the closet door and used her phone's flashlight to see inside.

The machine gun caught her attention first. Too big. She could never move quickly with that.

At the opposite end was a silver handgun, smaller than her original one. It was too simple to protect herself and Jess from Tony. She needed something as powerful as possible, but still portable.

Her gaze fell onto a mid-sized black one. Its grip was similar to her original pistol, but the barrel was long, and the magazine hung down past the grip.

She recognized it from video games. This was a submachine gun—fully automatic, able to do extensive damage, but reasonable to carry. Plus, there would be less recoil.

She snatched it from the wall. It was a manageable weight, about four pounds.

The air shifted, a hint of activity seeping under the closed bedroom door. Tony was getting out of bed.

Panicking, Halley shut the door and pulled out the bobby pins. She raced to the kitchen and opened the cupboard over the sink that was full of cans and flour and cereals. She stuffed the submachine gun behind the boxes and grabbed the Cap'n Crunch just as Tony's bedroom door opened.

"What are you doing?"

Halley popped open the box, shut the cupboard, and turned to the fridge. "Midnight snack. You've got better food up here."

Tony stared at her from the open door, wearing nothing. Halley averted her eyes.

Though she was anything but hungry, she continued making the cereal, pouring it into a bowl and covering it with milk.

He came over and stopped behind her. Halley wondered if he could feel her heart pounding, with the way it filled her eardrums.

He leaned his chin on her shoulder, breathing on her neck. His tongue came out to lick her earlobe.

"All I need to do is stand there and you get riled up," he said.

Halley exhaled slowly. If he thought her pounding heart was from arousal, she would roll with it.

His warm hands slid around her waist, slowly, and down into her panties. "Back to bed. We've got hours before we need to be up."

"Okay."

But he didn't let her move. His fingers pushed into her, massaging her. She was too disgusted with him to be turned on. The pain of his betrayal was fresh, her bruises tender, her heart broken.

She turned and kissed him. The time for the gun in the cupboard would come soon. She had to be patient.

Tony picked her up and carried her to his bedroom, where he dropped her on the bed and climbed on top of her. He had her roughly.

For the last time, Halley thought, turning her head so she could gaze out the crack in the curtains. The stars were out, the night sky the clearest she'd seen it since living in Tony's apartment.

It took a long while for Tony to fall asleep again. When he did, hours later, Halley padded back into the kitchen. She was trembling, but not from cold. She never got cold anymore.

Vancouver was beginning to awaken. The rising sun turned the snowy mountains a soft gold, so they looked like something from a different world.

Halley thought of her parents and how panicked they must be. The police and media were probably hounding them, given her status as the prime suspect. But she had to leave her parents out of this. She would reunite with them later—and apologize until her throat was raw.

First, she had to deal with Tony.

341

With the gun waiting in the kitchen cupboard, she went downstairs for her laptop.

Traditional locks were for picking. Modern locks were for hacking. Luckily, Tony had given her hours of hacking practice.

Halley turned on her laptop's receiver and let it scan for the lock. In her Downloads, she located the file with the encrypted password.

She crept to the front door with the laptop and felt around the lock pad for the pairing button. She pressed it until it activated pairing mode. Now, to link her laptop with the device. The standard 0000 code failed—which was expected. Tony would have changed the code to prevent others from pairing with it.

She'd written a quick program to slam it with every possible number combination, starting with numbers ending in 85 to 89—her best guess at his birth year.

She let her algorithm go to work, perfectly aware that in the worst case, this would take hours to crack. As soon as it did, though, her program would send the saved packets back to the lock. The lock would read the encrypted password, and *click.* Deactivated.

The question was, would Tony's phone receive an alert that the lock had been deactivated?

Either way, he would notice the draft of the front door opening. She would have to move quickly.

Halley let her laptop work and gathered her stuff. She loaded her backpack with all the usual tools, unsure of what she might need. She dropped it by the door. Moving with painstaking care, she opened the kitchen cupboard and retrieved the submachine gun from behind the cereal boxes.

Next, keys.

She hadn't made it out of the kitchen when the breath left her chest.

He was up.

No time to react. The bedroom door flew open. Tony stepped out, a wall between her and the entrance.

Halley gripped the submachine gun tighter, mind racing through options. Fight, flight, or feign innocence?

Tony said nothing. His gaze landed on the gun.

Then, as though he'd heard a shout in the hall, he snapped his attention to the front door.

Everything about the entrance screamed what Halley had done. Not only was the closet unlocked, but it was also slightly ajar, and air funneled through the crack. By the front door, the fan in her laptop whirred, overworked as it pounded the lock with passcodes.

Tony lunged with the speed of a striking cobra. Halley raised the submachine gun to defend herself. His arm crashed into hers and knocked it from her grip. It clattered to the floor.

His eyes met hers. For a split second she thought she saw surprise in their depths before they darkened with anger. He grabbed her throat and pushed her backward. Halley reached up with both hands, prying at his fingers.

He walked her back until she slammed into the wall with a gasp.

"Where are you skipping off to?" he hissed.

He squeezed her throat until she couldn't breathe. She tugged at his fingers, too panicked to think.

"What are you planning, my little comet?"

Abruptly, he let go. She coughed.

His hands were on her, searching for anything she might have been hiding.

Click.

She and Tony snapped their attention to the sound.

The door.

The LED on the lock pad glowed red. It was deactivated.

Halley gave a right hook, punching Tony in the nose. He shrieked with pain and hunched over. She gave her hardest roundhouse kick, getting him in the head. He fell onto the floor. She seized the submachine gun and raced for the door.

On the way out, she snatched up the Elion keys and her backpack.

She felt Tony struggling behind her. She'd kicked his head hard enough to disorient him.

And then she was out, past the door she hadn't left on her own accord for weeks.

Freedom!

He'd bought the lock days ago, but she'd been a prisoner since long before that. She was his prisoner the moment his fingers clasped hers when they danced to the jazz band in that crowded lounge.

Three steps across the hall, the elevator was waiting. Halley ran inside and jabbed the *close* button repeatedly. The doors moved painfully slowly.

Tony stumbled out the door of the suite, blood streaming from his nose, and lunged for her.

He was too slow. The elevator dropped, taking her on the long descent to the parkade.

When the doors finally opened, she sprinted through the elevator lobby and across the parkade. Tony's two cars were parked side-by-side.

Yes, he also had the Bentley as an option—but Halley had done advance research, like Tony had taught her. That was how she discovered the new Elion model outperformed it.

For good measure, she aimed the submachine gun at the Bentley's tires and peppered them with bullets. The car sank and went lopsided.

The door burst open behind her.

How? Already? Only one elevator led to the top floor.

Halley spun. The figure bursting out wasn't Tony—but Reah.

Wearing an oversized Rob Zombie concert tee and no pants, hair tousled, she pointed a silver handgun at Halley. Halley pointed the submachine gun back.

"I – can't –" said Reah, panting, "let you – go."

"Why not?" said Halley.

Reah adjusted her grip.

Halley looked past her. She had seconds before Tony would arrive.

"Reah, please. He was keeping me trapped up there."

Reah set her jaw, unwavering. But she didn't shoot. She said nothing.

"I know it's your job," said Halley, "and I know he probably threatened you into all sorts of obedience. But please. He's hurting me."

Reah glanced over her shoulder. The air vibrated around her. She was trembling.

Halley backed toward the Elion.

Reah didn't tell Halley to go—but she didn't tell her to stop, either.

Through the door behind Reah, the elevator light glowed.

Ding.

Halley spun. She jumped into the Elion and tossed her bag and the gun into the passenger's seat.

It was like operating a spaceship. Thank god she'd watched how Tony drove it.

Halley backed up so fast the tires shrieked against the concrete.

In the rear-view mirror, Tony burst into the parkade in a bathrobe, heaving. Reah ran up beside him, pistol ready, as though in the midst of chasing Halley.

Tony aimed the GN pistol at the back of the car. Halley squealed away, hearing bullets land and praying they didn't hit a tire.

She couldn't afford to wait for the gate to open. She winced as she crashed through it, metal squealing and shuddering against the car that was surely worth at least half a million dollars.

And then she was off, roaring down the streets of Vancouver at the speed of—

"Fuck."

It was 7:28 AM. Rush hour.

When a gap opened in the lane beside her, she swerved into oncoming traffic. At least, she tried to. The Elion jerked her back into place, flashing and beeping at her.

She tried again. The steering wheel refused to let it happen.

"Let me drive, dammit!" She slammed the button that had turned off autopilot mode before.

"Driver assist deactivated," said the Elion's dash, in what Halley imagined would have been a dejected, Marvin-the-manically-depressed-robot voice.

She spun the wheel. Oncoming cars honked and tires squealed, but they cleared the way.

She wove through the city, unable to open her speed, but making good time by endangering her life whenever a gap in the lanes opened.

Even with driver assist off, the car had an irritating collision-avoidance mode enabled that kept jerking her into the center of her lane and stopping her from getting close to the car in front. She cranked the radio to try and drown out the noise of all the warning beeps. The group singing informed her cheerily that they were here for a good time, not a long time.

It didn't take long for the police to pursue her—but then she hit the freeway. She slammed her foot down and accelerated so fast her stomach swooped.

Halley couldn't remember ever traveling so fast in her life. Cars going the speed limit passed by in a blur. The road became an obstacle course that demanded a reaction time so quick she couldn't afford to blink.

On the open road, she felt like a hippopotamus had been lifted off her shoulders. How had she not seen this in Tony earlier? She was a tool he needed for his business, not a partner—but she was too blinded by infatuation to notice.

Did he ever have feelings for her, or had he planned to use her to his advantage from the start?

She wiped a tear from her cheek, cursing him and the ache he left in her chest. She'd thought she found everything she wanted in Tony. Why had she been so naive?

She needed Jess back. More than Tony, Jess was the only person who understood everything she had been through and everything she needed. Halley was an idiot to let that girl out of her life.

She made it to the office and parked the car on the walkway out front. ("Goodbye, Tony!" said the dash.) She leapt out and sprinted to reception with the submachine gun.

Beth shrieked and raised her hands.

"Beth, I'm looking for someone. I need the office floor plan."

Beth looked perplexed at being addressed by name. Fair enough—the last time they'd met, Halley still had a face.

"Okay, don't shoot! It's on the computer."

Halley came around the reception desk and watched Beth navigate to the office directory with a trembling hand.

"Give me that," said Halley, shoving her aside.

She grabbed the mouse, knocking over a Bellatrix Lestrange figurine, and scrolled through the list of names until she landed on Jessica Curie. Squinting at the screen, she made a mental note of where she needed to go once she was on the third floor, and took off for the elevators. "Thanks!"

Beth would call the police any second. That gave Halley eleven minutes. Fewer until Tony arrived.

Some blonde guy was waiting for an elevator. His face turned to horror when he saw her coming.

Halley swung the gun toward him. "Stay here."

The elevator doors opened and she jumped inside, smashing the buttons.

Sprinting down the hall on the third floor, the mere sight of her cleared people out of her path. They gasped and shouted to each other. She flew past door after door, flashes of geeky toys and personal touches offering a glimpse into something that could have been her life.

Any other internship would have given her an office like those. She could have decorated a corkboard with pictures of family and friends. She could have displayed her Beanie Babies on her desk. She could have spent 9-to-5 coding instead of scaling walls and holding people at gunpoint.

She skidded to a stop at an intersection and turned.

Her heart gave a powerful thud.

Affixed to the closed door was a placard at eye level. The name on it was one she hadn't dared to think about in half a year.

Jessica Curie.

Chapter 28
Jess Gets a Security Clearance

Jess had seen a lot of weird things in her twenty-one years. She had walked past a man wearing nothing but roller skates and a horse mask. She had seen a kid jump out of a moving car to catch a Pokémon. She had lived through planking, the cinnamon challenge, and Salad Fingers. But never, in her entire life, did she expect to see her childhood friend burst through her office door with a submachine gun.

"Quick," said Halley, grabbing her hand.

Jess was too stunned to do anything but follow. She ran half a step behind, allowing Halley to pull her down the hallway.

The spill had done more damage than the photos revealed. Halley's skin looked ready to peel off, and her palm was stinging hot, like a fever. What had once been blonde hair was now a bald and scorched scalp.

The presence of Comet sent the office into chaos. People shouted as they passed, ducking behind furniture.

There was the sound of a door flying open, and Omar shouted, "Jess!"

Jess glimpsed his startled face poking out of a meeting room. Their team lead, Chuck, leaned out behind him, mouth agape.

"It's okay," said Jess. "Round everyone up and get out of here!"

Whether Omar would listen, she didn't know. She and Halley burst into the stairwell and thundered down the steps.

"Is he here?" said Jess.

"Any minute. His Elion has GPS tracking, so he'll know where I went."

They wound their way down to the lab, panting.

A lot of questions raced through Jess's mind. "You got to drive an Elion?"

"Oh my god, you should see it. It's gorgeous. At least, it was. I kind of drove it through a metal gate."

Jess gaped at her. "You wrecked an Elion for me?"

Halley's answering smile was the same as always. "And I kicked Anthony Ries in the face."

"Huh." Jess shouldn't have been surprised. It had been Halley's idea that they, Kayla, and Desi commandeered a swan float from their community Santa Claus parade. They'd driven it down a side street for a few minutes before hearing shouts and abandoning it. Maybe a swan float was a gateway drug to grand theft auto.

Halley pulled out her red badge and swiped it over the box by the lab door. It blinked green and let them in.

The room was stark white, all tile floor and tables of equipment. The only people inside were five men in lab coats. They turned as Jess and Halley burst in from the stairwell.

"Let us by," said Halley.

"Where's Doctor Ries?" said the man nearest, his face stony.

"He's on his way."

"Then you won't mind waiting for him."

"He gave me instructions."

"Us, too."

There was a pause. The men moved into the middle of the room. They and Halley glowered at each other. Evidently, Halley had no authority over them. Would they have a change of heart if Jess told them her life was in danger?

Halley raised the submachine gun. She hesitated, then aimed it beside them to the rocket on the table, which lay in pieces like a dissected cadaver.

"Let us by, or I'll blow whatever you're working on to shreds."

Jess snatched up an open notebook and a bunsen burner from the nearest table. "And I'll light this math on fire."

Everyone cringed.

The first man shouted, "No! God, you monsters. Just go."

They let Halley and Jess through, with Jess holding the notebook hostage as they crossed the white room.

Halley kicked open the double doors, and they plunged into the hollow depths of the warehouse.

Jess's jaw fell open. This was the room she'd watched on the Aries 181 imagery. It was even more vast in real life. The stacks of junk she'd seen on the images were enormous, dominating the room with little space left for walking. It reeked of motor oil and burnt metal, leaving a bad taste in her mouth.

They turned to face each other. Despite the changed appearance, the look in her friend's blue eyes was so familiar. She could have wept.

How did she ever think she could face life without Halley? She should have spent the time since the summer grieving with her friend, not trying to erase what happened and every memory that came before it.

"You sure you want to help?" said Halley. "We can get you out of—"

"Hal."

"This is my mess. You don't need to be a part of it."

Jess wanted to tell her it wasn't her fault. The Halley she knew was a rule-breaker, not a criminal. But the words stuck in her throat. She hated Tony for doing this to her friend— but she didn't know how much of this was a result of Halley's own recklessness.

Halley dropped her gaze, looking small. Jess reached out and lifted her chin. The feverish heat from her flesh warmed her fingers.

"The police are already on their way," said Halley.

Jess pulled her phone from her pocket. She had a weak Wi-Fi connection and a measly bar of service. "Time to inform your followers?"

Knowing the internet had risen to the challenge of catching Comet and Blitzen boosted Jess's confidence in crowdsourced heroism. Whatever the authorities were doing, the internet had given her firm reason to believe in power in numbers.

Halley nodded.

Jess raised her phone. "Gimme a duck face, then."

A large satellite was beside them, leaning on one of its solar panel wings. Halley posed against it like it was a sports car.

"Lift your chin more," said Jess, moving the phone to find the right lighting. "Put your hand on the solar panel. Like you're trying to seduce it. Yass, queen."

When they were satisfied with the photo, Jess tweeted it with the caption *"HELP #CometAndBlitzen attacking the Aries lab"* and tagged the location.

Halley looked around the sprawling warehouse. "Now to find something useful."

The ceiling was an assortment of fans, dim lights, LEDs, and a noise like a distant swarm of wasps. Hopefully, Tony hadn't engineered mutant wasps and the noise was just coming from the drones.

Alleyways between the equipment stretched endlessly through the warehouse. How were they supposed to decide which way to go?

Jess's gaze landed on a cone-shaped spacecraft near the center. It looked like one she'd seen years ago at a space museum. She raced toward it.

"Gemini."

Halley followed. "What?"

"This looks like the Gemini 3 Spacecraft. You can sit inside it."

She searched for the door. Halley found it instantly and heaved it open.

It was a claustrophobic space containing two seats and a control panel with about thirteen trillion buttons.

"Don't tell me you're envisioning us flying out of here like Willy Wonka's elevator," said Halley.

"This is what we'll use to trap him. Shove him in and slam it shut." She glanced back to the double doors, still visible from the alleyway between piles of junk. It was a good vantage point.

Halley stuck her head inside, looking around. "Good. As long as we disarm him before trapping him, the cops should be able to take it from here."

"Should we hide somewhere in all this crap until he comes?"

Halley shook her head. "You can't hide from him."

The way she said it, as though she were talking about a mountain lion, sent a shiver down Jess's spine.

"Something happened, J, when we became … Like, I feel where everything is in this room, just by the way the air is circulating. When I touch something—" She rested a hand on Jess's arm. "—I can feel the whole chemical composition."

Jess pulled away so Halley wouldn't feel how fast her pulse was racing. "And Tony?"

"If you hide, he'll feel your presence by the breaths you take and the way the air curls around you."

Ah. That explained a lot.

She swallowed. Just when Tony Ries couldn't get any more creepy.

"He'll come to me," said Halley.

"What if he shoots you?"

"Tony wouldn't kill me."

"You kicked him in the face and stole his car."

"J, I can handle him."

Jess rubbed a hand over her face. Was there a nice way to tell Halley she was never a good judge of character? More likely, arguing over the morality of the man she was in love with would go nowhere.

In love with.

An icy feeling slid into her stomach.

She met Halley's blue eyes—maybe the only constant part of her.

No. She wouldn't. Jess was embarrassed for letting herself think it.

"So we have to pretend you've tied me up here?"

Halley dropped her gaze and nodded.

Jess scoffed. "Humiliating. How about instead I kick him in the—"

"J, you can't act tough."

"What do you mean?"

"You need to act fragile. He needs to feel like you aren't threatening his power over the situation."

"Ew, that is so creepy."

"Trust me. I know Tony. That's how he is."

"Fine," said Jess. "I'll sit on the ground with my hands behind my back like a useless damsel. But I'll sit by Gemini's open door, and I'll kick it closed the second you've shoved him inside."

It sounded straightforward, but how easy would it be to stuff Tony inside?

Halley looked around. "We need something to tie your wrists."

"Can I just keep my wrists behind—?"

"No. You need something there. Tony will feel it."

Jess wrinkled her nose. "Okay. Also, we need to cut the inside handle off this thing so he can't get out."

They scoured through the piles of junk. Jess had barely begun searching when Halley returned with a coil of wire and a welding torch.

"I never thought I'd be down here," said Jess, unwinding some wire for her wrists. "I mean, since my first day here I hoped I would get to see it, but I never thought it would happen."

"Welcome to hell," said Halley, prodding at the door handle.

Jess grimaced. "When I started working here, even the thought of disagreeing with my team lead made me want to puke. Now look at me. I'm in the lab without permission, plotting to take out my boss."

"Feel like you're gonna puke, still?" said Halley.

"You can hold my hair back, for old times' sake."

Halley laughed.

"We weren't that bad, were we?" She wanted to hear it from someone else. She wanted to know she wasn't crazy for thinking Mandeep had spent months overreacting.

"What do you mean?"

"Last summer. We weren't out of control or anything."

"Jess, we were a bunch of preppy university students."

"It's just that Mandeep ... It's like she thinks we had it coming. Like we were so wild and reckless that an accident like that was bound to happen."

Halley's expression darkened. "That's bull. She's making you feel guilty for something you had no ..."

She trailed off, and Jess's heart gave a squeeze. That was the point. Jess had nothing to do with any of it. She should have been there for Halley when Brooke was mistreating her.

"What's Mandy got against having a wild streak, anyway?" said Halley.

"I dunno, but she doesn't like that side of me."

"Well, I do, and you shouldn't feel guilty for who you are. Sure, we did dumb things, but that's normal. Everyone does immature shit at our age. Making mistakes is part of life."

"So people tell me."

"Besides, you were an honors student and never tried a single drug, for god's sake. It wasn't *that* bad."

Jess stared at the twisted lines on her palms. "My sister said the same thing after it happened. But you know how she is. The devil on my shoulder."

Maybe Halley was as much of a loose cannon as Millie, but her words reassured Jess. According to Mandeep, Jess had been a terrible person until she came along and calmed her down. But it wasn't true. Jess didn't need to feel guilty over every irresponsible thing she'd done in her adolescence. She was adventurous and ambitious, and that type of person was bound to make mistakes.

Halley pulled back the sleeve from Jess's forearm. She uncurled her fingers, studying the scars.

"Titanium," she said. "I heard you shattered your arms."

"You feel the chemicals?" said Jess.

Halley nodded.

"It'll probably be in there forever. Depends how well my bones heal." Jess studied her friend's disfigured face. At least the worst of her own scars were hidden. "Hal, I should have

358

been there for you. I never should have broken us apart. I could have helped you avoid all of this."

"No," said Halley. "This was inevitable. Tony and I are— were—"

"Don't say destined to meet. He's a sociopath."

Halley sighed. "But I think I would have left our group sooner or later. We would have drifted, anyway."

A pang of sadness hit Jess. "Why do you say that?"

"I was always the outsider. Like, if one of us had to get voted off the island, it would have been me."

"That's not true." It ached to think Halley ever felt that way.

"I was the last one to join all of you when I moved here in grade six," said Halley. "The three of you had been friends for years before that. It was little things. Like I was the only one who wasn't an initial."

The initials. They'd all called each other by their first letter, because their names all happened to work that way. Jess was J, Desi was D, Kayla was K. Even Brooke had been promoted to B when Halley had brought her into the group when they were nineteen. 'H' never had the same ring.

"You're Hal," said Jess.

"I know it's dumb, but it was the tiny things like that. They added up and made me feel like the black sheep."

"Well, you weren't. And now the herd of sheep was eaten by wolves so it doesn't even matter."

Halley's gaze snapped to the double doors. "He's here."

Jess turned, but heard nothing. Was this Halley's new super-sense at work?

A moment later, someone shouted from the lab, distant and echoing.

Jess's breaths came faster. This was the situation North America had been most terrified of for weeks, and here she was, volunteering for a front row seat. While everyone else fled to safety, she was in the bowels of Aries—trapped in the warehouse with Comet and Blitzen.

Chapter 29
Halley's New Target

A jet of fire burst from the welding torch. Halley gritted her teeth against her fear as she cut through the steel. Gemini's door handle clattered to the floor.

Jess kicked it aside and sat on the concrete, positioning herself behind the capsule's open door—out of easy shooting range. She put her hands behind her back.

Halley looped the wire over her wrists.

"Not too tight," said Jess. "I need to get my hands out."

Halley did her best to keep the wire loose, but she didn't want to risk Tony feeling the free movement.

"It has to be a little tight. I can feel air flowing between your skin and the wire."

Jess gave a weak moan.

Halley's fingers trembled as she knotted the wire. After the short conversation with Jess, she was trusting they could repair their friendship. She trusted Jess would forgive her. But what if they couldn't get past what happened? What if Tony was the only person who would ever be close to her? She was about to make an irrevocable decision about her place in the world. She was about to dispose of her only chance at being loved.

As she worked, her fingers grazed Jess's soft, pure skin. Her dark hair cascaded down her back, over a chiffon blouse she must have bought specially for this job. Halley remembered that hair blowing back and forth on the swings when they were kids. Now, to see Jess sitting in front of her, making herself vulnerable, put a lump in Halley's throat. What would prove Jess's loyalty, if not this?

Halley had to trust their friendship. Jess would always be there for her. After everything she'd felt for Tony—the way he consumed her thoughts for weeks, the way her heart seemed to sprout wings every time she looked at him or heard his voice—she felt something stronger when she looked at Jess. It was different, not fueled by desperate passion and the need to make Jess love her. It was more comfortable than that. She knew Jess loved her unconditionally. With that security, she didn't need to focus all her energy on not losing her.

Tony would never give her that. He would never love her. She would always be chasing him, and she would never be able to focus on herself—on being happy.

With a noise like an oversized mosquito, a drone whirred overhead and disappeared into the LED-flecked ceiling. Halley shivered, rubbing her arms where they tingled from the vibration. Fuck this lab and everything in it.

She had to stop fearing what would happen if she left Tony. There had to be a better life waiting. It wasn't too late to be a good person—one deserving of Jess's friendship.

The double doors shuddered, like he was about to push through.

362

Halley's heart thumped faster. She left Jess and kicked the welding torch back into a pile of junk.

"You deserve better than him," whispered Jess. "Remember that."

Halley avoided her friend's eye, struggling to believe it. She was one of the most wanted criminals in North America.

Still, she wouldn't have done any of this if not for him. He was out of control—a storm of power and greed. She had to put an end to this while she had sanity left.

You sure about the sanity part? said a voice in her head, as she picked up the submachine gun.

The only option was to get rid of him, and she was the only one who could get close enough to do it. It was her responsibility.

She balled a fist, watching the charred flesh stretch over her knuckles, and thought of her Five T's.

Target, Tactic, Tools, Time, Takeoff.

She never thought Tony would fall under '*target*'.

The double doors opened.

Halley leaned against the Gemini capsule, hidden from view. The stark white light from the lab cast a glow across the ceiling.

"Honey, I'm home!"

Tony's voice echoed through the warehouse.

Carefully, she peeked around Gemini as the doors swung shut. He stepped inside and stopped next to the podium with the old satellite on it. He was holding something other than the pistol. It was shaped like the GN assault rifle, except bigger. Wires sprouted from various places, holding parts together.

She recognized the compression chamber in the stock. His engineers must have succeeded in making their own version of a chemical firearm.

But the material … What was it? It was white, like a skeleton, reminding Halley of—

Her mouth dropped open. She'd seen the material before.

This weapon was 3D printed.

Of course, they'd stolen a 3D printer weeks ago, and Tony's boys had been working on designs.

Either she and Jess had run right past the weapon in the lab, or it had been in pieces, and the engineers had just thrown it together for their boss.

However it was manufactured, Halley was sure this weapon was dangerously untested.

Hidden behind Gemini, she squared her shoulders, summoning courage. She thought of everything Tony's weapons stood for, and everything he'd done with them.

For weeks, she'd been running circles in the same rat maze, like little Peter taking wrong turns at every junction. This iteration was done. She'd lost. It was time to start over.

Chapter 30
Jess is Pretty Sure Guns like
This are Illegal in Canada

"I know you're here, Miss Lovelace." Tony's voice was magnified under the vast ceiling. "I feel you breathing."

Hearing his voice again sent Jess's heart into overdrive. She curled her trembling fingers over the wire binding her hands together.

Halley cast her a confirming glance. Jess nodded.

"I'm over here, baby." Halley's voice was strong and confident. "I have a present for you."

She stepped out from behind the Gemini capsule and into the alleyway, facing the doors.

Though they'd planned it this way, Jess couldn't help feeling defiled as she sat on the ground, hands behind her back. This was a pair of serial criminals. How many hostages had sat on the floor beneath them? She imagined what it must feel like to be truly trapped by them, a toy to be played with.

She shook her head. She couldn't lose her nerve. She was in control, and she had to keep it that way.

Tony moved silently, but he must have been close, because Halley's voice dropped.

"I wanted to surprise you. I got her."

Tony appeared in Jess's line of sight, bathed in the ring of light surrounding them. All the breath left her body. He was as she remembered from the day he'd threatened her—and nothing like the Doctor Ries who'd interviewed her. Or, was he? Had this version of him been beneath that businessman exterior all along?

Tony took in Jess's state, probably noting the sweat rolling down her temples.

She didn't have to fake her terror.

He turned back to Halley, his voice a growl. "*What – the – fuck –* is wrong with you?"

If Jess had been in Halley's place, she would have stepped back. But Halley stood taller, an arm's length from Tony, separated by the submachine gun and whatever monstrosity he was holding.

"You wanted me to take my job more seriously." Halley waved an arm at Jess. "Your target, ready for disposal."

"I didn't mean for you to—This wasn't a challenging task, baby."

"And what about staging a break-in at the office?"

Tony considered this for a half-second. "So you romp in here without a plan?"

Halley gave a mischievous smile. "Oh, honey. You think I don't have one?"

Tony eyed her. "Time?"

"Six minutes."

Jess's breaths came faster, making her light-headed.

Come on, Halley. Push him in.

What if she decided Jess wasn't worth it? She had a history of putting up with abuse. Maybe Jess was an idiot for assuming Halley would easily break free of Tony.

"Hostages?"

Halley stepped closer to Tony, biting her lip. "How many do you want?"

Tony closed the remaining distance. He traced the back of his fingers down her arm. "Enough to distract the—"

Halley front-kicked him in the groin with enough force to knock down a door. Tony curled over with an "OOMPH!"

Jess winced. She'd forgotten how strong Halley was.

Somehow, Tony kept a hold of his machine gun. Halley roundhouse kicked him, getting him in the hip. He stumbled sideways, landing with one hand on the Gemini capsule.

He was right by the door.

Jess resisted the urge to jump up and help. *Not yet.* She worked her wrists, ready to tear free.

Tony swung the machine gun toward Halley. Before he could shoot, Halley slammed the butt of her gun into his neck, sending him to his knees.

His upper body fell in front of the capsule opening.

Jess tore her wrists loose, the thin wire slicing her skin. She bit back a shriek of pain and leapt up.

Tony fought hard, but Halley fought harder. Jess grabbed one of his kicking legs. Halley grabbed the other.

Something hard cracked Jess in the head and she gasped, falling to her knees.

Tony was swinging his gun, hitting everything in reach.

Something clattered to the ground. A pistol.

367

Tony kicked, sending Halley sprawling backward. Jess got to her feet and slammed into him with both hands. Pain shot up her arms.

Tony dropped the machine gun to catch himself on the door frame. Jess aimed a kick at his groin, like Halley had done—but he caught her foot.

They locked eyes. There was a terrible moment where he had a hold of her, and Jess knew something painful was about to happen. He sneered.

"Don't—!"

He twisted.

Jess cried out as the force sent her crashing to the concrete. She caught herself with a forearm, sending a stabbing sensation to her shoulder.

She choked on the pain, taking gasping breaths.

There was a scuffle behind her.

"Jess, run," said Halley.

No. She couldn't leave Halley with him.

Tony grabbed the white machine gun and aimed it at her. Halley shoved the barrel out of the way, and Jess saw the shot go wide. She actually *saw it*, like a tiny meteor soaring past her ear.

That weapon wasn't a machine gun—it was a motherfucking bazooka.

The projectile hit something behind her and exploded with such force that it flattened all three of them with a wave of heat. Whatever Tony had hit was now in flames.

She got to her hands and knees, and her eyes fell to the fallen pistol. She recognized it, then. It was the one Halley had been pressing to the girl's temple in the viral photo.

She seized it and ran, limping on her twisted ankle, heading for the double doors that now seemed miles away. Another explosion sent her careening sideways. She collided with some kind of engine, seizing it to stop herself from falling.

A rocket twice the size of her toppled across her path, billowing smoke. Beside its base, the top of a steel barrel melted. The bottom glowed red hot. Jess hopped out of the way of its contents, which poured across the concrete floor, smelling like rotten eggs.

Halley screamed. Jess looked back to see Tony pick her up and stuff her inside Gemini.

"I'll deal with you later, my little comet."

"Let go of me!"

Jess aimed the pistol at Tony. She hesitated. The plan had been to get him arrested, not to kill him. She couldn't do it. Besides, she would never make the shot from this distance.

They needed the cops to get here. At the same time, she had to get Halley to safety. How was she supposed to get Halley out the trapdoor while keeping Tony in?

Tony kicked Halley in the ribs and slammed Gemini's door shut. He spun toward Jess, the bazooka hanging at hip level, ready to fire.

Jess had a fraction of time to act. She dove into the rubble behind her, landing between a propeller and a pile of hard drives.

The blast erupted, sending another wave of heat. She scrambled noisily away, tripping over the propeller and spilling a bottle of oil on her running shoes.

She could see a clear path beyond the rubble. If she could get to it and run back to Halley, the two of them could get away.

"It's a dead end, Jessica," shouted Tony. "It's time to pay the piper. Except instead of a piper, you get me. And instead of paying, you get to be blown to smithereens."

The sound of Halley kicking the Gemini door from the inside echoed through the warehouse.

Jess cursed. Tony wasn't lying. There were dead ends left and right.

"I expected more from *Blitzen*," said Jess, feigning confidence. "All you are is a fancy gun, aren't you?"

"Pardon me, dear, but this is the most advanced gun in the world."

There. Along the wall was one of the steel staircases that rose to the balcony tracing the warehouse perimeter. She recalled seeing the balcony on the drone images.

Climbing up might give Tony a clear shot at her—but it would also give her a clear shot at him.

He was leaving them little choice but to kill him. Could she bring herself to shoot someone? To save her own life and her friend's, she would have to.

She skirted a nearby forklift and sprinted up the stairs, taking them two at a time.

"A gun created from your own brainpower, eh?" She said once she'd made it to the balcony, her hands shaking on the rails. "Just like everything else in here?"

"Genius doesn't always mean numbers and formulas," said Tony from somewhere below.

Even with patches of fire to light the room, Jess's sight extended no more than a couple of meters in either direction along the balcony. Below, Gemini sat at the edge of a yellow halo of light, Halley trapped inside.

Tony ran for the staircase nearest him.

Jess ran in the opposite direction.

There was a clang of Gemini's door swinging open, and Halley shouted, "My ass, you'll deal with me later!"

Jess sprinted along the balcony, moving further from the doors to the warehouse, aware she only had one way to go. If anything lay ahead in the darkness, she would be trapped.

The room grew hotter, the further she ran. It was like she'd entered the mouth of a volcano.

Tony's footsteps pounded behind her, echoing, sending tremors through the steel.

This was her chance. She had to shoot him now. Bracing herself, Jess stopped and spun around. She gripped the pistol with two hands and fired. Several bullets left at once, like a tiny machine gun. There was no recoil.

"Oh ho!" said Tony. "Look at Jessica go!"

She couldn't see him past the veil of darkness. His footsteps had stopped. His breaths came quick and sharp. Sweat poured down her neck, her clothes clinging to her. The heat in this corner of the warehouse thickened the air like a sauna.

"I can feel your movements, Jessica. Every time you squeeze that trigger, I'll know. You can't shoot me."

Was he bluffing? The time it took to squeeze the trigger and send bullets at him was infinitesimal.

Jess gritted her teeth and held the trigger down, moving the gun to cover more space. When she stopped, and the racket of the gun had stopped ringing in her ears, Tony's laughter was echoing through the high ceiling.

With the pistol raised, she moved slowly backward, keeping an eye on the direction from which she could hear his taunting voice. Her hands shook, sweat sliding down her temples.

"J, stop moving!"

Her foot slipped off a ledge and she screamed, catching herself on the railing. Righting herself, she turned and saw a massive chunk had been taken out of the balcony, the steel completely ripped apart.

Of course. She'd watched it happen on Aries 181. The vat sitting below was broken, half its contents solidified on the concrete floor. A barrier had been partly drawn, shielding a third of the vat. What remained of the liquid churned inside, a pool of red, orange, and black magma. Smoke rose from it in wisps.

"Hold him off," Halley shouted from somewhere below.

Jess tried to spot her but saw only the mounds of junk.

"How noble of you, donating yourself to science," said Tony. His voice sounded much closer. Jess could see the whites of his eyes as he came out of the shadows. "My boys will be thrilled to study my weapon's effects on the human body."

"I'll leave behind quite the legacy," said Jess. "The only one to outsmart the great Doctor Anthony Ries."

He tipped his head back and laughed. "Is that what you call outsmarting me?" He gestured to the gap where she'd nearly fallen.

"The public thanks you for providing the technology needed to catch—"

"Oh, Jessica. Your cute little portal was decommissioned the second I found out about it."

Jess ground her teeth, rage flaring. Was this what her life had come to? Powerful dicks talking over her, interrupting her, calling her cute? Whether it was a coworker explaining her own project to her, or Floyd treating her like she was an idiot, or whatever shitshow this was, her place was always the same.

"It's *cute* you think you put a stop to my web portal," she said. "You didn't think a little intern could hack your API, Doctor Ries?"

Tony said nothing. Jess's lip curled.

"The page is still up, and if an API key gets revoked, my code just generates a new one. Anyone can use the key to see what your satellites are seeing. And right now, they know you're here."

He had moved steadily closer, the shadows sliding from his gruesome face like a cloak. He wore his anger like an exposed nerve, and for all his apparent genius, was about as subtle as a vat of rocket fuel. She knew what was coming before he lifted his rifle.

She dove, flattening herself on the steel floor, the shot erupting like a volcano in her ears. The projectile, glowing like a tiny sun, soared overhead. The force of it knocked the wind from her lungs.

She clenched her fist. Her hand was empty. She'd dropped the pistol.

"No!"

She whipped her head around in time to see it topple over the balcony. A moment later, it clattered to the concrete floor.

Another explosion of sound came. Halley was below, firing the submachine gun at Tony. She must have hit or grazed him, because he let out a roar that rang through the building.

Jess leapt to her feet.

Tony struggled toward her, grimacing in pain, when the sound of gunfire stopped.

Click, click, click.

"Shit," said Halley, small and distant.

He was a few steps away. She had nowhere to run.

He raised the bazooka.

Jess charged him, ducking under the weapon and slamming into his gut.

Tony grunted, trying to pry her off with his free hand. He couldn't blow her to smithereens while she was this close.

He forced her backward, slamming his knee into her, but she clung on and grabbed hold of the bazooka.

Tony thrust it away from him, Jess attached to the end. He wasn't going to win against her. She was strong enough to take him. She knew that, deep inside. She was tough, fierce, resilient. She always had been.

As he tried to shake her off, Jess was reminded of a spider that had once been attached to her by a single strand, and she couldn't for the life of her get rid of it.

Her foot slipped. She looked back to find herself at the lip of the balcony. The magma churned below.

Tony shoved her, but her grip on the weapon was firm.

Standing above the fiery blaze, that awful memory of a summer that seemed a lifetime ago forced its way back. She set her jaw, too determined to feel afraid. Anthony Ries would not defeat her. She was good, and good always won.

Their eyes met. As she looked into the empty black pools, she understood that nothing would stop this monster from killing her. Strength alone was not enough.

Don't, she thought, clinging to the vain hope that he had an ounce of humanity left.

He let go.

Jess sucked in a breath of surprise. How unfair the world was, to let her fail after all this—after she finally understood who she needed in her life, and that she was strong enough to fight for it.

Still holding the massive weapon, she toppled backward.

Chapter 31
Halley's Kingdom

An explosion broke the surface of the propellant as Tony's gun combusted. Flames roared into the ceiling, blue, green, and orange. The shockwave slammed into Halley, forcing her back a step.

"No! Jess!"

Ears ringing, she raced for the vat, searching for a way to get up there. She needed to climb in after Jess and pull her out. What if the propellant had become too imbalanced to keep her safe?

She couldn't find a ladder, and there was no sign of her friend. Tears sprang to her eyes.

The GN pistol lay on the floor, a crack in the stock. Gray bullet solution seeped across the concrete, shimmering like a puddle of unicorn blood.

Halley picked up the weapon. A splash of liquid was left inside. It would have to do. She looked to the balcony, cursing when she saw only darkness where Tony had been.

The pistol was a familiar weight in her hand. She would gut that asshole for doing this to Jess.

Movement stirred behind her and she whipped around, finger on the trigger.

Tony smashed into her. They fell to the floor, struggling for control. He pried her fingers from the pistol and she punched him in the throat before he could point it at her. He gagged.

They rolled over, grappling, until Halley slammed her knee down on Tony's wrist. He cried out, grip loosening, and she snatched the weapon.

She scrambled off him and stood, panting. "Consider this my letter of resignation."

Tony raised himself to his knees, rubbing his throat. "Aw, baby, did I hurt your feelings so bad that you want to kill me?"

Halley's grip tightened.

Blood flowed from three places on his arm, running down his mutilated flesh and hitting the concrete. *Drip, drip, drip.* She'd caught him with the submachine gun.

His thin lips curled into a snarl. "I made you. You'd be making nonfat double-shot cappuccinos and drawing little hearts in the foam if not for me."

"You didn't *make me*. I'm not some Bride of Frankenstein."

"Admit it. You belong to me and you love it that way." Tony opened his arms. "We're the king and queen of the tech industry, and this is our kingdom."

"Maybe I don't want to be your queen anymore."

"You think you have a choice? Your entire life has been one disgrace after another. Try as you might to erase your past, the scars will always be there."

Her insides ran cold. *Your entire life.*

He knew. Of course he did. Why hadn't it occurred to her that this man, this master of research and hacking and psychology, would know about her past?

"That girl died," he said, the words like a knife. "You could have stopped it. And look at you now. How do you expect anyone to love you?"

His words came from the end of a tunnel. The air left her lungs. He was right. She'd known for some time that the choices she made had doomed her. No one could love her. Maybe Jess had been ready to forgive—but where was Jess now? With each passing second, Halley's last hope at redemption slipped further away. She had no one but the man in front of her. He was the only person in the world who understood her, from her singed flesh to the constant, frantic impulses racing through her brain.

She could find a happy life with Tony. They could keep going on this crazy business venture, living outside of consequences, and Tony could achieve everything he dreamed of.

But at what cost?

The room was in flames around them, suffocating her.

Shoot him. End this.

Drip, drip, drip. Blood collected beneath him, forming a puddle.

"There is one man in the world who loves you, Halley, and you've got him at gunpoint."

The arm holding the pistol suddenly felt heavy. "You what?"

Tony stood, keeping his hands raised. "I've loved you since the moment I saw you. The tech show, do you remember?"

Halley's heart thrummed. All over again, the jazz band played in her ears, Tony's soft hands pulled her close, his breath tickled her skin, people swayed around them.

She shook her head violently, as though to dislodge him from it.

"Stop! You can't keep manipulating me, you nutcase."

He stepped closer.

"Stop!"

He reached out, carefully, and pushed the pistol aside. "We can work through this, baby. Don't let our kingdom crumble."

Take him out, said a voice in her head that sounded like Jess. *You deserve better.*

He gave her a lopsided grin that made her think of the Tony from weeks past. This was the one who took interest in her at the tech show, who defended her, who danced with her.

"I forgive you," he said. "Now, will you forgive me?"

Halley glanced to her disfigured hand, trembling over the pistol. He was, truly, the only person who could accept her.

"I want you to let me out whenever I feel like it," she said. "You're going to let me visit my parents."

Tony considered her. His expression softened. "Whatever you want, my little comet."

Halley extended a hand, as though to ask him to dance. He took it. She pulled him in—*But he's lying! Remember how he hurt you. He'll do it again*—and she shook that voice away. This was the only path left in her ruined life.

She kissed him.

He kissed her back, tasting sweet and familiar. Halley pressed closer, running her fingers down his back.

"See?" he murmured. "You'll always come back to me. It's the reason I hired you. Now let's stop this idiocy and blow outta here."

He pulled back, but Halley held on.

Tony had *hired* her. She was an assistant, not a partner—business or otherwise. She was his trained monkey. Business conquests had always taken priority.

Look what he did to Jess. He would always dispose of whomever got in his way—even Halley.

Maybe he loved her, or maybe it was a lie, but either way, she did deserve better. Nobody was allowed to disrespect her the way Tony had. Nobody had the right to make her feel worthless, to force her into anything, to hit her. Anthony Ries didn't deserve her. King and queen? *Ha.*

Her smile fell, and Tony's eyes widened. She tightened her grip around the back of his neck, nails digging into the tendons.

"Long live the queen," she said.

Before he could react, Halley raised the pistol to his temple and squeezed the trigger.

Nothing happened.

She squeezed again.

Tony's horror melted into a sneer. "Uh oh."

Halley cursed. The pistol was broken—it wouldn't compress the drops of solution left inside.

Tony attacked, wrapping his fingers around her neck. She kneed him but he held on. They fell, Halley clawing at his hands, driving her knee into his stomach. He was squeezing, suffocating her, his face contorted with rage. She felt blood pooling in her head as her mouth opened and closed. Spots erupted in her vision.

No. She couldn't die like this. Not because of him.

But she couldn't shake him off. Everything was numb. She needed air.

Then he snapped his head up, eyes wide. Something smashed into him and knocked him off her. Halley rolled over, taking a shuddering gasp.

"They're here," shouted a man's voice. "Someone bring the cops down!"

Someone's full weight landed on Halley's back, holding her to the cold floor. She struggled, still gasping for breath.

There was a scuffle beside her as a second man wrestled Tony to the floor.

"Don't move, Comet," said the one pinning Halley. "The cops are on their way."

With a roar, Tony threw his attacker off. The guy fell backward, and Tony sprinted down an alley between the piles of junk. There was an eruption of shouting and stampeding footsteps. She couldn't see who it was with her cheek pressed against the concrete floor.

She cursed herself. Why did she have to be so weak? It was pathetic. Now Tony was running loose again.

She squirmed, feeling the man's weight distribution, deciding how best to flip him off her. He was inexperienced, pinning her with the force of his body weight but with no strategy behind it. If she was quick, she could knock him off balance.

The man sank harder into her back, squeezing the air from her lungs and pressing her face into the concrete. As she was contemplating her move, she felt a rush of air coming toward them, then heard a thump. The man let out a sharp breath. She felt his body being dragged off of her and scrambled to her hands and knees, looking around to see who had been her savior.

Jess stood over Halley, panting. Her skin, hair, and clothes were dripping with a thick, red liquid.

Chapter 32
Jess's Weakness

Jess looked at her hands, making sure her mind was still attached to her body. She touched her face and arms. Yes, she was still a person, exactly the same, a young woman with ten fingers and the complexion of a snowflake. Her clothes had survived, though they were dripping with that awful, stinging liquid. Everything was blurry—but upon touching a goopy hand to her face, she discovered this was because she'd lost her glasses.

Damn. Those things were expensive.

Halley got to her feet, clutching her ribs. "It worked!"

Jess squinted at her. *Worked? What worked, exactly?*

"The rocket propellant. It preserved you," said Halley, and when Jess continued to stare in silence, she added, "It's supposed to leave organic matter untouched."

Jess didn't share Halley's awe. She might have avoided the same chemical burns as Halley, but something in her body felt off.

Shouts and footsteps echoed from further away in the warehouse.

"Don't let him go!"

There was a crash of equipment.

Jess chanced a look down one of the alleyways and found Anita, Kit, and Omar struggling to hold Tony down—and Floyd, getting to his feet some distance away.

Anita, using her knees to pin Tony, turned her blurry face toward Jess. "You okay?"

A glob of liquid rolled down Jess's arm. She wiped it away and nodded.

Fighting one of Tony's legs, Omar said, "Cops – are – here. We were supposed to evacuate, but—"

Tony's knee caught him in the jaw. Omar grunted and returned his focus to holding him down. Kit had both hands on Tony's throat, apparently trying to ease their effort by making him pass out.

"Jessica, go sit down and let us deal with protecting the lab." Floyd fiercely straightened his collared shirt, like he couldn't believe Jess had the nerve to throw him off Halley so forcefully.

Jess, too, was a bit surprised by her own strength.

Floyd moved closer, zeroing in on Halley.

Jess turned to her friend, struggling to understand what she'd seen. "You still love him?"

"I …" Halley glanced to the tangle of bodies, her expression holding every ounce of regret and apology. "I need your help. Please."

Jess wanted so badly to trust her. Yes, Halley had kissed Tony, but she also tried to shoot him. It seemed that even Halley didn't know how she felt.

Jess rounded on Floyd, who was feet away.

"Floyd, leave her alone. We need to help restrain Tony."

"Tony?"

Jess waved an arm at the others still grappling on the floor. "Blitzen! Anthony Ries!"

Anita, Kit, and Omar looked sharply at her, then back to Tony, then at each other.

Floyd looked at her like she was crazy. To his credit, with this red stuff dripping off her and hair plastered to her face, she probably resembled Carrie at prom.

"It's fine," Halley whispered in her ear. "I can take Mr. Comb Over."

But Jess didn't like the gleam in Floyd's eyes as he sized up Halley.

"Floyd, for once in your life, listen to me. Hal—Er, Comet isn't the problem."

"Back down, or I'll have you written up and dismissed," he said, coming close enough that he was nose-to-nose with her.

"Dismissed?" Jess let out a wild laugh. "You think I'm concerned about being fired right now? Do it! It's the only thing left for you to do to me, isn't it?"

Floyd sneered. "I've done my job to help you succeed. Listening to your manager is part of being a working girl."

There was a ringing in Jess's ears. Her breath came faster. Yes, she was definitely done with Mr. FF. She was done with every jerk who didn't give her the respect she deserved. From now on, nobody was allowed to step on her, or even hover over her with their boot.

"No," she said. "You don't understand in the slightest what's—"

Floyd grabbed her shoulders and shoved her aside. "Get out of my way."

"Don't touch me!" Jess pushed him off her—and a moment later, there was a crash on the other side of the alley. Floyd smashed into a metal container, denting it. He stayed there, unconscious, suspended inside the body-sized divot.

Jess blinked. *What the … ?* She looked around.

Halley, the Cloud Team, and Tony were all gaping at her.

Jess looked down at herself. A moment ago, Floyd had his hands on her, and then she'd pushed him, and now—

"Oh my god," whispered Halley, her eyes enormous.

Jess wiped the hot liquid oozing down her face. "What?"

Tentatively, Halley wrapped her fingers around Jess's forearm. She looked up at Jess, jaw unhinged.

Whatever was wrong, there was no time to find out. A commotion rose on the other side of the warehouse. In the distance, the ceiling was bathed in light as the double doors burst open.

"Doctor Ries?" someone shouted.

"I'm over—gah!"

His teeth cracked together as Kit punched him in the jaw.

"Crap," said Anita. "The Red Badges are on to us."

"What did you do?" said Jess.

"Took a chance, yelled something about how the cops are here and Doctor Ries says to deploy the emergency barrier … It worked. They told us to go out the trapdoor— wherever the hell that is—and let us through so they could barricade the entrance to the lab."

"You idiots!" shouted Tony.

Omar took off his shirt and stuffed it into Tony's mouth as a gag.

"Doctor Ries!" someone shouted again, closer this time. There was a stampede of footsteps.

Tony struggled harder, but between Anita, Kit, and Omar, they had him pinned and silenced.

Jess turned to Halley. "Where was that coil of wire?"

Halley gave a nod of understanding and sprinted off.

Pounding footsteps drew nearer as the Red Badges wove through the warehouse.

Where was that trapdoor? She recalled the picture of Halley and Tony emerging from the woods all those weeks ago.

"Why aren't you restraining her?" said Kit, nodding after Halley.

"She's all right," said Jess, coming over to join them. "It's him we need to hand over. You said the cops are coming down?"

"Any second. They were evacuating everyone."

There was a noise like a wasp buzzing by Jess's ear, and a drone swooped low. The others ducked as more drones followed suit.

"Piss off, robots!" shouted Omar, taking a swing at one.

Jess seized one before it collided with her skull and threw it onto the concrete, shattering it.

Halley returned with the wire.

"Where's the trapdoor?" said Jess.

Halley pointed to the far end of the warehouse. "Corner."

Another drone zoomed toward Halley and she grabbed it out of the air, snapped off two of its four propellers, and left it to spiral helplessly to the floor.

"Okay. Go," said Jess. "I'll meet you."

Halley gave her an 'are you kidding?' look and uncoiled the wire. Jess continued to beat away the drones dive-bombing them like angry crows.

"You should, though," said Anita. "Before the cops get down here."

She was avoiding looking at Halley, but Jess felt a surge of gratitude for Anita's trust.

"I'm not leaving until this is over for Tony," said Halley, pressing a foot into his throat so he let out a muffled gag.

"But—" Jess protested.

"You three can help by bringing the police over," said Halley.

Jess dropped to her knees to uncoil the wire. Whatever the plan, first they had to restrain Tony and get Halley out.

The Cloud Team looked at each other, hesitating.

"I'll stay," said Omar, leaning his weight into Tony. "You two go."

"Tell the cops Comet disappeared," said Jess, winding the wire around Tony's wrists.

"You continue to amaze me, Jessica Curie," said Anita, and she and Kit ran for the double doors, a swarm of drones chasing them.

Jess and Halley tightened the wire around Tony's limbs while he struggled. Blood gushed from the several bullet wounds on his arm. Omar tied his shirt behind Tony's head to secure it over his mouth, hopefully to the effect of giving Tony a face full of armpit sweat.

"Duck," said Halley.

"What?"

Something like a baseball soared past them and hit the magma vat. Jess found herself sprawled on the concrete as the explosion rang through the warehouse.

"That," said Halley, wincing.

Jess sprang up and pulled Halley to her feet. "Red Badges?"

"Yeah," said Halley. She was looking at Jess's hand as though she'd sprouted extra fingers.

Before Jess could ask, Halley turned. The Red Badges had arrived, and Jess found herself at the business end of five black handguns.

Halley reacted quickly, taking out the nearest guy with a kick to the gut and an arm around his neck. She yanked away his gun and pressed it to his temple. "Munchkin, is this really a fight you want to start?"

Tony gave a muffled shout through his gag.

Omar flicked his ear. "Shh."

Jess looked around at the other four men. Though she was an easy target, they had yet to open fire. They looked from Jess to Halley to Tony, shifting on their feet. These men definitely weren't the rumored trained ninjas. They were regular engineers who'd been given guns. They'd applied for a high-paying job at an aerospace company and found themselves threatened into an NDA.

"Who's controlling the drones?" said Jess, ready to snatch more out of the air.

The guy in Halley's chokehold croaked, "Don't insult me. They're in offensive mode. Totally autonomous."

"And totally annoying," said Halley. She used the handgun to shoot the drones down. They fell heavily, plummeting to the concrete with sad little whines.

"Boys," said Jess calmly. "None of us wants to kill each other. Get out of here and leave this to Comet and me."

"We won't kill you if you come quietly," said one engineer, a balding man with sweat gleaming off his scalp.

Jess sighed. "You won't kill me, anyway, buddy. I can see your hand shaking."

His face darkened, and he came at Jess, expression resolute. "Shut up. You're coming with us."

"Oh, for g—"

He swung at her and Jess jerked back reflexively, but the attack caught her off guard—she had not moved in time. She watched his fist connect with her jaw with a strange, distant feeling. That was to say, she felt it, and knew it was a hard hit, but there was no pain.

She met the man's startled eyes. Then she punched him in the face.

He flew through the air and hit the floor in a loose, unconscious heap.

There was a beat of silence. Then, as if exchanging some silent agreement, two of the engineers charged for Omar. The other went for Halley. The man already caught in Halley's grip elbowed her sharply in the gut.

Jess had none of Halley's martial arts training and no idea what she was doing, but the instinct to defend Halley took over logic. She raced over and threw the advancing Red Badge away from her. He, too, soared across the warehouse as though blasted by the force of a jet engine. Halley took care of the other guy, flipping him over and flattening him on the concrete.

Jess rushed to Omar, who was outnumbered and struggling to keep control of Tony. One guy was untying him. She shoved him aside, sending him cartwheeling. Halley delivered a blur of punches and kicks to the other, knocking him out.

But they were too late. Omar was sprawled flat on his back, and Tony leapt up, shaking the wire free and ripping off his gag. He faced them like a tiger ready to pounce.

With the vat of rocket fuel at his back, Jess and Halley had him cornered.

Omar labored to his feet.

"Omar, stay here." Jess pointed to the Red Badges, who were a semi-conscious mess on the floor. "Tie them up."

"Let me help—"

"Do it!" she said, baring her teeth.

Omar reached for the wire.

Jess rolled the tension loose in her wrists. "What the hell is going on with me, Halley?"

Halley straightened up, panting. "I think I know what element the propellant is meant to combust."

They faced Tony, Jess ready to clobber him, Halley ready to calculate his movements.

"You said it's supposed to preserve organic matter," said Jess, inching toward their target.

"Yes. And it did."

Jess pieced this together. She glanced to the scars running up her forearms, clear beneath the dripping rag that had been a nice chiffon blouse just a few hours ago. A sick feeling overcame her.

"What about my non-organic matter?"

Halley hesitated. "Your skin doesn't feel the same as before. You feel like—"

Before Jess knew what was happening, Halley took off, chasing Tony into the gap between the vat and the partly closed barrier. Dammit, there must have been an opening on the other side.

"Jess, you had titanium in your forearms," shouted Halley as they emerged into another alleyway.

"What do you mean, *had?*" said Jess, dashing after them.

"It's there. It's just … not isolated. Shit, he's going to the trapdoor."

They veered off the path, crashing through a pile of solar panels. In the dim light, Tony's dark figure was making a beeline for the far corner of the warehouse.

"Are you saying the titanium combusted inside my body?"

Halley leapt over a fallen barrel with the agility of a gazelle. "I think it fused with your cells. Like, I feel metal when I touch you. Part metal, part organic matter."

"What does that mean?!"

Tony reached a staircase to the balcony and ascended two at a time. They couldn't let him escape. Jess ran faster, overtaking Halley. She was feet away from him.

"It means your cells don't give out when organic matter would. They've been enhanced with titanium."

As her legs carried her toward Tony with no signs of exhaustion, Jess couldn't decide how to feel about this. At one time, she'd been uncomfortable with the idea of titanium rods holding her forearms together. Now, Halley was telling her she had titanium fused to her whole body.

At the top of the stairs, Tony lunged for the wall where a handle marked the exit. Jess dove after him. She caught him around the knees. Tony let out a "Guh!" as they crashed to the steel balcony.

Discomfort aside, she could live with this. She'd spent months thinking of the titanium implants as a weakness—but they weren't. They were a part of her, a representation of her inner strength.

She held Tony easily, stopping him from crawling further. The door was inches away. He struggled beneath her, his wounded arm slick with blood. The thrill of vengeance coursed through her. She could do this. She could own the titanium like Maleficent owned her horns.

Halley thundered up and stopped behind them, clutching her side, wheezing. "Nice – one – J."

Jess nodded.

Halley drew the small, black handgun she'd taken from the Red Badge. She adjusted her grip, and turned off the safety.

She pointed it at Tony's head.

Chapter 33
Halley's Job Description

"Step back," said Halley, waving Jess aside with the pistol.

Jess hesitated.

"I need to finish this," said Halley.

"Hal, I'm not letting you become a murderer."

"Jail time isn't enough for him."

"He'll get a life sentence, after everything he did."

Halley understood Jess's reluctance, but sometimes, vile decisions had to be made when dealing with vile people.

"J, move. I'll shoot anyway, and I'd rather you got out of the way so you don't get his brains on you."

Jess grimaced. She stepped carefully away from Tony, leaving him on his knees and at the mercy of Halley's pistol.

"Parting," said Tony, "is such sweet sorrow."

Halley clenched her jaw, the words delivering a jolt of pain.

The double doors whooshed open. Several people entered in a flurry, shouting, their words lost in the echoing rafters.

Police.

She tightened her finger over the trigger.

"You don't have the guts," said Tony. "Don't think I haven't noticed."

"I never wanted to kill innocent people."

"But you're willing to murder the man who loves you."

"You don't love me. I was just a business strategy."

Tony gave a strange smile. "Don't you care about the company vision?"

She scoffed. This relentless pursuit of his vision was the most infuriating part of him.

"We're literally surrounded by all the scientific potential you've ruined. Aries would be better off without you. You could say I'm taking you down in the name of science."

Tony's body shook. It took her a moment to realize he was laughing.

She pointed the gun more firmly at him. "What are you laughing at?"

Jess stepped closer to her.

Halley said it more desperately, a bleat of panic. "Tony, what are you laughing at?"

She considered the situation. She'd plotted against him. She'd called herself a business strategy. She'd admitted she was willing to murder him.

Her heart pounded faster.

"Is this what you wanted from me?"

"Look at you, putting the business first. I would say you've earned a promotion, darling."

The warehouse was a whirl of activity, the police drawing nearer.

"Doctor Ries, come out with your hands up!"

Jess stepped between Halley and the trapdoor. "Hal, we need to go." There was an urgency in her voice Halley had never heard before.

After weeks of trying to figure him out, it was like the last rotation in a Rubik's Cube snapped into place. He'd wanted her to be willing to do anything for Aries—even commit murder.

If she gave that to him, would that mean he'd won?

Jess grabbed Halley's arm. "Let's go!"

Tony leapt to his feet.

She peeled her gaze away from him and fixed it on Jess—her anchor.

"Let the cops take it from here, Hal. Please."

Tony ran.

Halley could distinguish each cop as they closed in. An entire team was here, fanning out, leaving no way through. Sprinting along the balcony, Tony was headed into a cavalry charge, and he had nothing with which to defend himself.

A gunshot fired. Halley and Jess ducked. The bullet hit something beside them with a *clink*.

They looked to the sound. An aluminum tower sprouted beside the balcony like a fir tree, solar panels covering half the surface. A 747 wing, maybe.

Jess drew a leg back and kicked. As though hit by a train, it skidded across the concrete with a deafening squeal, wobbling. Then, like a felled tree, it toppled. It landed with a shuddering boom, sending equipment flying, its corpse forming a wall between them and the approaching police.

Jess stepped toward the trapdoor. "Halley."

Something warm trickled down Halley's cheeks. She wiped an arm across her face.

Behind them, the air churned as the police encircled Tony. "Anthony Ries, you're under arrest ..."

Halley met Jess's eyes, finding the earnest, pure expression she'd known her whole life. This was the face of someone who truly loved her. Jess cared about Halley's life and her happiness.

The trapdoor was steps away. Beyond that stretched the forest and freedom.

Halley needed someone she could trust. She needed someone to help her stitch herself back together.

Jess held out a hand.

Chapter 34
Jess Completes her Perfectly Normal Internship

The office the next day was a strange combination of that *last-day-before-summer-vacation* feeling and a funeral service. Government officials had come to tell everyone to pack up, because the company was dissolving and everything in the lab was undergoing investigation. All Aries technology and algorithms were, for now, in no man's land.

The halls were a graveyard of desk ornaments and computers. Hazmat suits were involved downstairs, which got everyone's interest. Rumors about alien probes and organ farms increased. Jess helped them along by telling Steve 2 she saw a tentacle flop out of a body bag.

She removed her *Game of Thrones* map and rolled up her TARDIS poster. She prodded her desk, the temptation too much. She glanced into the hall, saw no one around, and lifted her desk off the floor with one hand. The thing was heavy, needing a smidge of effort, but *Jesus*. What was she supposed to do with this ability? Should she apply for a job as a firefighter or lifeguard? Try MMA?

She'd just put the desk down when Anita, Kit, and Omar appeared in her doorway. She breathed a sigh of relief to see them smiling and unharmed. She'd been unable to find them after all the chaos.

"You guys shouldn't have—"

They forced a group hug upon her. She didn't mind.

"—put yourselves at risk, coming down there," she finished, laughing.

"You're one to talk," said Kit as they broke apart.

"The second Kit and I left you with Comet and Blitzen, we doubted ourselves," said Anita.

"It all worked out," said Jess, though fear still gripped her over the near-misses. "But how did you even know to find me down there?"

The Cloud Team exchanged glances.

"We'd all been following the Comet and Blitzen story," said Kit.

"We found it interesting that the day we killed the servers, the portal stopped showing new images," said Anita. "So we re-launched them, and it came together. We realized that was what you'd been doing, *Lucy McGillicuddy*."

"Then I see you and Comet running down the hall," said Omar, "and a second later we get a lockdown notice because Beth says Comet just crashed the building."

"So you came after me?" said Jess, startled by their recklessness.

"We weren't going to let you get Comet-and-Blitzened!" said Kit.

There was a pause, and Jess got the impression they wanted her to go on and explain everything. She turned her gaze to her bag of stuff, wanting to keep Halley out of this.

"I stumbled on some drone imagery by accident," she said. "It's all a bit messy. I'm just happy Doctor Ries was caught."

"So are we," said Anita. "I mean, we all knew he was a bit eccentric, but no one expected that."

"I just feel awful that everyone here is out of a job."

"We'll find work," said Anita. "We're awesome."

Jess smiled.

"Plus," said Omar, "I'd rather be unemployed than keep working for the country's biggest jackass."

Jess said nothing more on the issue, and thankfully, the conversation turned to what other companies they would apply for. They exchanged emails and social media info, promising to stay in touch.

"If you want a reference …" Anita motioned to herself.

"Thanks," said Jess. "You have no idea how much you all helped me keep my sanity."

"Our pleasure."

"How are you feeling with, um … ?" said Omar, and pointed a tentative finger at her bicep.

"Good," said Jess quickly. "Yep, really good. Totally normal. Adrenaline, you know? Crazy what it does. Mothers lifting cars off children and stuff. I'm a bit stiff today, actually."

She rolled her shoulders and stretched. They didn't need to know the extent of this freaky situation—not when Jess had yet to understand it.

The others nodded, looking only mildly suspicious.

When Kit and Omar returned to their offices, Anita lingered behind, pulling a piece of paper from her pocket.

"I drew you something. I also wrote a link to my portfolio on there—if you want to see, I mean ..."

She broke off, looking more nervous than ever before. Jess unfolded the paper. It was a manga sketch of Jess wearing a cape and a black eye mask, crouched in a fighting stance.

"Oh, wow," she breathed. "It's adorable!"

"You inspired me to send out a few submissions," said Anita.

"I did?"

"Jess, if you can put your life at risk to save people from Comet and Blitzen, I can summon the bravery to share some artwork."

She gave Anita a hug—carefully. When she left, Jess deleted everything from her laptop, including any remaining traces of her Halley-tracking algorithm. Her human detection algorithm was forever in the Aries codebase and would probably be adopted by the CSA, but that one, at least, couldn't be used to locate her friend.

She shut down her laptop and gave the office a last sweep. She found a stack of sticky notes on the floor, and picked it up to find her own handwriting.

'Be Kind and Always Smile'.

It must have gotten dislodged from behind the desk when she picked it up.

She tossed it into an empty drawer. She'd smile when she felt like smiling, thank you very much.

Carrying her bag and rolled-up TARDIS poster, she said goodbye to the Steves, Jesus Chris, Shy Stanley, Grace, and Ethan (an ordeal full of empty niceties like "Let's keep in touch!" and "We should hang out!").

Wyatt shook her hand. "It's too bad Floyd didn't let you do more for the image analysis toolkit. Your demo was cool, you know. People were talking about it."

Jess blinked. "They were?"

"I heard some of the senior devs saying you should get a full-time offer. Anyway, guess that's not gonna happen, now."

Her insides inflated with pride. So, her demo hadn't been a total disaster.

They exchanged social media accounts. Then, she was free.

With a satisfied sigh, she stepped into the elevator—and had the immediate misfortune of running into Floyd. He had a bruise on his cheek and the expression of someone who found it painful to breathe.

"Leaving?" he said stiffly as the elevator began its descent.

"Yup."

They looked away from each other. Jess had nothing to say to him. Social expectations dictated she should thank him for being her manager, and wish him well, and shake his hand—but he hadn't earned any of that. He'd been a terrible human being to her since she started, never once giving her helpful advice, mentorship, or opportunities. He had not earned her gratitude. His appearance in the lab earlier was in the interest of protecting Aries, not her.

So she walked past him out of the elevator with her bag and poster.

"Bye."

She felt light as she strode from the building. Never again would she let someone make her feel diminished. She was smart, and likable, and strong. Nobody could change what she knew about herself. She wished she'd understood it sooner. She had all the power she needed to stand up to Floyd from the moment she walked into their first meeting.

The suite was empty when she came home. It was often empty, with Mandeep at school, spin, or wherever else, but this emptiness felt hollow. It was a pointed vacancy. Last night, Jess had checked Halley into a hotel and come home late, where Mandeep was in full panic over the news of Comet and Blitzen attacking the Aries office.

They'd had another fight over Jess's lack of communication—which, honestly, was fair—but when Jess informed her she would be spending time with Halley, Mandeep lost it. Jess was still hesitant to trust Halley, but that didn't mean she wanted to cut her out of her life. And she certainly wasn't letting someone else make that decision for her.

After that, their interactions had a finality to them. Jess would cherish the years they'd spent together, but they could never go back to the way they used to be. Mandeep's views were clear to Jess, now. But her crazy friends, her need for adventure, her outgoing look on life—they weren't the 'old Jess'. Those traits were who she was, and she was done pretending otherwise.

Mandeep was moving out. She would live with her parents while she finished school, leaving Jess by herself in that bare basement suite.

Jess wouldn't be there for long, given the cost of tuition and life. Her pay from the internship helped, but she would be back to broke quickly, and the remaining weeks of term weren't enough time to start another job. She would have to stay unemployed and worry about her growing debts later.

The following Monday, Jess put on a black sleeveless blouse she hadn't worn in months and headed to UBC for a meeting with the Computer Science department. She'd already had several calls with them and other authorities regarding what went down at the Aries office, and the school insisted on paying for her to see a psychologist in case of PTSD.

It had taken one therapy session for her to pour out what happened with Brooke and Desi last summer—and admittedly, she was feeling more accepting of the loss, and less guilty about surviving.

Today's meeting was a totally different topic: the faculty advisor, Mr. Berg, had asked her to come demo her Comet and Blitzen web portal. She explained that it wasn't part of the internship, and it wasn't even pulling in new images anymore, but he insisted on seeing it.

She was five minutes into explaining the cloud servers and showing him the webpage when the map crashed, a broken icon appearing in its place.

Jess's heart jumped, but she stopped herself there. She had to quit berating herself for mistakes. After all, the whole reason she'd been able to stop Tony and all the crimes he committed was because of that stupid, newbie coding error. It was time to accept that mistakes were a part of life, and especially a part of learning. To expect to avoid all of them was to set herself up for failure.

Jess refreshed the page. "Oops. Well, it never went through the full testing process."

When she finished her demo, Mr. Berg looked impressed. Jess let out a breath, and with it, her presentation jitters.

"Yes. Good. I can see why you received the nomination," he said.

"What nomination?"

"Congratulations, Miss Curie. The government awarded you the Canadian Junior Engineering Scholarship for the work you did at Aries."

Jess blinked at him. "I—what?"

"You'll be receiving the details via email."

"But I let the world see inside the high-security lab, knocked my team lead unconscious, and got my boss thrown in jail."

Mr. Berg waved it away. "Hiccups. Could happen to anyone."

When Jess eyed him, he smiled. "A few of your coworkers nominated you. This is very scholarship-worthy. Not only did you implement an advanced algorithm, but you also developed a complete web portal. You know this project would ordinarily take a team of senior-level engineers?"

Jess leaned back in her chair. Yes, she'd summoned all the knowledge she had to build that portal—machine learning, web interfaces, server systems—but she'd used it to take down the company that had hired her.

"You did a good thing, Jessica," said Mr. Berg. "Take it."

She let her face break into a smile. She shouldn't feel guilty for earning money from taking down Anthony Ries. In fact, wherever he was, she hoped he found out she won.

"I will!" said Jess. "Thank you."

With that to help her pay tuition, she could breathe a little.

She stopped by the comic store on the way home. With a contented sigh, she opened the door and headed for the glass case housing the Marvel statues.

She felt, somehow, it was important for her to buy something not related to building a sparkly resume. With a new toy, some video games, and the rest of the term off, it was time to have a bit of fun. She owed it to herself.

Chapter 35
Halley's Old Habits

Even the biggest bacon-cheeseburger at the greasiest pub on the Downtown Eastside couldn't lift Halley's spirits. The chocolate milkshake helped, but that was done in minutes. Now she was left with the dismal ambience of a pub that was empty at 8 o'clock in the evening.

She prodded the basket of soggy fries, fighting a trembling lip.

Across from her in the cracked leather booth, Jess poked at her own basket of fries, the corners of her mouth turned down.

Regret overwhelmed Halley—but she couldn't decipher what, exactly, she was regretting. These last few weeks? Years? Her whole life?

Her emotions swung between self-pity and self-hatred, leaving her flustered and wanting to drown herself in another milkshake.

What she really wanted was to be curled up in her living room, watching an animated movie with her parents. But as the country's most wanted criminal, she couldn't go home. Halley Lovelace was the prime suspect for Comet's identity, and her house was undoubtedly being monitored. Instead, she'd been living in a dirty hotel off the wages she'd made working for Tony, watching competitive cooking shows night after night.

She squashed a fry, watching vinegar ooze into the red and white checkered paper.

"I was thinking I could call your parents," said Jess, as if reading her thoughts. "I can invite them for dinner at my mom and dad's place. Reunion of old family friends, or whatever. I can smuggle you in through the backyard. The bunny trail's still there."

Halley felt a rush of affection for her friend.

"Thank you," she said, and the simple words weren't enough to express her gratitude.

After a pause, Jess said softly, "Do you forgive me?"

"For what?"

"For abandoning you. Leaving you to grieve alone after everything that happened."

"Jess, I—"

"It was a mistake, and I'm sorry. I thought it was better for me to pull away. I let someone else tell me who I was allowed to be friends with. I never want to do that again."

Halley studied Jess, trying to understand. She recalled what Jess said about Mandeep in the Aries warehouse.

"Mandeep is the reason you haven't talked to me since the summer?"

Jess's eyes welled with tears. "Kayla, too. I'm going to try contacting her."

"So … it wasn't because of my relationship with Brooke?"

"No! Why would——? Hal, do you think I blame you for what happened?"

Halley dropped her gaze to the table. "You, me, everyone. She was my girlfriend."

"Your girlfriend, but not your responsibility."

"But she was mad at me. I should have listened to her cries for help."

"Hal, you can't pin your self-worth on someone else's actions. Her cries for help weren't yours to fix, even if you were dating."

Halley hesitated. "You really don't think it was my fault?"

"Of course not. Just like Tony can't control you, and Mandeep can't control me, you couldn't have controlled Brooke. It was an awful thing she did, but no matter how close the two of you were, Brooke's actions don't reflect you."

Halley chewed her lip. So Jess was never mad at her, after all. At that thought, she let out a breath she felt like she'd been holding for months.

Halley had to show that same compassion to herself. She was a separate person from Brooke—from Tony—and could choose her own path. She could choose to be a good person.

"Tony picked me to be his dancing monkey," said Halley. "No one else. I get it, now. He picked me because I'm weak. I was easy to manipulate. All he had to do was pretend he loved and needed me—and that he was the only person who ever would."

Jess leaned across the table, expression serious. "Hal, listen to me. He came along at the worst possible time, when you were alone and needed someone to tell you you're worthy. He promised to stitch a wound that desperately needed attention.

You're not weak, you're broken. There's a difference. You're a strong person who's been through hell."

Halley dug a nail into a groove on the table. *Broken, not weak.* She hoped Jess was right.

"Another round of shakes, ladies?" said the waiter.

He was a twenty-something guy with a thick hipster beard and blue eyes that crinkled at the edges when he smiled.

Halley left it to Jess, too depleted to care.

Jess smiled and said, "Sure. Extra drizzle, please."

"My kinda girls."

He reached for their empties, arms muscular beneath a green polo shirt. Jess snapped her hand away, apparently afraid of accidentally crushing him.

"What brings two unicorns like yourselves into this end of town?"

He was referring to Halley's hair, no doubt. She'd bought the most colorful wig she could find. Better than purple, this one was a cascading rainbow that transformed her into a human My Little Pony. She also wore stage makeup so thick and opaque that it covered most of her burns. It gave her more of an 'acne scars' look than a 'taken out by a river of rocket propellant' look. That, plus long sleeves, gloves, and a scarf, was the best disguise she could manage.

"Drowning sorrows," said Jess.

The guy looked at Halley. She probably did look more heartbroken, beneath her puffy, teary face and her most *I-give-up* gym clothes.

"Need me to beat anyone up for you?" he said.

She almost smiled. "I've got that covered."

He cast her a strange look before turning away.

Halley stuffed a cold fry in her mouth.

"He's cute," said Jess.

"Go for it."

"For you, I mean. You might do with a rebound."

"And what happens when I take my makeup off? My dating life is over, J. I'm damaged goods."

Jess's face melted into some mixture of pity and amusement. Her arm jerked, like she wanted to reach across the table, but she stopped herself.

"You just need to find someone who isn't afraid of a girl who … who gets what she wants."

They accepted their new milkshakes and drank them in silence. Halley blinked a lot, willing the tears to stay put. Yes, she always did whatever it took to get what she wanted—but what did she want, anyway? Her future was a black hole.

"Move in with me," said Jess abruptly.

Halley choked on her milkshake. "What? Really?"

"It's a one-bedroom, but the couch has a pull-out bed."

"Rooming with you sounds like a recipe for disaster," said Halley.

Jess shrugged. "We make memorable disasters."

For the first time that day, Halley smiled.

"You're the best friend a girl can ask for, J."

Jess's lips quirked, but her eyes stayed sad.

"Mandeep moved out, then?"

"Took the video games with her, the jerk."

"Things any better between you?"

"No. She doesn't like that I—" She briefly met Halley's gaze. "She's way too controlling."

"We have terrible taste in partners," said Halley.

411

Jess leaned back in the booth, crossing her arms. "I'm done with relationships for a while."

"Me, too."

Still, Halley thought wistfully of Mae the hot engineer.

Across the barren room, the bartender hummed a melancholy rendition of a Johnny Cash song Dad liked to play.

Halley glanced to the bar. "You realize how easily we could knock out the staff and take what's in the cash register?"

"Halley! We're going to need to reintroduce you to society!"

"Kidding," she said, though they both knew she wasn't.

Alone in the pub, they sipped their milkshakes. Then Jess raised hers.

"To being roomies."

Halley met the toast. "Roomies."

She and Jess moved her stuff from the hotel that night (Jess handled all the heavy things) and set Halley up on the pull-out couch. After spending weeks in a Yaletown penthouse, she was more than relieved to get out of that hole.

Sleep came no easier than it had over the last few nights. She left for kickboxing at dawn, before Jess could wake and notice her puffy face.

Halley was the first one at the gym, bursting through the doors with purpose. She headed straight for the body opponent bag.

"Oh, no," said the trainer, shoulders sagging.

"I'm dressed properly this time," Halley snapped.

"But you need to start at the beginning of the circuit ..."

She withered under Halley's glare.

Halley set to work. She punched and kicked and elbowed the body opponent bag until her heart was ready to burst. Tears streamed down her cheeks.

She'd done everything she could to move on with her life. She'd refreshed her wardrobe, applied for a few distance education classes next term, and focused on filling all her free time that she otherwise would have spent with Tony. She and Jess went to movies, brunch, game night, and for runs, promising to hold each other accountable for adding more 'life' into their 'work-life balance'.

But Halley missed it all. She'd had a coach, a mentor. She'd had goals and assignments.

Jab, cross, hook, cross. Each combo brought Halley back to a memory. Granted, they were memories of her delivering that very combo to someone's face, but they were still memories. Tony had been there and Halley had been happy. Where had it gone so wrong?

She punched harder.

Something caught her eye on the television. She grabbed the body opponent bag to stop it moving and snapped her head around to look. It was a shaky video of Tony leaving a courtroom in handcuffs.

Halley gritted her teeth, forcing the tears to stop so she could read the subtitles.

Anthony Ries, known as Blitzen during his string of crimes these past weeks, was charged with manslaughter, theft, breaking-and-entering, possession of illegal firearms, and a slew of other crimes that could land him a life sentence.

They cut to a teary-eyed Reah.

Was there enough evidence to incriminate Reah? She'd known all along. She facilitated the crimes without question. Were those tears of remorse or regret?

They switched to a shot of the prison where Tony would presumably serve out his sentence.

He had too much money, though. He would buy his way out. Then what?

He would come for her.

Worse, he would come for Jess.

Halley stepped closer to the television, panting. She should have shot the bastard when she had the chance.

The fences were high. Barbed wire on top. The front door was guarded. Brick walls. CCTV cameras on every surface.

Focus switched back to the news anchor, who was filling the viewers in on the demise of Aries. The company was being dissolved. Everything in the warehouse was under investigation, most items being returned to their rightful owners. The propellant would be turned over to the CSA for examination.

Behind Halley, another girl entered the gym, engaging the trainer in chit-chat about how lovely and basic their days were. Off to get almond lattes and organic kale after this, no doubt.

Halley peeled her gaze from the TV, breathing hard.

Prison wouldn't hold him. She couldn't let him go free. She had a responsibility, especially to Jess.

CCTV was nothing. She'd handled barbed wire before, too. Short of a chemical firearm, she had all the resources she needed to get inside. She could stop Doctor Anthony Ries from hurting anyone ever again.

Target, Tactic, Tools, Time, Takeoff.

She went home for her laptop. This one would require careful planning.

Note from the Author

This book is dedicated to anyone who has been in Jess's or Halley's shoes. May you find your inner superpower and proceed to kick ass.

Thank you to my beta readers, Steph, Kelly, Deana, Bee, Joe, Ashley, Lindsay, Dmitri, and Alex, as well as my editor, Danielle, for your incredible suggestions and edits that made this book astronomically better.

If you enjoyed Jess and Halley's story, please consider rating it on Amazon or Goodreads. Reviews are the best way you can help an indie author keep writing. Thank you for your support! Connect with me on social media @tianawarner and on tianawarner.com.

Now a webcomic on Patreon

ICE MASSACRE

Book One in the Mermaids of Eriana Kwai trilogy

http://tianawarner.com/novels/graphic-novel/

★ "… thought provoking and intelligent … fresh and thoroughly entertaining … Warner does a fantastic job creating a tight plot and masterfully creates a sense of atmosphere through subtle yet potent descriptions … Ice Massacre is a truly exceptional book."
— *Foreword* Clarion Reviews, 5-star review

★ "Fascinating, unique, scary and written with a beautiful economy of words…"
— 23rd Annual Writer's Digest Self-Published Book Awards

Winner: Best Indie Book Award 2016
First Place Winner: Dante Rossetti Awards 2014
Foreword 10 Best Indie YA novels of 2014
Foreword Reviews' 2014 INDIEFAB Book of the Year Finalist